The Lee Shore

Rose Macaulay

Alpha Editions

This edition published in 2022

ISBN : 9789356716629

Design and Setting By
Alpha Editions
www.alphaedis.com
Email - info@alphaedis.com

Contents

CHAPTER I

A HEREDITARY BEQUEST

During the first week of Peter Margerison's first term at school, Urquhart suddenly stepped, a radiant figure on the heroic scale, out of the kaleidoscopic maze of bemusing lights and colours that was Peter's vision of his new life.

Peter, seeing Urquhart in authority on the football field, asked, "Who is it?" and was told, "Urquhart, of course," with the implication "Who else could it be?"

"Oh," Peter said, and blushed. Then he was told, "Standing right in Urquhart's way like that! Urquhart doesn't want to be stared at by all the silly little kids in the lower-fourth." But Urquhart was, as a matter of fact, probably used to it.

So that was Urquhart. Peter Margerison hugged secretly his two pieces of knowledge; so secret they were, and so enormous, that he swelled visibly with them; there seemed some danger that they might even burst him. That great man was Urquhart. Urquhart was that great man. Put so, the two pieces of knowledge may seem to have a certain similarity; there was in effect a delicate discrimination between them. If not wholly distinct one from the other, they were anyhow two separate aspects of the same startling and rather magnificent fact.

Then there was another aspect: did Urquhart know that he, Margerison, was in fact Margerison? He showed no sign of such knowledge; but then it was naturally not part of his business to concern himself with silly little kids in the lower-fourth. Peter never expected it.

But a few days after that, Peter came into the lavatories and found Urquhart there, and Urquhart looked round and said, "I say, you— Margerison. Just cut down to the field and bring my cap. You'll find it by the far goal, Smithson's ground. You can bring it to the lavatories and hang it on my peg. Cut along quick, or you'll be late."

Peter cut along quick, and found the velvet tasselled thing and brought it and hung it up with the care due to a thing so precious as a fifteen cap. The school bell had clanged while he was down on the field, and he was late and had lines. That didn't matter. The thing that had emerged was, Urquhart knew he was Margerison.

After that, Urquhart did not have occasion to honour Margerison with his notice for some weeks. It was, of course, a disaster of Peter's that brought them into personal relations. Throughout his life, Peter's relations were apt to be based on some misfortune or other; he always had such bad luck. Vainly on Litany Sundays he put up his petition to be delivered "from lightning and tempest, from plague, pestilence, and famine, from battle and murder, and from sudden death." Disasters seemed to crowd the roads on which he walked; so frequent were they and so tragic that life could scarcely be lived in sober earnest; it was, for Peter the comedian, a tragi-comic farce. Circumstances provided the tragedy, and temperament the farce.

Anyhow, one day Peter tumbled on to the point of his right shoulder and lay on his face, his arm crooked curiously at his side, remarking that he didn't think he was hurt, only his arm felt funny and he didn't think he would move it just yet. People pressed about him; suggested carrying him off the field; asked if he thought it was broken; asked him how he felt now; asked him all manner of things, none of which Peter felt competent to answer. His only remark, delivered in a rather weak and quavering voice, was to the effect that he would walk directly, only he would like to stay where he was a little longer, please. He said it very politely. It was characteristic of Peter Margerison that misfortune always made him very polite and pleasant in his manners, as if he was saying, "I am sorry to be so tiresome and feeble: do go on with your own businesses, you more fortunate and capable people, and never mind me."

As they stood in uncertainty about him, someone said, "There's Urquhart coming," and Urquhart came. He had been playing on another ground. He said, "What is it?" and they told him it was Margerison, his arm or his shoulder or something, and he didn't want to be moved. Urquhart pushed through the crowd that made way for him, and bent over Margerison and felt his arm from the shoulder to the wrist, and Margerison bit at the short grass that was against his face.

"That's all right," said Urquhart. "I wanted to see if it was sprained or broken anywhere. It's not; it's just a put-out shoulder. I did that once, and they put it in on the field; it was quite easy. It ought to be done at once, before it gets stiff." He turned Peter over on his back, and they saw that he was pale, and his forehead was muddy where it had pressed on the ground, and wet where perspiration stood on it. Urquhart was unlacing his own boot.

"I'm going to haul it in for you," he told Peter. "It's quite easy. It'll hurt a bit, of course, but less now than if it's left. It'll slip in quite easily, because you haven't much muscle," he added, looking at the frail, thin, crooked arm. Then he put his stockinged foot beneath Peter's arm-pit, and took the arm by the wrist and straightened it out. The other thin arm was thrown over Peter's pale face and working mouth. The muddy forehead could be seen getting visibly wetter. Urquhart threw himself back and pulled, with a long and strong pull. Sharp gasps came from beneath the flung-up left arm, through teeth that were clenched over a white jersey sleeve. The thin legs writhed a little. Urquhart desisted, breathing deeply.

"Sorry," he said; "one more'll do it." The one more was longer and stronger, and turned the gasps into semi-groans. But as Urquhart had predicted, it did it.

"There," said Urquhart, resting and looking pleased, as he always did when he had accomplished something neatly. "Heard the click, didn't you? It's in all right. Sorry to hurt you, Margerison; you were jolly sporting, though. Now I'm going to tie it up before we go in, or it'll be out again."

So he tied Peter's arm to Peter's body with his neck scarf. Then he took up the small light figure in his arms and carried it from the field.

"Hurt much now?" he asked, and Peter shook an untruthful head and grinned an untruthful and painful grin. Urquhart was being so inordinately decent to him, and he felt, even in his pain, so extremely flattered and exalted by such decency, that not for the world would he have revealed the fact that there had been a second faint click while his arm was being bound to his side, and an excruciating jar that made him suspect the abominable thing to be out again. He didn't know how the mechanism worked, but he was sure that the thing Urquhart had with such labour hauled in had slipped out and was disporting itself at large in unlawful territory. He said nothing, a little because he really didn't think he could quite make up his mind to another long and strong pull, but chiefly because of Urquhart and his immense decency. Success was Urquhart's rôle; one did not willingly imagine him failing. If heroes fail, one must not let them know it. Peter shut his eyes, and, through his rather sick vision of trespassing rabbits popping in and out through holes in a fence, knew that Urquhart's arms were carrying him very strongly and easily and gently. He hoped he wasn't too heavy. He would have said that he could walk, only he was rather afraid that if he said anything he might be sick. Besides, he didn't really want to walk; his shoulder was hurting him very much. He was so white about the cheeks and lips that Urquhart thought he had fainted.

After a little while, Urquhart was justified in his supposition; it was characteristic of Peter to convert, as promptly as was feasible, any slight error of Urquhart's into truth. So Peter knew nothing when Urquhart carried him indoors and delivered him into other hands. He opened his eyes next on the doctor, who was untying his arm and cutting his sleeve and saying cheerfully, "All right, young man, all right."

The next thing he said was, "I was told it had been put in."

"Yes," said Peter languidly. "But it came out again, I think."

"So it seems. Didn't they discover that down there?"

Peter moved his head limply, meaning "No."

"But you did, did you? Well, why didn't you say so? Didn't want to have it hauled at again, I suppose? Well, we'll have it in directly. You won't feel it much."

So the business was gone through again, and this time Peter not only half but quite groaned, because it didn't matter now.

When the thing was done, and Peter rigid and swathed in bed, the doctor was recalled from the door by a faint voice saying, "Will you please not tell anyone it came out again?"

"Why not?" The doctor was puzzled.

"Don't know," said Peter, after finding that he couldn't think of a reason. But then he gave the true one.

"Urquhart thought he'd got it in all right, that's all."

"Oh." The doctor was puzzled still. "But that's Urquhart's business, not yours. It wasn't your fault, you know."

"Please," said Peter from the bed. "Do you mind?"

The doctor looked and saw feverish blue lamps alight in a pale face, and soothingly said he did not mind. "Your shoulder, no one else's, isn't it?" he admitted. "Now you'd better go to sleep; you'll be all right directly, if you're careful not to move it or lie on it or anything."

Peter said he would be careful. He didn't at all want to move it or lie on it or anything. He lay and had waking visions of the popping rabbits. But they might pop as they liked; Peter hid a better thing in his inmost soul. Urquhart had said, "Sorry to hurt you, Margerison. You were jolly sporting, though." In the night it seemed incredible that Urquhart had stooped from Valhalla thus far; that Urquhart had pulled in his arm with his own hands and called him sporting to his face. The words, and the echo of the soft, pleasant, casual voice, with its unemphasised intonations, spread lifting wings for him, and bore him above the aching pain that stayed with him through the night.

Next morning, when Peter was wishing that the crumbs of breakfast that got between one's back and one's pyjamas were less sharp-cornered, and wondering why a dislocated shoulder should give one an aching bar of pain across the forehead, and feeling very sad because a letter from home had just informed him that his favourite guinea-pig had been trodden on by the gardener, Urquhart came to see him.

Urquhart said, "Hullo, Margerison. How are you this morning?" and Peter said he was very nearly all right now, thanks very much. He added, "Thanks awfully, Urquhart, for putting it in, and seeing after me and everything."

"Oh, that's all right." Urquhart's smile had the same pleasant quality as his voice. He had never smiled at Peter before. Peter lay and looked at him, the blue lamps very bright in his pale face, and thought what a jolly voice and face Urquhart had. Urquhart stood by the bed, his hands in his pockets, and looked rather pleasantly down at the thin, childish figure in pink striped pyjamas. Peter was fourteen, and looked less, being delicate to frailness. Urquhart had been rather shocked by his extreme lightness. He had also been pleased by his pluck; hence the pleasant expression of his eyes. He was a little touched, too, by the unmistakable admiration in the over-bright blue regard. Urquhart was not unused to admiration; but here was something very whole-hearted and rather pleasing. Margerison seemed rather a nice little kid.

Then, quite suddenly, and still in his pleasant, soft, casual tones, Urquhart dragged Peter's immense secret into the light of day.

"How are your people?" he said.

Peter stammered that they were quite well.

"Of course," Urquhart went on, "I don't remember your mother; I was only a baby when my father died. But I've always heard a lot about her. Is she..."

"She's dead, you know," broke in Peter hastily, lest Urquhart should make a mistake embarrassing to himself. "A long time ago," he added, again anxious to save embarrassment.

"Yes—oh yes." Urquhart, from his manner, might or might not have known.

"I live with my uncle," Peter further told him, thus delicately and unobstrusively supplying the information that Mr. Margerison too was dead. He omitted to mention the date of this bereavement, having always a delicate sense of what did and did not concern his hearers. The decease of the lady who had for a brief period been Lady Hugh Urquhart, might be supposed to be of a certain interest to her stepson; that of her second husband was a private family affair of the Margerisons.

(The Urquhart-Margerison connection, which may possibly appear complicated, was really very simple, and also of exceedingly little importance to anyone but Peter; but in case anyone feels a desire to have these things elucidated, it may here be mentioned that Peter's mother had made two marriages, the first being with Urquhart's father, Urquhart being already in existence at the time; the second with Mr. Margerison, a clergyman, who was also already father of one son, and became Peter's father later. Put so, it sounds a little difficult, chiefly because they were all married so frequently and so rapidly, but really is simplicity itself.)

"I live with my uncle too," Urquhart said, and the fact formed a shadowy bond. But Peter's tone had struck a note of flatness that faintly indicated a lack of enthusiasm as to the ménage. This note was, to Peter's delicately attuned ears, absent from Urquhart's voice. Peter wondered if Lord Hugh's brother (supposing it to be a paternal uncle) resembled Lord Hugh. To resemble Lord Hugh, Peter had always understood (till three years ago, when his mother had fallen into silence on that and all other topics) was to be of a charm.... One spoke of it with a faint sigh. And yet of a charm that somehow had lacked something, the intuitive Peter had divined; perhaps it had been too splendid, too fortunate, for a lady who had loved all small, weak, unlucky things. Anyhow, not long after Lord Hugh's death (he was killed out hunting) she had married Mr. Margerison, the poorest clergyman she could find, and the most devoted to the tending of the unprosperous.

Peter remembered her—compassionate, delicate, lovely, full of laughter, with something in the dance of her vivid dark-blue eyes that hinted at radiant and sad memories. She had loved Lord Hugh for a glorious and brief space of time. The love had perhaps descended, a hereditary bequest, with the deep blue eyes, to her son. Peter would have understood the love; the thing he would not have understood was the feeling that had flung her on the tide of reaction at Mr. Margerison's feet. Mr. Margerison was a hard liver and a tremendous giver. Both these things had come to mean a great deal to Sylvia Urquhart—much more than they had meant to the girl Sylvia Hope.

And hence Peter, who lay and looked at Lord Hugh Urquhart's son with wide, bright eyes. With just such eyes—only holding, let us hope, an adoration more masked—Sylvia Hope had long ago looked at Lord Hugh, seeing him beautiful, delicately featured, pale, and fair of skin, built with a strong fineness, and smiling with pleasant eyes. Lord Hugh's beauty of person and charm of manner had possibly (not certainly) meant more to Sylvia Hope than his son's meant to her son; and his prowess at football (if he had any) had almost certainly meant less. But, apart from the glamour of physical skill and strength and the official glory of captainship, the same charm worked on mother and son. The soft, quick, unemphasised voice, with the break of a laugh in it, had precisely the same disturbing effect on both.

"Well," Urquhart was saying, "when will they let you play again? You must buck up and get all right quickly.... I shouldn't wonder if you made a pretty decent three-quarter sometime.... You ought to use your arm as soon as you can, you know, or it gets stiff, and then you can't, and that's an awful bore.... Hurt like anything when I hauled it in, didn't it? But it was much better to do it at once."

"Oh, much," Peter agreed.

"How does it feel now?"

"Oh, all right. I don't feel it much. I say, do you think I ought to use it at once, in case it gets stiff?" Peter's eyes were a little anxious; he didn't much want to use it at once.

But Urquhart opined that this would be over-great haste. He departed, and his last words were, "You must come to breakfast with me when you're up again."

Peter lay, glorified, and thought it all over. Urquhart knew, then; he had known from the first. He had known when he said, "I say, you, Margerison, just cut down to the field ..."

Not for a moment did it seem at all strange to Peter that Urquhart should have had this knowledge and given no sign till now. What, after all, was it to a hero that the family circle of an obscure individual such as he should have momentarily intersected the hero's own orbit? School has this distinction—families take a back place; one is judged on one's own individual merits. Peter would much rather think that Urquhart had come to see him because he had put his arm out and Urquhart had put it in (really though, only temporarily in) than because his mother had once been Urquhart's stepmother.

Peter's arm did not recover so soon as Urquhart's sanguineness had predicted. Perhaps he began taking precautions against stiffness too soon; anyhow he did not that term make a decent three-quarter, or any sort of a three-quarter at all. It always took Peter a long time to get well of things; he was easy to break and hard to mend—made in Germany, as he was frequently told. So cheaply made was he that he could perform nothing. Defeated dreams lived in his eyes; but to light them there burned perpetually the blue and luminous lamps of undefeated mirth, and also an immense friendliness for life and mankind and the delightful world. Like the young knight Agenore, Peter the unlucky was of a mind having no limits of hope. Over the blue and friendly eyes that lit the small pale face, the half wistful brows were cocked with a kind of whimsical and gentle humour, the same humour that twitched constantly at the corners of his wide and flexible mouth. Peter was not a beautiful person, but one liked, somehow, to look at him and to meet his half-enquiring, half-amused, wholly friendly and sympathetic regard. By the end of his first term at school, he found himself unaccountably popular. Already he was called "Margery" and seldom seen by himself. He enjoyed life, because he liked people and they liked him, and things in general were rather jolly and very funny, even with a dislocated shoulder. Also the great Urquhart would, when he remembered, take a little notice of Peter—enough to inflate the young gentleman's spirit like a blown-out balloon and send him soaring skywards, to float gently down again at his leisure.

Towards the end of the term, Peter's half-brother Hilary came to visit him. Hilary was tall and slim and dark and rather beautiful, and he lived abroad and painted, and he told Peter that he was going to be married to a woman called Peggy Callaghan. Peter, who had always admired Hilary from afar, was rather sorry. The woman Peggy Callaghan would, he vaguely believed, come between Hilary and his family; and already there were more than enough of such obstacles to intercourse. But at tea-time he saw the woman, and she was large and fair and laughing, and called him, in her rich, amused voice "little brother dear," and he did not mind at all, but liked her and her laugh and her mirthful, lazy eyes.

Peter was a large-minded person; he did not mind that Hilary wore no collar and a floppy tie. He did not mind this even when they met Urquhart in the street. Peter whispered as he passed, "*That's* Urquhart," and Hilary suddenly stopped and held out his hand, and said pleasantly, "I am glad to meet you." Peter blushed at that, naturally (for Hilary's cheek, not for his tie), and hoped that Urquhart wasn't much offended, but that he understood what half-brothers who lived abroad and painted were, and didn't think it was Peter's fault. Urquhart shook hands quite pleasantly, and when Hilary added, "We shared a stepmother, you and I; I'm Peter's half-brother, you know," he amiably agreed. Peter hoped he didn't think that the Urquhart-Margerison connection was being strained beyond due bounds. Hilary said further, "You've been very good to my young brother, I know," and it was characteristic of Peter that, even while he listened to this embarrassing remark, he was free enough from self-consciousness to be thinking with a keen though undefined pleasure how extraordinarily nice to look at both Hilary and Urquhart, in their different ways, were. (Peter's love of the beautiful matured with his growth, but in intensity it could scarcely grow.) Urquhart was saying something about bad luck and shoulders; it was decent of Urquhart to say that. In fact, things were going really well till Hilary, after saying, "Good-bye, glad to have met you," added to it the afterthought, "You must come and stay at my uncle's place in Sussex some time. Mustn't he, Peter?" At the same time—fitting accompaniment to the over-bold words—Peter saw a half-crown, a round, solid, terrible *half-crown*, pressed into Urquhart's unsuspecting hand. Oh, horror! Which was the worse, the invitation or the half-crown? Peter could never determine. Which was the more flagrant indecency—that he, young Margerison of the lower fourth, should, without any encouragement whatever, have asked Urquhart of the sixth, captain of the fifteen, head of his house, to come and stay with him; or that his near relative should have pressed half-a-crown into the great Urquhart's hand as if he expected him to go forthwith to the tuck-shop at the corner and buy tarts? Peter wriggled, scarlet from his collar to his hair.

Urquhart was a polite person. He took the half-crown. He murmured something about being very glad. He even smiled his pleasant smile. And Peter, entirely unexpectedly to himself, did what he always did in the crises of his singularly disastrous life—he exploded into a giggle. So, some years later, he laughed helplessly and suddenly, standing among the broken fragments of his social reputation and his professional career. He could not help it. When the worst had happened, there was nothing else one could do. One laughed from a sheer sense of the completeness of the disaster. Peter had a funny, extremely amused laugh; hardly the laugh of a prosperous person; rather that of the unhorsed knight who acknowledges the utterness of his defeat and finds humour in the very fact. It was as if misfortune—and this misfortune of the half-crown and the invitation is not to be under-estimated—sharpened all the faculties, never blunt, by which he apprehended humour. So he looked from Hilary to Urquhart, and, mentally, from both to his cowering self, and exploded.

Urquhart had passed on. Hilary said, "What's the matter with *you*?" and Peter recovered himself and said "Nothing." He might have cried, with Miss Evelina Anvill, "Oh, my dear sir, I am shocked to death!" He did not. He did not even say, "Why did you stamp us like that?" He would not for the world have hurt Hilary's feelings, and vaguely he knew that this splendid, unusual half-brother of his was in some ways a sensitive person.

Hilary said, "The Urquharts ought to invite you to stay. The connection is really close. I believe your mother was devoted to that boy as a baby. You'd like to go and stay there, wouldn't you?"

Peter looked doubtful. He was nervous. Suppose Hilary met Urquhart again.... Dire possibilities opened. Next time it might be "Peter must go and stay at *your* uncle's place in Berkshire." That would be worse. Yes, the worst had not happened, after all. Urquhart might have met Peggy. Peggy would in that case have said, "You nice kind boy, you've been such a dear to this little brother of ours, and I hear you and these boys used to share a mamma, so you're really brothers, and so, of course, *my* brother too; and *what* a nice face you've got!" There were in fact, no limits to what Peggy might say. Peggy was outrageous. But it was surprising how much one could bear from her. Presumably, Peter used to reflect in after years, when he had to bear from her a very great deal indeed, it was simply by virtue of her being Peggy. It was the same with Hilary. They were Hilary and Peggy, and one took them as such. Indeed, one had to, as there was certainly no altering them. And Peter loved both of them very much indeed.

When Peter went home for the holidays, he found that Hilary's alliance with the woman Peggy Callaghan was not smiled upon. But then none of Hilary's projects were ever smiled upon by his uncle, who always said, "Hilary must do as he likes. But he is acting with his usual lack of judgment." For four years he had been saying so, and he said it again now. To Hilary himself he further said, "You can't afford a wife at all. You certainly can't afford Miss Callaghan. You have no right whatever to marry until you are earning a settled livelihood. You are not of the temperament to make any woman consistently happy. Miss Callaghan is the daughter of an Irish doctor, and a Catholic."

"It is," said Hilary, "the most beautiful of all the religions. If I could bring myself under the yoke of any creed at all ..."

"Just so," said his uncle, who was a disagreeable man; "but you can't," and Hilary tolerantly left it at that, merely adding, "There will be no difficulty. We have arranged all that. Peggy is not a bigot. As to the rest, I think we must judge for ourselves. I shall be earning more now, I imagine."

Hilary always imagined that; imagination was his strong point. His initial mistake was to imagine that he could paint. He did not think that he had yet painted anything very good; but he knew that he was just about to do so. He had really the artist's eye, and saw keenly the beauty that was, though he did not know it, beyond his grasp. His uncle, who knew nothing about art, could have told him that he would never be able to paint, simply because he had never been, and would never be, able to work. That gift he wholly lacked. Besides, like young Peter, he seemed constitutionally incapable of success. A wide and quick receptiveness, a considerable power of appreciation and assimilation, made such genius as they had; the power of performance they desperately lacked; their enterprises always let them through. Failure was the tragi-comic note of their unprosperous careers.

However, Hilary succeeded in achieving marriage with the cheerful Peggy Callaghan, and having done so they went abroad and lived an uneven and rather exciting life of alternate squalor and luxury in one story of what had once been a glorious roseate home of Venetian counts, and was now crumbling to pieces and let in flats to the poor. Hilary and his wife were most suitably domiciled therein, environed by a splendid dinginess and squalor, pretentious, tawdry, grandiose, and superbly evading the common.

Peggy wrote to Peter in her large sprawling hand, "You dear little brother, I wish you'd come and live with us. We have *such* fun...." That was the best of Peggy. Always and everywhere she had such fun. She added, "Give my sisterly regards to the splendid hero who shared your mamma, and tell him we too live in a palace." That was so like Peggy, that sudden and amused prodding into the most secret intimacies of one's emotions. Peggy always discerned a great deal, and was blind to a great deal more.

CHAPTER II

THE CHOICE OF A CAREER

Hilary, stretching his slender length wearily in Peter's fat arm-chair, was saying in his high, sweet voice:

"It's the merest pittance, Peter, yours and mine. The Robinsons have it practically all. The *Robinsons*. Really, you know ..."

The sweet voice had a characteristic, vibrating break of contempt. Hilary had always hated the Robinsons, who now had it practically all. Hilary looked pale and tired; he had been settling his dead uncle's affairs for the last week. The Margerisons' uncle had not been a lovable man; Hilary could not pretend that he had loved him. Peter had, as far as he had been permitted to do so; Peter found it possible to be attached to most of the people he came across; he was a person of catholic sympathies and gregarious instincts. Even when he heard how the Robinsons had it practically all, he bore no resentment either against his uncle or the Robinsons. Such was life. And of course he and Hilary did not make wise use of money; that they had always been told.

"You'll have to leave Cambridge," Hilary told him. "You haven't enough to keep you here. I'm sorry, Peter; I'm afraid you'll have to begin and try to earn a living. But I can't imagine how, can you? Has any paying line of life ever occurred to you as possible?"

"Never," Peter assured him. "But I've not had time to think it over yet, of course. I supposed I should be up here for two years more, you see."

At Hilary's "You'll have to leave Cambridge," his face had changed sharply. Here was tragedy indeed. Bother the Robinsons.... But after a moment's pause for recovery he answered Hilary lightly enough. Such, again, was life. A marvellous two terms and a half, and then the familiar barred gate. It was an old story.

Hilary's thoughts turned to his own situation. They never, to tell the truth, dwelt very long on anybody else's.

"We," he said, "are destitute—absolutely. It's simply frightful, the wear and strain of it. Peggy, of course," he added plaintively, "is *not* a good manager. She likes spending, you know—and there's so seldom anything to spend, poor Peggy. So life is disappointing for her. The babies, I needn't say, are growing up little vagabonds. And they will bathe in the canals, which isn't respectable, of course; though one is relieved in a way that they should bathe anywhere."

"If he was selling any pictures," Peter reflected, "he would tell me," so he did not enquire. Peter had tact as to his questions. One rather needed it with Hilary. But he wondered vaguely what the babies had, at the moment, to grow up upon, even as little vagabonds. Presently Hilary enlightened him.

"I edit a magazine," he said, and Peter perceived that he was both proud and ashamed of the fact. "At least I am going to. A monthly publication for the entertainment and edification of the Englishman in Venice. Lord Evelyn Urquhart is financing it. You know he has taken up his residence in Venice? A pleasant crank. Venice is his latest craze. He buys glass. And, indeed, most other things. He shops all day. It's a mania. When he was young I believe he had a very fine taste. It's dulled now—a fearful life, as they say. Well, his last fancy is to run a magazine, and I'm to edit it. It's to be called 'The Gem.' 'Gemm' Adriatica,' you know, and all that; besides, it's more or less appropriate to the contents. It's to be largely concerned with what Lord Evelyn calls 'charming things.' Things the visiting Englishman likes to hear about, you know. It aims at being the Complete Tourist's Guide. I have to get hold of people who'll write articles on the Duomo mosaics, and the galleries and churches and palaces and so on, and glass and lace and anything else that occurs to them, in a way calculated to appeal to the cultivated British resident or visitor. I detest the breed, I needn't say. Pampered hotel Philistines pretending to culture and profaning the sanctuaries, Ruskin in hand. *Ruskin*. Really, you know.... Well, anyhow, my mission in life for the present is to minister to their insatiable appetite for rhapsodising over what they feel it incumbent on them to admire."

"Rather fascinating," Peter said. It was a pity that Hilary always so disliked any work he had to do. Work—a terrific, insatiable god, demanding its hideous human sacrifices from the dawn of the world till twilight—so Hilary saw it. The idea of being horrible, all the concrete details into which it was translated were horrible too.

"If it was me," said Peter, "I should minister to my own appetite, no one else's. Bother the cultivated resident. He'd jolly well have to take what I gave him. And glass and mosaic and lace—what glorious things to write about.... I rather love Lord Evelyn, don't you."

Peter remembered him at Astleys, in Berkshire—Urquhart's uncle, tall and slim and exquisite, with beautiful waistcoats and white, attractive, nervous hands, that played with a monocle, and a high-pitched voice, and a whimsical, prematurely worn-out face, and a habit of screwing up short-sighted eyes and saying, with his queer, closed enunciation, "Quate charming. Quate." He had always liked Peter, who had been a gentle and amused boy and had reminded him of Sylvia Hope, lacking her beauty, but with a funny touch of her charm. Peter had loved the things he loved, too—the precious and admirable things he had collected round him through a recklessly extravagant life. Peter at fifteen, in the first hour of his first visit to Astleys, had been caught out of the incredible romance of being in Urquhart's home into a new marvel, and stood breathless before a Bow rose bowl of soft and mellow paste, ornamented with old Japan May flowers in red and gold and green, and dated "New Canton, 1750."

"Lake it?" a high voice had asked behind his shoulder. "Lake the sort of thing?" and there was the tall, funny man swaying on his heels and screwing his glass into his eye and looking down on Peter with whimsical interest. Little Peter had said shyly that he did.

"Prefer chaney to cricket?" asked Urquhart's uncle, with his agreeable laugh that was too attractive to be described as a titter, a name that its high, light quality might have suggested. But to that Peter said "No." He had been asked to Astleys for the cricket week; he was going to play for Urquhart's team. Not that he was any good; but to scrape through without disgrace (of course he didn't) was at the moment the goal of life.

Lord Evelyn had seemed disappointed. "If I could get you away from Denis," he said, "I'll be bound cricket wouldn't be in the 'also rans.'"

And at that moment Denis had sauntered up, and Peter's worshipping regard had turned from Lord Evelyn's rose bowl to his nephew, and it was Bow china that was not among the also rans. At that too Lord Evelyn had laughed, with his queer, closed mirth.

"Keep that till you fall in love," he had inwardly admonished Peter's back as the two walked away together. "I daresay she won't deserve it any better—but that's a law of nature, and this is sheer squandering. My word, how that boy does lake things—and people!" After all, it was hardly for any Urquhart to condemn squandering.

That was Lord Evelyn, as he lived in Peter's memory—a generous, whimsical, pleasant crank, touched with his nephew's glamour of charm.

When Peter said, "I rather love him, don't you," Hilary replied, "He's a fearful old spendthrift."

Peter demurred at the old. It jarred with one's conceptions of Lord Evelyn. "I don't suppose he's much over fifty," he surmised.

"No, I daresay," Hilary indifferently admitted. "He's gone the pace, of course. Drugs, and all that. He soon won't have a sound faculty left. Oh, I'm attached to him; he's entertaining, and one can really talk to him, which is exceptional in Venice, or, indeed, anywhere else. Is his nephew still up here, by the way?"

"Yes. He's going down this term."

"You see a good deal of him, I suppose?"

"Off and on," said Peter.

"Of course," said Hilary, "you're almost half-brothers. I do feel that the Urquharts owe us something, for the sake of the connexion. I shall talk to Lord Evelyn about you. He was very fond of your mother.... I am very sorry about you, Peter. We must think it over sometime, seriously."

He got up and began to walk about the room in his nervous, restless way, looking at Peter's things. Peter's room was rather pleasing. Everything in it had the air of being the selection of a personal and discriminating affection. There was a serene self-confidence about Peter's tastes; he always knew precisely what he liked, irrespective of what anyone else liked. If he had happened to admire "The Soul's Awakening" he would beyond doubt have hung a copy of it in his room. What he had, as a matter of fact, hung in his room very successfully expressed an aspect of himself. The room conveyed restfulness, and an immense love, innate rather than grafted, of the pleasures of the eye. The characteristic of restfulness was conveyed partly by the fat green sofa and the almost superfluous number of extremely comfortable arm-chairs, and Peter's attitude in one of them. On a frame in a corner a large piece of embroidery was stretched—a cherry tree in blossom coming to slow birth on a green serge background. Peter was quite good at embroidery. He carried pieces of it (mostly elaborately designed book-covers) about in his pockets, and took them out at tea-parties and (surreptitiously) at lectures. He said it was soothing, like smoking; only smoking didn't soothe him, it made him feel ill. On days when he had been doing tiresome or boring or jarring things, or been associating with a certain type of person, he did a great deal of embroidery in the evenings, because, as he said, it was such a change. The embroidery stood for a symbol, a type of the pleasures of the senses, and when he fell to it with fervour beyond the ordinary, one understood that he had been having a surfeit of the displeasures of the senses, and felt need to restore the balance.

Hilary stopped before a piece of extremely shabby, frayed and dingy tapestry, that had the appearance of having once been even dingier and shabbier. It looked as if it had lain for years in a dusty corner of a dusty old shop, till someone had found it and been pleased by it and taken possession, loving it through its squalor.

"Rather nice," said Hilary. "Really good, isn't it?"

Peter nodded. "Gobelin, of the best time. Someone told me that afterwards. When I bought it, I only knew it was nice. A man wanted to buy it from me for quite a lot."

Hilary looked about him. "You've got some good things. How do you pick them up?"

"I try," said Peter, "to look as if I didn't care whether I had them or not. Then they let me have them for very little. The man I got that tapestry from didn't know how nice it was. I did, but I cheated him."

"Well," Hilary said, passing his hand wearily over his forehead, "I must go to your detestable station and catch my train.... I've got a horrible headache. The strain of all this is frightful."

He looked as if it was. His pale face, nervous and strained, stabbed at Peter's affection for him. Peter's affection for Hilary had always been and always would be an unreasoning, loyal, unspoilably tender thing.

He went to the station to help Hilary to catch his train. The enterprise was a failure; it was not a job at which either Margerison was good. They had to wait in the detestable station for another. The annoyance of that (it is really an abnormally depressing station) worked on Hilary's nervous system to such an extent that he might have flung himself on the line and so found peace from the disappointments of life, had not Peter been at hand to cheer him up. There were certainly points about young Peter as a companion for the desperate.

Peter, having missed hall, as well as Hilary's train, went back to his room and put an egg on to boil. He lay back in his most comfortable chair to watch it; he needed comfort rather. He was going down. It had been so jolly—and it was over.

He had not got much to show for the good time he had had. Physically, he was more of a wreck than he had been when he came up. He was slightly lame in one leg, having broken it at football (before he had been forbidden to play) and had it badly set. He mended so badly always. He was also at the moment right-handed (habitually he used his left) and that was motor bicycling. He had not particularly distinguished himself in his work. He was good at nothing except diabolo, and not very good at that. And he had spent more money than he possessed, having drawn lavishly on his next year's allowance. He might, in fact, have been described as an impoverished and discredited wreck. But for such a one he had looked very cheerful, till Hilary had said that about going down. That was really depressing.

Peter, as the egg boiled, looked back rather wistfully over his year. It seemed a very long time ago since he had come up. His had been an undistinguished arrival; he had not come as a sandwich man between two signboards that labelled his past career and explained his path that was to be; he had been unaddressed to any destination. The only remark on his vague and undistinguished label had perhaps been of the nature of "Brittle. This side up with care." He had no fame at any game; he did not row; he was neither a sporting nor, in any marked degree, a reading man. He did a little work, but he was not very fond of it or very good. The only things one could say of him were that he seemed to have an immense faculty of enjoyment and a considerable number of friends, who knew him as Margery and ate muffins and chocolates between tea and dinner in his rooms.

He had been asked at the outset by one of these friends what sort of things he meant to "go in for." He had said that he didn't exactly know. "Must one go in for anything, except exams?" The friend, who was vigorously inclined, had said that one certainly ought. One could—he had measured Peter's frail physique and remembered all the things he couldn't do—play golf. Peter had thought that one really couldn't; it was such a chilly game. Well, of course, one might speak at the Union, said the persevering friend, insisting, it seemed, on finding Peter a career. "Don't they talk about politics?" enquired Peter. "I couldn't do that, you know. I don't approve of politics. If ever I have a vote I shall sell it to the highest female bidder. Fancy being a Liberal or a Conservative, out of all the nice things there are in the world to be! There are health-fooders, now. I'd rather be that. And teetotallers. A man told me he was a teetotaller to-day. I'll go in for that if you like, because I don't much like wine. And I hate beer. These are rather nice chocolates—I mean, they were."

The indefatigable friend had further informed him that one might be a Fabian and have a red tie, and encourage the other Fabians to wash. Or one might ride.

"One might—" Peter had made a suggestion of his own—"ride a motor bicycle. I saw a man on one to-day; I mean he had been on it—it was on him at the moment; it had chucked him off and was dancing on him, and something that smelt was coming out of a hole. He was such a long way from home; I was sorry about it."

His friend had said, "Serve him right. Brute," expressing the general feeling of the moment about men who rode motor bicycles.

"Isn't it funny," Peter had reflectively said. "They must get such an awful headache first—and then to be chucked off and jumped on so hard, and covered with the smelly stuff—and then to have to walk home dragging it, when it's deformed and won't run on its wheels. Unless, of course, one is blown up into little bits and is at rest.... But it is so awfully, frightfully ugly, to look at and to smell and to hear. Like your wallpaper, you know."

Peter's eyes had rested contentedly on his own peaceful green walls. He really hadn't felt in the least like "going in for" anything, either motor bicycling or examinations.

"I suppose you'll just footle, then," his friend had summed it up, and left him, because it was half-past six, and they had dinner at that strange hour. That was why they were able to run it into their tea, since obviously nothing could be done between, even by Peter's energetic friend. This friend had little hope for Peter. Of course, he would just footle; he always had. But one was, nevertheless, rather fond of him. One would like him to do things, and have a sporting time.

As a matter of fact, Peter gave his friend an agreeable surprise. He went in, or attempted to go in, for a good many things. He plunged ardently into football, though he had never been good, and though he always got extremely tired over it, which was supposed to be bad for him, and frequently got smashed up, which he knew to be unpleasant for him. This came to an abrupt end half way through the term. Then he took, quite suddenly, to motor bicycling. All this is merely to say that the incalculable factor that sets temperament and natural predilection at nought had entered into Peter's life. Of course, it was absurd. Urquhart, being what he was, could successfully do a number of things that Peter, being what *he* was, must inevitably come to grief over. But still he indomitably tried. He even profaned the roads and outraged all æsthetic fitness in the endeavour, clacking into the country upon a hired motor-bicycle and making his head ache badly and getting very cold, and being from time to time thrown off and jumped upon and going about in bandages, telling enquirers that he supposed he must have knocked against something somewhere, he didn't remember exactly. The energetic friend had been caustic.

"I've no intention of sympathising with you," he had remarked; "because you deserve all you get. You ass, you know when it's possible to get smashed up over anything you're safe to do it, so what on earth do you expect when you take up a thing like this?"

"Instant death every minute," Peter had truly replied. (His nerves had been a little shaken by his last ride, which had set his trouser-leg on fire suddenly, and nearly, as he remarked, burnt him to death.) "But I go on. I expect the worst, but I am resigned. The hero is not he who feels no fear, for that were brutal and irrational."

"What do you *do* it for?" his friend had querulously and superfluously demanded.

"It's so frightfully funny," Peter had said, reflecting, "that I should be doing it. That's why, I suppose. It makes me laugh. You might take to the fiddle if you wanted a good laugh. I take to my motor-bicycle. It's the only way to cheer oneself up when life is disappointing, to go and do something entirely ridiculous. I used to stand on my head when I'd been rowed or sat upon, or when there was a beastly wind; it cheered me a lot. I've given that up now; so I motor-bicycle. Besides," he had added, "you said I must go in for something. You wouldn't like it if I did my embroidery all day."

But on the days when he had been motor-bicycling, Peter had to do a great deal of embroidery in the evenings, for the sake of the change.

"I don't wonder you need it," a friend of the more æsthetically cultured type remarked one evening, finding him doing it. "You've been playing round with the Urquhart-Fitzmaurice lot to-day, haven't you? Nice man, Fitzmaurice, isn't he? I like his tie-pins. You know, we almost lost him last summer. He hung in the balance, and our hearts were in our mouths. But he is still with us. You look as if he had been very much with you, Margery."

Peter looked meditative and stitched. "Old Fitz," he murmured, "is one of the best. A real sportsman.... Don't, Elmslie; I didn't think of that, I heard Childers say it. Childers also said, 'By Jove, old Fitz knocks spots out of 'em every time,' but I don't know what he meant. I'm trying to learn to talk like Childers. When I can do that, I shall buy a tie-pin like Fitzmaurice's, only mine will be paste. Streater's is paste; he's another nice man."

"He certainly is. In fact, Margery, you really are *not* particular enough about the company you keep. You shun neither the over-bred nor the under-bred. Personally I affect neither, because they don't amuse me. You embrace both."

"Yes," Peter mildly agreed. "But I don't embrace Streater, you know. I draw the line at Streater. Everyone draws the line at Streater; he's of the baser sort, like his tie-pins. Wouldn't it be vexing to have people always drawing lines at you. There'd be nothing you could well do, except to draw one at them, and they wouldn't notice yours, probably, if they'd got theirs in first. You could only sneer. One can always sneer. I sneered to-day."

"You can't sneer," Elmslie told him brutally; "and you can't draw lines; and what on earth you hang about with so many different sorts of idiots for I don't know.... I think, if circumstances absolutely compelled me to make bosom friends of either, I should choose the under-bred poor rather than the over-bred rich. That's the sort of man I've no use for. The sort of man with so much money that he has to chuck it all about the place to get rid of it. The sort of man who talks to you about beagles. The sort of man who has a different fancy waistcoat for each day of the week."

"Well," said Peter, "that's nice. I wish I had."

His friend turned a grave regard on him. "The sort of man who rides a motor-bicycle.... You really should, Margery," he went on, "learn to be more fastidious. You mustn't let yourself be either dazzled by fancy waistcoats or sympathetically moved by unclean collars. Neither is interesting."

"I never said they were," Peter said. "It's the people inside them...."

Peter, in brief, was a lover of his kind, and the music life played to him was of a varied and complex nature. But, looking back, it was easy to see how there had been, running through all the variations, a dominant motive in the piece.

As Peter listened to the boiling of his egg, and thought how hard it would be when he took it off, the dominant motive came in and stood by the fire, and looked down on Peter. He jingled things in his pockets and swayed to and fro on his heels like his uncle Evelyn, and he was slim in build, and fair and pale and clear-cut of face, and gentle and rather indifferent in manner, and soft and casual in voice, and he was in his fourth year, and life went extremely well with him.

"It boils," he told Peter, of the egg.

Peter took it off and fished it out with a spoon, and began rummaging for an egg-cup and salt and marmalade and buns in the locker beneath his window seat. Having found these things, he composed himself in the fat arm-chair to dine, with a sigh of satisfaction.

"You slacker," Urquhart observed. "Well, can you come to-morrow? The drag starts at eleven."

"It's quite hard," said Peter, unreasonably disappointed in it. "Oh, yes, rather; I'll come." How short the time for doing things had suddenly become.

Urquhart remarked, looking at the carpet, "What a revolting mess. Why?"

"My self-filling bath," Peter explained. "I invented it myself. Well—it did fill itself. Quite suddenly and all at once, you know. It was a very beautiful sight. But rather unrestrained at present. I must improve it.... Oh, this is my last term."

"Sent down?" Urquhart sympathetically enquired. It was what one might expect to happen to Peter.

"Destitute," Peter told him. "The Robinsons have it practically all. Hilary told me to-day. I am thrown on the world. I shall have to work. Hilary is destitute too, and Peggy has nothing to spend, and the babies insist on bathing in the canals. Bad luck for us, isn't it. Oh, and Hilary is going to edit a magazine called 'The Gem,' for your uncle in Venice. That seems rather a nice plan. The question is, what am I to apply *my* great gifts to?"

Urquhart whistled softly. "As bad as all that, is it?"

"Quite as bad. Worse if anything.... The only thing in careers that I can fancy at the moment is art dealing—picking up nice things cheap and selling them dear, you know. Only I should always want to keep them, of course. If I don't do that I shall have to live by my needle. If they pass the Sweated Industries Bill, I suppose one will get quite a lot. It's the only Bill I've ever been interested in. My uncle was extremely struck by the intelligent way I took notice of it, when I had disappointed him so much about Tariff Reform and Education."

"You'd probably be among the unskilled millions whom the bill turns out of work."

"Then I shall be unemployed, and march with a flag. I shall rather like that.... Oh, I suppose somehow one manages to live, doesn't one, whether one has a degree or not. And personally I'd rather not have one, because it would be such a mortifying one. Besides," Peter added, after a luminous moment of reflection, "I don't believe a degree really matters much, in my profession. You didn't know I had a profession, I expect; I've just thought of it. I'm going to be a buyer for the Ignorant Rich. Make their houses liveable-in. They tell me what they want—I get hold of it for them. Turn them out an Italian drawing-room—Della Robbia mantel-piece, Florentine fire-irons, Renaissance ceiling, tapestries and so on. Things they haven't energy to find for themselves or intelligence to know when they see them. I love finding them, and I'm practised at cheating. One has to cheat if one's poor but eager.... A poor trade, but my own. I can grub about low shops all day, and go to sales at Christie's. What fun."

Urquhart said, "You'd better begin on Leslie. You're exactly what he wants."

"Who's Leslie?" Peter was eating buns and marmalade, in restored spirits.

"Leslie's an Ignorant Rich. He's a Hebrew. His parents weren't called Leslie, but never mind. Leslie rolls. He also bounds, but not aggressively high. One can quite stand him; in fact, he has his good points. He's rich but eager. Also he doesn't know a good thing when he sees it. He lacks your discerning eye, Margery. But such is his eagerness that he is determined to have good things, even though he doesn't know them when he sees them.

He would like to be a connoisseur—a collector of world-wide fame. He would like to fill his house with things that would make people open their eyes and whistle. But at present he's got no guide but price and his own pure taste. Consequently he gets hopelessly let in, and people whistle, but not in the way he wants. He's quite frank; he told me all about it. What he wants is a man with a good eye, to do his shopping for him. It would be an ideal berth for a man with the desire but not the power to purchase; a unique partnership of talent with capital. There you are. You supply the talent. He'd take you on, for certain. It would be a very nice little job for you to begin with. By the time you've decorated his town house and his country seat and his shooting-box and all his other residences, you'll be fairly started in your profession. I'll write to him about you."

Peter chuckled. "How frightfully funny, though. I wonder why anyone should want to have things unless they like to have them for themselves. Just as if I were to hire Streater, say, to buy really beautiful photographs of actresses for me!... Well, suppose he didn't like the things I bought for him? Suppose our tastes didn't agree? Should I have to try and suit his, or would he have to put up with mine?"

"There's only one taste in the matter," Urquhart told him. "He hasn't got any. You could buy him any old thing and tell him it was good and he'd believe you, provided it cost enough. That's why he has to have a buyer honest though poor—he couldn't check him in the least. I shall tell him that, however many the things you might lie about, you are a George Washington where your precious bric-a-brac is concerned, because it's the one thing you care about too much to take it flippantly."

Peter chuckled again. Life, having for a little while drifted perilously near to the shores of dullness, again bobbed merrily on the waters of farce. What a lot of funny things there were, all waiting to be done! This that Urquhart suggested should certainly, if possible, be one of them.

A week later, when Mr. Leslie had written to engage Peter's services, Urquhart's second cousin Rodney came into Peter's room (a thing he had never done before, because he did not know Peter much) and said, "But why not start a curiosity shop of your own? Or be a travelling pedlar? It would be so much more amusing."

Peter felt a little flattered. He liked Rodney, who was in his third year and had never before taken any particular notice of him. Rodney was a rather brilliant science man; he was also an apostle, a vegetarian, a fine football player, an ex-Fabian, and a few other things. He was a large, emaciated-looking person, with extraordinarily bright grey eyes, inspiring a lean, pale, dark-browed face—the face of an ascetic, lit by a flame of energising life. He looked as if he would spend and be spent by it to the last charred fragment, in pursuit of the idea. There was nothing in his vivid aspect of Peter Margerison's gentle philosophy of acquiescence; he looked as if he would to the end dictate terms to life rather than accept them—an attitude combined oddly with a view which regarded the changes and chances of circumstance as more or less irrelevant to life's vital essence.

Peter didn't know why Rodney wanted him to be a travelling pedlar—except that, as he had anyhow once been a Socialist, he presumably disliked the rich (ignorant or otherwise) and included Leslie among them. Peter always had a vague feeling that Rodney did not wholly appreciate his cousin Urquhart, for this same reason. A man of means, Rodney would no doubt have held, has much ado to save his soul alive; better, if possible, be a bricklayer or a mendicant friar.

"Some day," said Peter politely, "I may have to be a travelling pedlar. This is only an experiment, to see if it works."

He was conscious suddenly of two opposing principles that crossed swords with a clash. Rodney and Urquhart—poverty and wealth—he could not analyse further.

But Rodney was newly friendly to him for the rest of that term. Urquhart commented on it.

"Stephen always takes notice of the destitute. The best qualification for his regard is to commit such a solecism that society cuts you, or such a crime that you get a month's hard. Short of that, it will do to have a hole in your coat, or paint a bad picture, or produce a yesterday's handkerchief. He probably thinks you're on the road to that. When you get there, he'll swear eternal friendship. He can't away with the prosperous."

"What a mistake," Peter said. It seemed to him a singularly perverse point of view.

CHAPTER III

THE HOPES

It was rather fun shopping for Leslie. Leslie was a stout, quiet, ponderous person between thirty and forty, and he really did not bound at all; Urquhart had done him less than justice in his description. There was about him the pathos of the very rich. He was generous in the extreme, and Peter's job proved lucrative as well as pleasant. He grew curiously fond of Leslie; his attitude towards him was one of respect touched with protectiveness. No one should any more "do" Leslie, if he could help it.

"He's let me," Peter told his cousin Lucy, "get rid of all his horrible Lowestoft forgeries; awful things they were, with the blue hardly dry on them. Frightful cheek, selling him things like that; it's so insulting. Leslie's awfully sweet-tempered about being gulled, though. He's very kind to me; he lets me buy anything I like for him. And he recommends me to his friends, too. It's a splendid profession; I'm so glad I thought of it. If I hadn't I should have had to go into a dye shop, or be a weaver or something. It wouldn't have been good form; it wouldn't even have been clean. I should have had a day-before-yesterday's handkerchief and Rodney would have liked me more, but Denis would probably have cut me. As it is I'm quite good form and quite clean, and I move in the best circles. I love the Ignorant Rich; they're so amusing. I know such a nice lady. She buys potato rings. She likes them to be Dublin hall-marked and clearly dated seventeen hundred and something—so, naturally, they always were till I began to buy them for her. I've persuaded her to give away the most blatant forgeries to her god-children at their baptisms. Babies like them, sham or genuine."

Peter was having tea with his cousin Lucy and Urquhart in the White City. Peter and Lucy were very fond of the White City. Peter's cousin Lucy was something like a small, gay spring flower, with wide, solemn grey eyes that brimmed with sudden laughters, and a funny, infectious gurgle of a laugh. She was a year younger than Peter, and they had all their lives gone shares in their possessions, from guinea-pigs to ideas. They admired the same china and the same people, with unquestioning unanimity. Lucy lived in Chelsea, with an elder sister and a father who ran at his own expense a revolutionary journal that didn't pay, because those who would have liked to buy it couldn't, for the most part, afford to, and because those who could have afforded to didn't want to, and because, in short, journals run by nice people never do pay.

Lucy played the 'cello, the instrument usually selected by the small in stature. In the intervals of this pursuit, she went about the world open-eyed to all new-burnished joys that came within her vision, and lived by admiration, hope and love, and played with Peter at any game, wise or foolish, that turned up. Often Urquhart played with them, and they were a happy party of three. Peter and Lucy shared, among other things, an admiration of Urquhart.

Peter was finding the world delightful just now. This first winter in London was probably the happiest time he ever had. He hardly missed Cambridge; he certainly didn't miss the money that the Robinsons had. His profession was to touch and handle the things he loved; the Ignorant Rich were delightful; the things he bought for them were beyond all words; the sales he attended were revels of joy; it was all extremely entertaining, and Leslie a dear, and everyone very kind. The affection that always found its way to Peter through his disabilities spoke for something in him that must, it would seem, be there; possibly it was merely his friendly smile. He was anyhow of the genus comedian, that readily endears itself.

He and Urquhart and Lucy all knew how to live. They made good use of most of the happy resources that London offers to its inhabitants. They went in steamers to and fro between Putney and Greenwich, listening to concertinas and other instruments of music. They looked at many sorts of pictures, talked to many sorts of people, and attended many sorts of plays. Urquhart and Peter had even become associates of the Y.M.C.A. (representing themselves as agnostics seeking for light) on account of the swimming-baths. As Peter remarked, "Christian Young Men do not bathe very much, and it seems a pity no one should." On the day when they had tea at the White City, they had all had lunch at a very recherché café in Soho, where the Smart Set like to meet Bohemians, and you can only get in by being one or the other, so Peter and Lucy went as the Smart Set, and Urquhart as a Bohemian, and they liked to meet each other very much.

The only drawback to Peter's life was the bronchitis that sprang at him out of the fogs and temporarily stopped work. He had just recovered from an attack of it on the day when he was having tea at the White City, and he looked a weak and washed-out rag, with sunken blue eyes smiling out of a very white face.

"You would think, to look at him," Urquhart said to Lucy, "that he had been going in extensively for the flip-flap this afternoon. It's a pity Stephen can't see you, Margery; you look starved enough to satisfy even him. You never come across Stephen now, I suppose? You wouldn't, of course. He has no opinion of the Ignorant Rich. Nor even of the well-informed rich, like me. He's blindly prejudiced in favour of the Ignorant Poor."

Lucy nodded. "I know. He's nice to me always. I go and play my 'cello to his friends."

"I always keep him in mind," said Peter, "for the day when my patrons get tired of me. I know Rodney will be kind to me directly I take to street peddling or any other thoroughly ill-bred profession. The kind he despises most, I suppose, are my dear Ignorant Rich—the ill-bred but by no means breadless. (That's my own and not very funny, by the way.) Did I tell you, Denis, that Leslie is going to begin educating the People in Appreciation of Objects of Art? Isn't it a nice idea? I'm to help. Leslie's a visionary, you know. I believe plutocrats often are. They've so much money and are so comfortable that they stop wanting material things and begin dreaming dreams. I should dream dreams if I was a plutocrat. As it is my mind is earthly. I don't want to educate anyone. Well, anyhow we're going to Italy in the spring, to pick things up, as Leslie puts it. That always sounds so much as if we didn't pay for them. Then we shall bring them home and have free exhibits for the Ignorant Poor, and I shall give free and instructive lectures. Isn't it a pleasant plan? We're going to Venice. There's a Berovieri goblet that some Venetian count has, that Leslie's set his heart on. We are to acquire it, regardless of expense, if it turns out to be all that is rumoured."

Urquhart scoffed here.

"Nice to be infallible, isn't it. You and your goblets and your Ignorant Rich. And your brother Hilary and my uncle Evelyn. Your great gifts seem to run in the family. My uncle, I hear, is ruining himself with buying the things your brother admires. My poor uncle, Miss Hope, is getting so weak-sighted that he can't judge for himself as he used, so he follows the advice of Margery's brother. It keeps him very happy and amused, though he'll soon be bankrupt, no doubt."

Lucy, as usual, laughed at the Urquhart family and the Margerison family and the world at large. When she laughed, she opened her grey eyes wide, while they twinkled with dancing light.

Then she said, "Oh, I want to go on the flip-flap. Peter mustn't come, because it always makes him sick; so will you?"

Urquhart said he would, so they did, and Peter watched them, hoping Urquhart didn't mind much. Urquhart never seemed to mind being ordered about by Lucy. And Lucy, of course, had accepted him as an intimate friend from the first, because Peter had said she was to, and because, as she remarked, he was so astonishingly nice to look at and to listen to.

Among the visitors who frequented Lucy's home, people whom she considered astonishingly pleasant to look at and to listen to did not abound; so Lucy enjoyed the change all the more.

The first time Peter took Urquhart down to Chelsea to call on his Hope uncle and cousins, one Sunday afternoon, he gave him a succinct account of the sort of people they would probably meet there.

"They have oddities in, you know—and particularly on Sunday afternoons. They usually have one or two staying in the house, too. They keep open house for wastrels. A lot of them are aliens—Polish refugees, Russian anarchists, oppressed Finns, massacred Armenians who do embroidery; violinists who can't earn a living, decayed chimney-sweeps and so forth. 'Disillusioned (or still illusioned) geniuses, would-bes, theorists, artistic natures, failed reformers, knaves and fools incompetent or over-old, broken evangelists and debauchees, inebriates, criminals, cowards, virtual slaves' ... Anyhow it's a home for Lost Hopes. (Do you see that?) My uncle is keen on anyone who tries to revolt against anything—governments, Russians, proprieties, or anything else—and Felicity is keen on anyone who fails."

"And your other cousin—what is she keen on?"

"Oh, Lucy's too young for the Oddities, like me. She and I sit in a corner and look on. It's my uncle and Felicity they like to talk to. They talk about Liberty to them, you know. My uncle is great on Liberty. And they give them lemon in their tea, and say how wicked Russians are, and how stupid Royal Academicians are, and buy the Armenians' embroidery, and so forth. Lucy and I don't do that well. I disapprove of liberty for most people, I think, and certainly for them; and I don't like lemon in my tea, and though I'm sure Russians are wicked, I believe oppressed Poles are as bad—at least their hair is as bushy and their nails as long—and I prefer the embroidery I do myself; I do it quite nicely, I think. And I don't consider that Celtic poets or Armenian Christians wash their hands often enough.... They nearly all asked me the time last Sunday. I was sorry about it."

"You feared they were finding their afternoon tedious?"

"No; but I think their watches were up the spout, you see. So I was sorry. I never feel so sorry for myself as when mine is. I'm really awfully grateful to Leslie; if it wasn't for him I should never be able to tell anyone the time. By the way, Leslie's awfully fond of Felicity. He writes her enormous cheques for her clubs and vagabonds and so on. But of course she'll never look at him; he's much too well-off. It's not low to tell you that, because he makes it so awfully obvious. He'll probably be there this afternoon. Oh, here we are."

They found the Hopes' small drawing-room filled much as Peter had predicted. Dermot Hope was a tall, wasted-looking man of fifty-five, with brilliant eyes giving significance to a vague face. He had very little money, and spent that little on "Progress," whose readers were few and ardent, and whose contributors were very cosmopolitan, and full of zeal and fire; several of them were here this afternoon. Dermot Hope himself was most unconquerably full of fire. He could be delightful, and exceedingly disagreeable, full of genial sympathy and appreciation, and of a biting irony. He looked at Urquhart, whom he met for the first time, with a touch of sarcasm in his smile. He said, "You're exactly like your father. How do you do," and seemed to take no further interest in him. He had certainly never taken much in Lord Hugh, during the brief year of their brotherhood.

For Peter his glance was indulgent. Peter, not being himself a reformer, or an idealist, or a lover of progress, or even, according to himself, of liberty, but an acceptor of things as they are and a lover of the good things of this world, was not particularly interesting to his uncle, of course; but, being rather an endearing boy, and the son of a beloved sister, he was loved; and, even had he been a stranger, his position would have been regarded as more respectable than Urquhart's, since he had so far failed to secure many good things.

Felicity, a gracious and lovely person of twenty-nine, gave Peter and Urquhart a smile out of her violet eyes and murmured "Lucy's in the corner over there," and resumed the conversation she was trying to divide between Joseph Leslie and a young English professor who was having a holiday from stirring up revolutions at a Polish university. The division was not altogether easy, even to a person of Felicity's extraordinary tact, particularly as they both happened to be in love with her. Felicity had a great deal of listening to do always, because everyone told her about themselves, and she always heard them gladly; if she hastened the end a little sometimes, gently, they never knew it. She, in fact, wanted to hear about them as much—really as much, though the desire in these proportions is so rare as to seem incredible—as they wanted to let her hear. Her wish to hear was a temptation to egotism; those who disliked egotism in themselves had to fight the temptation, and seldom won. She did not believe—no one but a fool (and she was not that) could have believed—all the many things that were told her; the many things that must always, while pity and the need to be pitied endure, be told to the pitiful; but she seldom said so. She merely looked at the teller with her long and lovely violet eyes, that took in so much and gave out such continual friendship, and saw how, behind the lies, the need dwelt pleading. Then she gave, not necessarily what the lies asked for, but what, in her opinion, pity owed to that which pleaded. She certainly gave, as a rule, quite too much, in whatever coin she paid. That was inevitable.

"You give from the emotions," Joseph Leslie told her, "instead of from reason. How bad for you: how bad for them. And worse when it is friendship than when it is coin that you can count and set a limit to. Yes. Abominably bad for everyone concerned."

"Should one," wondered Felicity, "give friendship, as one is supposed to give money, on C.O.S. principles? Perhaps so; I must think about it."

But her thinking always brought her back to the same conclusion as before. Consequently her circle of friends grew and grew. She even included in it a few of the rich and prosperous, not wishing her chain of fellowship, whose links she kept in careful repair, to fail anywhere. But it showed strain there. It was forged and flung by the rich and prosperous, and merely accepted by Felicity.

Leslie, though rich and prosperous, stepped into the linked circle led by Peter, who was neither. Having money, and a desire to make himself conscious of the fact by using it, he consulted Miss Hope as to how best to be philanthropic. He wanted, it seemed, to be a philanthropist as well as a collector, and felt incapable of being either otherwise than through agents. His personal share in both enterprises had to be limited to the backing capital.

Miss Hope said, "Start a settlement," and he had said, "I can't unless you'll work it for me. Will you?" So he started a settlement, and she worked it for him, and he came about the place and got in the way and wrote heavy cheques and adored Felicity and suggested at suitable intervals that she should marry him.

Felicity had no intention of marrying him. She called him a rest. No one likes being called a rest when they desire to be a stimulant, or even a gentle excitement. Felicity was an immense excitement to Mr. Leslie (though he concealed it laboriously under a heavy and matter-of-fact exterior) and it is of course pleasanter when these things are reciprocal. But Mr. Leslie perceived that she took much more interest even in her young cousin Peter than in him. "Do you find him a useful little boy?" she asked him this afternoon, before Peter and Urquhart arrived.

Leslie nodded. "Useful boy—very. And pleasant company, you know. I don't know much about these things, but he seems to have a splendid eye for a good thing. Funny thing is, it works all round—in all departments. Native genius, not training. He sees a horse between a pair of shafts in a country lane; looks at it; says 'That's good. That would have a fair chance for the Grand National'—Urquhart buys it for fifty pounds straight away—

and it *does* win the Grand National. And he knows nothing special about horses, either. That's what I call genius. It's the same eye that makes him spot a dusty old bit of good china on a back shelf of a shop among a crowd of forged rubbish. I've none of that sort of sense; I'm hopeless. But I like good things, and I can pay for them, and I give that boy a free rein. He's furnishing my house well for me. It seems to amuse him rather."

"He loves it," said Felicity. "His love of pleasant things is what he lives by. Including among them Denis Urquhart, of course."

"Yes." Leslie pursed thoughtful lips over Denis Urquhart. He was perhaps slightly touched with jealousy there. He was himself rather drawn towards that tranquil young man, but he knew very well that the drawing was one-sided; Urquhart was patently undrawn.

"Rather a flash lot, the Urquharts, aren't they?" he said; and Peter, who liked him, would have had to admit that the remark was perilously near to a bound. "Seem to have a sort of knack of dazzling people."

"He's an attractive person, of course," Miss Hope replied; and she didn't say it distantly; she was so sorry for people who bounded, and so many of her friends did. "It's pleasing to see, isn't it—such whole-souled devotion?"

Mr. Leslie grunted. "I won't say pearls before swine—because Urquhart isn't a swine, but a very pleasant, ordinary young fellow. But worship like that can't be deserved, you know; not by anyone, however beautifully he motors through life. Margerison's too—well, too nice, to put it simply—to give himself to another person, body and soul, like that. It's squandering."

"And irritates you," she reflected, but merely said, "Is squandering always a bad thing, I wonder?"

It was at this point that Peter and Urquhart came in. Directed by Felicity to Lucy in an obscure corner, they found her being talked to by one of the Oddities; he looked rather like an oppressed Finn. He was talking and she was listening, wide-eyed and ingenuous, her small hands clasped on her lap. Peter and Urquhart sat down by her, and the oppressed Finn presently wandered away to talk to Lucy's father.

Lucy gave a little sigh of relief.

"*Wish* they wouldn't come and talk to me," she said. "I'm no good to them; I don't understand; and I hate people to be unhappy. I'm dreadfully sorry they are. I don't want to have to think about them. Why can't they be happy? There are so many nice things all about. 'Tis such *waste*." She looked up at Urquhart, and her eyes laughed because he was happy and clean, and shone like a new pin.

"It's nicest," she said, "to be happy and clean. And it's not bad to be happy and dirty; or *very* bad to be unhappy and clean; but ..." She shut her lips with a funny distaste on the remaining alternative. "And I'm horribly afraid Felicity's going to get engaged to Mr. Malyon, that young one talking to her, do you see? He helps with conspiracies in Poland."

"But he's quite clean," said Urquhart, looking at him.

Lucy admitted that. "But he'll get sent to Siberia soon, don't you see, and Felicity will go too, I know."

Peter said, "If I was Felicity I'd marry Leslie; I wouldn't hesitate for a moment. I wish it was me he loved so. Fancy marrying into all those lovely things I'm getting for him. Only I hope she won't, because then she'd take over the shopping department, and I should be left unemployed. Oh, Lucy, he's let me buy him the heavenliest pair of Chelsea *jardinières*, shaped like orange-tubs, with Cupids painted on blue panels. You must come and see them soon."

Lucy's eyes, seeing the delightful things, widened and danced. She loved the things Peter bought.

Suddenly Peter, who had a conscience somewhere, felt a pang in it, and, to ease it, regretfully left the corner and wandered about among his uncle's friends, being pleasant and telling them the time. He did that till the last of them had departed. Urquhart then had to depart also, and Peter was alone with his relatives. It was only after Urquhart had gone that Peter realised fully what a very curious and incongruous element he had been in the room. Realising it suddenly, he laughed, and Lucy laughed too. Felicity looked at them indulgently.

"Babies. What's the matter now?"

"Only Denis," explained Peter.

"That young man," commented Dermot Hope, without approbation, "is remarkably well-fed, well-bred, and well-dressed. Why do you take him about with you?"

"That's just why, isn't it, Peter," put in Lucy. "Peter and I *like* people to be well-fed and well-bred and well-dressed."

Felicity touched her chin, with her indulgent smile.

"Baby again. You like no such thing. You'd get tired of it in a week."

"Oh, well," said Lucy, "a week's a long time."

"He's got no fire in all his soul and body," complained Dermot Hope. "He's a symbol of prosperous content—of all we're fighting. It's people like him who are the real obstructionists; the people who don't see, not because they're blind, but because they're too pleased with their own conditions to look beyond them. It's people like him who are pouring water on the fires as they are lit, because fires are such bad form, and might burn up their precious chattels if allowed to get out of hand. Take life placidly; don't get excited, it's so vulgar; that's their religion. They've neither enthusiasm nor imagination in them. And so ..."

And so forth, just as it came out in "Progress" once a month. Peter didn't read "Progress," because he wasn't interested in the future, being essentially a child of to-day. Besides, he too hated conflagrations, thinking the precious chattels they would burn up much too precious for that. Peter was no lover either of destruction or construction; perhaps he too was an obstructionist; though not without imagination. His uncle knew he had a regrettable tendency to put things in the foreground and keep ideas very much in the background, and called him therefore a phenomenalist. Lucy shared this tendency, being a good deal of an artist and nothing at all of a philosopher.

CHAPTER IV

THE COMPLETE SHOPPER

Six months later Peter called at the Hopes' to say good-bye before he went to Italy. He found Lucy in, and Urquhart was there too, talking to her in a room full of leaping fire-shadows. Peter sat down on the coal-scuttle (it was one of those coal-scuttles you can sit on comfortably) and said, "Leslie's taking me to Italy on Sunday. Isn't it nice for me. I wish he was taking you too."

Lucy, clasping small hands, said, "Oh, Peter, I wish he was!"

Urquhart, looking at her said, "Do you want to go?" and she nodded, with her mouth tight shut as if to keep back floods of eloquence on that subject. "So do I," said Urquhart, and added, in his casual way, "Will you and your father come with me?"

"You paying?" said Lucy, in her frank, unabashed way like a child's; and he smiled down at her.

"Yes. Me paying."

"'Twould be nice," she breathed, her grey eyes wide with wistful pleasure. "I would love it. But—but father wouldn't, you know. He wouldn't want to go, and if he did he'd want to pay for it himself, and do it his own way, and travel third-class and be dreadfully uncomfortable. Wouldn't he, Peter?"

Peter feared that he would.

"Thank you tremendously, all the same," said Lucy, prettily polite.

"I shall have to go by myself, then," said Urquhart. "What a bore. I really am going, you know, sometime this spring, to stay with my uncle in Venice. I expect I shall come across you, Margery, with any luck. I shan't start yet, though; I shall wait for better motoring weather. No, I can't stop for tea, thanks; I'm going off for the week-end. Good-bye. Good-bye, Margery. See you next in Venice, probably."

He was gone. Lucy sat still in her characteristic attitude, hands clasped on her knees, solemn grey eyes on the fire.

"He's going away for the week-end," she said, realising it for herself and Peter. "But it's more amusing when he's here. When he's in town, I mean, and comes in. That's nice and funny, isn't it."

"Yes," said Peter.

"But one can go out into the streets and see the people go by—and that's nice and funny too. And there are the Chinese paintings in the British Museum ... and concerts ... and the Zoo ... and I'm going to a theatre to-night. It's *all* nice and funny, isn't it."

"Yes," said Peter again. He thought so too.

"Even when you and he are both gone to Italy," said Lucy, reassuring herself, faintly interrogative. "Even then ... it can't be dull. It can't be dull ever."

"It hasn't been yet," Peter agreed. "But I wish you were coming too to Italy. You must before long. As soon as ..." He left that unfinished, because it was all so vague at present, and he and Lucy always lived in the moment.

"Well," said Lucy, "let's have tea." They had it, out of little Wedgwood cups, and Lucy's mood of faint wistfulness passed over and left them chuckling.

Lucy was a little sad about Felicity, who was now engaged to the young professor who was conspiring in Poland.

"I knew she would, of course. I told you so long ago. He's quite sure to get arrested before long, so that settled it. And they're going to be married directly and go straight out there and plot. He excites the students, you know; as if students needed exciting by their professors.... I shall miss Felicity horribly. *'Tis* too bad."

Peter, to cheer her up, told her what he and Leslie were going to do in Italy.

"I'll write, of course. Picture post cards, you know. And if ever I've twopence halfpenny to spare I'll write a real letter; there'll be a lot to tell you." Peter expected Leslie to be rather funny in Italy, picking things up.

"A great country, I believe, for picking things up," he had said. "Particularly for the garden." He had been referring to his country seat.

"I see," said Peter. "You want to Italianise the garden. I'm not quite sure.... Oh, you might, of course. Iron-work gates, then; and carved Renaissance oil-tanks, and Venetian well-heads, and such-like. All right; we'll see what we can steal. But it's rather easy to let an Italianised garden become florid; you have to be extremely careful with it."

"That's up to you," said Mr. Leslie tranquilly.

So they went to Italy, and Peter picked things up with judgment, and Leslie paid for them with phlegm. They picked up not only carved olive-oil tanks and well-heads and fifteenth-century iron-work gates from ancient and impoverished gardens, but a contemporarily copied Della Robbia fireplace, and designs for Renaissance ceilings, and a rococo carved and painted altarpiece from a mountain church whose *parroco* was hard-up, and a piece of 1480 tapestry that Peter loved very much, whereon St. Anne and other saints played among roses and raspberries, beautiful to behold. These things made both the picker-up and the payer exceedingly contented. Meanwhile Peter with difficulty restrained Leslie from "picking up" stray pieces of mosaic from tessellated pavements, and other curios. Oddly together with Leslie's feeling for the costly went the insane and indiscriminate avidity of the collecting tourist.

"You can't do it," Peter would shrilly and emphatically explain. "It's like a German tripper collecting souvenirs. Things aren't interesting merely because you happen to have been to the places they belong to. What do you want with that bit of glass? It isn't beautiful; when it's taken out of the rest of its pattern like that it's merely ridiculous. I thought you wanted *beautiful* things."

Leslie would meekly give in. His leaning on Peter in this matter of what he wanted was touching. In the matter of what he admired, where no questions of acquisition came in, he and his shopping-man agreed less. Leslie here showed flashes of proper spirit. He also read Ruskin in the train. Peter had small allegiance there; he even, when irritated, called Ruskin a muddle-head.

"He's a good man, isn't he?" Leslie queried, puzzled. "Surely he knows what he's talking about?" and Peter had to admit that that was so.

"He tells me what to like," the self-educator said simply. "And I try to like it. I don't always succeed, but I try. That's right, isn't it?"

"I don't know." Peter was puzzled. "It seems to me rather a funny way of going about it. When you've succeeded, are you much happier? I mean, what sort of a liking is it? Oh, but I don't understand—there aren't two sorts really. You either like a thing, or ... well."

At times one needed a rest from Leslie. But outside the province of art and the pleasures of the eye he was lovable, even likeable, having here a self-dependence and a personality that put pathos far off, and made him himself a rest. And his generosity was limitless. It was almost an oppression; only Peter, being neither proud nor self-conscious, was not easily oppressed. He took what was lavished on him and did his best to deserve it. But it was perhaps a little tiring. Leslie was a thoroughly good sort—a much better sort than most people knew—but Italy was somehow not the fit setting for him. Nothing could have made Peter dislike things pleasant to look at; but Leslie's persevering, uncomprehending groping after their pleasantness made one feel desirous to dig a gulf between them and him. It was rather ageing. Peter missed Urquhart and Lucy; one felt much younger with them. The thought of their clean, light, direct touch on life, that handled its goods without fumbling, and without the need of any intervening medium, was as refreshing as a breath of fresh air in a close room.

Rodney too was refreshing. They came across him at Pietrasanta; he was walking across Tuscany by himself, and came to the station, looking very dusty and disreputable, to put the book he had finished into his bag that travelled by train and get out another.

"Come out of that," he said to Peter, "and walk with me to Florence. Trains for bags; roads for men. You can meet your patron in Florence. Come along."

And Peter, after a brief consultation with the accommodating Leslie, did come along. It was certainly more than amusing. The road in Tuscany is much better than the railway. And Rodney was an interesting and rather attractive person. Since he left Cambridge he had been pursuing abstruse chemical research in a laboratory he had in a Westminster slum. Peter never saw him in London, because the Ignorant Rich do not live in slums, and because Rodney was not fond of the more respectable quarters of the city.

Peter was set speculating vaguely on Rodney's vivid idealism. To Peter, ideas, the unseen spirits of life, were remote, neither questioned nor accepted, but simply in the background. In the foreground, for the moment, were a long white road running through a river valley, and little fortress cities cresting rocky hills, and the black notes of the cypresses striking on a background of silver olives. In these Peter believed; and he believed in blue Berovieri goblets, and Gobelin tapestries, and in a great many other things that he had seen and saw at this moment; he believed intensely, with a poignant vividness of delight, in all things visible. For the rest, it was not that he doubted or wondered much; he had not thought about it enough for that; but it was all very remote. What was spirit, apart from form? Could it be? If so, would it be valuable or admirable? It was the shapes and colours of things, after all, that mattered. As to the pre-existence of things and their hereafter, Peter seldom speculated; he knew that it was through entering the workshop (or the play-room, he would rather have said) of the phenomenal, where the idea took limiting lines and definite shape and the tangible charm of the sense-apprehended, that life for him became life. Rodney attained to his real by looking through the manifold veils of the phenomenal, as through so much glass; Peter to his by an adoring delight in their complex loveliness. He was not a symbolist; he had no love of mystic hints and mist-veiled distances; he was George Herbert's

Man who looks on glassAnd on it rests his eye,

because glass was so extremely jolly. Rodney looked with the mystic's eyes
on life revealed and emerging behind its symbols; Peter with the artist's on
life expressed in the clean and lovely shapes of things, their colours and
tangible sweetness. To Peter Rodney's idealism would have been impossibly
remote; things, as things, had a delightful concrete reality that was its own
justification. They needed to interpret nothing; they were themselves; no
veils, but the very inner sanctuary.

Both creeds, that of things visible and that of the idea, were good, and
suited to the holders; but for those on whom fortune frequently frowns, for
those whose destiny it is to lose and break and not to attain, Peter's has
drawbacks. Things do break so; break and get lost and are no more seen;
and that hurts horribly. Remains the idea, Rodney would have said; that,
being your own, does not get lost unless you throw it away; and, unless you
are a fool, you don't throw it away until you have something better to take
its place.

Anyhow they walked all day and slept on the road. On the third night they
slept in an olive garden; till the moon, striking in silver slants between silver
trees, lit on Rodney's face, and he opened dreamy eyes on a pale, illumined
world. At his side Peter, still in the shadows, slept rolled up in a bag.
Rodney slept with a thin plaid shawl over his knees. He glanced for a
moment at Peter's pale face, a little pathetic in sleep, a little amused too at
the corners of the lightly-closed lips. Rodney's brief regard was rather
friendly and affectionate; then he turned from the dreaming Peter to the
dreaming world. They had gone to sleep in a dark blue night lit by golden
stars, and the olive trees had stood dark and unwhispering about them,
gnarled shapes, waiting their transformation. Now there had emerged a
white world, a silver mystery, a pale dream; and for Rodney the reality that
shone always behind the shadow-foreground dropped the shadows like a
veil and emerged in clean and bare translucence of truth. The dome of
many-coloured glass was here transcended, its stain absorbed in the white
radiance of the elucidating moon. So elucidating was the moon's light that it
left no room for confusion or doubt. So eternally silver were the still ranks
of the olives that one could imagine no transformation there. That was the
pale and immutable light that lit all the worlds. Getting through and behind
the most visible and obvious of the worlds one was in the sphere of true
values; they lay all about, shining in unveiled strangeness, eternally and
unalterably lit. So Rodney, who had his own value-system, saw them.

Peter too was caught presently into the luminous circle, and stirred, and
opened pleased and friendly eyes on the white night—Peter was nearly
always polite, even to those who woke him—then, half apologetically, made

as if to snuggle again into sleep, but Rodney put out a long thin arm and shoved him, and said, "It's time to get up, you slacker," and Peter murmured:

"Oh, bother, all right, have you made tea?"

"No," said Rodney. "You can do without tea this morning."

Peter sat up and began to fumble in his knapsack.

"I see no morning," he patiently remarked, as he struck a match and lit a tiny spirit-lamp. "I see no morning; and whether there is a morning or merely a moon I cannot do without tea. Or biscuits."

He found the biscuits, and apparently they had been underneath him all night.

"I thought the ground felt even pricklier than usual," he commented. "I do have such dreadfully bad luck, don't I. Crumbs, Rodney? They're quite good, for crumbs. Better than crusts, anyhow. I should think even you could eat crumbs without pampering yourself. And if crumbs then tea, or you'll choke. Here you are."

He poured tea into two collapsible cups and passed one to Rodney, who had been discoursing for some time on his special topic, the art of doing without.

Then Peter, drinking tea and munching crumbs, sat up in his bag and looked at what Rodney described as the morning. He saw how the long, pointed olive leaves stood with sharp edges against pale light; how the silver screen was, if one looked into it, a thing of magic details of delight, of manifold shapes and sharp little shadowings and delicate tracery; how gnarled stems were light-touched and shadow-touched and silver and black; how the night was delicate, marvellous, a radiant wonder of clear loveliness, illustrated by a large white moon. Peter saw it and smiled. He did not see Rodney's world, but his own.

But both saw how the large moon dipped and dipped. Soon it would dip below the dim land's rim, and the olive trees would be blurred and twisted shadows in a still shadow-world.

"Then," said Peter dreamily, "we shall be able to go to sleep again."

Rodney pulled him out of his bag and firmly rolled it up.

"Twelve kilometres from breakfast. Thirty from tea. No, we don't tea before Florence. Go and wash."

They washed in a copper bucket that hung beside a pulley well. It was rather fun washing, till Peter let the bucket slip off the hook and gurgle down to the bottom. Then it was rather fun fishing for it with the hook, but it was not caught, and they abandoned it in sudden alarm at a distant sound, and hastily scrambled out of the olive garden onto the white road.

Beneath their feet lay the thick soft dust, unstirred as yet by the day's journeyings. The wayfaring smell of it caught at their breath. Before them the pale road wound and wound, between the silver secrecy of the olive woods, towards the journeying moon that dipped above a far and hidden city in the west. Then a dim horizon took the dipping moon, and there remained a grey road that smelt of dust and ran between shadowed gardens that showed no more their eternal silver, but gnarled and twisted stems that mocked and leered.

One traveller stepped out of his clear circle of illumined values into the shrouded dusk of the old accustomed mystery, and the road ran faint to his eyes through a blurred land, and he had perforce to take up again the quest of the way step by step. Reality, for a lucid space of time emerging, had slipped again behind the shadow-veils. The ranks of the wan olives, waiting silently for dawn, held and hid their secret.

The other traveller murmured, "How many tones of grey do you suppose there are in an olive tree when the moon has set? But there'll be more presently. Listen...."

The little wind that comes before the dawn stirred and shivered, and disquieted the silence of the dim woods. Peter knew how the stirred leaves would be shivering white, only in the dark twilight one could not see.

The dusk paled and paled. Soon one would catch the silver of up-turned leaves.

On the soft deep dust the treading feet of the travellers moved quietly. One walked with a light unevenness, a slight limp.

CHAPTER V

THE SPLENDID MORNING

"Listen," said Peter again; and some far off thing was faintly jarring the soft silence, on a crescendo note.

Rodney listened, and murmured, "Brute." He hated them more than Peter did. He was less wide-minded and less sweet-tempered. Peter had a gentle and not intolerant æsthetic aversion, Rodney a fervid moral indignation.

It came storming over the rims of twilight out of an unborn dawn, and the soft dust surged behind. Its eyes flamed, and lit the pale world. It was running to the city in the dim west; it was in a hurry; it would be there for breakfast. As it ran it played the opening bars of something of Tchaichowsky's.

Rodney and Peter leant over the low white wall and gazed into grey shivering gardens. So could they show aloof contempt; so could they elude the rioting dust.

The storming took a diminuendo note; it slackened to a throbbing murmur. The brute had stopped, and close to them. The brute was investigating itself.

"Perhaps," Rodney hoped, but not sanguinely, "they'll have to push it all the way to Florence." Still contempt withheld a glance.

Then a pleasant, soft voice broke the hushed dusk with half a laugh, and Peter wheeled sharply about. The man who had laughed was climbing again into his seat, saying, "It's quite all right." That remark was extremely characteristic; it would have been a suitable motto for his whole career.

The next thing he said, in his gentle, unsurprised voice, was to the bare-headed figure that smiled up at him from the road.

"You, Margery?... What a game. But what have you done with the Hebrew? Oh, that's Stephen, isn't it. That accounts for it: but how did he get you? I say, you can't have slept anywhere; there's *been* nowhere, for miles. And have you left Leslie to roam alone among the Objects of Beauty with his own unsophisticated taste for guide? I suppose he's chucked you at last; very decent-spirited of him, I think, don't you, Stephen?"

"I chucked him," Peter explained, "because he bought a sham Carlo Dolci. I drew the line at that. Though if one must have a Carlo Dolci, I suppose it had better be a sham one, on the whole. Anyhow, I came away and took to the road. We sleep in ditches, and we like it very much, and I make tea every morning in my little kettle. I'm going to Florence to help Leslie to buy bronze things for his grates—dogs, you know, and shovels and things. Leslie will have been there for three days now: I do wonder what he's bought."

"You'd better come on in the car," Urquhart said. "Both of you. Why is Stephen looking so proud? I shall be at Florence for breakfast. *You* won't, though. Bad luck. Come along; there's loads of room."

Rodney stood by the wall. He was unlike Peter in this, that his resentment towards a person who motored across Tuscany between dusk and dawn was in no way lessened by the discovery of who it was.

Peter stood, his feet deep in dust, and smiled at Urquhart. Rodney watched the two a little cynically from the wall. Peter looked what he was—a limping vagabond tramp, dust-smeared, bare-headed, very much part of the twilight road. In spite of his knapsack, he had the air of possessing nothing and smiling over the thought.

Peter said, "How funny," meaning the combination of Urquhart and the motor-car and Tuscany and the grey dawn and Rodney and himself; Urquhart was smiling down at them, his face pale in the strange dawn-twilight. The scene was symbolical of their whole relations; it seemed as if Urquhart, lifted triumphantly above the road's dust, had always so smiled down on Peter, in his vagabond weakness.

"I don't think," Urquhart was saying, "that you ought to walk so far in the night. It's weakening." To Urquhart Peter had always been a brittle incompetent, who could not do things, who kept breaking into bits if roughly handled.

"Rodney and I don't think," Peter returned, in the hushed voice that belonged to the still hour, "that you ought to motor so loud in the night. It's common. Rodney specially thinks so. Rodney is sulking; he won't come and speak to you."

Urquhart called to his cousin: "Come with me to Florence, you and Margery. Or do you hate them too much?"

"Much too much," Rodney admitted, coming forwards perforce. "Thank you," he added, "but I'm on a walking tour, and it wouldn't do to spoil it. Margery isn't, though. You go, Margery, if you like."

Urquhart said, "Do, Margery," and Peter looked wistful, but declined. He wanted horribly badly to go with Urquhart; but loyalty hindered.

Urquhart said he was going to Venice afterwards, to stay with his uncle Evelyn.

"Good," said Peter. "Leslie and I are going to do Venice directly we've cleared Florence of its Objects of Beauty. You can imagine the way Leslie will go about Florence, his purse in his hand, asking the price of the Bargello. 'Worth having, isn't it? A good thing, I think?' If we decide that it is he'll have it, whatever the price; he always does. He's a sportsman; I can't tell you how attached I am to him." Peter had not told even Urquhart that one was ever glad of a rest from Leslie.

Urquhart said, "Well, if you *won't* come," and hummed into the paling twilight, and before him fled the circle of golden light and after him swept the dust. Peter's eyes followed the golden light and the surging whiteness till a bend in the road took them, and the world was again dim and grey and very still. Only the little cool wind that soughed among the olive leaves was like the hushed murmuring of quiet waves. Eastwards, among the still, mysterious hills and silver plains, a translucent dawn was coming.

Peter's sigh was very unobtrusive. "After all," he murmured, "motoring does make me feel sick."

Rodney gave half a cynical smile with the corner of his mouth not occupied with his short and ugly pipe. Peter was pipeless; smoking, perhaps, had the same disastrous effect.

"But all the same," said Peter, suddenly aggrieved, "you might be pleasant to your own cousin, even if he is in a motor. Why be proud?"

He was really a little vexed that Rodney should look with aloofness on Urquhart. For him Urquhart embodied the brilliance of life, its splendidness and beauty and joy. Rodney, with his fanatical tilting at prosperity, would, Peter half consciously knew, have to see Urquhart unhorsed and stripped bare before he would take much notice of him.

"Too many things," said Rodney, indistinctly over his thick pipe. "That's all."

Peter, irritated, said, "The old story. The more things the better; why not? You'd be happy on a desert island full of horrid naked savages. You think you're civilised, but you're really the most primitive person I know."

Rodney said he was glad; he liked to be primitive, and added, "But you're wrong, of course. The naked savages would like anything they could get— beads or feathers or top hats; they're not natural ascetics; the simple life is enforced.... St. Francis took off all his clothes in the Piazza and began his new career without any."

"Disgusting," murmured Peter.

"That," said Rodney, "is what people like Denis should do. They need to unload, strip bare, to find themselves, to find life."

"Denis," said Peter, "is the most alive person I know, as it happens. He's found life without needing to take his clothes off—so he scores over St. Francis."

Denis had rushed through the twilight vivid like a flame—he had lit it for a moment and left it grey. Peter knew that.

"But he hasn't," Rodney maintained, "got the key of the thing. If he did take his clothes off, it would be a toss-up whether he found more life or lost what he's got. That's all wrong, don't you see. That's what ails all these delightful, prosperous people. They're swimming with life-belts."

"You'll be saying next," said Peter, disgusted, "that you admire Savonarola and his bonfire."

"I do, of course. But he'd only got hold of half of it—half the gospel of the empty-handed. The point is to lose and laugh." For a moment Rodney had a vision of Peter standing bare-headed in the dust and smiling. "To drop all the trappings and still find life jolly—just because it *is* life, not because of what it brings. That's what St. Francis did. That's where Italy scores over England. I remember at Lerici the beggars laughing on the shore, with a little maccaroni to last them the day. There was a man all done up in bandages, hopping about on crutches and grinning. Smashed to bits, and his bones sticking out of his skin for hunger, but there was the sun and the sea and the game he was playing with dice, and he looked as if he was saying, '*Nihil habentes, omnia possidentes*; isn't it a jolly day?' When Denis says that, I shall begin to have hopes for him. At present he thinks it's a jolly day because he's got money to throw about and a hundred and one games to play at and friends to play them with, and everything his own way, and a new motor.... Well, but look at that now. Isn't it bare and splendid—all clean lines—no messing and softness; it might be cut out of rock. Oh, I like Tuscany."

They had rounded a bend, and a spacious country lay there stretched to the morning, and over it the marvel of the dawn opened and blossomed like a flower. From the basin of the shining river the hills stood back, and up their steep sides the vine-hung mulberries and close-trimmed olives climbed (olives south of the Serchio are diligently pruned, and lack the generous luxuriance of the north), and against the silver background the sentinel cypresses stood black, like sharp music notes striking abruptly into a vague symphony; and among the mulberry gardens and the olives and the cypresses white roads climbed and spiralled up to little cresting cities that took the rosy dawn. Tuscany emerging out of the dim mystery of night had a splendid clarity, an unblurred cleanness of line, an austere fineness, as of a land hewn sharply out of rock.

Peter would not have that fine bareness used as illustration; it was too good a thing in itself. Rodney the symbolist saw the vision of life in it, Peter the joy of self-sufficient beauty.

The quiet road bore them through the hushed translucence of the dawn-clear land. Everything was silent in this limpid hour; the little wind that had whitened the olives and set the sea-waves whispering there had dropped now and lay very still.

The road ran level through the river basin. Far ahead they could see it now, a white ribbon laid beside a long golden gleam that wound and wound.

Peter sighed, seeing so much of it all at once, and stopped to rest on the low white wall, but instead of sitting on it he swayed suddenly forward, and the hill cities circled close about him, and darkened and shut out the dawn.

The smell of the dust, when one was close to it, was bitter and odd. Somewhere in the further darkness a voice was muttering mild and perplexed imprecations. Peter moved on the strong arm that was supporting him and opened his eyes and looked on the world again. Between him and the rosy morning, Rodney loomed large, pouring whisky into a flask.

It all seemed a very old and often-repeated tale. One could not do anything; one could not even go a walking-tour: one could not (of this one was quite sure) take whisky at this juncture without feeling horribly sick. The only thing that occurred to Peter, in the face of the dominant Rodney, was to say, "I'm a teetotaller." Rodney nodded and held the flask to his lips. Rodney was looking rather worried.

Peter said presently, still at length in the dust, "I'm frightfully sorry. I suppose I'm tired. Didn't we get up rather early and walk rather fast?"

"I suppose," said Rodney, "you oughtn't to have come. What's wrong, you rotter?"

Peter sat up, and there lay the road again, stretching and stretching into the pink morning.

"Thirty kilometres to breakfast," murmured Peter. "And I don't know that I want any, even then. Wrong?... Oh ... well, I suppose it's heart. I have one, you know, of a sort. A nuisance, it's always been. Not dangerous, but just in the way. I'm sorry, Rodney—I really am."

Rodney said again, "You absolute rotter. Why didn't you tell me? What in the name of anything induced you to walk at all? You needn't have."

Peter looked down the long road that wound and wound into the morning land. "I wanted to," he said. "I wanted to most awfully.... I wanted to try it.... I thought perhaps it was the one thing.... Football's off for me, you know—and most other things.... Only diabolo left ... and ping-pong ... and jig-saw. I'm quite good at those ... but oh, I did want to be able to walk. Horribly I wanted it."

"Well," said Rodney practically, "it's extremely obvious that you aren't. You ought to have got into that thing, of course. Only then, as you remarked, you would have felt sick. Really, Margery...."

"Oh, I know," Peter stopped him hastily. "*Don't* say the usual things; I really feel too unwell to bear them. I know I'm made in Germany and all that— I've been hearing so all my life. And now I should like you to go on to Florence, and I'll follow, very slow. It's all very well, Rodney, but you were going at about seven miles an hour. Talk of motors—I couldn't see the scenery as we rushed by. That's such a Vandal-like way of crossing Tuscany."

"Well, you can cross the rest of Tuscany by train. There's a station at Montelupo; we shall be there directly."

Peter, abruptly renouncing his intention of getting up, lay back giddily. The marvellous morning was splendid on the mountains.

"How extremely lucky," remarked Peter weakly, "that I wasn't in this position when Denis came by. Denis usually does come by at these crucial moments you know—always has. He probably thinks by now that I am an escaped inhabitant of the Permanent Casualty Ward. Bother. I wish he didn't."

"Since it's obvious," said Rodney, "that you can't stand, let alone walk, I had better go on to Montelupo and fetch a carriage of sorts. I wonder if you can lie there quietly till I come back, or if you'll be having seizures and things? Well, I can't help it. I must go, anyhow. There's the whisky on your left."

Peter watched him go; he went at seven miles an hour; the dust ruffled and leapt at his heels.

Peter sat very still leaning back against the rough white wall, and thought what a pity it all was. What a pity, and what a bore, that one could not do things like other people. Short of being an Urquhart, who could do everything and had everything, whose passing car flamed triumphant and lit the world into a splendid joy, and was approved under investigation with "quite all right"—short of that glorious competence and pride of life, one might surely be an average man, who could walk from San Pietro to Florence without tumbling on the road at dawn. Peter sighed over it, rather crossly. The marvellous morning was insulted by his collapse; it became a remote thing, in which he might have no share. As always, the inexorable "Not for you" rose like a barred gate between him and the lucid country the white road threaded.

Peter in the dust began to whistle softly, to cheer himself, and because he was really feeling better, and because anyhow, for him or not for him, the land at dawn was a golden and glorious thing, and he loved it. What did it matter whether he could walk through it or not? There it lay, magical, clear-hewn, bathed in golden sunrise.

Round the turn of the road a bent figure came, stepping slowly and with age, a woodstack on his back. Heavier even than a knapsack containing a spirit kettle and a Decameron and biscuit remainders in a paper bag, it must be. Peter watched the slow figure sympathetically. Would he sway and topple over; and if he did would the woodstack break his fall? The whisky flask stood ready on Peter's left.

Peter stopped whistling to watch; then he became aware that once more the hidden distances were jarring and humming. He sat upright, and waited; a little space of listening, then once again the sungod's chariot stormed into the morning.

Peter watched it grow in size. How extremely fortunate.... Even though one was again, as usual, found collapsed and absurd.

The woodstack pursued its slow advance. The music from Tchaichowsky admonished it, as a matter of form, from far off, then sharply, summarily, from a lessening distance. The woodstack was puzzled, vaguely worried. It stopped, dubiously moved to one side, and pursued its cautious way a little uncertainly.

Urquhart, without his chauffeur this time, was driving over the speed-limit, Peter perceived. He usually did. But he ought to slacken his pace now, or he would miss Peter by the wall. He was nearing the woodstack, just going to pass it, with a clear two yards between. It was not his doing: it was the woodstack that suddenly lessened the distance, lurching over it, taking the middle of the road.

Peter cried, "Oh, don't—oh, *don't*," idiotically, sprawling on hands and knees.

The car swung sharply about like a tugged horse; sprang to the other side of the road, hung poised on a wheel, as near as possible capsized. A less violent jerk and it would have gone clean over the woodstack that lay in the road on the top of its bearer.

By the time Peter got there, Urquhart had lifted the burden from the old bent figure that lay face downwards. Gently he turned it over, and they looked on a thin old face gone grey with more than age.

"He can't be," said Urquhart. "He can't be. I didn't touch him."

Peter said nothing. His eyes rested on the broken end of a chestnut-stick protruding from the faggot, dangling loose by its bark. Urquhart's glance followed his.

"I see," said Urquhart quietly. "That did it. The lamp or something must have struck it and knocked him over. Poor old chap." Urquhart's hand shook over the still heart. Peter gave him the whisky flask. Two minutes passed. It was no good.

"His heart must have been bad," said Urquhart, and the soft tones of his pleasant voice were harsh and unsteady. "Shock, I suppose. How—how absolutely awful."

How absolutely incongruous, Peter was dully thinking. Urquhart and tragedy; Urquhart and death. It was that which blackened the radiant morning, not the mercifully abrupt cessation of a worn-out life. For Peter death had two sharply differentiated aspects—one of release to the tired and old, for whom the grasshopper was a burden; the other of an unthinkable blackness of tragedy—sheer sharp loss that knew no compensation. It was not with this bitter face that death had stepped into their lives on this clear morning. One could imagine that weary figure glad to end his wayfaring so; one could even imagine those steps to death deliberately taken; and one did imagine those he left behind him accepting his peace as theirs.

Peter said, "It wasn't your fault. It was his doing—poor chap."

The uncertain quaver in his voice brought Urquhart's eyes for a moment upon his face, that was always pale and was now the colour of putty.

"You're ill, aren't you?... I met Stephen.... I was coming back anyhow; I knew you weren't fit to walk."

He muttered it absently, frowning down on the other greyer face in the grey dust. Again his hand unsteadily groped over the still heart, and lay there for a moment.

Abruptly then he looked up, and met Peter's shadow-circled eyes.

"I was over-driving," he said. "I ought to have slowed down to pass him."
He stood up, frowning down on the two in the road.

"We've got to think now," he said, "what to do about it."

To that thinking Peter offered no help and no hindrance. He sat in the road
by the dead man and the bundle of wood, and looked vaguely on the
remote morning that death had dimmed. Denis and death: Peter would
have done a great deal to sever that incredible connection.

But it was, after all, for Denis to effect that severing, to cut himself loose
from that oppressing and impossible weight.

He did so.

"I don't see," said Denis, "that we need ... that we can ... do anything about
it."

Above the clear mountains the sun swung up triumphant, and the wide
river valley was bathed in radiant gold.

CHAPTER VI

HILARY, PEGGY, AND HER BOARDERS

When Leslie and Peter went to Venice to pick up Berovieri goblets and other things, Leslie stayed at the Hotel Europa and Peter in the Palazzo Amadeo. The Palazzo Amadeo is a dilapidated palace looking onto the Rio delle Beccarie; it is let in flats to the poor; and in the sea-story suite of the great, bare, dingy, gilded rooms lived Hilary and Peggy Margerison, and three disreputable infants who insisted on bathing in the canals, and the boarders. The boarders were at the moment six in number; Peter made seven. The great difficulty with the boarders, Peggy told him, was to make them pay. They had so little money, and such a constitutional reluctance to spend that little on their board.

"The poor things," said Peggy, who had a sympathetic heart. "I'm sure I'm sorry for them, and I hate to ask them for it. But one's got to try and live."

She was drying Illuminato (baptized in that name by his father's desire, but by his mother called Micky) before the stove in the great dining-room. Illuminato had just tumbled off the bottom step into the water, and had been fished out by his uncle Peter; he was three, and had humorous, screwed-up eyes and a wide mouth like a frog's, so that Hilary, who detested ugliness, could really hardly be fond of him. Peggy was; but then Peggy always had more sense of humour than Hilary.

A boarder looked in to see if lunch was ready. It was not, but Peggy began preparations by screaming melodiously for Teresina. They heard the boarder sigh. He was a tall young man with inspired eyes and oily hair. Peter had observed him the night before, with some interest.

"That's Guy Vyvian," Peggy told him, looking for Illuminato's dryer suit in the china cupboard.

"Fancy," said Peter.

"Yes," said Peggy, pulling out a garment and dropping a plate out of its folds on the polished marble floor. "There now! Micky, you're a tiresome little ape and I don't love you. Guy Vyvian's an ape, too, entirely; his one merit is that he writes for 'The Gem,' so that Hilary can take the rent he won't pay out of the money he gives him for his articles. It works out pretty well, on the whole, I fancy; they're neither of them good at paying, so it saves them both bother. ("È pronto, Teresina?" "Subito, subito," cried Teresina from the kitchen.) "I can't abide Vyvian," Peggy resumed. "The babies hate him, and he makes himself horrid to everyone, and lets Rhoda Johnson grovel to him, and stares at the stains on the table-cloth, as if his own nails weren't worse, and turns up his nose at the food. Poor little Rhoda! You saw her? The little thin girl with a cough, who hangs on Vyvian's words and blushes when her mother speaks. She's English governess to the Marchesa Azzareto's children. Mrs. Johnson's a jolly old soul; I'm fond of her; she's the best of the boarders, by a lot. Now, precious, if you tumble in again this morning, you shall sit next to Mr. Vyvian at dinner. You go and tell the others that from me. It isn't respectable, the way you all go on. Here's the minestra at last."

Teresina, clattering about the marble floor with the minestra, screamed "Pronto," very loud, and the boarders trailed in one by one. First came Mr. Guy Vyvian, sauntering with resignedly lifted brows, and looking as if it ought to have been ready a long time ago; he was followed by Mrs. Johnson, a stout and pleasant lady, who looked as if she was only too delighted that it was ready now, and the more the better; her young daughter, Rhoda, wearing a floppy smocked frock and no collar but a bead necklace, coughed behind her; she looked pale and fatigued, and as if it didn't matter in the least if it was never ready at all. She was being talked to by a round-faced, fluffy-haired lady in a green dress and pince-nez, who took an interest in the development of her deplorably uncultured young mind—a Miss Barnett, who was painting pictures to illustrate a book to be called "Venice, Her Spirit." The great hope for young Rhoda, both Miss Barnett and Mr. Vyvian felt, was to widen the gulf between her and her unspeakable mother. They, who quarrelled about everything else, were united in this enterprise. The method adopted was to snub Mrs. Johnson whenever she spoke. That was no doubt why, as Peggy had told Peter, Rhoda blushed on those frequent occasions.

The party was completed by a very young curate, and an elderly spinster with mittens and many ailments, the symptoms of which she lucidly specified in a refined undertone to any lady who would listen; with gentlemen, however, she was most discreet, except with the curate, who complained that his cloth was no protection. Finally Hilary came in and took the head of the table, and Peggy and the children took the other end. Peter found himself between Mrs. Johnson and Miss Barnett, and opposite Mr. Vyvian and Rhoda.

Mrs. Johnson began to be nice to him at once, in her cheery way.

"Know Venice?" and when Peter said, "Not yet," she told him, "Ah, you'll like it, I know. So pleasant as it is. Particlerly for young people. It gives me rheumatics, so much damp about. But my gel Rhoder is that fond of it. Spends all her spare time—not as she's got much, poor gel—in the gall'ries and that. Art, you know. She goes in for it, Rhoder does. I don't, now. I'm a stupid old thing, as they'll all tell you." She nodded cheerfully and inclusively at Mr. Vyvian and Rhoda and Miss Barnett. They did not notice. Vyvian, toying disgustedly with his burnt minestra, was saying in his contemptuous voice, "Of course, if you like *that*, you may as well like the Frari monuments at once and have done."

Rhoda was crimson; she had made another mistake. Miss Barnett, who disputed the office of mentor with Vyvian, whom she jealously disliked, broke in, in her cheery chirp, "I don't agree with you, Mr. Vyvian. I consider it a very fine example of Carpaccio's later style; I think you will find that some good critics are with me." She addressed Peter, ignoring the intervening solidity of Mrs. Johnson. "Do you support me, Mr. Margerison?"

"I've not seen it yet," Peter said rather timidly. "It sounds very nice."

Miss Barnett gave him a rather contemptuous look through her pince-nez and turned to Hilary.

"Lor!" whispered Mrs. Johnson to Peter. "They do get so excited about pictures. Just like that they go on all day, squabblin' and peckin' each other. Always at Rhoder they are too, tellin' her she must think this and mustn't think that, till the poor gel don't know if she's on her head or her heels. She don't like *me* to interfere, or it's all I can do sometimes not to put in my word and say, 'You stick to it, Rhoder my dear; you stand up to 'em and your mother'll back you.' But Rhoder don't like that. 'Mother,' she says, quite sharp, 'Mother, you don't know a thing about Art, and they do. You let be, and don't put me to shame before my friends.' That's what she'd like to say, anyhow, if she's too good a gel to say it. Rhoder's ashamed of my ignorance, that's what it is." This was a furtive whisper, for Peter's ear alone. Having thus unburdened herself Mrs. Johnson cleared her throat noisily and said very loud, "An' what do you think of St. Mark's?" That was a sensible and intelligent question, and she hoped Rhoda heard.

Peter said he thought it was very nice. That Rhoda certainly heard, and she looked at him with a curious expression, in which hope predominated. Was this brother of the Margerisons another fool, worse than her? Would he perhaps make her folly shine almost like wisdom by comparison? She exchanged a glance with Vyvian; it was extraordinarily sweet to be able to do that; so many glances had been exchanged àpropos of *her* remarks between Vyvian and Miss Barnett. But here was a young man who thought St. Mark's was very nice. "The dear Duomo!" Miss Barnett murmured, protecting it from Tourist Insolence.

Mrs. Johnson agreed enthusiastically with Peter.

"I call it just sweet. You should see it on a Sunday, Mr. Margerison—Mr. Peter, as I should say, shouldn't I?—all the flags flying, and the sun shining on the gilt front an' all, and the band playing in the square; an' inside half a dozen services all at once, and the incense floatin' everywhere. Not as I'm partial to incense; it makes me feel a bit squeamish—and Miss Gould there tells me it affects her similarly, don't it, Miss Gould? Incense, I say—don't it give you funny feelin's within? Seem to upset you, as it were?"

Miss Gould, disturbed in her intimate conversation with the curate, held up mittened hands in deprecating horror, either at the delicacy of the question called across the table with gentlemen present, or at the memory it called up in her of the funny feelings within.

Mrs. Johnson took it as that, and nodded. "Just like me, she is, in that way. But I like to see the worship goin' on, all the same. Popish, you know, of course," she added, and then, bethinking herself, "But perhaps you're a Roman, Mr. Peter, like your dear brother and sister? Well, Roman or no Roman, I always say as how Mrs. Margerison is one of the best. A dear, cheery soul, as has hardships to contend with; and if she finds the comforts of religion in graven images an' a bead necklace, who am I to say her no?"

"Peggy," said Hilary wearily across the table, "Illuminato is making a little beast of himself. Put him out."

Peggy scrubbed Illuminato's bullet head dry with her handkerchief (it had been lying in his minestra bowl), slapped him lightly on the hands, and said absently, "Don't worry poor Daddy, who's so tired." She was wishing that the *risotto* had been boiled a little; one gathered from the hardness of the rice that that process had been omitted. Vyvian, who was talking shop with Hilary, sighed deeply and laid down his fork. He wondered why he ever came in to lunch. One could get a much better one nearly as cheap at a restaurant.

Miss Barnett, with an air of wishing to find out how bad a fool Peter was, leaned across Mrs. Johnson and said, "What are you to Venice, Mr. Margerison, and Venice to you? What, I mean, are you going to get out of her? Which of her aspects do you especially approach? She has so infinitely many, you know. What, in fact, is your connecting link?" She waited with some interest for what Peter would say. She had not yet "placed" him.

Peter said, "Oh, well ... I look at things, you know ... much the same as anyone else, I expect. And I go in gondolas; and then there are the things one would like to buy."

Mrs. Johnson approved this. "Lovely, ain't they! Only one never has the money to spend."

"I watch other people spending theirs," said Peter, "which is the next best thing, I suppose ... I'm sorry I'm stupid, Miss Barnett—but it's all so jolly that I don't like to be invidious."

"Do you write?" she enquired.

"Sometimes," he admitted. "You're illustrating a book about Venice, aren't you? That must be awfully interesting."

"I am trying," she said, "to catch the most elusive thing in the world—the Spirit of Venice. It breaks my heart, the pursuit. Just round the corner, always; you know Browning's 'Love in a Life'?

Heart, fear nothing, for heart, thou shalt find her,Next time herself!—not the trouble behind her ...Still the same chance! she goes out as I enter.Spend my whole day in the quest;—who cares? ...

It's like that with me and my Venice. It hurts rather—but I have to go on."

"You shouldn't, my dear," Mrs. Johnson murmured soothingly. "I'm sure you should be careful. We mustn't play tricks with our constitutions."

Rhoda kicked Peter under the table in mistake for her mother, and never discovered the error.

"Can you tell me," Miss Barnett added abruptly, in her cheerful voice, "where it hides?"

Peter looked helpful and intelligent, and endeared himself to her thereby. She thought him a sympathetic young man, with possibilities, probably undeveloped.

Vyvian, who regarded Miss Barnett and "Venice, Her Spirit," with contemptuous jealousy, thought that Rhoda was paying them too much attention, and effectually called her away by saying, "If you care to come with me to the Schiavoni, I can better explain to you what I mean."

Rhoda kindled and flushed and looked suddenly pretty. Peter heard a smothered sigh on his left.

"I don't like it," Mrs. Johnson murmured to him. "No, I don't. If it was you, now, as offered to take her—But there, I daresay you wouldn't be clever enough to suit Rhoder; she's so partic'lar. You and me, now—we get on very well; seems as if we liked to talk on the same subjects, as it were; but Rhoder's different. When we go about together, it's always, 'Mother, not so loud! Oh, mother, you mustn't! Mother, that ain't really beautiful at all, and you're givin' of us away. Mother, folks are listening.' Let 'em listen is what I say. They won't hear anything that could hurt 'em from me. But Rhoder's so quiet; she hates a bit of notice. Not that she minds when she's with *him*; he talks away at the top of his voice, and folks do turn an' listen—I've seen 'em. But I suppose that's clever talk, so Rhoder don't mind."

She raised her voice from the thick and cautious whisper which she thought suitable for these remarks, and addressed Peggy.

"Well, we've had a good dinner, my dear—plenty of it, if the rice *was* a bit underdone."

"A grain," Miss Gould was murmuring to the curate, "a single grain would have had unspeakable effects...."

Peggy was endeavouring to comb Caterina's exceedingly tangled locks with the fingers of one hand, while with the other she slapped Silvio's (Larry's) bare and muddy feet to make him take them off the table-cloth. Not that they made much difference to the condition of the table-cloth; but still, there are conventions.

"It is a disgrace," Hilary remarked mechanically, "that my children can't behave like civilised beings at a meal ... Peter, what are you going to do this afternoon?"

The boarders rose. Mrs. Johnson patted Peter approvingly on the arm, and said, "I'm glad to of had the pleasure. One day we'll go out together, you and me. Seem as if we look at things from the same point of view, as it were. You mayn't be so clever as some, but you suit me. Now, my dear, I'm goin' to help you about the house a bit. The saloon wants dustin', I noticed."

Peggy sighed and said she was sure it did, and Teresina was hopeless, and Mrs. Johnson was really too kind, but it was a shame to bother her, and the saloon could go another while yet. She was struggling with the children's bibs and rather preoccupied.

The boarders went out to pursue their several avocations; Rhoda and Mr. Vyvian to the church of San Giorgio degli Schiavoni, that Mr. Vyvian might the better explain what he meant; Miss Barnett, round-about and cheerful, sketch-book in hand, to hunt for "Venice, Her Spirit," in the Pescaria; Miss Gould to lie down on her bed and recover from lunch; the curate to take the air and photographs for his magic lantern lectures to be delivered in the parish-room at home; and Mrs. Johnson to find a feather broom.

Hilary sat down and lit a cigar, and Illuminato crawled about his legs.

"I'm going out with Leslie," said Peter. "We're going to call on the prince and see the goblet and begin the haggling. We must haggle, though as a matter of fact Leslie means to have it at any price. It must be a perfectly ripping thing.... Now let me have a number of 'The Gem' to read. I've not seen it yet, you know."

"It's very dull, my dear," Peggy murmured, rinsing water over the place on the table-cloth where Silvio's feet had been.

Hilary was gazing into the frog-like countenance of his youngest son. It gave him a disappointment ever new, that Illuminato should be so plain. "But your mother's handsome, frog," he murmured, "and I'm not worse than my neighbours to look at." (But he knew he was better than most of them). "Let's hope you have intellect to make up. Now crawl to your uncle Peter, since you want to."

Illuminato did want to. He adored his uncle Peter.

"The Gem, Peter?" said Hilary. "Bother the Gem. As Peggy remarks, it's very dull, and you won't like it. I don't know that I want you to read it, to say the truth."

Peter was in the act of doing so. He had found three torn pages of it on the floor. He was reading an article called "Osele." Hilary glanced at it, with the slight nervous frown frequent with him.

"What have you got hold of?... Oh, that." His frown seemed to relax a little. "I really don't recommend the thing for your entertainment, Peter. It'll bore you. I have to provide two things—food for the interested visitor, and guidance for Lord Evelyn's mania for purchasing."

"So I am gathering," Peter said. "I'm reading about *osele*, marked with the Mocenigo rose. Signor Antonio Sardi seems to be a man worth a visit. I must take Leslie there. That's just the sort of thing he likes. And sixteenth-century visiting cards. Yes, he'd like those too. By all means we'll go to your friend Sardi. You wrote this, I suppose?"

Hilary nodded. His white nervous fingers played on the arm of his chair. It seemed to be something of an ordeal to him, this first introduction of Peter to the Gem.

Peggy, assisting Teresina to bundle the crockery off the table, shot a swift glance at the group—at Hilary lying back smoking, with slightly knitted forehead, one unsteady hand playing on his chair; at Peter sitting on the marble floor with the torn fragments of paper in his hands and Illuminato astride on his knee. Peggy's grey, Irish eyes were at the moment a little speculative, touched with a dispassionate curiosity and a good deal of sisterly and wifely and maternal and slightly compassionate affection. She was so fond of them all, the dear babes.

Peter had gone on from *osele* to ivory plaques. He was not quite so much interested in reading about them because he knew more about them for himself, but he took down the name of a dealer who had, according to the Gem, some good specimens, and said he should take Leslie there too.

Hilary got up rather suddenly, and jerked his cigar away into a corner (marble floors are useful in some ways) and said, "Is Leslie going to buy the whole place up? I'm sick of these wealthy Jews. They're ruining Venice. Buying all the palaces, you know. I suppose Leslie'll be wanting to do that next. There's altogether too much buying in this forsaken world. Why can't people admire without wanting to acquire? Lord Evelyn can't. The squandering old fool; he's ruining himself over things he's too blind even to look at properly. And this Leslie of yours, who can't even appreciate, still must get and have, of course; and the more he gets the more he wants. Can't you stop him, Peter? It's such a monstrous exhibition of the vice of the age."

"It's not my profession to stop him," Peter said. "And, after all, why shouldn't they? If it makes them happy—well—" His finality conveyed his creed; if it makes them happy, what else is there? To be happy is to have reached the goal. Peter was a little sad about Hilary, who seemed as far as ever from that goal. Why? Peter wondered. Couldn't one be happy in this lovable water-city, which had, after all, green ways of shadow and gloom between the peeling brick walls of ancient houses, and, beyond, the broad spaces of the sea? Couldn't one be happy here even if the babies did poise muddy feet on a table-cloth, not, after all, otherwise clean; and even if the poor boarders wouldn't pay their rent and the rich Jews would buy palaces and plaques? Bother the vice of the age, thought Peter, as he crossed the sun-bathed piazza and suddenly smelt the sea. There surely never was such a jolly world made as this, which had Venice in it for laughter and breathless wonder and delight, and her Duomo shining like a jewel.

"An' the sun shinin' on the gilt front an' all," murmured Peter. "I call it just sweet."

He went in (he was to meet Leslie there), and the soft dusk rippled about him, and beyond the great pillars stretched the limitless, hazy horizons of a dream.

Presently Leslie came. He had an open "Stones of Venice" in his hand, and said, "Now for those mosaics." Leslie was a business-like person, who wasted no time. So they started on the mosaics, and did them for an hour. Leslie said, "Good. Capital," with the sober, painstaking, conscientious appreciation he was wont to bestow on unpurchasable excellence; and Peter said, "How jolly," and felt glad that there were some excellences unpurchasable even by rich Jews.

They then went to the Accademia and looked at pictures. There Leslie had a clue to merit. "Anything on hinges, I presume," he remarked, "is worth inspection. Only why don't they hinge *more* of the good ones? They ought to give us a hint; they really ought. How's a man to be sure he's on the right tack?"

After an hour of that they went to see the prince who had the goblet. Half an hour's conversation with him, and the goblet belonged to Leslie. It was a glorious thing of deep blue glass and translucent enamel and silver, with the Berovieri signature cut on it. Peter looked at it much as he had seen a woman in the Duomo look up at her Lady's shrine, much as Rodney had looked on the illumined reality behind the dreaming silver world.

Peter said, "My word, suppose it broke!" It was natural that he should think of that; things so often broke. Only that morning his gold watch had broken, in Illuminato's active hands. Only that afternoon his bootlace had broken, and he had had none to replace it because Caterina had been sailing his other boots in the canal. Peter sighed over the lovely and brittle world.

Then he and Leslie visited Signor Sardi's shop and looked at *osele* and sixteenth-century visiting cards. Peter said he knew nothing about either personally, but quoted Hilary in the Gem, to Leslie's satisfaction.

"Your brother's a good man," said Leslie. "Knows what's what, doesn't he? If he says these are good *osele*, we may take it that they *are* good *osele*, though we don't know one *osele* from another. That's right, isn't it?"

Peter said he supposed it was, if one wanted *osele* at all, which personally he didn't care about; but one never knew, of course, what might come in useful. Anyhow Leslie bought some, and a visiting card belonging to the Count Amadeo Vasari, which gave him much satisfaction. Then they visited the person who, the Gem had said, had good plaques, and inspected them critically. Then they had tea at Sant' Ortes' tearoom, and then Peter went home.

Hilary, who was looking worried, said, "Lord Evelyn wants us to dine with him to-night," and passed Peter a note in delicate, shaky handwriting.

"Good," said Peter. Hilary wore a bored look and said, "I suppose we must go," and then proceeded to question Peter concerning Leslie's shopping adventures. He seemed on the whole more interested in the purchase of *osele* than of the Berovieri goblet.

"But," said Peter presently, "your plaque friend wasn't in form to-day. He had only shams. Rather bright shams, but still—So we didn't get any, which, I suppose, will please you to hear. Leslie was disappointed. I told your friend we would look in on a better day, when he had some of the real thing. He wasn't pleased. I expect he passes off numbers of those things on people as antiques. You ought to qualify your remarks in the Gem, Hilary—add that Signor Leroni has to be cautiously dealt with—or you'll be letting the uncritical plaque-buyer through rather badly."

"I daresay they can look after themselves," Hilary said, easily; and Peggy added:

"After all, so long as they *are* uncritical, it can't matter to them what sort of a plaque they get!" which of course, was one point of view.

CHAPTER VII

DIANA, ACTÆON, AND LORD EVELYN

Hilary and Peter gondoled to Lord Evelyn Urquhart's residence, a rather exquisite little old palace called Ca' delle Gemme, and were received affectionately by the tall, slim, dandified-looking young-old man, with his white ringed hands and high sweet voice and courtly manner. He had aged since Peter remembered him; the slim hands were shakier and the near-sighted eyes weaker and the delicate face more deeply lined with the premature lines of dissipation and weak health. He put his monocle in his left eye and smiled at Peter, with the old charming smile that was like his nephew's, and tilted to and fro on his heels.

"Not changed at all, as far as I can see," he said to Peter, with the same mincing, finicking pronunciation that had pleased the boy Peter eight years ago. "Only my sight isn't what it was. *Are* you changed at all? Do you still like Bow rose-bowls better than anything except Denis? Denis is coming here soon, you know, so I shall be able to discover. Oh, I beg pardon—Mr. Peter Margerison, Mr. Cheriton."

Mr. Cheriton was a dark, sturdy young man with an aggressive jaw, who bowed without a smile and looked one rather hard in the face. Peter was a little frightened of him—these curt, brisk manners made him nervous always—and felt a desire to edge behind Hilary. He gathered that Hilary and Cheriton did not very much like one another. He knew what that slight nervous contraction of Hilary's forehead meant.

Dinner was interesting. Lord Evelyn told pleasant and funny stories in his high, tittering voice, addressing himself to all his guests, but looking at Peter when he came to his points. (People usually looked at Peter when they came to the points of their stories.) Hilary talked a good deal and drank a good deal and ate very little, and was obviously on very friendly terms with Lord Evelyn and on no terms at all with Mr. Cheriton. Cheriton looked a good deal at Peter, with very bright and direct eyes, and flung into the conversation rather curt and spasmodic utterances in a slightly American accent. He seemed a very decided and very much alive young man, a little rude, thought Peter, but possibly that was only his trans-Atlantic way, if, as his voice hinted, he came from America. Once or twice Peter met the direct and vivid regard fixed upon him, and nearly was startled into "I beg your pardon," for there seemed to him an odd element of accusation in the look.

"But it isn't my fault," he told himself reassuringly. "I've not done anything, I'm sure I haven't. It's just the way he's made, I expect. Or else people have done him badly once or twice, and he's always thinking it's going to happen again. Rough luck on him; poor chap."

After dinner they went into what Lord Evelyn called the saloon. "Where I keep my especial treasures," he remarked to Peter. "You'd like to walk round and look at some of them, I expect. These bronzes, now—," he indicated two statuettes on brackets by the door.

Peter looked at them, then swiftly up at Lord Evelyn, who swayed at his side, his glass screwed into one smiling eye.

Lord Evelyn touched the near statuette with his light, unsteady, beautifully-ringed hand.

"Rather lovely, isn't she," he said, caressing her. "We found her and the Actæon in a dusty hole of a place in a miserable little *calle* off the Campo delle Beccarie, kept by a German Jew. Quite a find, the old sinner. What an extortioner, though! Eh, Margerison? How much has the old Schneller got out of my pocket? It was your brother who discovered him for me, young Peter. He took me there, and we found the Diana together. Like her? Giacomo Treviso, a pupil of Verrocchio's. Heard of him? The Actæon's not so good now. Same man, but not so happy."

He turned the Diana about; he posed her for Peter's edification. Peter looked from her to the Actæon, from the Actæon to Lord Evelyn's face. He opened his lips to say something, and closed them on silence. He looked past Lord Evelyn to Hilary, who stood in the background, leaning a little against a chair. It seemed to Peter that there was a certain tensity, a strain, in his face.

Then Peter met full the bright, hard, vivid gaze of the alert Cheriton. It had an odd expression at this moment; unmistakably inimical, observantly curious, distinctly sardonic. A faint ironic smile just touched the corners of his determined mouth. Peter returned the look with his puzzled, enquiring eyes that sought to understand.

This much, anyhow, he seemed to understand: his rôle was silence. If Cheriton didn't speak (and Cheriton's expression showed that he knew) and if Hilary didn't speak ... well, he, Peter, couldn't speak either. He must acquiesce in what appeared to be a conspiracy to keep this pathetic, worn-out dilettante in a fool's paradise.

The pathos of it gripped Peter's heart. Lord Evelyn had once known so well. What havoc was this that one could apparently make of one's faculties? It wasn't only physical semi-blindness; it was a blindness of the mind, a paralysis of the powers of discrimination and appreciation, which, was pitiful. Peter was angry. He thought Hilary and Cheriton so abominably, unmitigatedly wrong. And yet he himself had said, "If it makes them happy"—and left that as the indubitable end. Ah, but one didn't lie to people, even for that.

Peter was brought up sharply, as he had often been before, against Hilary's strange Hilaryish, perverted views of the conduct of life's businesses. Then, as usual when he should have felt furthest from mirth, he abruptly collapsed into sudden helpless laughter.

Lord Evelyn turned the eye-glass on him.

"Eh?" he queried. "Why so? But never mind; you always suffered in that way, I remember. Get it from your mother, I think; she did, too. Never explain jokes; they lose so in the telling. Now I want to show you something over here."

Peter crossed the room, his laughter dead. After all, funny wasn't what it really was. Mainly, it was perplexing. Till he could have it out with Hilary, he couldn't understand it at all.

He saw more of Lord Evelyn's treasures, and perplexity grew. He did not laugh again; he was very solemn and very silent and very polite where he could not admire. Where he could he did; but even here his admiration was weighed down to soberness by the burden of the things beyond the pale.

Lord Evelyn found him lukewarm, changed and dulled from the vivid devotee of old, who had coloured up all over his pale face at the sight of a Bow rose-bowl. He coloured indeed now, when Lord Evelyn said "Like it?"—coloured and murmured indistinguishable comments into his collar. He coloured most when Lord Evelyn said, as he frequently did, "Your brother's find. A delicious little man in some *sotto-portico* or other—quite an admirable person. Eh, Margerison?"

Hilary in the background would vaguely assent. Peter, who looked at him no more, felt the indefinable challenge of his tone. It meant either, "I've as much right to my artistic taste as you have, Peter, and I'm not ashamed of it," or, "Speak out, if you want to shatter the illusions that make the happiness of his ridiculous life; if not, be silent."

And all the time the vivid stare of Jim Cheriton was turned like a search-light on Peter's face, and his odd smile grew and grew. Cheriton was watching, observing, taking in something new, trying to solve some problem.

At the end of half an hour Lord Evelyn said, "Peter Margerison, you've lost some of the religious fervour of your youth. The deceitfulness of riches and the cares of this world—is that it? What's come to you that you're so tepid about this Siena chalice? Don't be tepid, young Peter; it's the symptom of a ruined soul."

He polished his glass, screwed it into his left eye, and looked down on Peter with his whimsical, kindly scrutiny. Peter did not return the look; he stood with bent head, looking vaguely down at the Sienese chalice. That too was one of Hilary's finds. Hilary it seemed, had approved its seller in an article in the Gem.

"Damme," said Lord Evelyn suddenly, with unusual explosiveness, "if I didn't like you better when you were fifteen! Now, you *blasé* and soulless generation, I suppose you want to play bridge. Do you play as badly as ever, Peter? A remarkable player you were, I remember—quite remarkable. Denis always told you so. Now Cheriton will tell you so, because he's rude."

Bridge was a relief to Peter, though he was still a rather remarkable player. He played with Cheriton, who was not rude, because he was absolutely silent. It was an absurd game. Cheriton was a brilliant player, even when he was only giving half his mind to it, as he seemingly was to-night. Lord Evelyn had been a brilliant player once, and was now brilliant with alternations of eccentricity; he talked most of the time, making the game the centre of his remarks, from which he struck out along innumerable paths of irrelevancy. The Margerisons too were irrelevant; Hilary thought bridge a bore, and Peter, who thought nothing a bore, was always a little alarmed by anything so grown-up. But to-night he didn't much mind what he did, so long as he stopped looking at Lord Evelyn's things. Peter only wanted to get away; he was ashamed and perplexed and sorry and angry, and stabbed through with pity. He wanted to get out of Lord Evelyn's house, out of the range of his kindly, whimsical smile and Cheriton's curious hostile stare; he wanted to be alone with Hilary, and to understand.

The irony of Cheriton's look increased during bridge; it was certainly justified by the abstraction of Peter's play.

Lord Evelyn laughed at him. "You need Denis to keep you in order, young Peter. Lord, how frightened you used to be when Denis was stern. Smiled and pretended you weren't, but I knew...." He chuckled at the painted ceiling. "Knew a man at Oxford, Peter ... well, never mind that story now, you're too young for it.... Anyhow I make it no trumps."

At eleven o'clock Hilary and Peter went home. Lord Evelyn shook hands with Peter rather affectionately, and said, "Come and see me again soon, dear boy. Lunch with me at Florian's to-morrow—you and your wealthy friend. Busy sight-seeing, are you? How banal of you. Morning in the Duomo, afternoon on the Lido, and the Accademia to fill the spare hours; I know the dear old round. Never could be worried with it myself; too much else to do. But one manages to enjoy life even without it, so don't overwork. And come and see my toys again by daylight, and try to enthuse a little more over them next time. You're too young to be *blasé*. You'd better read the Gem, to encourage yourself in simple pleasures. Good-night. Good-night, Margerison."

He shook hands with them both again, possibly to make up for Cheriton, who did not shake hands at all, but stood with his own in his pockets, leaning against the wall, his eyes still on Peter's face.

"Queer manners you have, dear Jim," was what they heard Lord Evelyn say as they stepped into the Ca' delle Gemme gondola, that was taking them back to the Rio delle Beccarie.

They swung out into the faintly-shining darkness of the water-road, into which the climbing moon could not look—a darkness crossed and flecked by the red gleamings of the few gondola and sandolo lights abroad at this hour in the quiet street. They sent their own red path before them as they softly travelled; and round it the stars flickered and swam, deep down. Peter could have sworn he heard their thin, tinkling, submerged, funny song, somewhere above or beneath the soft and melodious "Chérie Birri-Bim," that someone (not Lord Evelyn's beautifully trained and taciturn *poppe*) was crooning near at hand.

The velvet darkness of a bridge drowned the stars for a moment; then, with a musical, abrupt cry of "Sta—i!" they swung round a corner into a narrow way that was silver and green in the face of the climbing moon.

The musically lovely night, the peace of the dim water-ways, the shadowing mystery of the steep, shuttered houses, with here and there a lit door or window ajar, sending a slant of yellow light across the deep green lane full of stars and the moon, the faint crooning of music far off, made a cool marvel of peace for strung nerves. Peter sat by Hilary in silence, and no longer wanted to ask questions. In the strange, enveloping wonder of the night, minor wonders died. What did it matter, anyhow? Hilary and Venice—Venice and Hilary—give them time, and one would explain the other.

It was Hilary who began to talk, and he talked about Cheriton, his nervous voice pitched on a high note of complaint.

"I do intensely dislike that man. The sort of person I've no use for, you know. So horribly on the spot; such sharp, unsoftened manners. All the terrible bright braininess of the Yankee combined with the obstreperous energy of the Philistine Briton. His mother is a young American, about to be married for the third time. The sort of exciting career one would expect from a parent of the delightful Jim. I cannot imagine why Lord Evelyn, who is a person of refinement, encourages him. Really, you know!"

He grew very plaintive over it. Peter really did not wonder.

Peter's subconscious mind registered a dim impression that this was defensive talk, to fill the silence. Hilary was a nervous person, easily agitated. Probably the evening had agitated him. But he was no good at defence. His complaint of Jim Cheriton broke weakly on an unsteady laugh. Peter nodded assent, and looked up the street of dim water, his chin propped in his hands, and thought how extraordinarily pleasant was the red light that slanted across the dark water from green doors ajar in steep house-walls.

Hilary tried to light a cigar, and flung broken matches into spluttering darkness. At last he succeeded; and then, when he had smoked in silence for two minutes, he turned abruptly on Peter and said, "Well?"

Peter, dreamily turning towards him, felt the nervous challenge of his tone, and read it in his pale, tired face.

Peter pulled himself together and collected his thoughts. After all, one might as well know.

"Oh, well ... what? Yes, what about those ghastly statuettes, and all the rest of them? Why, when, how ... and what on earth for?"

Hilary, after a moment of silence, said, with a rather elaborate carelessness, "I saw you didn't like them."

At that Peter started a little, and the dreaminess of the night fell away from him.

"You saw ... oh." For a moment he couldn't think of anything else to say. Then he laughed a little. "Why, yes, I imagine you did.... But what's the object of it all? Have you and Cheriton (by the way, why does he glare at us both so?) come to the conclusion that it's worth while playing that sort of game? If you have, I can't tell you how utterly wrong I think you are. Make him happy—oh, I know—but what extraordinary cheek on your part! I as near as possible gave you away—I did really. Besides, what did he mean by saying you'd advised him to buy the things—praised them in the Gem, and all that? You can't have gone so far as that—did you?"

After a moment of silence, Hilary turned abruptly and looked Peter in the face, taking the long cigar out of his mouth and holding it between two white, nervous fingers.

"Upon my word," said Hilary, speaking rather slowly, "Talk of cheek! Do you know what you're accusing me of? You and your precious taste! Leslie and your other fool patrons seem to have given you a fair opinion of yourself. Because you, in your omniscience, think a thing bad, which I ... which I obviously consider good, and have stated so in print ... you don't so much as deign to argue the question, but get upon your pedestal and ask me why I tell lies. You think one thing and I think another; of course, you must know best, but I presume I may be allowed to hold my misguided and ill-informed opinion without being accused blankly of fraud. Upon my word, Peter ... it's time you took to some other line of life, I think."

His high, unsteady voice trailed away into silence. Peter, out of all the dim beauty of the night, saw only the pale, disturbed, frowning face, the quivering hand that held the lean cigar. All the strangeness and the mystery of the mysterious world were here concentrated. Numbly and dully he heard the soft, rhythmic splashing of the dipping oar, the turning cry of "Premié!" Then, sharper, "Sciar, Signori, sciar!" as they nearly jostled another gondola, swinging round sharply into a moonless lane of ancient palaces.

Peter presently said, "But ..." and there stopped. What could he say, beyond "but?"

Hilary answered him sharply, "Well?" and then, after another pause, Peter pulled himself together, gave up trying to thread the maze of his perplexity, and said soberly, "I beg your pardon, Hilary. I'm an ass."

Hilary let out his breath sharply, and resumed his cigar.

"It's possible, of course," he said, more quietly, "that you may be right and I wrong about the things. That's another question altogether. I may be a fool: I only resent being called a knave. *Really*, you know!"

"I never meant that," Peter hopelessly began to explain. And, indeed, now that Hilary disclaimed it, it did seem a far too abominable thing that he had implied. He had hurt Hilary; he deserved to be kicked. His anger with himself rose. To hurt anyone was atrocious; to hurt Hilary unforgivable. He would have done a great deal now to make amends.

He stammered over it. "I did think, I'm afraid, that you and Cheriton were doing it to make him happy or something. I'm awfully sorry; I was an ass; I ought to have known. But it never occurred to me that you didn't kn—that you had a different opinion of the things. I say, Hilary—Cheriton knows! I saw him know. He knew, and he was wondering what I was going to say."

"Knew, knew, knew!" Hilary nervously exploded. "There you go again. You're intolerable, Peter, really. All the spoiling you've had has gone to your head."

"I beg your pardon," said Peter again. "I meant, Cheriton agreed with me, I'm sure.... But, Hilary—those statuettes—you can't really.... They're mid-Victorian, and positively offensive!" His voice rose shrilly. They had been so horrible, Diana and Actæon. He couldn't forget them, in their podgy sentimentality. "And—and that chalice ..." he shuddered over it—"and—"

"That'll do, thanks," Hilary broke in. "You can say at once that you disagree with me about everything I admire, and leave it there. But, if I may ask you, don't say so to Lord Evelyn, if you can resist the temptation to show me up before him. It will only bother and disturb him, whichever of us he ends by agreeing with. He's shown that he trusts my taste more or less, by giving me his paper to edit, and I should think we might leave it at that."

"Yes, the paper"—Peter was reminded of it, and it became a distracting puzzle. Hilary thought Diana and Actæon and the Siena chalice good things—and Hilary edited an art paper. What in the name of all that was horrible did he put in it? A light was shed on Signor Leroni, who was, said the Gem, a good dealer in plaques, and who was, Peter had thought, a bare-faced purveyor of shams. Peter began to question the quality of the *osele*, that Leslie had purchased from Signor Sardi.

How curious it was; and rather tragic, too. For Hilary, like Lord Evelyn, had known once. Had Hilary too, in ruining much else of himself, ruined his critical faculties? And could one really do that and remain ignorant of the fact? Or would one rather have a lurking suspicion, and therefore be all the more defiantly corroborative of one's own judgment? In either case one was horribly to be pitied; but—but one shouldn't try to edit art papers. And yet this couldn't be conveyed without a lacerating of feelings that was unthinkable. There was always this about Hilary—one simply couldn't bear to hurt him. He was so easily hurt and so often; life used him so hardly and he felt it so keenly, that it behoved Peter, at least, to insert as many cushions as possible between him and the sharp edges of circumstance. Peter was remorseful. He had taken what he should have seen before was an unforgivable line; he had failed abominably in comprehension and decent feeling. Poor Hilary. Peter was moved by the old impulse to be extraordinarily nice to him.

They turned out of the Rio della Madonnetta into the narrow rio that was the back approach to the Palazzo Amadeo. It is a dark little canal, a rio of the poor. The doors that stood open in the peeling brick walls above the water let out straggling shafts of lamplight and quarrelling voices and singing and the smell of wine. The steep house walls leant to meet one another from either side; from upper windows the people who hadn't gone to bed talked across a space of barely six feet.

The gondola crept cautiously under two low bridges, then stopped outside the water-washed back steps of the Palazzo Amadeo.

One pleasant thing about Lord Evelyn's exquisitely mannered *poppe* was that one didn't feel that he was thinking "I am not accustomed to taking my master's visitors to such low haunts." In the first place, he probably was. In the second, he was not an English flunkey, and not a snob. He was no more a snob than the Margerisons were, or Lord Evelyn himself. He deposited them at the Palace back door, politely saluted, and slipped away down the shadowy water-street.

Hilary and Peter stepped up two water-washed steps to the green door, and Peggy opened it from within. Peggy (Peter occasionally wondered when, if ever, she went to bed) was in the hall, nursing Illuminato, who couldn't sleep—a small bundle of scarlet night-shirt and round bullet head, burrowing under his mother's left arm and staring out from that place of comfort with very bright and wakeful eyes. When, indeed, it might have been asked, did any of the Margerison family take their rest? No one of them ever felt or expressed any surprise at finding any other awake and active at any hour of the night.

Peggy looked at her three male infants with her maternal serenity touched with mirth. There were nearly always those two elements in Peggy's look—a motherly sympathy and desire to cheer and soothe, and a glint from some rich and golden store of amusement.

She patted Peter on the arm, softly.

"Was it a nice evening, then? No, not very, I think. Dear, dear! You both look so unutterably tired. I wonder had you better go to bed, quite straight?"

It seemed to be suggested as a last resource of the desperate, though the hour was close on midnight.

"And the children have been pillow-fighting, till Mr. Vyvian—the creature—came down with nothing in particular on, to complain to me that he couldn't sleep. Sleep, you know! It wasn't after ten—but it seems he had a headache, as usual, because Mrs. Johnson had insisted on going to look at pictures with him and Rhoda, and her remarks were such—Nervous prostration, poor Mr. Vyvian. So I've had Illuminato down here with me since then. He wants to go to you, Peter, as usual."

Peter took the scarlet bundle, and it burrowed against his shirt-front with a contented sigh. Peggy watched the two for a moment, then said to the uncle, "You poor little boy, you're tireder than Hilary even. You must surely go to bed. But isn't Lord Evelyn rather a dear?"

"Quite a dear," Peter answered her, his face bent over the round cropped head. "Altogether charming and delightful. Do you know, though, I'm not really fond of bridge. Jig-saw is my game—and we didn't have it. That's why I'm tired I expect. And because there was a Mr. Cheriton, who stared, and seemed somehow to have taken against us—didn't he, Hilary? Or perhaps it was only his queer manners, dear Jim. Anyhow, he made me feel shy. It takes it out of one, not being liked. Nervous prostration, like poor Mr. Vyvian. So let's go to bed, Hilary, and leave these two to watch together."

"Give me the froglet." She took it from his arms, gently, and kissed first one then the other.

"Good night, little Peter. You are a darling entirely, and I love you. And don't worry, not over not being liked or anything else, because it surely isn't worth it."

She was always affectionate and maternal to Peter; but to-night she was more so than usual. Looking at her as she stood in her loose, slatternly *negligé*, beneath the extravagantly blazing chandelier, the red bundle cuddling a round black head into her neck, her grey eyes smiling at him, lit with love and laughter and a pity that lay deeper than both, Peter was caught into her atmosphere of debonair and tranquil restfulness, that said always, "Take life easy; nothing's worth worrying over, not problems or poverty or even one's sins." How entirely true. Nothing *was* worth worrying over; certainly other people's strange points of view weren't. It was a gospel of ease and *laissez-faire* well suited to Peter's temperament. He smiled at Peggy and Hilary and their son, and went up the marble stairs to bed. He was haunted till he slept by the memory of Hilary's nervous, tired face as he had seen it in the moonlight in the gondola, and again in the hall as he said good night. Hilary wasn't coming to bed yet. He stayed to talk to Peggy. If anything could be good for Hilary's moods of depression, thought Peter, Peggy would. How jolly for Hilary to be married to her! She was such a refreshment always. She was so understanding; and was there a lapse somewhere in that very understandingness of her that made it the more restful—that made her a relaxation to strained minds? To those who were breaking their moral sense over some problem, she would return simply, "There isn't any problem. Take things as they come and make the best of them, and don't, don't worry!" "I'm struggling with a temptation to steal a purse," Peter imagined himself saying to her, "What can I do about it?" And her swift answer came, with her indulgent, humorous smile, "Dear little boy, if it makes you any happier—do it!" And then she would so well understand the ensuing remorse; she would be so sympathetic, so wholly dear and comforting. She would say anything in the world to help, except "Put it back." Even that she would say if one's own inclinations were tending in that direction. But never if they weren't. She would never be so hard, so unkind. That sort of uncongenial admonition might be left to one's confessor; wasn't that what confessors were there for?

But why think of stealing purses so late at night? No doubt merely because it was late at night. Peter curled himself up and drew the sheet over his ears and sighed sleepily. He seemed to hear the rich, pleasant echoes of Peggy's best nursery voice far off, and Hilary's high, plaintive tones rising above it.

But above both, dominant and insistent, murmured the lapping voice of the wonderful city at night. A faint rhythm of snoring beyond a thin wall somehow suggested Mrs. Johnson, and Peter laughed into his pillow.

CHAPTER VIII

PETER UNDERSTANDS

On the shores of the Lido, three days later, Peter and Leslie came upon Denis Urquhart. He was lying on the sand in the sun on the Adriatic side, and building St. Mark's, rather well. Peter stood and looked at it critically.

"Not bad. But you'd better let us help you. We've been studying the original exhaustively, Leslie and I."

"A very fine and remarkable building," said Leslie, ponderously, and Peter laughed for the sheer pleasure of seeing Urquhart's lazy length stretched on the warm sand.

"Cheriton's somewhere about," said Urquhart. "But he wouldn't help me with St. Mark's. He was all for walking round the island at a great pace and seeing how long it took him. So superfluously energetic, isn't he? Fancy being energetic in Venice."

Peter was thankful that he was. The thought of Cheriton's eyes upon him made him shudder.

"He has his good points," Urquhart added; "but he excites himself too much. Always taking up some violent crusade against something or other. Can't live and let live. Another dome here, I think."

Peter wondered if Cheriton's latest crusade was against Hilary's taste in art, and if so what Urquhart thought on that subject. It was an uncomfortable thought. He characteristically turned away from it.

"The intense blue of the sea, contrasted with the fainter blue of the Euganean Hills," said Leslie suddenly, "is most remarkable and beautiful. What?"

He was proud of having noticed that. He was always proud of noticing beauty unaided. He made his remark with the simple pleasure of a child in his own appreciation. His glance at Peter said, "I am getting on, I think?"

The others agreed that he was correct. He then bent his great mind to the completion of St. Mark's, and Urquhart discovered what Peter had long known, that he could really play in earnest. The reverse art—handling serious issues with a light touch—he was less good at. Grave subjects, like the blue of the sea or the shape of a goblet, he approached with the same solidity of earnestness which he brought to bear on sand cathedrals. It was just this that made him a little tiring.

But the three together on the sands made a happy and congruous party of absorbed children, till Cheriton the energetic came swinging back over the sand-hills. Peter saw him approaching, watched the resolute lunge of his stride. His mother was about to be married for the third time: one could well believe it.

"I hope he is going to be nicer to me to-day," Peter thought. Even as he hoped it, and before Cheriton saw the party on the sands, Peter saw the determined face stiffen, and into the vivid eyes came the blank look of one who is cutting somebody. Peter turned and looked behind him to see who it was, and saw Mr. Guy Vyvian approaching. It was obvious from his checked recognition that he thought he knew Cheriton, and that Cheriton did not share the opinion. Peter saw Vyvian's mortified colour rise; he was a vain and sensitive person.

Cheriton came and sat down among them. His words as he did so, audibly muttered, were, "The most unmitigated cad!" He looked angry. Then he saw Peter, and seemed a little surprised, but did not cut him; he hardly could. Peter supposed that he owed this only to the accident of Urquhart's presence, since this young man seemed to go about the world ignoring everyone who did not please his fastidious fancy, and Peter could not hope that he had done that.

Peter looked after Vyvian's retreating figure. He could detect injured pride in his back.

He got up and brushed the sand from him.

"I must go and talk to that man," he said. "He's lodging with my brother."

The situation for a moment was slightly difficult. Leslie and Urquhart had both heard Cheriton's description of Peter's brother's lodger. Besides, they had seen him, and that was enough.

It was unlike Peter to make awkward situations. He ended this one abruptly by leaving it to itself, and walking away after his brother's lodger.

Vyvian greeted him huffily. It needed all Peter's feeling for a hurt man to make him anything but distantly aloof. Cheriton's description was so manifestly correct. The man was a cad—an oily bounder with a poisonous mind. Peter wondered how Hilary could bear to have his help on the Gem.

Vyvian broke out about Cheriton.

"Did you see that grand fellow who was too proud to know me? Driven you away too, has he? We don't know people in boarding-houses—we're in our private flat ourselves! It makes me sick!"

But his vulgarity when he was angry was a shade less revolting, because more excusable, than when he wasn't. So Peter bore it, and even tried to be comforting, and to talk about pictures. Vyvian really knew something about art; Peter was a little surprised to find that he knew so much, remembering certain curious blunders of his in the Gem.

He did not talk about the Gem to Vyvian; instinctively he avoided it. Peter had a rather useful power of barring his mind against thoughts that he did not desire to have there; without reasoning about it, he had placed the Gem in this category.

He was absently watching the dim blue of the Euganean Hills against the clearer blue of the sky when he discovered that Vyvian was talking about Rhoda Johnson.

"A dear little gurl, with real possibilities, if one could develop them. I do my best. She's fond enough of me to let me mould her atrocious taste. But what can one do to fight the lifelong influence of a home like that—a mother like that? Oh, frightful! But she *is* fond of me, and there's her hope—"

"Good-bye," said Peter. "I must go." He could not for the life of him have said any of the other things he was thinking. He would have given a lot to have been Cheriton for the moment, so that he wouldn't mind being rude and violent. It was horribly feeble; all he could say was "Good-bye." Having said it, he went abruptly.

He sighed as he went back to Urquhart and Leslie. Things were so difficult to manage. One left one's friends to comfort a hurt bounder; that was all very well, but what if the bounder comforted was much more offensive than the bounder hurt? However, it was no good reasoning about these things. Peter knew that one had to try and cheer up the hurt, in the face of all reason, simply because one felt so uncomfortable oneself if one didn't.

But it was almost worth while to have a few rather revolting people about; they threw the others into such glorious relief. As long as there were the nice people, who laughed at life and themselves, playing about the world, nothing else in particular mattered. And it was really extraordinarily good luck that Urquhart should happen to be playing about Venice at the same time as Peter. In spite of Cheriton, they would have a good time together. And Cheriton would perhaps become friendly in time—dear Jim, with his queer manners. People mostly did become friendly, in quite a short time, according to Peter's experience.

That the time, as far as Cheriton was concerned, had not yet arrived, was rather obvious, however. His manners to Peter on the sands were still quite queer—so queer that Peter and Leslie only stayed a few minutes more. Peter refused Urquhart's suggestion that they should have tea together on the island, and they crossed over to the lagoon side and got into their waiting gondola.

The lagoon waters were smooth like glass, and pale, and unflushed as yet with the coming sunset. Dark lines of stakes marked the blue ship-ways that ran out to open sea, and down them plied the ships, spreading painted wings to the evening breeze.

Leslie said, "I see in the Gem that there is a good old well-head to be had from a man on the Riva Ca' di Dio. I want well-heads, as you know. We'll go and see, shall we?"

The crystal peace of the lagoon was shattered for Peter. He had been getting into a curious mood of late; he almost disliked well-heads, and other purchasable forms of beauty. After all, when one had this limpid loveliness of smooth water and men walking on its surface like St. Peter, why want anything more? Because, Leslie would say, one wants to possess, to call beauty one's own. Bother, said Peter, the vice of the age, which was certainly acquisitiveness. He was coming to the conclusion that he hated buying things. And it was so awkward to explain to Leslie about Hilary and the Gem. He had spent the last few days in trying, without too much giving Hilary away, to restrain Leslie from following his advice. He said now, "All right; we'll go and see. But, to say the truth, I'm not sure that Hilary is a very good authority on well-heads." He blushed a little as he said it; it seemed to him that he had been saying that sort of thing very often of late. Leslie was so persistent, so incorrigibly intent on his purpose.

Leslie looked at him now over his large cigar a little speculatively.

"According to you," he remarked placidly after a moment, "your brother is uncommonly little of an authority on anything he mentions. Fraternal scepticism developed to its highest point."

Peter nodded. "Our family way," he said; and added, "Besides, that Vyvian man does as much of the Gem as Hilary. There's a young man, Leslie! My word, what a dog! Talks about gurls. So I left him. I turned upon him and said, 'Sir, this is no talk for a gentleman to listen to.' I said it because I knew it was what he would expect. Then I turned on my heel and left him without a word. He ground his teeth and hissed, 'A time will come.' But Cheriton seems rather a rude man, all the same. He hurts my feelings too, whenever I meet him. I too hiss, 'A time will come.' But I don't believe it ever will. Do you suppose the water is shallow over there, or that the men walking on it are doing miracles? It must be fun, either way. Let's do it instead of buying well-heads, Leslie. The fact is, buying so many things is rather demoralising, I think. Let's decide to buy no more. I'm beginning to believe in the simple life, like Rodney. Rodney hates men like you and Urquhart—rolling plutocrats. He wanted me to leave you and the other plutocrats and be a travelling pedlar. I'm not sure that I shan't, before long."

"Can't spare you," Leslie grunted.

Peter flattered himself that he had successfully turned the conversation from well-heads.

When, after having tea with Leslie at Florian's, he returned to the Palazzo Amadeo, Teresina told him that someone had called to see the Signore, and the Signore, being out, was waiting in the saloon. Peter went to the saloon to see if he would do instead of the Signore, and found a stout gentleman with a black moustache and up-brushed hair, spitting on the saloon floor. A revolting habit, as Hilary was wont wearily to remark; but Peter always accepted it with anyhow outward equanimity.

"My brother is unfortunately away from the house," he explained, with his polite smile and atrocious Italian. "But perhaps I can give him a message?"

The visitor gave him a sharp look, bowed ceremoniously, and said, "Ah! The Signore is the brother of Signor Margerison? Truly the brother?"

Peter assured him, not even halving the relationship; and indeed, he seldom did that, even in his thoughts.

The visitor gave him a card, bearing the name of Signor Giacomo Stefani, sat down, at Peter's request, spat between his feet, and said, "I have had various affairs with your Signor brother before. I am come to solicit his patronage in the matter of a pair of vases. If he would recommend them for me in his paper, as before. They are good; they might easily be antiques."

"You wish my brother to mention them in his paper?" Peter gathered. He was correct.

"Exactly so," Signor Stefani told him. "Of course, on the same terms as before, if the Signor would be satisfied with them."

"Terms?" Peter repeated after him.

Signor Stefani became more explicit. He named the terms.

"That was what I paid Signor Margerison before, for an article on a pseudo-Sienese chalice. But the vases are better; they are good; they might deceive an expert. Truly, they might be antiques!"

He continued to talk, while Peter listened. He was taking it in rather slowly. But at last, not being stupid, he no longer thought Hilary so. He understood.

He stood up presently, looking a little dazed.

"It appears," he said slowly, in his broken Italian, to Signor Stefani, "that you are making a rather bad mistake, which is a pity. I think you had better go home."

Signor Stefani gave a startled upward twist to his moustache, and stood up too.

"Excuse me," he said rather angrily, "there is no mistake. Your brother and I have very frequently had affairs together."

Peter looked at him, frowning doubtfully as he collected his words.

"I am right, I think," he said slowly, "that you are offering my brother a bribe to publish a fraudulent article on fraudulent goods of yours? That is so? Then, as I said, you are making a very serious mistake, and ... and you had better go home. Will you come this way, please?"

Signor Stefani continued to talk, but so rapidly and loudly now that Peter couldn't follow him. He merely shook his head and opened the door, saying, "This way, please. I can't understand you when you talk so fast."

Signor Stefani, with a final angry shrug and expectoration, permitted himself to be ushered out of the room.

On the stairs outside they met Vyvian coming up, who nodded affably to both of them. Signor Stefani, as he passed, shrugged his shoulders up to his ears and spread his two hands wide, with a look of resigned despair over his shoulder at Peter, and Vyvian's brows went up at the gesture. Peter ushered his guest out at the street entrance. Signor Stefani's last words were, "I shall return shortly and see your brother in person. I have made a foolish mistake in thinking that you were in his confidence. Good evening."

So they parted, more in sorrow than in anger.

Peter met Vyvian again on the stairs. He was passing on, but Vyvian stopped and said, "What have you been doing to Stefani to put him out so?"

Peter stopped and looked at him for a moment. He felt rather dazed, as if someone had hit him a blow on the head. He had to remember what was this funny bounder's place in the newly-revealed scheme of things. Not merely a funny bounder after all, it seemed, but just what Cheriton had called him. But one couldn't let him know that one thought so; one was ostensibly on Hilary's side, against honesty, against decency, against all the world.

So Peter, having located Vyvian and himself in this matter, said nothing at all, but went on upstairs.

Vyvian, staring after him in astonishment (none of Hilary's boarders had seen Peter discourteous before), raised his eyebrows again, and whistled beneath his breath.

"So we're too fine for our brother's dirty jobs! I'm dashed if I don't believe it's that!"

Peter went upstairs rather too quickly for his heart. He returned to the saloon and collapsed suddenly into a chair, feeling giddy. Mrs. Johnson came in a moment later and found him leaning back with closed eyes. She was disturbed about his complexion.

"The colour of putty, poor Mr. Peter! You've bin excitin' yourself, tearin' about sight-seein', I know. Tell me now just how you feel. I'm blest if I don't believe you've a-bin in the Cathedral, smellin' at that there choky incense! It takes me like that, always; and Miss Gould says she's just the same. Funny feelin's within, haven't you now?"

"Yes," said Peter, "just exactly that"; and they so overcame him that he began to laugh helplessly.

"I'm sorry, Mrs. Johnson," he said presently. "I'm an ass. But I'm all right now. I came upstairs in a hurry, that's all. And before that a man talked so loud and so fast that it took my breath away. It may be silly, but I *am* like that, as Miss Barnett says. My brother and sister-in-law are both out, aren't they?"

Mrs. Johnson, sitting down opposite him and studying the returning tints of his complexion, nodded.

"That's it," she said, more cheerfully. "You're gettin' a wholesome white again now. I didn't like that unhealthy greeny-grey. But you've none of you any colour, you gentlemen—not you nor your brother nor that pasty Vyvian. None of you but the little curate; he had a nice little pink face. I'm sure I wish some gals cared more for looks, and then they wouldn't go after some as are as well let alone." This cryptic remark was illuminated by a sigh. Mrs. Johnson, now that she saw Peter improving in complexion, reverted to her own troubles.

Peter replied vaguely, "No, I suppose they wouldn't. People ought to care for looks, of course. They matter so much more than anything else, really."

"Without goin' all that way with you, Mr. Peter," said Mrs. Johnson, "and with all due respect to Great Minds (which I haven't got and never shall have, and nor had my poor dear that's gone, so I'm sure I don't know where Rhoder got her leanin's from), I will say I do like to see a young man smart and well-kept. It means a respect for himself, not to mention for those he takes out, that is a stand-by, at least for a mother. And the young fellows affect the gals, too. Rhoder, now—she'd take some pains with herself if she went out with a smart fellow, that was nicely turned out himself and expected her to be the same. But as it is—hair dragged and parted like a queer picture, and a string of green beads for a collar, as if she was a Roman with prayers to say—and her waist, Mr. Peter! But there, I oughtn't to talk like this to a gentleman, as Miss Gould would say; (I do keep on shockin' Miss Gould, you know!) But I find it hard to rec'lect that about you, Mr. Peter; you're so sympathetic, you might be a young lady. An' I feel it's all safe with you, an' I do believe you'd help me if you could."

"I should be glad to," said Peter, wondering whether it was for the improvement of Rhoda's hair, waist, or collar that his assistance might be acceptable.

Mrs. Johnson was looking at him very earnestly; it was obvious that something was seriously amiss, and that she was wondering how much she could venture to say to this sympathetic young man who might be a young lady. She made a sudden gesture with her stout hands, as if flinging reticence to the winds, and leant forward towards him.

"Mr. Peter ... I don't hardly like to say it ... but could you take my gal out sometimes? It does sound a funny thing to ask—but I can't abide it that she should be for ever with that there Vyvian. I don't like him, and there it is. And Rhoder does ... And he's just amusin' himself, and I can't bear it for my little gal, that's where it is.... Mr. Peter, I hate the fellow, though you may say I'm no Christian for it, and of course one is bidden not to judge but to love all men. But he fair gives me the creeps, like a toad.... Do you know that feelin'?"

"Oh, yes," said Peter readily. "And of course, I should like immensely to go out with Miss Rhoda sometimes, if she'll let me. But do you think she will? I'm afraid she would be dreadfully bored with me. I haven't a Great Mind, you know."

"Rhoder likes you," said Mrs. Johnson, a smile of relief overspreading her jolly face. "She was sayin' so only the other day. She has a great respect for your knowledge of art, too. 'You wouldn't think it just to talk with him,' she

said, 'but he knows the most surprisin' things. Knows them for himself'—
that was how she put it—'without needin' to depend on any books, or what
anyone else says. I wish I was like that, mother,' she says, and sighs. And of
course, I knew why she wished that, and I said to her, 'Rhoder, my dear,
never you mind about knowin' things; gals don't need to bother their heads
about that. You look after the *outside* of your head,' I said, chaffing her
about her hair, you know, 'and leave the inside to look after itself.' I made
her cross, of course; I'm for ever makin' Rhoder cross without meanin' it.
But that just shows what she feels towards you, you see. And you'd talk
healthy-like to her, which is more than some does, if I know anythin'. One
feels that of you, Mr. Peter, if you'll excuse my sayin' it, that your talk is as
innocent as a baby's prattle, though it mayn't always mean much."

"Thank you very much," said Peter. "I will certainly prattle to Miss Rhoda
whenever she will let me. I should enjoy it, of course."

"Then that's settled." Mrs. Johnson rose, and shook out her skirts with
relief. "And a weight off my mind it will be.... You could make a third with
Rhoder and that Vyvian to-morrow afternoon, if you were so good and not
otherwise employed. They're off together somewhere, I know."

"Making a third" was a little beyond even Peter's readiness to be helpful,
and he looked dubious.

"I wonder if Mr. Vyvian would let me do that. You see, he doesn't much
like me. I expect I give him the creeps, like a toad...." Then, seeing Mrs.
Johnson's relieved face cloud, he added, "Oh, well, I'll ask them to take
me," and she smiled at him as at a good child. "I knew you would!"

Hilary didn't come in to dinner. That was as well; it gave Peter more time.
Perhaps it would be easier late at night to speak of the hopeless, weary,
impossible things that had suddenly risen in the way; easier to think of
things to say about them that wouldn't too much hurt Hilary or himself.

At dinner Peter was very quiet and polite to everyone. Vyvian's demeanour
towards him was touched with irony; his smile was a continual reference to
the fellowship of secrecy that bound them. Rhoda was very silent; Peter
supposed that Vyvian had been snubbing her.

Hilary came home late. Peter and Peggy and Vyvian were sitting in the
dimly-lighted saloon, and the ubiquitous Illuminato was curled up, a sleepy
ball, on the marble top of a book-case. Peggy had a habit of leaving him
lying about in convenient corners, as a little girl her doll.

"You look tired to death, my dear," she commented, as Hilary came in. Her
kindly grey eyes turned from him to Peter, who had looked up from the
book he was reading with a nervous movement. Peter's sweet-tempered

companionableness had been oddly obscured this evening. Perhaps he too was tired to death. And poor little Rhoda had been so unmercifully snubbed all the evening that at last she had crept up to bed all but in tears. Peggy felt very sorry for everyone to-night; they all seemed to need it so much.

Vyvian, as usual, had a headache. When Hilary came in, he rose and said he was going upstairs to try and get some sleep—an endeavour seldom successful in this noisy and jarring world, one gathered. Before he embarked on it he said to Peter, squirting soda into a large tumbler of whisky, "Stefani want anything particular to-day?"

He had waited to say it till Hilary came in. Peter supposed that he said it merely out of his general desire to be unpleasant, and perhaps to revenge himself for that unanswered enquiry on the stairs. Or possibly he merely wished to indicate to Peter how entirely he was privy to Stefani's business with Hilary, and that it might just as well be discussed in his presence. Or again, he might be desirous of finding out how far Peter himself was in the know.

Peter said, "Nothing very particular," and bent over Illuminato, that he might not meet Hilary's eyes or Peggy's. He knew that Hilary was violently startled, and he heard Peggy's softly let out breath, that might have been a sigh or a gentle whistle, and that conveyed in either case dismay touched with a laugh.

Vyvian, who had been watching the three with a covert smile, drained his glass and said, "Well, it's supposed to be partly my business, you know. But since you don't think so, I'll say good-night."

He included the three in a supercilious nod, and left the room.

He left a queer silence behind him. When it had lasted for a moment, Peter looked up from his inspection of Illuminato's screwed-up face, with an effort, and met Hilary's eyes searching his own. Peggy was in the background; later she would be a comforting, easing presence; but for the moment the situation held only these two, and Peter's eyes pleaded to Hilary's, "Forgive me; I am horribly sorry," and in Hilary's strained face shame intolerably grew, so that Peter looked away from it, bending over Illuminato in his arms.

It was Peggy who broke the silence with a tearful laugh.

"Oh, don't look like that, you poor darling boys! Peter, little dear Peter ... you must try and understand! You're good at understanding, you know. Oh, take it easy, my dear! Take it easy, and see how it's nothing to matter, how it's all one great joke after all!" Her arm was round his shoulders as he sat on the table's edge; she was comforting him like a child. To her he was always about Illuminato's age, a most beloved infant.

Peter smiled a little at her. "Why, yes, of course it's a joke. Everything is, isn't it. But ... but...."

He was more than ever a child, stammering unwordable protest, blindly reaching out for help.

Hilary stood before him now, with his hands in his pockets, nervous, irritable, weary, shame now masked by self-defence. That was better; but still Peter kept his eyes for the curled-up child.

"My dear boy," said Hilary, in his sweet, plaintive tones, edged with irritation, "if people like to be taken in, is it my business?"

And Peggy echoed, "Yes, Peter darling, *is* it Hilary's business?"

Then Peter laughed suddenly. After all, it was all too hopeless, and too absurd, for anything else.

"You can't go on, you know," he said then. "You've got to resign." And Peggy looked at him in surprise, for he spoke now like a man instead of a child, with a man's finality. He wasn't giving a command, but stating an obvious fact.

"Darling—we've got to live!" Peggy murmured.

"You mayn't see the necessity," Hilary ironically put the approved answer into Peter's mouth, "but we, unfortunately, do."

"Oh, don't be silly," said Peter unusually. "You *are* being silly, you know; merely absurd. Because, of course, it's simply a question between resigning and being chucked out before long. You can't go on with this sort of thing indefinitely. You see," he explained, apologetic now, "it isn't even as if you did it well. You really don't. And it's an awfully easy thing to see through, if once anyone gets on the track. All that rubbish you've saddled Lord Evelyn with—anyone who isn't as blind as a bat can spot it in a minute. I did; Cheriton has (that's why he's so queer-mannered, by the way, I suppose); probably Denis has. Well, with everyone knowing about it like that, someone is bound before long to ferret out the real facts. Cheriton won't be long, I fancy, before he gets hold of it all. And then—and then it will be so frightfully awkward. Oh, you can't go on, Hilary; you've got to drop it."

"You're talking very lightly," said Hilary, "of throwing up one's entire income."

Peter sighed. "Not lightly; I'm really not. I know what a bore it will be—but not such a bore as the other thing.... Well, then, don't throw it up: simply chuck Stefani and the rest, and run the thing on different lines. I'd help, if you'd let me. I'd chuck Leslie and stay on here and write for you. I would love to. I made a start to-day, you see; I told Stefani he was out of his reckonings, so he'll be prepared. We'll tell all the rest the same.... I suppose Vyvian's in it, too? Can't you get rid of the man? I do so dislike him, you know. Well, never mind; anyhow, we'll tell him he's got to run on new lines now. Oh, we'll make a decent thing of the Gem after all; Hilary, do let's. Peggy, don't you think that would be jolly?"

He looked up into his sister-in-law's face, and met smiling eyes suddenly tear-dimmed. She smiled down at him.

"Very jolly, you beloved child.... So you'll chuck your Mr. Leslie and your own profession and help to run the Gem? I don't think we can let him do that, Hilary, can we?"

Hilary's strained face had softened and relaxed.

"I confess," he said, "that it would be in many ways a great relief to me to drop that side of the business, if I could see my way to it. But it won't be easy now, Peter. It will mean a certain amount of going back on former statements, for one thing."

"Oh, that'll be all right. Papers are always doing that. We'll manage all right and put a good face on it. And we'll make the thing sell—make it funny and interesting and nice. Of course, if Leslie is willing for me to give part of my time to it, there's no reason why I should leave him, as long as he stays in Venice. It will be all in his interests really, because he can get tips from the Gem. I've warned him off it lately because I thought you were such an awful muddler, Hilary. By the way, it's rather a relief that you aren't quite so wanting as I was beginning to fear; seriously, I was wondering how on earth you were going to get through this difficult world. There's no remedy for a muddler; he can't mend."

But a swindler can; a swindler certainly must, that was conveyed by the appeal in Peter's tired face. So tired it was that Peggy gently took Illuminato from his uncle's arms and said, "And now we'll all go to bed. My beloved little brother—you're an angel in the house, and we'll all do just as you say, if it's only to make you smile again. Won't we, Hilary?"

She leant a soft cheek against Hilary's shoulder, smiling at Peter; but Peter waited for Hilary's reply before he smiled back.

Hilary's reply came after a moment.

"Of course, if Peter can contrive a way of keeping our heads above water without having recourse to these detestable methods, I shall be only too relieved. I loathe having to traffic with these dirty swindlers; it's too insufferably wearying and degrading.... By the way, Peter, what did Stefani want to-day?"

Peter said, "Oh, bother Stefani. I'm tired of him. Really, I can't remember—oh, yes, it was antique vases, that might deceive an expert. But let's stop thinking about Stefani and go to bed. I'm so awfully sleepy; do let's go upstairs and try to get a little rest, as Vyvian puts it."

Peggy patted him softly on the cheek as he passed her, and her smile for him was curiously pitiful.

"We'll do our best to mend, my dear; we'll do our best," was what she soothingly murmured; and then, to Illuminato, "There, my froglet; cuddle up and sleep," and to Hilary, "You poor old dear, will we let the little brother have his way, because he's a darling entirely, and quite altogether in the right?"

CHAPTER IX

THE FAT IN THE FIRE

Peter, self-appointed sub-editor to the Gem, was revising a dissertation of Vyvian's on lace. It was a difficult business, this. Vyvian, in Peter's opinion, needed so much expurgation; and yet one couldn': be unkind. Peter wished very much that Hilary would get rid of Vyvian. Vyvian often wrote such tosh; though he was clever, too. Came of being a bounder, perhaps. Peter had often noticed that bounders were apt to write tosh, even clever bounders. Such a sensitive bounder, too; that made it extraordinarily difficult to edit him satisfactorily. Decidedly Hilary ought to get rid of him, gently but finally. That would have the added advantage of freeing Peter from the obligation of "making a third" with him and Rhoda Johnson. Also, one would feel safer; one didn't really trust Vyvian not to be doing little private deals of his own; so little, in fact, did one trust him that the names of dealers were rigorously taboo now on the Gem.

Peter sighed over this rather tiresome article on lace. He wanted to be finishing one of his own on well-heads; and then he wanted to go out with Leslie and look for stone lions for Leslie's gate-posts; and then he and Leslie were going to dine with Lord Evelyn Urquhart. There were a lot of jolly things to be done, when he had finished with Vyvian's lace.

Peter was quite enjoying life just now; it was interesting trying to set the Gem on its legs; there were immense potentialities in the Gem now that toshery with dealers had been put an end to. And to be allowed to write *ad infinitum* about well-heads or anything else was simply splendid.

Peter heard, with a small, abstracted part of his mind, someone talking to Hilary in the hall. The low-toned conversation vaguely worried his subconscious self; he wished people would converse more audibly. But probably it was private.... Peter suddenly frowned irritably and sat upright, biting at his pen. He was annoyed with himself. It was so impertinent, so much the sort of thing he most disliked, to be speculating, as he had suddenly found himself doing, on the nature of another person's private business. Had he come to that? It must be some emanation from that silly, syrupy article of Vyvian's; Vyvian, Peter felt sure, would have towards a private conversation just such an attitude that he had detected in himself. He settled himself to his job again, and made a rather savage excision of two long sentences.

The outer door shut. Peter heard Hilary's steps crossing the hall alone, rather slowly, till they stopped at the door of the saloon. Hilary came in; his head was thoughtfully bent, and he didn't at first see Peter at the table in a corner. When he did see him, he started violently. Hilary had such weak nerves; he was always starting for no reason.

Peter said, "Things going on all right?" and Hilary said, "Yes, quite," and stood silent for a moment, his mobile face flickering nervously, as it did when he was tired or embarrassed.

"I was looking for Peggy," he added, and went out. He had forgotten, apparently, that Peggy had told them an hour ago that she was going shopping and would be out all the afternoon.

Peter sat quite still in his chair and bit his pen. From his expression, Mrs. Johnson might have inferred that he had been in the Cathedral again, smelling at the choky incense, and had got "funny feelin's" within. They were like the nauseating reminiscence of an old sickness. He tried to ignore them. He said to himself, "I'm an ass. I'm a suspicious, low-minded ass."

But he was somehow revolted by the thought of going on with the work for "The Gem" just then. He was glad when Leslie called to fetch him out.

Leslie said, "What's the matter, my son?"

Leslie had, with all his inapprehensiveness of things, an extraordinary amount of discernment of people; he could discern feelings that had no existence. Or, if they had any existence in this case, they must have been called into it by Vyvian's sugary periods. Peter conceded that to that extent he ailed.

"A surfeit of Vyvian. Let's come out and take the air and look for little stone lions."

Leslie was restful and refreshing, with his direct purposes and solid immobility. You could be of use to Leslie, because he had a single eye; he knew what he wanted, and requested you to obtain it for him. That was simple; he didn't make your task impossible by suddenly deciding that after all he didn't really want what you were getting for him. He was a stable man, and perhaps it is only the stable who are really susceptible of help, thought Peter vaguely.

At seven o'clock Peter and Leslie went to the Ca' delle Gemme. They found Cheriton there. Cheriton was talking when they arrived, in his efficient, decisive, composed business tones. Lord Evelyn was pacing up and down the room, his fine, ringed hands clasped behind his back. He looked extraordinarily agitated; his delicate face was flushed crimson. Denis was lying back in a low chair, characteristically at ease.

When Leslie and Peter came in, Cheriton stopped speaking, and Lord Evelyn stopped pacing, and absolute silence momentarily fell.

Then Denis gave his pleasant, casual "Hullo."

Cheriton's silence continued. But Lord Evelyn's did not. Lord Evelyn, very tall and thin, and swaying to and fro on his heels, looked at Peter, turning redder than before; and Peter turned red too, and gave a little apprehensive, unhappy sigh, because he knew that the fat was at last in the fire.

There ensued an uncomfortable scene, such as may readily be imagined.

Lord Evelyn said, and his sweet voice quavered distressingly up and down, "I suppose it's been a good joke. But I wouldn t have thought it of you, Peter Margerison; I wouldn't have thought it of you. Of your brother I say nothing; it's a dishonest world, and he's like the rest, and I can't say he ever gave me any reason to trust him, so I've myself to blame. But you—I did trust you. I thought you were a nice boy, and cared too much for nice things to lie about them." He broke off, and looked round the room—at the Diana and Actæon, at the Siena chalice, at all the monstrous collection. They weren't nearly all monstrous, either—not even most—but he didn't know that; they might be for all he could tell. He looked at them all with the same bewildered, hurt, inimical eyes, and it was that which gave Peter his deepest stab of pitiful pain.

"You've made a fool of me between you," said Lord Evelyn, and suddenly sat down, as if very tired. Leslie sat down too, ponderous and silent in the shadowed background. But Peter remained standing before them all, his head a little bent, his eyes on Denis Urquhart's profile. He was wondering vaguely if Denis would say anything, and if so what it would be.

Still looking at Denis, he made foolish apologies because he was always polite.

"I'm frightfully sorry.... I've been frightfully sorry all along...."

Lord Evelyn lifted a white hand, waving his absurdities contemptuously aside.

"All along! Oh, I see. At least you're honest now: you don't attempt to deny that you've known all about it, then." There was perhaps a fresh ring of bitterness in his voice, as if some last faint hope had been killed by Peter's words.

Cheriton, whose eyes were studying the floor, lifted them sharply for a moment, and glanced at Denis, who was lighting a cigarette and didn't look at him.

"You knew that first evening, when you looked at the things," said Lord Evelyn, half a question still in his querulous voice. "You saw through them at once, of course. Anyone but a blind fool would have, I've no manner of doubt. Cheriton here says he saw you see through them."

Peter stammered over it. "I—I—knew they weren't much."

Lord Evelyn turned to Cheriton whose face was still bent down as if he didn't much like the scene now he had brought it about.

"You were right, as usual, Jim. And Denis was wrong. Denis, you know," he added to Peter, "was inclined to put your morals above your intelligence. He said you couldn't have known. Cheriton told him he was sure you had. It seems Cheriton was right."

It seemed that he was. Peter imagined that Cheriton would always be right.

After a moment's silence Peter gathered that they were all waiting to hear if he had anything to say about it. He hadn't much, but he might as well say it, such as it was.

"It won't make much difference, of course," he began, and his voice sounded odd and small and tired in the great room, "but I think I should like you to know that all this stopped three weeks ago. Hilary—we—decided then to—to give it up, and run 'The Gem' on different lines in future. We couldn't easily undo the past—but—but there's been nothing of the sort since then, and we didn't mean there to be again. Oh, I know that doesn't make much difference, of course...."

The only difference that mattered was that Denis frowned. Incidentally—only that didn't matter—Cheriton laughed curtly, and Lord Evelyn wearily said, "Oh, stop lying, stop lying. I'm so unutterably tired of your lies.... You think we don't know that your brother accepted a bribe this very afternoon.... Tell him, Jim."

So Jim told him. He told him shortly, and in plain words, and not as if he was pleased with his triumph in skilful detection, which he no doubt was.

"I rather wanted to sift this business, Margerison, as I had suspected for a good while more than I could prove. So to-day I sent a man to your brother, commissioning him to pretend to be an art-dealer and offer a sum of money for the insertion in 'The Gem' of an appreciative notice of some spurious objects. As perhaps you are aware, the offer was accepted.... It may seem to you an underhand way of getting evidence—but the case was peculiar."

He didn't look at Peter; his manner, though distant, was not now unfriendly; perhaps, having gained his object and sifted the business, there was room for compassion. It was a pity that Peter had made things worse by that last lie, though.

"I see," said Peter. "It's all very complete."

And then he laughed, as he always did when disasters were so very complete as to leave no crevice of escape to creep through.

"You laugh," said Lord Evelyn, and rose from his chair, trembling a little. "You laugh. It's been an admirable joke, hasn't it? And you always had plenty of sense of humour."

Peter didn't hear him. He wasn't laughing any more; he was looking at Denis, who had never looked at him once, but sat smoking with averted face.

"Shall I go now?" said Peter. "There isn't much more to say, is there? And what there is, perhaps you will tell us to-morrow.... It seems so silly to say one is sorry about a thing like this—but I am, you know, horribly. I have been all along, ever since I found out. You think that must be a lie, because I didn't tell. But things are so mixed and difficult—and it's not a lie." He was looking at Lord Evelyn now, at the delicate, working face that stabbed at his pity and shame. After all, it was Lord Evelyn, not Denis, whom they had injured and swindled and fooled; one must remember that. To Lord Evelyn he made his further feeble self-exculpation. "And, you know, I did really think Hilary had dropped it weeks ago; he said he would. And that's not a lie, either." But he believed they all thought it was, and a silly one at that.

It was Lord Evelyn who laughed now, with his high, scornful titter.

"You and your sorrow! I've no doubt your brother will be sorry too, when he hears the news. I may tell you that he'll have very good reason to be.... Yes, by all means go now—unless you'd like to stay and dine, which I fancy would be carrying the joke too far even for you.... Will you stay one moment, though? There's a little ceremony to be performed."

He crossed the room, and took the Sienese chalice between his hands, holding it gingerly for a moment as if it had been some unclean thing; then he dashed it on to the marble floor and it lay in splinters about his feet. He took up the pair of vases next it, one in each hand (they happened to be of great value), and threw them too among the splinters; he had cleared the shelf of all its brittle objects before Leslie, who had sat motionless in the background until now, rose and laid a heavy hand on his arm.

"My dear sir," said Leslie tranquilly, "don't be melodramatic. And don't give the servants so much trouble and possible injury when they do the room to-morrow. If you want to part with your goods, may I ask to be allowed to inspect them with a view to purchase? Some of them, as you are no doubt aware, are of considerable intrinsic value, and I should be happy to be allowed to buy."

Lord Evelyn looked at the man of commerce with distant contempt.

"As you please, sir. I've no doubt that Mr. Peter Margerison will be equally happy to give you his valuable advice in the business. He is your counsellor in these matters, isn't he. An excellent adviser, of sound judgment and most disinterested honesty!"

He bowed to Peter, who took it as a dismissal, and said "Good night."

Denis, at the opposite side of the room, nodded in his casual way, neither hostile nor friendly, but gentle and indifferent. You couldn't make Denis seem angry, or hurt, or agitated in any way whatever. He had always the air of reserving his opinion; and he extremely disliked scenes. To be present at this one must have been painful to him. Peter, who knew him so well, knew that. He liked things to go easily and smoothly always. He had winced at the crash of glass on marble; it seemed to him in such bad taste. This, no doubt, was his attitude towards the whole business; towards the Magerisons' behaviour, Cheriton's exposure of it, and this final naked, shameful scene of accusation and confession.

Peter was realising this as he put on his coat in the hall, when the door he had shut behind him was opened, and steps followed him. He started and faced round, a hope leaping in his face. The swift dying of it left him rather pale.

Leslie said, "I'm coming too."

It was good of Leslie, thought Peter dully, and not caring in the least. He said, "No, stay and dine. Really, I'd like you to.... We'll talk to-morrow."

Leslie put on his overcoat and said to the footman, "Call a gondola," and the footman stood on the steps and cried "*Poppe*" till a *poppe* came; then they swung away down a rose-flushed water-street with the after-glow in their eyes.

Leslie was restful; he didn't bother one. He merely said, "We'll dine to-night at Luigi's."

It was not until they had done so, and were having coffee outside, that Peter said, "We'll have to leave Venice, of course, directly we can."

"You too?" said Leslie. "You go with them?"

"I go with them," said Peter. "Well, I can't well stay here, can I. And we may as well stick together—a family party..... You see, I haven't a notion what Hilary will do to live now. I can go into business of sorts. Hilary can't; he'd hate it so. Hilary's not business-like, you know. Nor is Peggy. I couldn't trust them by themselves; they'd tumble into something and get broken. They need my common sense to sustain them."

Leslie said, "What's the matter with your own line of life, that you want to chuck it?"

Peter looked at him in surprise.

"It's chucked me," he said. "Violently—with a smash. You don't suppose anyone will hire me again to buy their things for them? There'll be something of a crab on the Margerison family in future. It's going to be made very public, you know, this business; I gathered that. We shall be— rather notorious, in a very few days."

Leslie said, after a moment, "I've hired you to buy my things for me. Are you going to chuck me?"

And Peter, leaning his forehead on his hand as if tired, returned beneath his breath, "Don't be good to me, please, just now. And you must see I've got to chuck it all—all that side of things. We must do something quite new, Hilary and I. We—we've spoiled this."

After a pause, Leslie said gently, afraid of blundering, "You stick together, you and your brother? You go through it together—all the way?"

Peter answered hopelessly, "All the way. We're in it together, and we must get out together, as best we can," and Leslie accepted that, and asked no further question.

CHAPTER X

THE LOSS OF A PROFESSION

Peter went back to the Palazzo Amadeo and said to Hilary, who was writing an article for "The Gem" in the saloon, "I wouldn't go on with that, Hilary. It's no use."

The flatness of his voice, the pallor of his face, startled Hilary and Peggy.

Peggy said, "You're tired to death, child. Take the big chair."

Hilary said, "How do you mean, no use?"

And Peter told him. While he did so, he stood at the window, looking down at the canal between the green shutters that swung ajar, and did not look at Hilary's face.

It was an impossible position for Hilary, so utterly impossible that it was no use trying to make the best of it; one could only look away, and get through it quickly.

Peter didn't say much. He only said, "We've been found out. That man who came to you this afternoon was a spy sent by Cheriton. He reported the result of his interview with you, and Lord Evelyn knows all about everything. Cheriton suspected from the first, you see.... From what Lord Evelyn said, I gather he means to prosecute.... He is ... very angry indeed.... They all are...."

On the last statement Peter's voice sank a little in pitch, so that they hardly heard it. But the last statement mattered to no one but Peter.

Hilary had got up sharply at the first words, and stood very still to listen, letting out one long breath of weary despair. Peggy came and stood close to him, and took one slim white hand in her large kind ones, and gently held it. The fat was indeed in the fire. Poor old Hilary! How he would feel it! Peggy divined that what stung Hilary most deeply at the moment was Peter's discovery of his faithlessness.

It was of that that his first shamed, incoherent words were.

"What was I to do? How could I break abruptly with the old methods, as you suggested? It had to come gradually. You know nothing of business, Peter—nothing." His voice ran up the scale of protesting self-defence.

"Nothing," Peter admitted drearily. Hilary's shame before him could hardly now add to the badness of the situation, as it had once done; the badness of situations has a limit, and this one had reached its limit some three hours since, just before he had laughed in Lord Evelyn's drawing-room.

"Oh," said Peter, very tired suddenly, "never mind me; what does that matter? The point is ... well, you see the point, naturally."

Yes, Hilary saw the point. With a faint groan he ran his fingers through his hair and began to pace up and down the room in agitation.

He said, "That brute Cheriton.... An execrable bounder; I always knew it. What *right* had he?... It's too horrible, too abominable.... Just when we were doing our best to get the thing onto straight lines...." He wheeled about and paced back again, with quick, uneven steps. Between him and the motionless Peter, Peggy stood, looking from one to the other. Her merry eyes were quite grave now. The situation was certainly appalling.

"We must leave Venice," said Peggy, on a sigh. That seemed, certainly, the only thing to be done.

Hilary groaned again.

"Oh, Lord, what are we let in for? What will be the result, if he prosecutes? It may be utter ruin.... I know nothing of these things. Of course, in justice nothing could be done to us—for, after all, what harm have we done? Anyone may insert advertisements for pay, and it only amounted to that.... But justice isn't taken into much account in the law-courts.... It is a horrible, cast-iron system—the relic of a barbarous age.... I don't know what we mayn't be in for, or how we shall come out of it. You don't know either, Peter; you know nothing of law—nothing. It mustn't come into court; that is unthinkable. We will make full apologies—any restitution within our power that Lord Evelyn demands.... I shall go there; I shall see him about it, and appeal to his better feelings. He has been a friend of mine. He has always been good to you, Peter. The memory of your mother.... Appeal to that. You must go to him and see what can be done. Yes, it had better be you; he has a kinder feeling for you, I believe, than for me."

"He has no kind feeling for me," said Peter dully. "He is more annoyed with me than with you."

Hilary jerked his head impatiently.

"Nonsense. You want to shirk; you want to leave me to get out of the mess for myself. Oh, of course, you're not legally involved; I am aware of that; you can leave the sinking ship if you choose, and save yourself."

Peggy said, "Don't be ridiculous, darling. Peter's doing his best for us, as he always has," and came and stood at her brother-in-law's side, kind and big and comforting, with a hand on his arm.

Hilary went on querulously, "I'm asking Peter to do a simple thing—to use his friendship with the Urquharts to help me out of this mess. If you don't want to see Lord Evelyn, Peter, you can go to Denis. He's a friend of yours; he's—he's your kind of step-brother. You can easily persuade him to get the thing hushed up. You've always pretended that he was a friend of yours. Go and see him, then, for heaven's sake, and help us all out of this miserable predicament."

Peter was still silent, staring down at the dark ribbon of shining water that lapped against two old brick walls, a shut lane full of stars.

Peggy, her hand on his arm, said gently, "Oh, Peter'll do his best for us, of course he will, won't you, Peter."

Peter sighed very faintly into the dark night.

"I will do anything I can, naturally. It won't be much, you know."

"You will go to the Urquharts to-morrow morning, and appeal to them?" said Hilary.

"Yes," said Peter. "I will do that."

Hilary breathed a sigh of relief, and flung himself into a chair.

"Thanks, Peter. I believe that is the best we can do. You will persuade them at least to be just, not to push the matter to unfair extremes.... *Oh, my God, what a life!*" His beautiful, unhappy face was hidden in his hands; he shuddered from head to foot, feeling horribly sick. The Margerison organism was sensitive.

Peggy, bending over him, drew caressing fingers through his dark hair and said, "Go to bed, you poor old dear, and don't worry any more to-night. Worry won't help now, will it?"

"Bed?" said Hilary. "Bed? What's the use of that? I shouldn't sleep a wink. I have a frightful head, and I must go and find Vyvian and tell him."

Peggy sniffed. "Much Vyvian'll care! He's been in bad odour all his life, I should fancy. One more row won't bother *him* much. I wish it would; it would be almost worth while to be upset if Guy Vyvian was going to be upset too—the waster. Well, I wonder anyhow will this show that silly little Rhoda what sort of a creature she's been making a golden calf of.... Well, go and wake Vyvian, then, darling, and then come and tell me what he said to it. Peter, you're dropping to sleep as you stand."

Peter went to bed. There didn't seem to be anything to stay up for, and bed is a comforting friend on these occasions. Hilary had a perverse tendency to sit up all night when the worst had happened and he had a frightful head; Peter's way with life was more amenable; he always took what comfort was offered him. Bed is a good place; it folds protecting, consoling arms about you, and gives at best oblivion, at worst a blessed immunity from action.

In the morning, about eleven o'clock, Peter went to the Ca' delle Gemme. That had to be done, so it was no use delaying. He asked for Lord Evelyn Urquhart, and supposed that the servant who showed him in was astonished at his impudence. However, he was permitted to wait in the reception-room while the servant went to acquaint Lord Evelyn with his presence. He waited some time, standing in the middle of the big room, looking at some splinters of glass and china which had been left on the marble floor, forming on his tongue what he was going to say. He could form nothing that was easy to say; honestly he didn't know whether, when the door should open and that tall, elegant, fastidious figure should walk in, he would find himself able to say anything at all. He feared he might only grow hot, and stammer, and slink out. But he pulled himself together; he must do his best; it was quite necessary. He would try to say, "Lord Evelyn, I know it is abominably impertinent of me to come into your house like this. Will you forgive me this once? I have come to ask you, is there any consideration whatever, any sort of reparation my brother and I can make, which will be of any use as amends for what we did? If so, of course we should be grateful for the chance...."

That was what he would try to say. And what he would mean was: "Will you let Hilary off? Will you let him just go away into obscurity, without further disgrace? Isn't he disgraced enough already? Because you are kind, and because you have been fond of me, and because I ask you, will you do this much?"

And what the answer would be, Peter had not the faintest idea. To him personally the answer was indifferent. From his point of view, the worst had already happened, and no further disgrace could affect him much. But Hilary desperately cared, so he must do his best; he must walk into the fire and wrest out of it what he could.

And at last the door opened, and Denis Urquhart came in.

He was just as usual, leisurely and fair and tranquil, only usually he smiled at Peter, and to-day he did not smile. One might have fancied under his tranquillity a restrained nervousness. He did not shake hands; but then Peter and he never did shake hands when they met.

He said, "Sit down, won't you. My uncle isn't available just now, so I have come instead.... You have something to say to him, haven't you?"

He sat down himself, and waited, looking at the splinters of glass on the floor.

Peter stood, and his breath came shortly. Yes, he had something to say to Lord Evelyn, but nothing to Lord Evelyn's nephew. He grew hot and cold, and stammered something, he did not know what.

"Yes?" said Denis, in his soft, casual voice, politely expectant.

Peter, who did not, after all, lack a certain desperate courage, walked into the fire, with braced will. It was bad that Denis should be brought into the business; but it had to be gone through, all the same.

"I only wanted to know ... to know ... what Lord Evelyn is going to do about this matter." He jerked out the words like stones from a catapult.

Denis was silent for a moment. He disliked being dragged into this revolting affair; but he had had to come and see Peter, since his uncle refused and he could not let Peter go unseen away. He didn't want to see him ever again, since he had behaved as he had behaved, but neither did he want to violate the laws of courtesy and hospitality.

"I don't quite know," he said, after a moment.

"Is he ... does he intend to prosecute?" Peter asked, blushing.

Denis answered to that at once: "I shall certainly do my best to prevent anything of the sort. I don't think he will. At present he is still very angry; but I think when he cools down he will see reason. To prosecute would be to make himself absurd; he will see that, no doubt. He values his reputation as an art connoisseur, you see." At the faint, cool irony in the words, Peter winced.

"Of course," went on Denis, lighting a cigarette, "your brother will leave Venice at once, I suppose?" He passed Peter his cigarette box; Peter refused it.

"Naturally. We mean to leave as soon as we can.... Thank you, that is all I had to say.... Good-bye."

Denis got up, and Peter saw relief through the mask of politeness.

"Good-bye.... I needn't say how sorry I am about all this. It was hard lines on you being brought into it."

He was making a transparent effort after friendliness; Peter almost smiled at it. Poor Denis; what a relief it would be to him when the disreputable Margerisons were off the scenes.

Peter paused at the door and said, in a low, embarrassed voice, "Would you mind telling Lord Evelyn what I told him myself last night—that I'm horribly sorry about it—sorrier than I have ever been for anything.... It won't make any difference to him, I know—but if you will just tell him.... And I'm sorry it happened while you were here, too. You've been dragged in.... Good-bye."

"Good-bye, Margerison." Denis was grave, embarrassed, restrained, and not unkind. It was obvious that he had nothing to say about it all.

Peter left the Ca' delle Gemme.

That afternoon Hilary received a note from Lord Evelyn. It was to the effect that Lord Evelyn had decided not to bring an action, on the understanding that Hilary and his brother and Vyvian left Venice at once and discontinued for ever the profession of artistic advisers. If any of the three was discovered engaging again in that business, those who employed them should promptly be advised of their antecedents. They were, in fact, to consider themselves warned off the turf. There was also to be a paragraph about them in the English art papers.

"Well," was Peggy's comment, "it hasn't been such a grand trade that we need mind much. We'll all come back to England and keep a boarding-house there instead, and you shall paint the great pictures, darling, and have ever so much more fun. And we'll never need to see that Vyvian again; there's fine news for the babies, anyhow. And I will be relieved to get them away from the canals; one of them would have been surely drowned before long. In London they'll have only gutters."

Hilary, who was looking tired and limp after a distressing night and day, said, "What shall you do, Peter?"

"I don't know," said Peter. "I must find something, I suppose. Some sort of work, you know." He pronounced the word gingerly, distastefully, as if it were a curious, unwonted one. "Perhaps I shall be able to get a post as door-keeper somewhere; in some museum, you know, or perhaps a theatre, or the White City. I've always thought that might be amusing."

"You wouldn't earn much that way," Hilary said hopelessly.

"Need one earn much?" Peter wondered; then remembered how exceedingly little Hilary would be earning, and that perhaps one need, because of the babies.

"Or perhaps I can get taken on as a clerk in some business," he amended. "Or in a bank; only I don't believe my sums or manners are good enough for a bank, really.... Oh, well, I must see what I can squeeze into. Perhaps Leslie can think of something. And perhaps the Robinsons will interest themselves in me, though they'll be even more disgusted at our downfall than they were when I took up my profession, and they thought that perfectly idiotic. They always do think we're perfectly idiotic, and now they'll know we're something worse. But they may help me to a job, if I bother them enough.... Anyhow, I'll be one of your boarders, if I may."

"You darling," said Peggy, beaming at him. "It'll give the house quite a different feeling if you're in it. And how delighted the babies will be. I believe we're going to have the fine time, after all, in spite of this bothersome business. Hurrah for London and no mosquitoes! And we'll be quite near a Catholic church, the way the children'll be able to run in and out as they do here, and not pick up heathen customs. Why, Hilary, I'm really pleased!"

Peggy was splendid. She was nearly always really pleased.

They started for England a week later. In the course of that week two things happened. One was that Leslie gave Peter the Berovieri goblet for his own.

"You've got to take it," he said. "If you don't, I shall give it back to the prince. I've no right to it; I can't appreciate it properly. Since I first saw you look at the thing I knew it was really yours. Take it and keep it. You won't let me do anything else for you, but you shall let me do that."

Peter looked at it with wistful love. His fingers lingered about its exquisiteness.

"It will break," he said. "My things do break. Break and get lost, and go with the dust. Or thieves will break in and steal it. I shan't be able to keep it, I know; I'm such a bad hand at keeping things."

"Well, well, have a try," said Leslie. So Peter took it and was glad. It was his one link with the world of exquisiteness and new-burnished joys out of which he was being thrust; he would keep it if he could.

Leslie also said that he could get him a place in a business, if he really wanted one.

"I shall be extremely little use," said Peter.

"Extremely little," Leslie agreed. "You'd much better not try. But if you must you must."

"I'm afraid I must," said Peter.

So Leslie wrote letters about him, and secured him a humble post in a warehouse. Leslie was not going to return to England at present. He was going a tour round the world. Since Peter refused to accompany him, he went alone.

"There's no one else I can fancy hanging round me day and night," he said. "I wanted you, Margery"—the nickname fell from him with a clumsy pathos—"but if you won't you won't. I shall acquire an abominable collection of objects without you to guide me; but that can't be helped."

The other thing that happened was that Mrs. Johnson fell suddenly ill and died. Before she died, she talked to Peter about Rhoda.

"It's leaving of her as I can't bear," she whispered. "All alone and unprotected like. I can't leave her by herself in this heathen country. I want to get her back to England. But she's got no relatives there as'll do for her; none, you know, as I should care to trust her to, or as 'ud be really good to her. And I'm afraid of what'll come to the child without me; I'm *afraid*, Mr. Peter. That man—it gives me the creeps of nights to think of him comin' after Rhoder when I'm gone. I'm just frightened as he'll get her; you know what Rhoder is, like a soft wax candle that gets droopy and gives before his bold look; he can do anythin' with her. And if he gets her, he won't be good to her, I know that. He'll just break her and toss her away, my little gal. Oh, what can I do, Mr. Peter, to save that?"

She was in great pain; drops of sweat kept gathering on her forehead and rolling on to the pillow. Peter took her hand that picked at the blanket.

"May we try to take care of her?" he gently asked. "If she will come and stay with us, in London, it would be better than being alone among strangers, wouldn't it? She could get work near, and live with us. Peggy is fond of her, you know; we all are. We would try to make her as happy as we could."

She smiled at him, between laboured breaths.

"God bless you, dear Mr. Peter. I somehow thought as how you'd be good to my little gal.... You are so sympathetic to everyone always.... Yes, Rhoder shall do that; I'll have her promise. And that man—you'll keep him off of her?"

"I will try," said Peter. "I will do my very best."

"Oh, Lord, oh, dear Lord," said Mrs. Johnson, "the pain!"

But it didn't last long, for she died that night.

And four days later the boarding-house was broken up, and the Margerison family and Rhoda Johnson left Italy together.

Rhoda was very quiet and still and white. She was terribly alone, for her mother was gone, and the man she loved was gone, hurriedly, without a word to her. There remained the Margerisons; Peter, with his friendly smile and gentle companionableness; Hilary, worried and weary and hardly noticing her unobtrusive presence; Silvio, Caterina, and Illuminato sucking gingerbread and tumbling off the rack, and Peggy, on whose broad shoulder Rhoda suddenly laid her head and wept, all through the Mont Cenis tunnel.

CHAPTER XI

THE LOSS OF AN IDEA

Peter's room was the smallest and highest in the boarding-house. It was extremely small and high, and just above the bed was a ceiling that got hot through and through like a warming-pan, so that the room in summer was like a little oven below. What air there was came in came through a small skylight above the wash-stand; through this also came the rain when it rained; the dirtiest rain Peter had ever seen.

It was not raining this morning, when Peter, after passing a very warm night, heard the bells beginning. A great many bells begin on Sunday mornings in this part of London, no doubt in any part of London, but here they seem particularly loud. The boarding-house was in a small street close to a large English church and a small Roman church; and the English church had its first Mass at seven, and the Roman church at six, and each had another an hour later, and bells rang for all. So Peter lay and listened.

Sometimes he went with Hilary and Peggy to the Roman Mass. That pleased Peggy, who had hopes of some day converting him. And occasionally he went alone to the English Mass, and he liked that better, on the whole, because the little Roman church was rather ugly. Peter didn't think he would ever join the Roman church, even to please Peggy. It certainly seemed to him in some ways the most finely expressive of the churches; but equally certainly it often expressed the wrong things, and (like all other churches) left whole worlds unexpressed. And so much of its expression had a crudity.... It kept saying too little and too much, and jarring.

Anyhow, this morning Peter, who had a headache after his warm night, lay and heard the bells and thought what a nice day Sunday was, with no office to go to. Instead, he would take Rhoda on the river in the morning, and go and see Lucy in the afternoon, and probably have tea there. When Peter went to see Lucy he always had a faint hope that Urquhart would perhaps walk in, and that they would all be friendly and happy together in the old way, for one afternoon. It hadn't happened yet. Peter hadn't seen Urquhart since they had left Venice, two months ago. Sunday was his day for going to see Lucy, and it wasn't Urquhart's day, perhaps because Urquhart was so often away for week-ends; though last Sunday, indeed, he had just left the Hopes' house when Peter arrived.

Lucy, when Peter had told her his tale of dishonour two months ago, had said, half laughing at him, "How *stupid* of all of you!" She hadn't realised quite how much it mattered. Lucy judged everything by a queer, withdrawn standard of her own.

Peter had agreed that it had been exceedingly stupid of all of them. Once, since then, when he heard that Urquhart had returned and had seen Lucy, he had asked her, "Does he dislike us all very much? Is he quite too disgusted to want to see me again?"

Lucy had wrinkled her forehead over it.

"He's not angry," she had said. "You can fancy, can't you? Merely—merely ..."

"Detached," said Peter, who had more words, and always expressed what Lucy meant; and she nodded. "Just that, you know." She had looked at him wistfully, hoping he wasn't minding too horribly much.

"It's *stupid* of him," she had said, using her favourite adjective, and had added, dubiously, "Come and meet him sometime. You can't go on like this; it's too silly."

Peter had shaken his head. "I won't till he wants to. I don't want to bother him, you see."

"He does want to," Lucy had told him. "Of course he does. Only he thinks *you* don't. That's what's so silly."

They had left it there for the present. Some day Peter meant to walk into Denis's rooms and say, "Don't be stupid. This can't go on." But the day hadn't come yet. If it had been Denis who had done the shady thing and was in penury and dishonour thereby, it would have been so simple. But that was inconceivable; such things didn't happen to Denis; and as it was it was not simple.

Peter got out of his hot bed on to his hot floor, and made for the bathroom. There was only one bathroom in the boarding-house, but there was no great competition for it, so Peter had his bath in peace, and sang a tune in it as was his custom, and came back to his hot room and put on his hot clothes (his less tidy clothes, because it was the day of joy), and came down to breakfast at 9:25.

Most of the other boarders had got there before him. It was a mixed boarding-house, and contained at the moment two gentlemen besides Hilary and Peter, and five ladies besides Peggy and Rhoda. They were on the whole a happy and even gay society, and particularly on Sundays.

Peggy, looking up from the tea-cups, gave Peter a broad smile, and Rhoda gave him a little subdued one, and Peter looked pleased to see everyone; he always did, even on Mondays.

"I'm sure your brother hasn't a care in the world," an envious lady boarder had once said to Peggy; "he's always so happy-looking."

This was the lady who was saying, as Peter entered, "And my mother's last words were, 'Find Elizabeth Dean's grave.' Elizabeth Dean was an author, you know—oh, very well known, I believe. She treated my mother and me none too well; didn't stand by us when she should have—but we won't say anything about that now. Anyhow, it was a costly funeral—forty pounds and eight horses—and my mother hadn't an idea where she was laid. So she said, 'Find Elizabeth Dean's grave,' just like that. And the strange thing was that in the first churchyard I walked into, in a little village down in Sussex, there was a tombstone, 'Elizabeth Dean, 65. The Lord gave and the Lord hath taken away.' Wasn't that queer, now? So I went straight and...."

"The woman's a fool," muttered the gentleman next Peter, a cynical-faced commercial traveller. Peter had heard the remark from him frequently before, and did not feel called upon to reply to it.

But the tale of Elizabeth Dean was interrupted by a lady of a speculative habit of mind.

"Now I want to ask you all, *should* one put up a tombstone to the departed? I've been having quite a kick-up with my sisters about it lately. Hadn't one better spend the money on the living? What do *you* think, Miss Matthews?"

Miss Matthews said she liked to see a handsome headstone.

"After all, one honours them that way. It's all one can do for them, isn't it."

"Oh, Miss Matthews, *all?*" Several ladies were shocked. "What about one's prayers for the dead?"

"I don't pray for the dead," said Miss Matthews, who was a protestant, and did not attend the large church in the next street. "I do not belong to the Romish religion. I'm not saying anything against those who do, but I consider that those who do *not* should confine their prayers to those who may require them in this troubled world, and not waste them upon those whose fate we have every reason to believe is settled once and for all."

The lady who always quarrelled with her on this subject rose to the occasion. Peggy, soothing them down, said mechanically, "There now.... Three lumps, Peter?... Micky, one doesn't suck napkin rings; naughty."

Peter was appealed to by his neighbour, who knew that he occasionally attended St. Austin's church. People were always drawing him into theological discussions, which he knew nothing at all about.

"Mr. Peter, isn't that against all reason, to stop praying for our friends merely because they've passed through the veil?"

"Yes," Peter agreed. "I should have thought so." But all he really thought was that beyond the veil was such darkness that he never looked into it, and that it was a pity people should argue on a holiday.

"Now," said someone else, wishing to be a peace-maker, "I'm afraid you'll all say I'm very naughty, but *I* attend the early Mass at St. Austin's, high Mass at the Roman church"—she nodded at Peggy—"and the City Temple in the evening"—she smiled at the commercial traveller, who was believed to be a New Theologian. "Aren't I naughty, now?"

Mademoiselle, the French governess, came down at this point, saying she had had a dream about a hat with pink roses. The peace-making lady said, "Bad little thing, she's quite frisky this morning." Hilary, to whom Mademoiselle was the last straw, left the room.

Rhoda followed his example. She had sat very silent, as usual, over breakfast, eating little. Peter came out with her, and followed her into the sitting-room, where she stood listlessly playing with the tassel of the blind. Rhoda was thinner than ever, and floppier, and took even less pains to be neat. She had left off her beads, but had not replaced them by a collar.

Peter said, "Are you coming out with me this morning?"

She replied, listless and uncaring, "If you like."

"We might go," said Peter, "and see if the New English Art Club is open on Sunday mornings. And then we'll go on the river. Shall we?"

She assented again. "Very well."

A moment later she sighed, and said wearily, "How it does go on, day after day, doesn't it!"

Peter said it did.

"On and on," said Rhoda. "Same stupid people saying the same stupid old things. I do wonder they don't get tired. They don't *know* anything, do they?"

Rhoda's hankering was still after Great Minds.

"They're funny sometimes," suggested Peter tentatively; but she was blind to that.

"They don't know a thing. And they talk and talk, so stupidly. About religion—as if one religion was different from another. And about dead people, as if they knew all about them and what they were doing. They seem to make sure souls go on—Miss Matthews and Miss Baker were both sure of that. But how can they tell? Some people that know lots more than them don't think so, but say ... say it's nothingness."

Peter recognised Guy Vyvian's word. Rhoda would have said "nothing to follow."

"People say," he agreed, "quite different things, and none of them know anything about it, of course. One needn't worry, though."

"*You* never worry," she accused him, half fretfully. "But," she added, "you don't preach, either. You don't say things are so when you can't know.... Do you *think* anything about that, Peter—about going on? I don't believe you do."

Peter reflected. "No," he said. "I don't believe I do. I can't look beyond what I can see and touch; I don't try. I expect I'm a materialist. The colours and shapes of things matter so awfully much; I can't imagine anything of them going on when those are dead. I rather wish I could. Some people that know lots more than me do, and I think it's splendid of them and for them. They're very likely right, too, you know."

Rhoda shook her head. "*I* believe it's nothingness."

Peter felt it a dreary subject, and changed it.

"Well, let's come and look at pictures. And I can't imagine nothingness, can you? We might have lunch out somewhere, if you don't mind."

So they went out and looked at pictures, and went up the river in a steamer, and had lunch out somewhere, and Rhoda grew very gentle and more cheerful, and said, "I didn't mean to be cross to *you*, Peter. You're ever so good to me," and winked away tears, and the gentle Peter, who hated no one, wished that some catastrophe would wipe Guy Vyvian off the face of the earth and choke his memory with dust. Whenever one thought Rhoda was getting rather better, the image of Vyvian, who knew such a lot more than most people, came up between her and the world she ought to have been enjoying, and she had a relapse.

Peter and Rhoda came home together, and Rhoda said, "Thank you ever so much for taking me. I've liked it ever so," and went up to her room to read poetry. Rhoda read a good deal of the work of our lesser contemporary poets; Vyvian had instilled that taste into her.

Peter, about tea-time, went to see Lucy. He went by the Piccadilly tube, from Holborn to South Kensington—(he was being recklessly extravagant to-day, but it was a holiday after all, and very hot).

Peter climbed the stairs to the Hopes' drawing-room and opened the door, and what he had often dreamed of had come about, for Denis was there, only in a strange, undreamed-of way that made him giddy, so he stood quite still for a moment and looked.

He would have turned away and gone before they saw him; but they had seen him, and Lucy said, "Oh, Peter—come in," and Denis said, "Oh ... hullo," and held out his hand.

Peter, who was dizzily readjusting certain rather deeply-rooted ideas, said, "How do you do? I've come ... I've come to tea, you know."

"'Course you have," said Lucy. Then she looked up into Peter's face and smiled, and slipped her hand into his. "How nice; we're three again."

"Yes," said Peter.

"But I must go," said Urquhart. "I'm awfully sorry, but I've got to meet a man.... I shall see you some time, shan't I, Margery? Why don't you ever come and see me, you slacker? Well, good-bye. Good-bye, Lucy. Lunch to-morrow; don't forget."

He was gone.

Peter sat on the coal-scuttle, and Lucy gave him tea, with three lumps in it.

"Thank you," said Peter.

Lucy looked at him. "You *did* know, didn't you? All this time, I mean? I didn't tell you, because I never tell you things, of course. You always know them. And this particularly. You *did* know it, Peter? But when you came in you looked ... you looked as if you didn't."

"I was stupid," said Peter. "I ought to have known."

Looking back, he saw that he certainly ought. He certainly must have, only that his vision had been blocked by a certain deeply-rooted idea, that was as old as his growth. He had assumed, without words. He had thought that she too had assumed; neither had ever required words to elucidate their ideas one to the other; they had kept words for the other things, the jolly, delightful things of the foreground.

"How long?" asked Peter, drinking his tea to warm him, for, though it was so hot outside, he felt very cold in here.

She told him. "Oh, since the beginning, I think. I thought you knew, Peter.... We didn't say anything about it till quite lately. Only we both knew."

She came and sat on the rug by his side, and slipped her hand into his. "Are you glad, Peter? Please, Peter, be glad."

"I will presently," said Peter, with one of his fainter smiles. "Let me just get used to it, and I will."

She whispered, stroking his hand, "We've always had such fun, Peter, we three. Haven't we? Let's go on having it."

"Yes," said Peter. "Let's."

He was vague still, and a little dizzy, but he could smile at her now. After all, wasn't it splendid? Denis and Lucy—the two people he loved best in the world; so immeasurably best that beside them everyone else was no class at all.

He sat very still on the coal-scuttle, making a fresh discovery about himself. He had known before that he had a selfish disposition, though he had never thought about it particularly; but he hadn't known that it was in him to grudge Denis anything—Denis, who was consciously more to him than anyone else in the world. Lucy was different; she was rooted in the very fibre of his being; it wasn't so much that he consciously loved her as that she was his other self. Well, hadn't he long since given to Denis, to use as he would, all the self he had?

But the wrench made him wince, and left him chilly and grown old.

"It's perfectly splendid for both of you," said Peter, himself again at last. "And it was extraordinarily stupid of me not to see it before.... Do you think Denis really meant I could go and see him? I think I will."

"'Course he did. 'Course you will. Go to-morrow. But now it's going to be just you and me and tea. And honey sandwiches—oh, Peter!" Her eyes danced at him, because it was such a nice world. He came off the coal-scuttle and made himself comfortable in a low chair near the honey sandwiches.

"Will you and Denis try always to have them when I come to tea with you? I do love them so. Have you arranged when it is to be, by the way?"

"No. Father won't want it to be for ages—he won't like it to be at all, of course, because Denis isn't poor or miserable or revolutionary. But Felicity has done so nicely for him in that way (Lawrence is getting into horrid rows in Poland, you know) that I think I've a *right* to someone happy and clean, don't you?... And Denis wants it to be soon. So I suppose it will be soon."

"Sure to be," Peter agreed.

The room was full of roses; their sweetness was exuberant, intoxicating; not like Lucy, who usually had small, pale, faint flowers.

"Isn't it funny," she said, "how one thinks one can't be any happier, and then suddenly something happens inside one, and one sees everything new. I used to think things couldn't be brighter and shine more—but now they glitter like the sun, all new."

"I expect so," said Peter.

Then she had a little stab of remorse; for Peter had been turned out of the place of glittering things, and moved in a grey and dusty world among things no one could like.

"'Tis so *stupid* that your work is like that," she said, with puckered forehead. "I wish you could find something nice to do, Peter dear."

"Oh, I'm all right," said Peter. "And there are all the nice things which aren't work, just the same. Rhoda and I went a ride in a steamer this morning. And the sun was shining on the water—rather nice, it was. Even Rhoda grew a little brighter to see it. Poor Rhoda; the boarders do worry her so. I'm sorry about it; they don't worry me; I rather like them. Some day soon I want you to come and see Rhoda; it would cheer her up. I wish she liked things more. She's left off her bead necklace, you know. And she gets worried because people discuss the condition of 'the departed' (that's what we call them in the boarding-house). Rhoda is sure they are in nothingness. I told her it was impossible for me to speculate on such things. How can one, you know? People have so much imagination. Mine always sticks at a certain point and won't move on. Could you do it if someone asked you to imagine Denis, say, without his body?"

She wrinkled her forehead, trying to.

"Denis's body matters a lot," was her conclusion. "I suppose it's because it's such a nice one."

"Exactly," said Peter. "People's bodies are nice. And when they're not I don't believe their minds are very nice either, so I'd rather not think about them. Now I must go home."

It was very hot going home. London was a baked place, full of used air— Peter's bedroom on a large scale. Peter tried walking back, but found he was rather giddy, so got into a bus that took him the wrong way, a thing he often did. Riding across London on the top of a bus is, of course, the greatest fun, even if it is the wrong bus. It makes up for almost any misfortune.

A few days later, after office hours, Peter took Urquhart at his word and went to his rooms. Urquhart wasn't there, but would be in some time, he was told, so he sat and waited for him. It was a pleasant change after the boarding-house rooms. Urquhart's things were nice to look at, without being particularly artistic. There was nothing dingy, or messy, or second-rate, or cheap. A graceful, careless expensiveness was the dominant note. An aroma of good tobacco hung about. Peter liked to smell good tobacco, though he smoked none, good or bad.

Urquhart came in at seven o'clock. He was going to dine somewhere at eight, so he hadn't much time.

"Glad to see you, Margery. Quite time you came."

Peter thought it nice of him to speak so pleasantly, seeming to ignore the last time Peter had come to see him. He had been restrained and embarrassed then; now he was friendly, in the old casual, unemphasised way.

"How splendid about you and Lucy," said Peter. "A very suitable alliance, I call it."

"So do I," said Denis, lighting a cigarette. "She's so much the nicest person I know. I perceived that the day you introduced us."

"Of course," said Peter. "You would."

"Do you mind," said Denis, "if I dress? We can talk meanwhile. Rotten luck that I'm booked for dinner, or we could have had it together. You must come another day."

While he dressed he told Peter that he was going to stand at the next elections. Peter had known before that Denis was ultimately destined to assist in the government of his country, and now it appeared that the moment had arrived.

"Do you *really* take a side?" Peter enquired. "Or is it just a funny game?"

"Oh, of course it's a game too; most things are. But, of course, one's a Conservative and all that, if one's a person of sense. It's the only thing to be, you know."

"I rather like both sides," said Peter. "They're both so keen, and so sure they're right. But I expect Conservatives are the rightest, because they want to keep things. I hate people who want to make a mess and break things up and throw them away. Besides, I suppose one couldn't really be on the same side as what's his name—that man everyone dislikes so—could one? or any of those violent people."

Urquhart said one certainly couldn't. Besides, there were Free Trade and Home Rule, and dozens of other things to be considered. Obviously Conservatives were right.

"I ought to get in," he said, "unless anything upsets it. The Unionist majority last time was two hundred and fifty."

Peter laughed. It was rather nice to hear Denis talking like a real candidate.

When Denis was ready, he said, "I'm dining in Norfolk Street. Can you walk with me part of the way?"

Peter said it was on the way to Brook Street, where he lived. Denis displayed no interest in Brook Street. As far as he intended to cultivate Peter's acquaintance, it was to be as a unit, detached from his disgraceful relatives. Peter understood that. As he hadn't much expected to be cultivated again at all, he was in good spirits as he walked with Denis to Norfolk Street. No word passed between them as to Peter's past disgrace or present employment; Denis had an easy way of sliding lightly over embarrassing subjects.

They parted, and Denis dined in Norfolk Street with a parliamentary secretary, and Peter supped in Brook Street with the other boarders.

CHAPTER XII

THE LOSS OF A GOBLET AND OTHER THINGS

Denis and Lucy were married at the end of September. They went motoring in Italy for a month, and by the beginning of November were settled at Astleys. Astleys was in Berkshire, and was Urquhart's home. It was rather beautiful, as homes go, with a careless, prosperous grace about it at which Lucy laughed because it was so Urquhartesque.

Almost at once they asked some people to stay there to help with the elections and the pheasant shooting. The elections were hoped for in December. Urquhart did not propose to bother much about them; he was a good deal more interested in the pheasants; but he had, of course, every intention of doing the usual and suitable things, and carrying the business through well. Lucy only laughed; to want to get into Parliament was so funny, looked at from the point of view she had always been used to. Denis, being used by inheritance and upbringing to another point of view, did not see that it was so funny; to him it was a very natural profession for a man to go into; his family had always provided a supply of members for both houses. Lucy and Peter, socially more obscure, laughed childishly together over it. "Fancy being a Liberal or a Conservative out of all the things there are in the world to be!" as Peter had once commented.

But it was delightfully Urquhart-like, this lordly assumption of a share in the government of a country. No doubt it was worth having, because all the things Urquhart wanted and obtained were that; he had an eye for good things, like Peter, only he gained possession of them, and Peter could only admire from afar.

They were talking about the election prospects at dinner on the evening of the fifteenth of November. They were a young and merry party. At one end of the table was Denis, looking rather pale after a hard day's hunting, and very much amused with life; at the other Lucy, in a white frock, small and open-eyed like a flower, and very much amused too; and between them were the people, young mostly, and gay, who were staying with them. Lucy, who had been brought up in a secluded Bohemianism, found it very funny and nice having a house-party, and so many servants to see after them all that one needn't bother to run round and make sure everyone had soap, and so on.

One person, not young, who was staying there, was Lord Evelyn Urquhart. Lucy loved him. He loved her, and told funny stories. Sometimes, between the stories, she would catch his near-sighted, screwed up eyes scanning her face with a queer expression that might have been wistfulness; he seemed at times to be looking for something in her face, and finding it. Particularly when she laughed, in her chuckling, gurgling way, he looked like this, and would grow grave suddenly. They had talked together about all manner of things, being excellent friends, but only once so far about Lucy's cousin Peter. Once had been too much, Lucy had found. The Margerisons were a tabooed subject with Lord Evelyn Urquhart.

Denis shrugged his shoulders over it. "They did him brown, you see," he explained, in his light, casual way. "Uncle Evelyn can't forgive that. And it's because he was so awfully fond of Peter that he's so bitter against him now. I never mention him; it's best not.... You know, you keep giving the poor dear shocks by looking like Peter, and laughing like him, and using his words. You *are* rather like, you know."

"I know," said Lucy. "It's not only looking and laughing and words; we think alike too. So perhaps if he gets fond of me he'll forgive Peter sometime."

"He's an implacable old beggar," Denis said. "It's stupid of him. It never seems to me worth while to get huffy; it's so uncomfortable. He expects too much of people, and when they disappoint him he—"

"Takes umbrage," Lucy filled in for him. That was another of Peter's expressions; they shared together a number of such stilted, high-sounding phrases, mostly culled either out of Adelphi melodrama or the fiction of a by-gone age.

To-night, when the cloth had been removed that they might eat fruit, Denis was informed that there was a gentleman waiting to see him. The gentleman had not vouchsafed either his name or business, so he could obviously wait a little longer, till Denis had finished his own business. In twenty minutes Denis went to the library, and there found Hilary Margerison, sitting by the fire in a great coat and muffler and looking cold. When he rose and faced him, Denis saw that he also looked paler than of old, and thinner, and less perfectly shaved, and his hair was longer. He might have been called seedy-looking; he might have been Sidney Carton in "The Only Way"; he had always that touch of the dramatic about him that suggested a stage character. He had a bad cough.

"Oh," said Urquhart, polite and feeling embarrassed; "how do you do? I'm sorry to have kept you waiting; they didn't tell me who it was. Sit down, won't you?"

Hilary said thanks, he thought not. He had a keen sense of the fit. So he refused the cigarette Urquhart offered him, and stood by the fire, looking at the floor. Urquhart stood opposite him, and thought how ill and how little reputable he looked.

Hilary said, in his high, sweet, husky voice, "It is no use beating about the bush. I want help. We are in need; we are horribly hard up, to put it baldly. That has passed between your family and mine which makes you the last person I should wish to appeal to as a beggar. I propose a business transaction." He paused to cough.

Urquhart, feeling impatient at the prospect of a provoking interview when he wanted to be playing bridge, said "Yes?" politely.

"You," said Hilary, "are intending to stand as a candidate for this constituency. You require for that, I fancy, a reputation wholly untarnished; the least breath dimming it would be for you a disastrous calamity. I have some information which, if sent to the local Liberal paper, would seriously tell against you in the public mind. It is here."

He took it out of his breast pocket and handed it to Urquhart—a type-written sheet of paper. He must certainly have been to a provincial theatre lately; he had hit its manners and methods to a nicety, the silly ass.

Urquhart took the paper gingerly and did not look at it.

"Thanks; but ... I don't know that I am interested, do you know. Isn't this all rather silly, Mr. Margerison?"

"If you will oblige me by reading it," said Mr. Margerison.

So Urquhart obliged him. It was all about him, as was to be expected; enough to make a column of the Berkshire Press.

"Well?" said Hilary, when he had done.

"Well," said Urquhart, folding up the paper and returning it, "thank you for showing it me. But again I must say that I am not particularly interested. Of course you will send anything you like to any paper you like; it is no business of mine. There's the libel law, as of course you know; newspapers are as a rule rather careful about that. No respectable paper, I needn't say, would care to use such copy as this of yours.... Well, good night.... Oh, by the way, I suppose your brother told you all that?"

Hilary said, "I had it from various reliable sources." He stood uncertain, with wavering eyes, despair killing hope. "You will do nothing at all to save your reputation, then?"

Urquhart laughed, unamused, with hard eyes. He was intensely irritated.

"Do you think it likely? I don't care what you get printed in any dirty rag about me, man. Why on earth should I?"

The gulf between them yawned; it was unbridgeable. From Hilary's world insults might be shrieked and howled, dirt thrown with all the strength of hate, and neither shrieks nor dirt would reach across the gulf to Urquhart's. They simply didn't matter. Hilary, realising this, grew slowly, dully red, with the bitterness of mortified expectation. Urquhart's look at him, supercilious, contemptuous, aloof, slightly disgusted, hurt his vanity. He caught at the only weapon he had which could hurt back.

"I must go and tell Peter, then, that his information has been of no use."

Urquhart said merely, "Peter won't be surprised. It's no good your trying to make me think that Peter is joining in this absurdity. He has too much sense of the ridiculous. He seems to have talked to you pretty freely of my concerns, which I certainly fancied he would keep to himself; I suppose he did that by way of providing entertaining conversation; Peter was always a chatterbox"—it was as well that Peter was not there to hear the edge in the soft, indifferent voice—"but he isn't quite such a fool as to have countenanced this rather stagey proceeding of yours. He knows me—used to know me—pretty well, you see.... Good night. You have plenty of time to catch your train, I think."

Hilary stopped to say, "Is that all you have to say? You won't let your connexion with our family—with Peter—induce you to help us in our need?... I've done an unpleasant thing to-night, you know; I've put my pride in my pocket and stooped to the methods of the cad, for the sake of my wife and little children. I admit I have made a mistake, both of taste and judgment; I have behaved unworthily; you may say like a fool. But are you prepared to see us go under—to drive by and leave us lying in the road, as you did to that old Tuscan peasant? Does it in no way affect your feelings towards us that you are now Peter's cousin by marriage—besides being practically, his half-brother?"

"I am not practically, or in any other way, Peter's half-brother," said Urquhart casually. "But that is neither here nor there. Peter and I are—have been—friends, as you know. I should naturally give him help if he asked me for it. He has not done so; all that has happened is that you have tried to blackmail me.... I really see no use in prolonging this interview, Mr. Margerison. Good night." Urquhart was bored and impatient with the absurd scene.

Into the middle of it walked Peter, pale and breathless. He stood by the door and looked at them, dazed and blinking at the light; looked at Urquhart, who stood leaning his shoulder against the chimney-piece, his hands in his pockets, the light full on his fair, tranquil, bored face, and at Hilary, pale and tragic, with wavering, unhappy eyes. So they stood for a type and a symbol and a sign that never, as long as the world endures, shall Margerisons get the better of Urquharts.

They both looked at Peter, and Urquhart's brows rose a little, as if to say, "More Margerisons yet?"

Hilary said, "What's the matter, Peter? Why have *you* come?"

Peter said, rather faintly, "I meant to stop you before you saw Denis. I suppose I'm too late.... I made Peggy tell me. I found a paper, you see; and I asked Peggy, and she said you'd come down here to use it. *Have* you?"

"He has already done his worst," Denis's ironic voice answered for him. "Sprung the awful threat upon me."

Peter leant back against the door, feeling rather sick. He had run all the way from the station; and, as always, he was too late.

Then he laughed a little. The contrast of Hilary's tragedian air and Urquhart's tranquil boredom was upsetting to him.

Urquhart didn't laugh, but looked at him enquiringly.

"It's certainly funny rather," he said quietly. "You must have got a good deal of quiet fun out of compiling that column."

"Oh," said Peter. "But I didn't, you know."

"I gather you helped—supplied much of the information. That story of the old man I brutally slew and then callously left uncared for on the road— you seem to have coloured that rather highly in passing it on.... I suppose it was stupid of me to fancy that you weren't intending to make that public property. Not that I particularly mind: there was nothing to be ashamed of in that business; but it somehow never happened to occur to me that you were relating it."

"I didn't," said Peter. "I have never told anyone."

Urquhart said nothing; his silence was expressive.

Peter stammered into speech incoherently.

"At least—at least—yes, I believe I did tell Peggy the story, months ago, in Venice—but I didn't say it was you. I merely said, if someone had done that ... what would she think? I wanted to know if she thought we ought to have found the old man's people and told them."

"I see," said Urquhart. "And did she?"

"No. She thought it was all right." Peter had known beforehand that Peggy would think it was all right; that was why he had asked her, to be reassured, to have the vague trouble in his mind quieted.

And she, apparently, had seen through his futile pretence, had known it was Urquhart he spoke of, needed reassuring about (Peter didn't realise that even less shrewd observers than Peggy might easily know when it was Urquhart he spoke of) and had gone and told Hilary. And Hilary, in his need, had twisted it into this disgusting story, and had typed it and brought it down to Astleys to-night, with other twisted stories.

"I suppose the rest too," said Urquhart, "you related to your sister-in-law to see what she would think."

Peter stammered, "I don't think so. No, I don't believe anything else came from me. Did it, Hilary?"

Hilary shrugged his shoulders, and made no other answer.

"It really doesn't particularly matter," said Urquhart, "whether the informant was you or some other of my acquaintances. I daresay my gyp is responsible for the story of the actresses I brought down to the St. Gabriel's dance; he knew about it at the time, I believe. I am not in the least ashamed of that either; the 'Berkshire Press' is extremely welcome to it, if it can find space for it.... Well, now, will you both stay the night with me, or must you get back? The last good train goes at 10.5, I think."

Peter said, "Come along, Hilary."

Urquhart stood and watched them go.

As they turned away, he said, in his gentle, inexpressive voice, that hadn't been raised in anger once, "Can I lend you any money, Peter?"

Peter shook his head, though he felt Hilary start.

"No, thank you. It is very good of you.... Good night."

"Good night."

Going out of the room, they came face to face with Lord Evelyn Urquhart coming in. He saw them; he stiffened a little, repressing a start; he stood elaborately aside to let them pass, bowing slightly.

Neither Margerison said anything. Hilary's bow was the stage copy of his own; Peter didn't look at him at all, but hurried by.

The servant let them out, and shut the hall door behind them.

Lord Evelyn said to his nephew in the library, swinging his eye-glass restlessly to and fro, "Why do you let those people into your house, Denis? I thought we had done with them."

"They came to call," said Denis, who did not seem disposed to be communicative. "I can't say why they chose this particular hour."

Lord Evelyn paced up the room, restless, nervous, petulant.

"It's monstrous," he said querulously. "Perfectly monstrous. Shameless. How dare they show their faces in this house?... I suppose they wanted something out of you, did they?"

Denis merely said, "After all, Peter is my cousin by marriage, you must remember. And I have never broken with him."

Lord Evelyn returned, "The more shame to you. He's as great a swindler as his precious brother; they're a pair, you can't deny that."

Denis didn't attempt to deny it; probably he was feeling a little tired of the Margerisons to-night.

"I'm not defending Peter, or his brother either. I only said that he's Lucy's cousin, and she's very fond of him, and I'm not keen on actually breaking with him. As to the brother, he's so much more of an ass than anything else that to call him a swindler is more than he deserves. He simply came here to-night to play the fool; he's no more sense than a silly ass out of a play."

That was what Peter was telling Hilary on the way to the station. Hilary defended himself rather feebly.

"My good Peter, we must have money. We are in positive want. Of course, I never meant to proceed to extremities; I thought the mere mention of such a threat would be enough to make him see that we really were desperately hard up, and that he might as well help us. But he doesn't care. Like all rich people, he is utterly callous and selfish.... Do you think Lucy would possibly give us any help, if you asked her?"

"I shan't ask her," said Peter. "Don't, please, Hilary," he added miserably. "Can't you *see*...."

"See what? I see that we get a little more destitute every day: that the boarders are melting away; that I am reduced to unthinkably sordid hackwork, and you to the grind of uncongenial toil; that Peggy can't afford to keep a cook who can boil a potato respectably (they were like walnuts to-day) that she and the children go about with their clothes dropping off them. I see that; and I see these Urquharts, closely connected with our family, rolling in unearned riches, spending and squandering and wasting and never giving away. I see the Robinsons, our own relations, fattening on the money that ought to have come to us, and now and then throwing us a loan as you throw a dog a bone. I see your friend Leslie taking himself off to the antipodes to spend his millions, that he may be out of the reach of disturbing appeals. I see a world constituted so that you would think the devils in hell must cry shame on it." His cough, made worse by the fog, choked his relation of his vision.

Peter had nothing to say to it: he could only sigh over it. The Haves and the Have-Nots—there they are, and there is no getting round the ugly fact.

"Denis," said Peter, "would lend me money if I asked him. You heard him offer. But I am not going to ask him. We are none of us going to ask him. If I find that you have, and that he has given it you, I shall pay it straight back.... You know, Hilary, we're really not so badly off as all that; we get along pretty well, I think; better than most other people." The other Have-Nots; they made no difference, in Hilary's eyes, to the fact that of course the Margerisons should have been among the Haves.

Hilary said, "You are absolutely impervious, Peter, to other people's troubles," and turned up his coat-collar and sank down on a seat in the waiting-room. (Of course, they had missed the 10.5, the last good train, and were now waiting for the 11.2, the slow one.)

Peter walked up and down the platform, feeling very cold. He had come away, in his excitement, without his overcoat. The chill of the foggy night seemed to sink deep into his innermost being.

Hilary's words rang in his ears. "I see that we get a little more destitute every day." It was true. Every day the Margerisons seemed to lose something more. To-night Peter had lost something he could ill afford to part with—another degree of Denis Urquhart's regard. That seemed to be falling from him bit by bit; perhaps that was why he felt so cold. However desperately he clung to the remnants, as he had clung since that last interview in Venice, he could not think to keep them much longer at this rate.

As he walked up and down the platform, his cold hands thrust deep into his pockets, he was contemplating another loss—one that would hurt absurdly much.

If Hilary felt that he needed more money so badly, he must have it. There were certain things Peter declined to do. He wouldn't borrow from the Urquharts; but he would sell his last treasured possession to soothe Hilary for a little while. The Berovieri goblet had been bought for a lot of money, and could at any moment be sold for a lot of money. The Berovieri goblet must go.

That evening, in the tiny attic room, Peter took the adorable thing out of the box where it lay hid, and set it on the chest of drawers, in front of the candle, so that the flame shone through the blue transparency like the setting sun through a stained-glass window.

It was very, very beautiful. Peter sat on the bed and looked at it, as a devotee before a shrine. In itself it was very beautiful, a magic thing of blue colour and deep light and pure shadow and clear, lovely form. Peter loved it for itself, and for its symbolic character. For it was a symbol of the world of great loveliness that did, he knew, exist. When he had been turned out of that world into a grey and dusty place, he had kept that one thing, to link him with loveliness and light. Peter was a materialist: he loved things, their shapes and colours, with a passion that blinded him to the beauty of the colourless, the formless, the super-sensuous.

He slipped his fingers up the chalice's slim stem and round its cool bowl, and smiled for pleasure that such a thing existed—had existed for four hundred years—to gladden the world.

"Well, anyone would have thought I should have smashed you before now," he remarked, apostrophising it proudly. 'But I haven't. I shall take you to Christie's myself to-morrow, as whole as you were the day Leslie gave you me."

It was fortunate that Leslie was out of reach, and would not hear of the transaction. If he had been in England, Peter would have felt bound to offer him the goblet, and he would have paid for it too enormous a price to be endured. Leslie's generosity was sometimes rather overwhelming.

When Peter took Hilary and Peggy the cheque he had received, and told them what he had received it for, Hilary said, "I suppose these things must be. It was fortunate you did not ask my advice, Peter; I should have hesitated what to say. It is uncommonly like bartering one's soul for guineas. To what we are reduced!"

He was an artist, and cared for beautiful goblets. He would much rather have borrowed the money, or had it given him.

Peggy, who was not an artist, said, "Oh, Peter darling, how sweet of you! Now I really *can* pay the butcher; I've had to hide from him the last few mornings, in the coal-hole. You dear child, I hope you won't miss that nice cup too much. When our ship comes in you shall have another."

"*When*," sighed Hilary, who was feeling over-worked that evening. (He did advertisement pictures for a weekly paper; a sordid and degrading pursuit.)

"Well," said Peggy hopefully, "the boarders we have now really do pay their rent the way they never did in Venice. That's such a comfort. If only Larry's cough gets off his chest without turning to bronchitis, I will be quite happy. But these loathsome fogs! And that odious man coming round wanting to know why aren't the children attending school! 'I'm sure,' I said to him, 'I wish they were; the house would be the quieter missing them; but their father insists on educating them himself, because he won't let them mix up with the common children in the school; they're by way of being little gentry, do you see,' I said, 'though indeed you mightn't think it to look at them.' Oh dear me, he was so impolite; he wouldn't believe that Hilary was doing his duty by them, though I assured him that he read them all the 'Ancient Mariner' yesterday morning while they watched him dress, and that I was teaching them the alphabet whenever I had a spare minute. But nothing would satisfy him; and off the two eldest must go to the Catholic school next week to be destroyed by the fog and to pick up with all the ragamuffins in the district."

"An abominable, cast-iron system," Hilary murmured mechanically. "Of a piece with all the other institutions of an iniquitous state."

"And what do you think," added Peggy, who was busy putting a patch in Silvio's knickerbockers, "Guy Vyvian turned up out of nowhere and called this afternoon, bad manners to him for a waster. When he found you were out, Hilary, he asked where was Rhoda; he'd no notion of sitting down to listen to *me* talking. Rhoda was out at work too, of course; I told him it wasn't most of us could afford to play round in the afternoons the way he did. I suppose he'll come again, bothering and upsetting the child just when she's settling down a bit. I've thought her seeming brighter lately; she likes going about with you, Peter. But there'll be pretty doings again when that man comes exciting her."

"Vyvian is a cad and a low fellow," Hilary said, "and I always regretted being forced into partnership with him; but I suppose one can't kick one's past acquaintances from the door. I, at least, cannot. Some people can and do; they may reconcile it with their standards of decency if they choose; but I cannot. Vyvian must come if he likes, and we must be hospitable to him. We must ask him to dinner if he comes again."

"Yes," sniffed Peggy, "I can see him! Sticking his fork into the potatoes and pretending he can't get it through! Oh, have him to dinner if you like; he must just make the best of what he gets if he comes. He'll be awfully rude to the rest, too, but I'll apologise for him beforehand."

"Though a cad," Hilary observed, "Vyvian is less of a vacuous fool than most of the members of our present delightful house-party. He at least knows *something* of art and literature, and can converse without jarring one's taste violently by his every word. He is not, after all, a Miss Matthews or a Mr. Bridger. Apologies, therefore, are scarcely called for, perhaps."

Peggy said, "What a solemn face, Peter. Is it the Vyvian man, or the beautiful cup, that we've never half thanked you for getting rid of yet?"

Peter said, "It's the Vyvian man. He makes me feel solemn. You see, I promised Mrs. Johnson faithfully to keep Rhoda out of his clutches, if I could."

"Darling, what a silly promise. Oh, of course, we'll all do our best; but if he wants to clutch her, the silly little bird, he'll surely do it. Not that I'm saying he does want to; I daresay he only wants to upset her and make her his slave and then run away again to his own place, the Judas."

"But I don't want him to do that. Rhoda will be unhappier than ever again."

"Oh, well, I wouldn't wonder if, when Rhoda sees him again now, she sees what a poor creature it is, after all. It may be a turning-point with her, and who knows will she perhaps settle down afterwards and be a reasonable girl and darn her stockings and wear a collar?"

"If one *is* to talk of stockings," began Hilary, "I noticed Caterina's to-day, and really, you know...."

Peggy bit off her cotton and murmured, "Oh dear, oh dear, oh dear, what's to become of us all?"

CHAPTER XIII

THE LOSS OF THE SINGLE STATE

The man Vyvian came. He came again and again, but not to dinner. Perhaps he suspected about the potatoes, and thought that they would not even be compensated for by the pleasure of sneering at the boarders. He came in the evenings and sat in the sitting-room and drank coffee (the only thing that was well cooked in Peggy's household), and talked to Hilary, and looked at Rhoda. Rhoda, embroidering apple-boughs on a green dress-front, shivered and trembled under his eyes.

"Now I know," thought Peter, seeing Vyvian look, "what villains in books are really like. Vyvian is just like one; specially about the eyes." He was sitting near Rhoda, playing that sort of patience called calcul, distinguished from other patiences by the fact that it comes out; that was why Peter liked it. He had refused to-night to join in the game the others were playing, which was animal grab, though usually he enjoyed it very much. Peter liked games, though he seldom won them. But this evening he played patience by himself and sat by Rhoda and consulted her at crucial moments, and babbled of many things and knew whenever Vyvian looked and Rhoda shook. At half-past nine Vyvian stopped talking to Hilary and crossed the room and took the arm-chair on Rhoda's other side.

"Enthralling evenings you spend here," he remarked, including in his glance Rhoda's embroidery, Peter's patience, and the animal grab table, from which cheerfully matter-of-fact farmyard and jungle cries proceeded with spirit.

Rhoda said nothing. Her head was bent over her work. The next moment she pricked her finger violently, and started. Before she could get her handkerchief out, Vyvian had his, and was enveloping her small hand in it.

"Too bad," he said, in a voice so low that the farmyard cries drowned it as far as Peter was concerned. "Poor little finger." He held it and the handkerchief closely in his two hands.

Rhoda, her colour flooding and ebbing over her thin face and thin neck down to the insertion yoke of her evening blouse, trembled like a captured bird. Her eyes fell from his look; a bold, bad look Peter thought, finding literary terminology appropriate.

The next moment the little table on which Peter was playing toppled over onto the floor with a small crash, and all his cards were scattered on the carpet.

Rhoda started and looked round, pulling her hand away as if a spell was broken.

"Dear me," said Peter regretfully, "it was just on coming out, too. I shan't try again to-night; it's not my night, obviously." He was picking up the cards. Rhoda watched him silently.

"Do you know calcul, Mr. Vyvian?" Peter enquired, collecting scattered portions of the pack from under the arm-chair.

Mr. Vyvian stared at Peter's back, which was the part of him most visible at the moment.

"I really can't say I have the pleasure; no." (That, Peter felt certain, was an insolent drawl.)

"Would you like to learn it?" said Peter politely. "Are you fond of patience?"

"I can't say I am," said Mr. Vyvian.

"Oh! Then you *would* like calcul. People who are really fond of other patiences don't; they despise it because it comes out. I don't like any other sort of patience; I'm not clever enough; so I like this. Let me teach you, may I?"

Vyvian got up.

"Thanks; you're quite too kind. On the whole, I think I can conduct my life without any form of patience, even one which comes out."

"You have a turn, then, Miss Johnson," said Peter, arranging the cards. "Perhaps it'll come out for you, though it won't for me to-night."

"Since you are all so profitably occupied," said Vyvian, "I think I will say good night."

Peter said, "Oh, must you?... Good night, then. We play calcul most nights, so you can learn it some other time if you'd like to."

"A delightful prospect," Vyvian murmured, his glance again comprehensively wandering round the room. "A happy family party you seem here.... Good night." He bent over Rhoda with his ironic politeness.

"I was going to ask you if you would come out with me to-morrow evening to a theatre.... But since your evenings seem to be so pleasantly filled otherwise...."

She looked up at him a moment, wavered, met his dark eyes, was caught by the old domination, and swept off her feet as of old.

"Oh, ... I should like to come...." She was a little breathless.

"Good! I will call for you then, at seven, and we will dine together. Au revoir."

"He swept her a mocking bow and was gone," Peter murmured to himself.

Then he looked at Rhoda, and found her eyes upon his face, wide, frightened, bewildered, and knew in a flash that she had never meant to consent to go out with Vyvian, that she had been caught by the old power he had over her and swept off her feet. That knowledge gave him confidence, and he could say, "You don't want to go, do you? Let me go after him and tell him."

"Oh," she pressed her hands together in front of her. "But I must go—I said I would."

Peter was on his feet and out of the door in a second. He saw Vyvian in the passage downstairs, putting on his coat. He spoke from half-way down the stairs:

"Oh, Miss Johnson asks me to say she is sorry she can't go with you to-morrow night after all; she finds she has another engagement."

Vyvian turned and looked up at him, a slight smile lifting his lip.

"Really?" was all he said. "All the same, I think I will call at seven and try to persuade her to change her mind again. Good night."

As plainly as possible he had said to Peter, "I believe you to be lying." Peter had no particular objection to his believing that; he was not proud; but he did object to his calling at seven and trying to persuade Rhoda to change her mind again, for he believed that that would be a task easy of achievement.

He went back into the sitting-room. Rhoda was sitting still, her hands twisted together on the green serge on her lap. Peter sat down by her and said, "Will you come out with me instead to-morrow evening?" and she looked at him, her teeth clenched over her lower lip as if to steady it, and said after a moment, forlornly, "If you like."

It was so much less exciting than going with Vyvian would have been, that Peter felt compunction.

"You shall choose the play," he said. "'Peter Pan,' do you think? Or something funny—'The Sins of Society,' or something?"

Rhoda whispered "Anything," nearly on the edge of tears. A vividness had flashed again into her grey life, and she was trying to quench it. She had heroically, though as an afterthought, flung an extinguishing douche of water at it; but now that she had done so she was melting into unheroic self-pity.

"I want to go to bed," she said shakily, and did so, feeling for her pocket-handkerchief as she crossed the room.

At a quarter to seven the next evening Peter looked for Rhoda, thinking it well that they should be out of the house by seven o'clock, but couldn't find her, till Miss Clegson said she had met her "going into church" as she herself came out. Peter went to the church to find her. Rhoda didn't as a rule frequent churches, not believing in the creeds they taught; but even to the unbelieving a church is often a refuge.

Peter, coming into the great dim place out of the wet fog, found it again, as he had long since known it to be, a refuge from fogs and other ills of living. Far up, the seven lamps that never go out burned dimly through the blurred air. It was a gaudy place, no doubt; over-decorated; a church for the poor, who love gaudiness. Perhaps Peter too loved gaudiness. Anyhow, he loved this place and its seven lamps and its shrines and statued saints.

Surely, whatever one believed of the mysterious world and of all the other mysterious worlds that might be floating behind the veils, surely here was a very present help in trouble, a luminous brightness shining in a fog-choked world.

Peter, sitting by the door, sank into a great peace. Half-way up the church he saw Rhoda sitting very still. She too was looking up the church towards the lamps and the altar beyond them.

Presently a cassocked sacristan came and lit the vesper lights, for evensong was to be at seven, and the altar blazed out, an unearthly brilliance in the dim place. The low murmur of voices (a patient priest had been hearing confessions for an hour) ceased, and people began coming in one by one for service. Rhoda shivered a little, and got up and came down the church. Peter joined her at the door, and they passed shivering into the fog together.

"I was looking for you," said Peter, when they were out in the alley that led to the church door.

"It's time we went, isn't it," she said apathetically.

Then she added, inconsequently, "The church seems the only place where one can find a bit of peace. I can't think why, when probably it's all a fairy-tale."

"I suppose that's why," said Peter. "Fairyland is the most peaceful country there is."

"You can't get peace out of what's not true," Rhoda insisted querulously.

"Oh, I don't know.... Besides, fairy-tales aren't necessarily untrue, do you think? I don't mean that, when I call what churches teach a fairy-tale. I mean it's beautiful and romantic and full of light and colour and wonderful things happening. And it's probably the truer for that."

"D'you *believe* it all?" queried Rhoda; but he couldn't answer her as to that.

"I don't know. I never do know exactly what I believe. I can't think how anyone does. But yes, I think I like to believe in those things; they're too beautiful not to be true."

"It's the ugly things that are true," she said, coughing in the fog.

"Why, yes, the ugly things and the beautiful; God and the devil, if one puts it like that. Oh, yes, I believe very much in the devil; I can't believe that any street of houses could look quite like this without the help of someone utterly given over to evil thinking. *We* aren't, you see; none of us are ugly enough in our minds to have thought out some of the things one sees; so there must be a devil."

Rhoda was silent. He thought she was crying. He said gently, "I say, would you like to come out to-night, or would you rather be quiet at home?" It would be safe to return home by half-past seven, he thought.

She said, in a small muffled voice, that she didn't care.

A tall figure passed by them in the narrow alley, looming through the fog. Rhoda started, and shrank back against the brick wall, clutching Peter's arm. The next moment the figure passed into the circle of light thrown down by a high lamp that glimmered over a Robbia-esque plaque shrine let into the wall, and they saw that it was a cassocked priest from the clergy-house going into church. Rhoda let out her breath faintly in a sigh, and her fingers fell from Peter's coat-sleeve.

"Oh," she whispered, "I'm frightened.... Let's stay close to the church; just outside the door, where we can see the light and hear the music. I don't want to go out into the streets to-night, Peter, I want to stay here. I'm ... so frightened."

"Come inside," suggested Peter, as they turned back to the church. "It would be warmer."

But she shook her head. "No. I'd rather be outside. I don't belong in there."

Peter said, "Why not?" and she told him, "Because for me it's the ugly things that are true."

So together they stood in the porch, outside the great oak door, and heard the sound of singing stealing out, fog-softened, and smelt the smell of incense (it was the festal service of some saint) that pierced the thick air with its pungent sweetness.

They sat down on the seat in the porch, and Rhoda shivered, not with cold, and Peter waited by her very patiently, knowing that she needed him as she had never needed him before.

She told him so. "You don't *mind* staying, Peter? I feel safer with you than with anyone else.... You see, I'm afraid.... Oh, I can't tell you how it is I feel. When he looks at me it's as if he was drawing me and dragging me, and I feel I must get up and follow him wherever he goes. It's always been like that, since first I met him, more than a year ago. He made me care; he made me worship the ground he walked on; if he'd thrown me down and kicked me, I'd have let him. But he never cared himself; I know that now. I've known it a long time. And I've vowed to myself, and I vowed to mother when she lay dying, that I wouldn't let him have anything more to do with me. He frightens me, because he can twist me round his finger and make me care so ... and it hurts.... And he's just playing; he'll never really care. But for all I know that, I know he can get me whenever he wants me. And he's come back again to amuse himself seeing me worship him ... and he'll make me follow him about, and all the time he'll be thinking me a little fool, and I shall know it ... but I can't help it, Peter, I can't help it.... I've nothing to hold on to, to save me. If I could be religious, if I could pray, like the people in there ... but he says there's nothing in that; he's made me believe like him, and I sometimes think he only believes in himself, and that's why I can only believe in him too. So I've got nothing in the world to hold on to, and I shall be carried away and drowned...."

She was crying with strangled sobbings, her face in her thin hands.

Peter's arm was put gently about her shoulders, comforting her.

"No, you won't, Rhoda. Rhoda dear, you won't be carried away, because I shall be here, holding you. Is that any help at all?"

He felt her relax beneath his arm and lean back against him; he heard her whisper, "Yes; oh, yes. If I can hold onto you, Peter, I shall feel safe."

"Hold on, then," said Peter, "as tight as you like."

She looked up at him with wet eyes and he felt the claim and the appeal of her piercing straight into his heart.

"I could care ..." she whispered. "Are you sure, Peter?"

His arm tightened about her. He hadn't meant precisely what she had understood him to mean; at least, he hadn't translated his purpose to help her to the uttermost into a specified relation, as she was doing; but if the purpose, to be fulfilled, had to be so translated, he was ready for that too. So he said, "Quite sure, Rhoda. I want to be the most to you that you'll let me be," and her face was hidden against his coat, and her tension relaxed utterly, and she murmured, "Oh, I can be safe like that."

So they sat in silence together, between the lit sanctuary and the desolate night, and heard, as from a long way off, the sound of chanting:—

"Lord, now lettest thou thy servant depart in peace: according to thy word;

"For mine eyes have seen ..."

Later on, Rhoda said, quiet and happy now, "I've thought you cared, Peter, for some time. And last night, when I saw you hated Guy to be near me, I felt sure. But I feel I've so little to give you. So much of me is burnt away and spoilt. But it'll come back, Peter, I think, if you love me. I do love you, very much; you've been such a dear to me always, from the very first night at the Palazzo, when you spoke to me and smiled. Only I couldn't think of anyone but Guy then. But lately I've been thinking, 'Peter's worth a hundred Guys, and if only I could care for him, I should feel safe.' And I do care, ever so much; and if it's a different sort of caring from what I've felt for Guy, it's a better sort. That's a bad, black sort, that hurts; I never want any more of that. Caring for you will keep me from that, Peter."

"It's dear of you to care for me at all," said Peter. "And we won't let Guy come near us, now or ever."

"You hate him, don't you?" said Rhoda. "I know you do."

"Oh, well, I don't know that it's as bad as all that. He's more funny than anything else, it seems to me. He might have walked straight out of a novel; he does all the things they do in books, you know, and that one never thinks people really do outside them. He sneers insolently. I watch him sometimes, to see how it's done. He curls his upper lip, too, when he's feeling contemptuous; that's another nice trick that I should like to acquire. Oh, he's quite an interesting study really. You've taken him wrong, you know. You've taken him seriously. He's not meant for that."

"Oh," said Rhoda, vaguely uncomprehending. "You *are* a funny boy, Peter. You do talk so.... I never know if you mean half you say."

"About two-thirds, I think," said Peter. "The rest is lies. We all lie in my family, and not well either, because we're rather weak in the intellect....

Now do you feel like supper, because I do? Let's come home and have it, shall we?"

They went home through the fog, Rhoda clinging to Peter's arm as to an anchor in a sweeping sea. A great peace and security possessed her; she no longer started at the tall figures that loomed by.

They let themselves into 51 Brook Street, and blinked at one another in the lamp-lit, linoleumed little hall. Rhoda looked at herself in the glass, and said, "What a fright I am!" seeing her tear-stained countenance and straggling fog-wet locks. The dinner-bell rang, and she ran upstairs to tidy herself. Peter and she came into the dining-room together, during the soup.

"Let's tell them at once, Peter," whispered Rhoda; so Peter obediently said, as he sat down by Peggy, "Rhoda and I have just settled to marry."

"*Marry*?" Hilary queried, from the end of the table. "Marry whom?" And Rhoda, blushing, laughed for the first time for some days.

Peggy said, "Don't be silly, Hilary. Each other, of course, the darlings mean. Well, well, and to think I never guessed that all this time!"

"Oh," said Miss Clegson, "I did, Mrs. Margerison; I had a very shrewd suspicion, I assure you. And this evening, when Mr. Peter asked me where Miss Johnson was gone, and I told him into church, and he followed her straight away, I said to myself, 'Well, *that* looks like something we all know about very well!' I didn't say it to anyone else; I wouldn't breathe a word till all was settled; I knew you asked me in confidence, Mr. Peter; but I thought the more. I was always one to see things; they used to tell me I could see through a stone wall. Well, I'm sure I offer my congratulations to both of you."

"And I too, with all my heart," said Miss Matthews, the lady who did not attend ritualistic churches. "Do I understand that the happy arrangement was made *in church*, Miss Johnson? I gather from Miss Clegson that Mr. Peter followed you there."

"Oh, not inside, Miss Matthews," said Rhoda, blushing again, and looking rather pretty. "In the porch, we were."

Miss Matthews sniffed faintly. Such goings-on might, she conveyed, be expected in the porch of St. Austin's, with all that incense coming through the door, and all that confessing going on inside.

"Well," said Mr. Bridger, "we ought to have some champagne to drink success to the happy event. Short of that, let us fill the festive bumpers with the flowing lemonade. Pass the jug down. Here's *to* you, Miss Rhoda; here's *to* you, Mr. Peter Margerison. May you both be as happy as you deserve. No one will want me to wish you anything better than that, I'm sure."

"Here's luck, you dears," said Peggy, drinking. Engagements in general delighted her, and Peter's in particular. And poor little Rhoda was looking so bright and happy at last. Peggy wouldn't have taken it upon herself to call it a remarkably suitable alliance had she been asked; but then she hadn't been asked, and Peter was such a sweet-natured, loving, lovable dear that he would get on with anyone, and Rhoda, though sometimes a silly and sometimes fractious, was a dear little girl too. The two facts that would have occurred to some sisters-in-law, that they had extremely few pennies between them, and that Rhoda wasn't precisely of Peter's gentle extraction, didn't bother Peggy at all.

They occurred, however, to Hilary. It occurred to him that Peter would now require all his slender earnings for himself and wife, which was awkward; also that Peter really needn't have looked down to the lower middle classes for a wife. Hilary believed in gentle birth; through all his vicissitudes a pathetic pride of breeding clung to him. One might be down at heels; one might be reduced to sordid means of livelihood, even to shady schemes for enlarging one's income; but once a gentleman always so, and one was not to be ranked with the bounders, the Vyvians, the wealthy Leslies even.

Hilary looked resigned and weary. Why should Peter want to marry a commonplace and penniless little nobody, and not so very pretty either, though she looked nice and bright when she was animated, as now.

"Well," he said, "when is it to be?"

Peter looked across at Rhoda.

"I should hope very soon," he said. It was obviously safer, and safety was the object, to have it very soon.

"How soon can one get married? There have to be banns and so on, don't there? The third time of asking—that brings it to the eighteenth of December. What about the nineteenth, Rhoda? That's a Monday."

"Really, Peter ..." Rhoda blushed more than ever. "That seems awfully soon."

"Well," said Peter, blind to the unusualness of such a discussion at the dinner-table, "the sooner the better, don't you think? There's nothing to wait for. I don't suppose we shall ever have more money to do it on than we have now. I know of a man who waited years and years because he thought he hadn't got quite enough, and he got a little more each year, and at the end of six years he thought to double his fortune by putting it all on a winner, because he was getting so impatient. And the horse came in last. So the girl broke it off and married someone else, and the man's heart broke and he took to drink."

"Well?" enquired Miss Matthews, who thought Peter habitually irrelevant in his remarks.

"Well—so let's be married on December the nineteenth."

"I'm sure," said Rhoda, "we're quite embarrassing everybody, being so public. Let's settle it afterwards, Peter, when we're alone."

But she too meant to have it as soon as might be after the third time of asking; it was safer, much safer, so.

"Well," said Miss Clegson, as the ladies rose from the table, "now we're going to carry Miss Johnson away to tell us all about it; and we'll leave Mr. Peter to tell you gentlemen *his* secrets. And after that we'll have a good round game; but two of the present company can be left out if they like better to sit in the window-seat!"

But when the other gentlemen repaired to the drawing-room for the good round game, Peter stayed behind, with Hilary. He didn't want to talk or be talked to, only to stay where he was and not to have to sit in the window-seat.

"The insufferable vulgarity of this class of person on this subject is really the limit," Hilary remarked plaintively, as if it had jarred him beyond endurance.

"They're awfully kind, aren't they," said Peter, who looked tired. Then he laughed to himself. Hilary looked at him enquiringly.

"I suppose you know your own business, Peter. But I must confess I am surprised. I had literally no idea you had such a step in mind."

"I hadn't any idea either," Peter admitted frankly. "I thought of it quite suddenly. But I think it is a good plan, you know. Of course," he added, wording what he read in Hilary's face, "I know my life will cost me more. But I think it is worth while."

"It's quite entirely your own business," Hilary said again, throwing responsibility from him with a gesture of the hands. Then he leant back and shut his eyes.

Peter looked at him as he lay in the arm-chair and smoked; his eyes rested on the jaded, still beautiful face, the dark lock of hair falling a little over the tired forehead, the brown velvet smoking coat and large red silk tie. He knew that he had hurt and puzzled Hilary. And he knew that Hilary wouldn't understand if he were to explain what he couldn't ever explain. At the most he would say, "It is Peter all over," and shrug his shoulders at Peter and Peter's vagaries.

A great desire to smooth Hilary's difficult road, as far as might be, caught and held Peter. Poor old Hilary! He was so frightfully tired of life and its struggles; tired of being a Have-Not.

To help the other Have-Nots, to put pleasant things into their hands as far as might be, seemed to Peter at this moment the thing for which one existed. It is obviously the business of the Have-Nots to do that for one another; for the Haves do not know or understand. It is the Have-Nots who must give and give and give, with emptying hands; for from him that hath not shall be taken away even that which he hath.

Peter went upstairs to the drawing-room to play animal grab.

CHAPTER XIV

PETER, RHODA, AND LUCY

When Mr. Vyvian called at 51 Brook Street one evening and was informed by the assembled company that Miss Johnson had got engaged to Mr. Peter Margerison, he sneered a little and wished them both joy, and said good-night rather markedly early.

"He won't come back," said Rhoda in Peter's ear when he had gone. "He's gone for good." She sat very still, realising it, and shivered a little. Then, casting off that old chain of the past, she turned on Peter eyes full of tears and affection.

"Now I'm going to forget all about him and be happy," she whispered. "He's not going to be part of my life any more at all. How queer that seems!"

If in her heart she wished a little that Peter had had Guy Vyvian's handsome face and person (Peter had no presence: one might overlook him; the only vivid note about him, except when he smiled, was the blue of his eyes), she stifled the wish with firm pressure. What were looks, after all? And that bold, handsome stare of Guy's had burnt and hurt; in the blue of Peter's she found healing and coolness, as one finds it in a summer sea.

So, after the third time of asking, they were married, in St. Austin's Church, and Rhoda, coming out of it, whispered to Peter, "Some of the beautiful things are true after all, I do believe;" and he smiled at her and said, "Of course they are."

They left the boarding-house, because Rhoda was tired of the boarders and wanted a little place to themselves. Peter, who didn't really care, but who would have rather liked to stay and be with Peggy and Hilary, pretended that he too wanted a little place to themselves. So they took lodgings in Greville Street, which runs out of Brook Street. Rhoda gave up her work and settled down to keep house and do needlework. They kept a canary in the sitting-room, and a kitten with a blue bow, and Rhoda took to wearing blue bows in her own hair, and sewed all the buttons on her frocks and darned her gloves and stockings and Peter's socks, and devoted herself to household economy, a subject in which her mother had always tried to interest her without success. Rhoda thought it a great relief to have escaped from the tiresome boarders who chattered so about things they knew nothing about, and from her own daily drudgery, that had tired her back.

(She had been a typist.) It was nice to be able to sit at peace with one's needlework and one's own reflections, and have Peter, who was always kind and friendly and cheerful, to brighten breakfast and leave her in peace during the day and come in again to brighten the evening. Peter's chatter didn't worry her, though she often thought it childish and singularly inconsequent; Peter, of course, was only a boy, though such a dear, kind, affectionate boy. He would spend his evenings teasing the kitten and retying the blue bow, or lying on the rug before the fire, talking nonsense which made Rhoda laugh even when she was feeling low. Sometimes they would go to Brook Street and spend the evening there; and often Hilary would drop in and smoke with Peter; only Rhoda didn't much care for these evenings, for she never felt at ease with Hilary, who wasn't at ease with her either. The uncultured young creatures of either sex never quite knew where they were with the æsthetic Hilary; at any moment they might tread heavily on his sensitive susceptibilities and make him wince visibly, and no one likes being winced at. Rhoda in particular was very sensitive; she thought Hilary ill-mannered and conceited, and vaguely resented his attitude towards her without understanding it, for (now that she was removed from the crushing influence of a person who had always ruthlessly shown her her limitations and follies) she didn't think of herself as uncultured, she with her poetical and artistic tastes, sharpened and refined by contact with the culture of Guy Vyvian and broadened by acquaintance with the art of foreign cities. On the contrary, she felt in herself yearnings for a fuller and freer life of beauty and grace. She wasn't sure that Peter ever felt such yearnings; he seemed quite contented with the ugly rooms in the ugly street, and the dingy lace curtains and impossible pictures; he could make a joke of it all; and things one could make a joke of couldn't really hurt, thought Rhoda.

But anyhow, cramped and squalid and dingy though 9 Greville Street might be, it held security and peace.

"The Snuggery, that's what we call it at fifty-one," said Miss Clegson, who sometimes looked in to rally them.

Fifty-one was getting less of a snuggery than ever. Fifty-one, Peter feared, was going down the hill. The Berovieri goblet had made a little piece of level road for it, but that was soon over, and the descent began again. Peggy, try as she would, could not make both ends meet. Hilary, despise his job as he might, found it slipping from him more and more. Week by week he seemed to earn a little less; week by week they seemed to spend a little more. Peggy, as Hilary had frequently remarked, was *not* a good manager. One or two of the boarders left, to seek more commodious quarters elsewhere. More frequently, as the winter advanced, Peggy wailed, "Whatever is to become of us, dear only knows! What with Larry drinking pints of cough-syrup, and Micky rolling in the gutter in his best suit, and Norah, the creature, letting the crockery fly about as if it was alive, and Hilary insisting on the table cloth being cleaner than it ever is, and the boarders having to have food they can eat, and now Lent's coming on and half of them don't take any notice of it but eat their joints just the same, bad manners to them for heretics. Oh, *dear*, oh dear, oh dear!"

Whenever Peter could spare any money he gave it to Peggy. But his own fortunes were not exactly on the make. He was not proving good at his job. Recommended to his employers by Leslie, he had begun, of course, on a very small salary, to learn his trade; he hadn't so far learnt enough of it to justify his promotion. Every day he went through the same drudgery, with the same lack of intelligence,—(it is odd how discernment and talent in one trade serve so little for another)—and every week came home with the same meagre sum.

As far as he hated anything, he hated this work of his; long ago, had he been alone concerned, he would have dropped it, and taken to tramping the roads with boot-laces to sell, or some other equally unstrenuous and unlucrative avocation. But he had not, from the first, been alone concerned; first he had had to help Hilary and Peggy, and now he had to keep a wife too. Eventually there would probably be also children to keep; Peter didn't know how much these cost, but vaguely believed them to be expensive luxuries. So there seemed no prospect of his being able to renounce his trade, though there was a considerable prospect of its renouncing him, as he was from time to time informed.

The winter dragged quietly through, and the spring came; the queer London ghost of spring, with its bitter winds and black buds and evasive hints of what is going on in the real world, where things change. Peter dreamt of green things coming up and hawthorn hedges growing edible. Rhoda's cough grew softer and her eyes more restless, as if she too had her dreams. She developed a new petulance with Peter and with the maid-of-all-work, and left off tying the kitten's neck-ribbon. It was really a cat now, and cats are tiresome. She said she was dull all day with so little to do. Peter, full of compunction, suggested asking people to the house more, and she assented, rather listlessly. So Peter hinted to Peggy, who had a cheering presence, that Rhoda would be glad to see her more often, and Peggy made what time she could to come round. Their circle of friends was limited; they chiefly consisted of the inhabitants of fifty-one, and a few relatives of Rhoda's, who amused and pleased Peter but vexed Rhoda by being common.

"But I like them," said Peter.

"You like to see me put to shame, I suppose," said Rhoda, with tears in her eyes. "As if it was *my* fault that my parents came of common people. I've cried myself sick over it sometimes, when I was younger, and now I just want to forget it."

Peter said no more. It was one of the sides of Rhoda with which he felt he had no connexion; it was best let alone, as Peter always let alone the things he could not like. But he was sorry she felt like that, for her nice, common, friendly relations might have been company for her.

Peter sometimes brought friends home from his office; Peter could not have been in an office without collecting friends, having the social instinct strongly developed. But Rhoda didn't much care about seeing his fellow-clerks; they hadn't, she was sure, great minds, and they made silly jokes.

Another person who came to see Peter sometimes was Rodney. Ever since the Margerisons' abrupt fall into ignominy, Rodney had cultivated Peter's acquaintance. Peter perceived that he had at last slipped into the ranks of those unfortunates who were qualified for Rodney's regard; it was enough for that, Urquhart had long since told him, to be cut by society or to produce a yesterday's handkerchief. Peter, driven from the faces of the rich, found Rodney waiting to receive him cheerfully among the ranks of the poor. Rodney was a much occupied person; but when he found time from his other pursuits he walked up from his Westminster slum to Holborn and visited 9 Greville Street. He hadn't known quite what to make of Peter's marriage; though when he got to know Rhoda a little he began to understand rather more. She, being very manifestly among the Have-Nots, and a small, weak, and pitiable thing, also entered in a manner into the circle of his tolerance. He was gentle with her always, though not expansive. She was a little in awe of the gaunt young man, with his strange eyes that seemed to see so much further than anyone else's. She pronounced him "queer."

"I suppose he's very clever," she said to Peter.

"Yes," Peter agreed.

But even that didn't further him in Rhoda's regard. She thought him rude, as indeed he was, though he tried to conceal it. He seldom spoke to her, and when he did it was with an unadorned brevity that offended her. Mostly he let her alone, and saw Peter when he could outside his home. Rodney, himself a celibate, thought matrimony a mistake, though certainly a necessary mistake if the human race was to continue to adorn the earth—a doubtful ornament to it, in Rodney's opinion.

Rhoda said one evening to Peter, "You don't see anything of your friends the Urquharts now, do you?"

"No," said Peter, who was stroking the kitten's fur the wrong way, to bring sparks out of it before the gas was lit. "They've been in the country all the winter."

"Mr. Urquhart got elected a member, didn't he?" said Rhoda, without much interest.

"Yes," said Peter.

"I suppose they'll be coming up to town soon, then, for him to attend Parliament."

Peter supposed they would.

"When last Lucy wrote, she said they were coming up this month."

"Have you heard from her again, since Monday week?" enquired Rhoda.

"No. We write alternate Sundays, you know. We always have. Last Sunday it was my turn."

"Fancy going on all these years so regular," said Rhoda. "I couldn't, not to any of my cousins. I should use up all there was to say."

"Oh, but there are quite new things every fortnight," Peter explained.

Certainly it wasn't easy to picture Rhoda corresponding with any of the Johnson relatives once a fortnight.

"I expect you and she have heaps to tell each other always when you meet," said Rhoda, a little plaintive note in her weak voice.

Peter considered.

"Not so much to tell exactly as to talk about. Yes, there's lots to say.... She's coming to see you, Rhoda, directly they come up to town. It's so funny to think you and she have never met."

"Is it? Well, I don't know. I've not met any of your cousins really, have I?"

Rhoda was in one of her slightly pettish moods this evening. Peter didn't better matters by saying, "Oh, well, none of the others count. Lucy and I have always been different from most cousins, I suppose; more like brother and sister, I daresay."

Rhoda looked at him sharply. She was in a fault-finding mood.

"You think more of her than you do of anyone else. Of course, I know that."

Peter was startled. He stopped stroking the kitten and looked at her through the dim firelight. The suspicion of a vulgar scene was in the air, and frightened him. Then he remembered that Rhoda was in frail health, and said very gently, "Oh, Rhoda darling, don't say silly things, like a young gurl in a novelette," and slithered along the floor and laid his arm across her lap and laughed up into her face.

She sniffed a little, and dabbed her handkerchief at her eyes.

"It's all very well, Peter, but you do care for her a lot, you know you do."

"But of course I do," said Peter, laying his cheek against her knee. "You don't *mind*, Rhoda, do you?"

"You care for her," said Rhoda, but softening under his caresses, "and you care for her husband. You care for him awfully, Peter; more than for her really, I believe; more than for anyone in the world, don't you?"

"Don't," said Peter, his voice muffled against her dress. "I can't compare one thing with another like that, and I don't want to. Isn't one's caring for each of the people one knows quite different from every other? Isn't yours? Can you say which you love best, the sun rising over the river, or St. Mark's, or a Bellini Madonna? Of course you can't, and it's immoral to try. So I'm not going to place Lucy and Denis and you and Rodney and Peggy and the kitten in a horrid class-list. I won't. Do you hear?"

He drew one of her small thin hands down to his lips, then moved it up and placed it on his head, and drew it gently to and fro, ruffling his hair.

"You're a silly, Peter," said Rhoda, and there was peace.

Very soon after that Lucy came. She came in the afternoon before Peter got home, and Rhoda looked with listless interest at the small, wide-eyed person in a grey frock and big grey hat that made her small, pale face look like a white flower. Pretty? Rhoda wasn't sure. Very like Peter; so perhaps not pretty; only one liked to look at her. Clever? It didn't transpire that she was. Witty? Well, much more amused than amusing; and when she was amused she came out with Peter's laugh, which Rhoda wasn't sure was in good taste on her part. Absurdly like Peter she was, to look at and to listen to, and in some inner essence which was beyond definition. The thought flashed through Rhoda's mind that it was no wonder these two found things to tell each other every other Sunday; they would be interested in all the same things, so it must be easy.

Remotely, dully, Rhoda thought these things, as things which didn't concern her particularly. Less and less each day she had grown to care whether Peter found his cousin Lucy a kindred spirit or not. She could work herself up into a fit of petulant jealousy about it at times; but it didn't touch her inmost being; it was a very surface grievance.

So she looked at Lucy dispassionately, and let herself, without a struggle, be caught and held by that ingenuous charm, a charm as of a small woodland flower set dancing by the winds of spring. She noticed that when the kitten that was now nearly a cat sprang on to Lucy's lap, she stroked its fur backwards with her flat hand and spread fingers precisely as Peter always did.

Then Peter came in, and he and Lucy laughed the same laugh at one another, and then they had tea. After all, Rhoda didn't see now that they were so like. Peter talked much more; he said twenty words to Lucy's one; Lucy wasn't a great talker at all. Peter was a chatterbox; there was no denying that. And their features and eyes and all weren't so like, either. But when one had said all this, there was something... something inner, essential, indefinable, of the spirit, that was not of like substance but the same. So it is sometimes with twins. Rhoda, her intuitive faculties oddly sharpened, took in this. Peter might care most for Denis Urquhart; he might love Rhoda as a wife; but Lucy, less consciously loved than either, was intimately one with himself.

Peter asked "How is Denis?" and Lucy answered "Very well, of course. And very busy playing at being a real member. Isn't it fun? Oh, he sent you his love. And you're to come and see us soon."

That last wasn't a message from Denis; Peter knew that. He knew that there would be no more such messages from Denis; the Margerisons had gone a little too far in their latest enterprise; they had strained the cord to breaking-point, and it had broken. In future Denis might be kind and friendly to Peter when they met, but he wouldn't bring about meetings; they would embarrass him. But Lucy knew nothing of that. Denis hadn't mentioned to her what had happened at Astleys last November; he never dwelt on unpleasant subjects or made a talk about them. So Lucy said to Peter and Rhoda, "You must come and see us soon," and Peter said, "You're so far away, you know," evading her, and she gave him a sudden wide clear look, taking in all he didn't say, which was the way they had with one another, so that no deceits could ever stand between them.

"Don't be *silly*, Peter," she told him; then, "'*Course* you must come"; but he only smiled at her and said, "Some day, perhaps."

"Honey sandwiches, if you come at tea-time," she reminded him. "D'*you* like them, Rhoda?" She used the name prettily, half shyly, with one of her luminous, friendly looks. "They're Peter's favourite food, you know."

But Rhoda didn't know; Peter had never told her; perhaps because it would be extravagant to have them, perhaps because he never put even foods into class-lists. Only Lucy knew without being told, probably because it was her favourite food too.

When Lucy went, it was as if a ray of early spring sunshine had stolen into the room and gone. A luminous person: that was the thing Rhoda felt her to be; a study in clear pale lights; one would not have been surprised if she had crept in on a wind from a strange fairy world with her arms full of cold wet primroses, and danced out, taking with her the souls of those who dwelt within. Rhoda wasn't jealous now, if she had ever had a touch of that.

Neither Peter nor Rhoda went to the Urquharts' house, which was a long way off. But Lucy came again, many times, to Greville Street, through that spring and summer, stroking the cat's fur backwards, laughing at Peter, shyly friendly to Rhoda.

And then for a time her laughter was sad and her eyes wistful, because her father died. She said once, "I feel so stranded now, Peter; cut off from what was my life; from what really is my life, you know. Father and Felicity and I were so disreputable always, and as long as I had father I could be disreputable too, whenever I felt I couldn't bear being prosperous. I had only to go inside the house and there I was—you know, Peter?—it was all round me, and I was part of it.... Now I'm cut off from all that sort of thing. Denis and I *are* so well off, d'you know. Everything goes right. Denis's friends are all so happy and successful and beautifully dressed. I *like* them to be, of course; they are joys, like the sun shining; only..."

"The poor are always with you," suggested Peter. "You can always come to Greville Street, if you can't find them nearer at hand. And when you come we'll take Algernon's blue neck-ribbon off, that none of us may appear beautifully dressed."

"But I *like* Algernon's blue bow," Lucy protested. "I love people to be bright and beautiful.... That's why I like Denis so much, you know. Only I'm not sure I properly belong, that's all."

Obviously the remedy was to come to Greville Street. Lucy came more and more as the months went by.

Rhoda said once, "Doesn't it bother you to come all this way, into these ugly streets?" and she shook her head.

"Oh, I *like* it. I like these streets better than the ones round us. And I like your house better than ours too; it's smaller."

Rhoda could have thought she looked wistful, this fortunate person who was in love with her splendid husband and lived in the dwellings of the prosperous.

"Don't you like large houses?" she asked, without much caring; for she was absorbed in her own thoughts in these days.

Lucy puckered her wide forehead.

"Why, no. No, I don't believe I do," she said, as if she was finding it out with a little surprise.

Rhoda saw her one day in July. In a few weeks, she told Rhoda (Peter was out that afternoon), she and Denis were going up to Scotland, to stay with people.

"We shall miss you," said Rhoda dully.

"And me you," said Lucy, with a more acute sense of it.

"Peter'll miss you dreadfully," said Rhoda. She was lying on the sofa, pale and tired in the heat.

"Only," said Lucy, "next month you'll both be feeling too interested to miss anyone."

"Peter," said Rhoda, "cares more about the baby coming than I do."

Lucy said, "Peter loves little weak funny things like that." She was a little sad that Rhoda didn't seem to care more about the baby; babies are such entrancing toys to those who like toys, people like her and Peter.

Suddenly Lucy saw that two large tears were rolling down Rhoda's pale cheeks as she lay. Lucy knelt by the sofa side and took Rhoda's hand in both of hers and laid her cheek upon it.

"Please, little Rhoda, not to cry. Please, little Rhoda, tell me."

Rhoda, with her other hand, brushed the tears away.

"I'm a silly. I suppose I'm crying because I can't feel to care about anything in the world, and I wish I could. What's the use of a baby if you can't love it? What's the use of a husb—"

Lucy's hand was over her lips, and Lucy whispered, "Oh, hush, little Rhoda, hush!"

But Rhoda pushed the hand away and cried, "Oh, why do we pretend and pretend and pretend? It's Guy I care for—Guy, Guy, Guy, who's gone for good and all."

She fell to crying drearily, with Lucy's arms about her.

"But you *mustn't* cry," said Lucy, her own eyes brimming over; "you mustn't, you mustn't. And you do care for Peter, you know you do, only it's so hot, and you're tired and ill. If that horrible Guy was here—oh, I know he's horrible—you'd know you cared for Peter most. You mustn't *say* things, Rhoda; it makes them alive." Her eyes were wide and frightened as she looked over Rhoda's head out of the window.

Slowly Rhoda quieted down, and lay numb and still.

"You won't tell Peter," she said; and Lucy said, "Oh, Rhoda!"

"Well, of course I know you wouldn't. Only that you and Peter tell one another things without saying anything.... Peter belongs to you really, you know, not to me at all. All he thinks and says and is—it's all yours. He's never really been near *me* like that, not from the beginning. I was a silly to let him sacrifice himself for me the way he's done. We don't belong really, Peter and I; however friendly we are, we don't belong; we don't understand each other like you two do.... You don't mind my saying that, do you?" for Lucy had dropped her hands and fallen away.

"I mind your saying anything," said Lucy, "just now. Don't say things: it makes them alive. It's hot, and you're tired, and I'm not going to stay any more."

She got up from the floor and stood for a moment looking down at Rhoda. Rhoda saw her eyes, how they were wet and strange and far-away, and full of what seemed an immense weight of pity; pity for all the sadnesses of mankind.

The next moment Lucy's cool finger-tips touched her forehead in a light caress, and Lucy was gone.

CHAPTER XV

THE LOSS OF A WIFE

In September Peter and Rhoda had a son, whom they called Thomas, because, Peter said, he had a sceptical look about the eyes and nose. Peter was pleased with him, and he with Peter. Rhoda wasn't much interested; she looked at him and said he was rather like Peter, and might be taken away now, please.

"Like me?" Peter wondered dubiously. "Well, I know I'm not handsome, but..."

Peggy, a born mother, took Thomas into her large heart at once, with her out-at-elbows infants, and was angry with Rhoda for not showing more interest.

"You'd think, from the way of her, that it was her thirteenth instead of her first," she complained to Hilary. "I've no patience with the silly, mooning child. She's nothing like good enough for Peter, and that's a fact, and she'd have a right to realise it and try to improve for very shame, instead of moping the way she does. It's my belief, Hilary, that her silly little heart's away after the Vyvian man, whatever haunt of wickedness he's adorning now. I don't want to believe it of her; but there's no end to the folly of the human heart, is there, now? I wish she was a Catholic and had a priest to make her take shame to herself; but there's no hold one has over her as it is, for she won't say a word to me beyond 'Yes' and 'No,' and 'Take him away, please, he tires me.' I nearly told her she'd a right not to be so easily tired by her own son now she's getting her health. But there, she's a poor frail thing and one can't speak roughly to her for fear she breaks in two."

Hilary said, "After all, there's no great cause for rejoicing in a man's being born into the world to trouble; I suppose she feels that. It will make it more difficult than ever for them and for us to make both ends meet."

"Oh, meet," groaned Peggy, "that's not what there's any thought of their doing in these days, my dear. If one can bring them within a mile of one another, one's thankful for small mercies."

Hilary rested his head on his hand and sighed.

"Have you spoken to Peter yet about appealing to the Urquharts?" he asked.

"Darling, I have not, and I'm not going to. Why should I annoy the poor child to no purpose? He'll not appeal to the Urquharts, we know that well, and I'm not going to waste my breath. I'd far rather—"

"What?" asked Hilary, as she paused.

"Oh well, I don't know. Don't you worry about ways and means; something will surely turn up before long." Peggy was an optimist.

"And anyhow," went on Peggy, to change the subject from ways and means, which was a depressing one, "isn't our little Peter a darling with his baby? I love to see them together. He washes it himself as often as not, you know; only he can't always catch it again when it slips through his hands, and that worries him. He's dreadfully afraid of its getting drowned or spoilt or lost or something."

"It probably will," said Hilary, who was a pessimist. "Peter is no hand at keeping things. We are not a fortunate family."

"Never mind, darling; we've kept three; and more by token Kitty *must* have a new pair of boots this winter; she's positively indecent the way she goes about now. I can't help it, Hilary; you must pawn your ring again or something."

Peggy didn't want to say anything else depressing, so she didn't mention that Miss Matthews had that morning given notice of her departure. But in Peggy's own mind there was a growing realisation that something drastic must really be done soon.

October went by. When Peter knew that the Urquharts had come back to London, he wondered why Lucy didn't come to see Thomas. So he wrote and asked her to, and on that she came.

She came at tea-time, one day when Rhoda happened to have gone out. So Peter and Lucy had tea alone together, and Thomas lay in his crib and looked at them, and Algernon snored on Lucy's knee, and the November fog shut out the outer world like a blanket, and blurred the gas-light in the dingy room.

Peter thought Lucy was rather quiet and pale, and her chuckle was a little subdued. Her dominant aspect, of clear luminousness, was somehow dimmed and mystified, with all other lights, in this blurred afternoon. Her wide clear eyes, strange always with the world's gay wonder and mystery, had become eyes less gay, eyes that did not understand, that even shrank a little from what they could not understand. Lucy looked a touch puzzled, not so utterly the glad welcomer of all arriving things that she had always been.

But for Thomas, the latest arrived thing, she had a glad welcome. Like Peter, she loved all little funny weak things; and Thomas seemed certainly that, as he lay and blinked at the blurred gas and curled his fingers round one of Peter's. A happy, silent person, with doubts, one fancied, as to the object of the universe, but no doubts that there were to be found in it many desirable things.

When Lucy came in, Peter was reading aloud to him some of Traherne's "Divine Reflections on the Native Objects of an Infant-Eye," which he seemed rather to like.

"I that so long [Peter told him he was thinking,
Was *Nothing* from Eternity,
Did little think such Joys as Ear and Tongue
To celebrate or see:
Such Sounds to hear, such Hands to feel, such Feet,
Such Eyes and Objects on the Ground to Meet.

"New burnisht Joys!
Which finest Gold and Pearl excell!"

"Oo," said Thomas expectantly.

"A Stranger here, [Peter told him further,
Strange things doth meet, strange Glory see;
Strange Treasures lodg'd in this fair World appear
,Strange all and New to me:
But that they *mine* should be who Nothing was,
That strangest is of all; yet brought to pass."

"Ow," said Thomas, agreeing.

Peter turned over the pages. "Do you like it? Do you think so too? Here's another about you."

"But little did the Infant dream
That all the Treasures of the World were by,
And that himself was so the Cream
And Crown of all which round about did ly.
Yet thus it was!..."

"I don't think you'd understand the rest of that verse, Thomas; it's rather more difficult. 'Yet thus it was!' We'll end there, and have our tea."

Turning his head he saw that Lucy had come in and was standing behind him, looking over his shoulder at Thomas in his crib.

"Oh, Lucy," he said, "I'm reading to Thomas. Thomas is that. Do you like him? He is surprised at life, but quite pleased. He that was *Nothing* from Eternity did little think such Joys to celebrate or see. Yet thus it is. He is extraordinarily happy about it all, but he can't do anything yet, you know— not speak or sit up or anything. He can only make noises, and cry, and drink, and slither about in his bath like a piece of wet soap. Wasn't there a clergyman once who thought his baby ought to be baptised by immersion unless it was proved not well able to endure it, as it says in the rubric or somewhere, so he put it in a tub to try if it could endure it or not, and he let it loose by accident and couldn't catch it again, it was so slippery, just like a horrid little fish, and its mother only came in and got hold of it just in time to prevent its being drowned? So after that he felt he could honestly certify that the child couldn't well endure immersion. I'm getting better at catching Thomas, though. He isn't supposed to slip off my hand at all, but he kicks and slithers so I can't hold him, and swims away and gets lost. After tea will you come and help me wash him? Rhoda's out to tea; I'm so sorry. But there's tea, and Thomas and Algernon and me, and—and rather thick bread and butter only, apparently; but I shall have jam now you've come. First I must adjust Thomas's drinking-bottle; he always likes a drink while we have our tea. He's two months old. Is he good for that, do you think, or should he be a size larger? But I rather like them small, don't you? They're lighter so, for one thing. Is he nice? Do you like him?"

Lucy, kneeling by the crib, nodded.

"He's very old and wise, Peter; very old and gay. Look at his eyes. He's much—oh very much—older than you or me. That's as it should be."

"He'll rejuvenate with years, won't he?" said Peter. "At present he's too old to laugh when I make jokes; he thinks them silly; but he'll be sillier than anyone himself in about six months, I expect. Now we'll have tea."

Lucy left Thomas and came to the tea-table and poured out tea for both of them.

"I'm trying to learn to do without three lumps," said Peter, as Lucy put them in. "I expect it's extravagant to have three, really. But then Rhoda and Thomas don't take any, so it's only the same as if we each had one, isn't it. Thomas shan't be allowed more than one in each cup when he grows young enough to want any; Rhoda and I mean him to be a refined person."

"I don't think he will be," said Lucy, looking thoughtfully into the future. "I expect he'll be as vulgar as you and me. He's awfully like you to look at, Peter."

"So I am informed. Well, I'm not vain, and I don't claim to be an Adonis, like Denis. Is Denis flourishing? The birds were splendid; they came so thick and fast that I gathered it was being a remarkable season. But as you only answered my numerous letters by one, and that àpropos merely of Thomas's arrival, I could only surmise and speculate on your doings. I suppose you thought the grouse were instead of letters."

"They were Denis's letters. *I* didn't shoot the grouse, dear darlings, nor send them."

"What were your letters, then?"

"Well, I sent rowan berries, didn't I? Weren't they red?"

"Yes. Even Thomas read them. We're being rather funny, aren't we? Is Denis going on with Parliament again this autumn, or has he begun to get tired of it?"

"Not a bit tired of it. He doesn't bother about it particularly, you know; not enough to tire himself; he sort of takes it for granted, like going up to Scotland in August."

Peter nodded. "I know. He would take it just like that if he was Prime Minister, or Archbishop of Canterbury. I daresay he will be one day; isn't it nice the way things drop into his hands without his bothering to get them."

He didn't see the queer, silent look Lucy turned on him as he spread his thick bread and butter with blackberry jam.

"Thomas," she said after a moment, "has dropped into your hands, Peter." It was as if she was protesting against something, beating herself against some invisible, eternal barrier that divided the world into two unequal parts.

Peter said, "Rather, he has. I do hope he'll never drop out. I'm getting very handy about holding him, though. Oh, let's take him upstairs and tub him now; do you mind?"

So they took him upstairs and tubbed him, and Lucy managed to hold him so firmly that he didn't once swim away and get lost.

As they were drying him (Lucy dried him with a firmer and more effective hand than Peter, who always wiped him very gingerly lest he should squash) Rhoda came in. She was strange-eyed and pale in the blurred light, and greeted Lucy in a dreamy, absent way.

"I've had tea out.... Oh, have you bathed baby? How good of you. I meant to be in earlier, but I was late.... The fog's awful; it's getting thicker and thicker."

She sat down by the fire and loosened her coat, and took off her hat and rubbed the fog from her wet hair, and coughed. Rhoda had grown prettier lately; she looked less tired and listless, and her eyes were brighter, and the fire flushed her thin cheek to rose-colour as she bent over it.

Peter took her wet things from her and took off her shoes and put slippers on her feet, and she gave him an absent smile. Rhoda had had a dreamy way with her since Thomas's birth; moony, as Peggy, who didn't approve, called it.

A little later, when Thomas was clean and warm and asleep in his bed, they were told that Mrs. Urquhart's carriage had come.

Lucy bent over Thomas and kissed him, then over Rhoda. Rhoda whispered in her ear, without emotion, "Baby ought to have been yours, not mine," and Lucy whispered back:

"Oh hush, hush!"

Rhoda still held her, still whispered, "Will you love him? Will you be good to him, always?"

And Lucy answered, opening wide eyes, "Why, of course. No one could help it, could they?" and on that Rhoda let her go.

Peter thought that Lucy must have infected Rhoda with some of her own appreciation of Thomas, opened her eyes to his true worth; for during the next week she was newly tender to him. She bathed him every evening herself, only letting Peter help a little; she held him in her arms without wearying of his weight, and wasn't really annoyed even when he was sick upon her shoulder, an unfortunate habit of Thomas's.

But a habit, Peter thought, that Thomas employed with some discrimination; for the one and only one time that Guy Vyvian took him in his arms—or rather submitted to his being put there by Rhoda—Thomas was sicker than he had ever been before, with an immense completeness.

"Just what I always feel myself," commented Peter in his own mind, as Thomas was hastily removed. "I'm glad someone has shown him at last what the best people feel about him."

Vyvian had come to call. It was the first time Peter had met him since his marriage; he hoped it would be the last. The object of the call was to inspect Thomas, Rhoda said. Thomas was inspected, produced the impression indicated above, and was relegated to the region of things for which Vyvian had no use. He detested infants; children of any sort, in fact; and particularly Thomas, who had Peter's physiognomy and expressed Peter's sentiments in a violently ill-bred way.

Peter, a little later, was very glad that Thomas had revealed himself thus openly on this occasion. For it quite sealed Thomas's fate, if anything more was needed to seal it than the fact that Thomas would be an impossible burden, and also belonged by right to Peter. Anyhow, they left Thomas behind them when they went.

Rhoda wrote a scrawled note for Peter one foggy Monday morning, and hugged Thomas close and cried a little, and slipped out into the misty city with a handbag. Peter, coming in at tea-time, found the note on the sitting-room chimney-piece. It said:—

Don't try to follow me, Peter, for I can't come back. I *have* tried to care for you more than him and be a good wife, but I can't. You know I told you when we got engaged that I cared for him, and I tried so hard to stop, and I thought I would be able, with you to help me, but I couldn't do it. For the first few months I thought I could, but all the time it was there, like a fire in me, eating me up; and later on he began writing to me, but for a long time I wouldn't answer, and then he came to see me, and I said he mustn't, but he's been meeting me out and I couldn't stop him, and at last it grew that I knew I loved him so that it was no use pretending any more. I'd better go, Peter, for what's the use of trying to be a good wife to you when all I care for is him. I know he's not good, and you are, but I love him, and I must go when he wants me. It was all a mistake; you and I ought never to have married. You meant it kindly, I know; you meant to help me and make me happy, but it was no use. You and I never properly belonged. When I saw you and Lucy together, I knew we didn't belong, not like that; we didn't properly understand each other's ways and thoughts, like you two did. I love Lucy, too. You and she are so like. And she'll be good to Baby; she said she would. I hate to leave Baby, but Guy won't let me bring him, and anyhow I suppose I couldn't, because he's yours. I've written a list of his feeds, and it's on the chimney-piece behind the clock; please make whoever sees to him go by it or he gets a pain. Please be careful when you bath him; I think Mrs. Adams had better do it usually. She'll take care of him for you, or Peggy will, perhaps. You'll think I never cared for him, but I do, I love him, only I must love Guy most of all. I don't know if I shall be happy or miserable, but I expect miserable, only I must go with Guy. Please, dear Peter, try and understand this, and forgive me. I think you will, because you always do understand things, and forgive them too; I think you are the kindest person I ever knew. If I thought you loved me really, I don't think I'd go, even for Guy; but I know you've only felt kindly to me all along, so I think it is best for you too that I should go, and you will be thankful in the end. Good-bye. You promised mother to see after me, I know, for she told me before she died; well, you've done your best, and mother'd be grateful to you if she could know. I suppose some would say she does know, perhaps; but I don't believe those stories; I believe it's all darkness beyond, and silence. And if it is, we must try and get all the light and warmth here that we can. So I'm going.

Good-bye, Peter.

RHODA.

Peter read it through, sitting on the rug by the fire. When he had finished it, he put it into the fire and watched it burn. Then he sighed, and sat very still for a while, his hands clasped round one knee.

Presently he got up and looked behind the clock, and saw that the next feeding-time was due now. So he rang for Mrs. Adams, the landlady, and asked her if she would mind bringing Thomas's bottle.

When Thomas had it, Peter stood and looked down upon him as he drank with ill-bred noises.

"Gently, Thomas: you'll choke. You'll choke and die, I know you will. Then you'll be gone too. Everything goes, Thomas. Everything I touch breaks; everything I try to do fails. That's because I'm such an ass, I suppose. I did think I could perhaps make one little unlucky girl decently happy; but I couldn't, you see. So she's gone after light and warmth, and she'll—she'll break her heart in a year, and it'll be my fault. Follow her? No, I shan't do that. I shouldn't find her, and if I did what would be the use? If she must go, she must; she was only eating her heart out here; and perhaps it's better to break one's heart on something than eat it out in emptiness. No, it isn't better in this case. Anything in the world would have been better than this; that she should have gone with that—that person. Yet thus it is. And they'll all set on her and speak against her, and I shall have to bear it. You and I will have to bear it together, Thomas.... I suppose I ought to be angry. I ought to want to go after them, to the end of the world or wherever they've gone and kill him and bring her back. But I can't. I should fail in that too. I'm tired of trying to do things; simply horribly tired of it, Thomas." He sat down on the rug with Thomas in his arms; and there, an hour later, Peggy found them. She swung in breezily, crying, "Oh, Peter, all alone in the dark? Where's Rhoda? Why, the silly children haven't had their tea!" she added, looking at the unused cups on the tea-table.

Peter looked up vaguely. "Oh, tea. I forgot. I don't think I want any tea to-day. And Thomas has had his. And Rhoda's gone. It's no good not telling you—is it?—because you'll find out. She's gone away. It's been my fault entirely; I didn't make her happy, you see. And she's written out a list of the times Thomas has to feed at. I suppose Mrs. Adams will do that if I ask her, and generally look after him when I'm out."

Peggy stood aghast before him for a moment, staring, then collapsed, breathless, on the sofa, crying, with even more r's than usual.

"*Peter!*... Why, she's gone and rrun off with that toad, that rreptile man! Oh, I know it, so it's not a bit of use your trying to keep it from me."

"Very well," said Peter; "I suppose it's not."

"Oh, the little fool, the little, silly, wicked fool! But if ever a little fool got her rich deserts without needing to wait for purgatory, that one'll be Rhoda.... Oh, Peter, be more excited and angry! Why aren't you stamping up and down and vowing vengeance, instead of sitting on the hearth saying, 'Rhoda's gone,' as if it was the kitten?"

"I'm sorry, Peggy." Peter sighed a little. "I'm nursing Thomas, you see."

Peggy at that was on her knees on the floor, taking both of them into her large embrace.

"Oh, you two poor little darling boys, what's to become of you both? That child has a heart of stone, to leave you to yourselves the way she's done. Don't defend her, Peter; I won't hear a word said for her again as long as I live; she deserves Guy Vyvian, and I couldn't say a worse word for her than that. You poor little Tommy; come to me then, babykins. You must come back to us now, Peter, and I'll look after you both."

She cuddled Thomas to her breast with one arm, and put the other round Peter's shoulders as he sat huddled up, his chin resting on his knees. At the moment it was difficult to say which of the two looked the most forsaken, the most left to himself. Only Thomas hadn't yet learnt to laugh, and Peter had. He laughed now, softly and not happily.

"It *has* been rather a ghastly fiasco, hasn't it," he said. "Absurd, you know, too, in a way. I thought it was all working out so nicely, Thomas coming and everything. But no. It wasn't working out nicely at all. Things don't as a rule, do they?"

There was a new note of dreariness in his voice, a note that had perhaps been kept out of it of set purpose for a long time. Now there seemed at the moment no particular reason to keep it out any more, though fresh reasons would arrive, no doubt, very soon; and Thomas when waking was a reason in himself. But in this dim hour between two roads, this hour of relaxation of tension in the shadowy firelight, when Thomas slept and only Peggy listened, Peter, having fallen crashing through floor after floor of his pleasant house of life, till he was nearly at the bottom, looked up at all the broken floors and sighed.

Peggy's arm was comfortingly about him. To her he was always a little, brittle, unlucky boy, as she had first seen him long ago.

"Never you mind, Peterkin. There's a good time coming, I do believe. She'll come back, perhaps; who knows? Vyvian wouldn't do for long, not even for Rhoda. Besides, you may be sure he'll throw her off soon, and then she'll want to come back to you and Tommy. I wouldn't say that to any other man, because, of course, no other man would have her back; but I do believe, Peterkin, that you would, wouldn't you now? I expect you'd smile and say, 'Oh, come in, you're just in time for tea and to see me bath Thomas,' and not another word about it."

"Probably," said Peter. "There wouldn't be much to say, would there? But she won't come back; I know that. Even if she leaves him she won't. Rhoda's horribly proud really, you know. She'd sooner sweep a crossing, or trim hats or something, than come near us again. I don't know what to hope about it. I suppose one must hope they'll go on together, as Rhoda seems to like him as he is; but it's an awful thought.... She's right that we never understood each other. I couldn't, you know, bear to think of spending even one day alone with Vyvian. I should be sick, like Thomas. The mere sight of his hair is enough, and his hand with that awful ring on it. I—I simply draw the line at him. *Why* does Rhoda care for him? How can she?" Peter frowned over it in bewilderment.

Peggy said, "Girls are silly things. And I suppose the way one's been brought up counts, and what one's inherited, and all that."

"Well, if Rhoda'd taken after Mrs. Johnson she wouldn't have liked Vyvian. He used to give her the creeps, like a toad. She told me so. She disliked him more than I did.... Well, I shall never understand. I suppose if I could Rhoda would have found me more sympathetic, and might have stayed."

"Now, darling, you're not to sit up and brood any more; that won't help. You're coming straight back with me to dinner, and Tommy's coming too, to sleep. I shall ask Mrs. Adams to help me get his things together."

"He hasn't many things," said Peter, looking vaguely round for them. "I got him a rattle and a ball, but he doesn't seem to care about them much; Lucy says he's not young enough yet. Here's his bottle. And his night clothes are upstairs, and his other day clothes, and his bath. Thomas leads the simple life, though; he really possesses very little; I think he's probably going to be a Franciscan later on. But he can sleep with me here all right; I should like to have him; only it would be awfully good of you if you'd have him to-morrow, while I'm out at work. But in the night he and I rather like each other's company."

"Rubbish," said Peggy. "You're both coming along to fifty-one this minute. You don't suppose I'm going to leave you two infants alone together like that. We've heaps of room at fifty-one"—she sighed a little—"people have been fading away like the flowers of the forest, and we should be thankful to have you back."

"Oh, we'll come then; thanks very much, Peggy." Peter's ready sympathy was turned on again, having temporarily been available only for himself and Rhoda and Thomas. He remembered now that Peggy and Hilary needed it too. He and Thomas would go and be boarders in the emptying boarding-house; it might amuse Thomas, perhaps, to see the other boarders.

"And we'll have him baptized," went on Peggy, thinking of further diversions for Thomas and Peter. "You'll let him be a Catholic, Peter, won't you?"

"Thomas," said Peter, "can be anything he likes that's nice. As long as he's not a bigot. I won't have him refusing to go into one sort of church because he prefers another; he mustn't ever acquire the rejecting habit. Short of that, he may enter any denomination or denominations he prefers."

They were collecting Thomas's belongings as they talked. Thomas lay and looked at them with the very blue slits that were like his father's eyes grown old. And suddenly Peggy, looking from son to father, saw that Peter's eyes had grown as old as Thomas's, looking wearily out of a pale, pinched face.

Peggy's own eyes brimmed over as she bent over Thomas's night-shirt.

CHAPTER XVI

A LONG WAY

Lord Evelyn Urquhart dined with his nephew on the last evening in February. It was a characteristic Urquhart dinner-party; the guests were mostly cheerful, well-bred young people of high spirits and of the worldly station that is not much concerned with any aspect of money but the spending of it. High living, plain thinking, agreeable manners and personal appearance, plenty of humour, enough ability to make a success of the business of living and not enough to agitate the brain, a light tread along a familiar and well-laid road, and a serene blindness to side-tracks and alleys not familiar nor well-laid and to those that walked thereon—these were the characteristics of the pleasant people who frequented Denis Urquhart's pleasant house in Park Lane.

Lucy was among them, small and pale, and rather silent, and intensely alive. She, of course, was a native not of Park Lane but of Chelsea; and the people who had frequented her home there were of a different sort. They had had, mostly, a different kind of brain, a kind more restless and troublesome and untidy, and a different type of wit, more pungent and ironic, less well-fed and hilarious, and they were less well-dressed and agreeable to look at, and had (perhaps) higher thoughts (though how shall one measure height?) and ate (certainly) plainer food, for lack of richer. These were the people Lucy knew. Her father himself had been of these. She now found her tent pitched among the prosperous; and the study of them touched her wide gaze with a new, pondering look. Denis hadn't any use for cranks. None of his set were socialists, vegetarians, Quakers, geniuses, anarchists, drunkards, poets, anti-breakfasters, or anti-hatters; none of them, in fine, the sort of person Lucy was used to. They never pawned their watches or walked down Bond Street in Norfolk coats. They had, no doubt, their hobbies; but they were suitable, well-bred hobbies, that did not obtrude vulgarly on other people's notice. Peter had once said that if he were a plutocrat he would begin to dream dreams. Lucy supposed that the seemingly undreaming people who were Denis's friends were not rich enough; they hadn't reached plutocracy, where romance resides, but merely prosperity, which has fewer possibilities. Lucy began in these days to ponder on the exceeding evil of Socialism, which the devil has put it into certain men's hearts to desire. For, thought Lucy, sweep away the romantic rich, sweep away the dreaming destitute, and what have you left? The prosperous; the comfortable; the serenely satisfied; the sanely reasonable.

Dives, with his purple and fine linen, his sublime outlook over a world he may possess at a touch, goes to his own place; Lazarus, with his wallet for crusts and his place among the dogs and his sharp wonder at the world's black heart, is gathered to his fathers: there remain the sanitary dwellings of the comfortable, the monotonous external adequacy that touches no man's inner needs, the lifeless rigour of a superintended well-being. Decidedly, thought Lucy, siding with the Holy Roman Church, a scheme of the devil's. Denis and his friends also thought it was rot. So no doubt it was. Denis belonged to the Conservative party. Lucy thought parties funny things, and laughed. Though she had of late taken to wandering far into seas of thought, so that her wide forehead was often puckered as she sat silent, she still laughed at the world. Perhaps the more one thinks about it the more one laughs; the height and depth of its humour are certainly unfathomable.

On this last night of February, Lord Evelyn, when the other guests had gone, put his unsteady white hand under Lucy's chin and raised her small pale face and looked at it out of his near-sighted, scrutinising eyes, and said:

"Humph. You're thinner."

Lucy's eyes laughed up at him.

"Am I? I suppose I'm growing old."

"You're worrying. What's it about?" asked Lord Evelyn.

They were in the library. Lord Evelyn and Denis sat by the fire in leather chairs and smoked, and Lucy sat on a hassock between them, her chin in her hands.

She was silent for a moment. Then she looked up at Denis, who was reading Punch, and said, "I've had a letter from Peggy Margerison this morning."

Denis gave a sound between a grunt and a chuckle. The grunt element was presumably for Peggy Margerison, the chuckle for Punch.

Lord Evelyn, tapping his eye-glass on the arm of his chair, said, "Well? Well?" impatiently, nervously.

Lucy drew a note from her pocket (she was never pocketless) and spread it on her knees. It was a long letter on crinkly paper, written in a large, dashing, sprawling hand, full of curls, generosities, extravagances.

"She says," said Lucy, "(Please listen, Denis,) that—that they want money."

"I somehow thought that would be what she said," Denis murmured, still half preoccupied. "I'm sure she's right."

"A woman who writes a hand like that," put in Lord Evelyn, "will always spend more than she has. A hole in the purse; a hole in the purse."

"She says," went on Lucy, looking through the letter with wrinkled forehead, "that they're all very hard-up indeed. Of course, I knew that; I can see it whenever I go there; only Peter will never take more than silly little clothes and things for Thomas. And now Peggy says they're in great straits; Thomas is going to teethe or something, and wants better milk, all from one cow, and they're all awfully in debt."

"I should fancy that was chronic," remarked Denis, turning to Essence of Parliament.

"A hole in the purse, a hole in the purse," muttered Lord Evelyn, tapping with his eye-glass.

"Peggy says that Peter won't ask for help himself, but he's let her, it seems. And their boarders are nearly all gone, one of them quite suddenly, without paying a sixpence for all the time he was there."

"I suppose he didn't think he'd had sixpence worth," said Denis. "He was probably right."

"And Thomas is still very delicate after his bronchitis, and Peter's got a bad cold on the chest and wants more cough-mixture than they can afford to buy; and they owe money to the butcher and the fishmonger and the baker and the doctor and the tailor, and Hilary's lost his latest job and isn't earning anything at all. So I suppose Peter is keeping the family."

"Scamps; scamps all," muttered Lord Evelyn. "Deserve all they get, and more. People like the Margerisons an't worth helping. They'd best go under at once; best go under. Swindlers and scamps, the lot of them. I daresay the woman's stories are half lies; of course, they want money, but it's probably only to spend on nonsense. Why can't they keep themselves, like decent people?"

"Oh," said Lucy, dismissing that as absurd, "they can't. Of course they can't. They never could ... Denis."

"Lucy." Denis absently put out a hand to meet hers.

"How much shall we give them, Denis?"

Denis dropped Punch onto the floor, and lay back with his hands clasped behind his fair head. Lucy, looking at his up-turned, foreshortened, cleanly-modelled face, thought with half of her mind what a perfect thing it was. Sudden aspects of Denis's beauty sometimes struck her breathless, as they struck Peter.

"The Margerison family wants money, I understand," said Denis, who hadn't been listening attentively.

"Very badly, Denis."

Denis nodded. "They always do, of course.... Well, is it our business to fill the bottomless Margerison purse?"

Lucy sat very still, looking up at him with wide eyes.

"Our business? I don't know. But, of course, if Peter and Peter's people want anything, we shall give it them."

"But I gather it's not Peter that asks? Peter never asks, does he?"

"No," said Lucy. "Peter never asks. Not even for Thomas."

"Well, I should be inclined to trust Peter rather than his charming family. Peter's name seems to be dragged into that letter a good deal, but it doesn't follow that Peter sanctioned it. I'm not going to annoy Peter by sending him what he's never asked for. I should think probably Peter knows they can get on all right as they are, and that this letter must be taken with a good deal of salt. I expect the egregious Hilary only wants the money for some new enterprise of his own, that will fail, as usual. Anyhow, I really don't fancy having any further dealings with Hilary Margerison or his wife; I've had enough there. He's the most impossible cad and swindler."

"Swindlers all, swindlers all," said Lord Evelyn, getting up and pacing up and down the room, his hands behind his back.

Lucy, after a moment, said simply, "I shall give them something, Denis. I must. Don't you see? Whoever it was, I would. Because anyhow, they're poor and we're rich, and they want things we can give them. It's so obvious that when people ask one for things they must have them if one can give them. And when it's Peter who's in want, and Peter's baby, and Peter's people ..."

"You see," said Denis, "I doubt about Peter or the baby benefiting by anything we give them. It will all go down the drain where Hilary Margerison's money flows away. Give it to Peter or give it to his relations, it'll come to the same thing. Peter gives them every penny he gets, I don't doubt. You know what Peter is; he's as weak as a baby in his step-brother's hands; he lets himself be dragged into the most disgraceful transactions because he can't say no."

Lucy looked up at him, open-eyed, pale, quiet.

"You think of Peter like that?" she said, and her voice trembled a little.

Lord Evelyn stopped in his walk and listened.

"I'm sorry, Lucy," said Denis, throwing away his cigar-end. "I don't want to say anything against Peter to you. But ... one must judge by facts, you know. I don't mean that Peter means any harm; but, as I say, he's weak. I'm fond of Peter, you know; I wish to goodness he wouldn't play the fool as he does, mixing himself up with his precious relations and helping them in their idiotic schemes for swindling money out of people—but there it is; he will do it; and as long as he does it I don't feel moved to have much to do with him. I should send him money if he asked me personally, of course, even if I knew it would only go into his brother's pocket; but I'm not going to do it at his sister-in-law's command. If you ask me whether I feel inclined to help Hilary Margerison and his wife, my answer is simply no I don't. They're merely scum; and why should one have anything to do with scum?"

Lucy looked at him silently for a while. Then she said slowly, "I see. Yes, I see you wouldn't want to, of course. They *are* scum. And you're not. But I am, I think. I belong to the same sort of people they do. I could swindle and cheat too, I expect. It's the people at the bottom who do that. They're my relations, you see, not yours."

"My dear Lucy, only Peter is your relation."

"Peter and Thomas. And I count the rest too, because they're Peter's. So let me do all that is to be done, Denis. Don't you bother. I'll take them money."

"Let them alone, Lucy. You'd better, you know. What's the good?"

"I don't know," said Lucy. "None, I expect. None at all; because Peter wouldn't take it from me without you."

She came a little nearer him, and put her hand on his knee like a wistful puppy.

"Denis," she said, "I wish *you* would. They know already that I care. But I wish *you* would. Peter'd like you to. He'd be more pleased than if I did; much more. Peter cares for you and me and Thomas extraordinarily much; and you can't compare carings, but the way he cares for you is the most wonderful of all, I believe. If you went to him ... if you showed him you cared ... he'd take it from you. He wouldn't take it from me without you, because he'd suspect you weren't wanting him to have it. Denis, won't you go to Peter, as you used to do long ago, before he was in disgrace and poor, before he was scum? Can't you, Denis?"

Denis had coloured faintly. He always did when people were emotional. Lucy seldom was; she had a delicious morning freshness that was like the cool wind on the hills in spring.

"Peter never comes here, Lucy, does he. If he wanted to see me, I suppose he would."

Lucy was looking strangely at the beautiful face with the faint flush rising in it. She apparently thought no reply necessary to his words, but said again, "*Can't* you, Denis? Or is it too hard, too much bother, too much stepping out of the way?"

"Oh, it's not the bother, of course. But ... but I really don't see anything to be gained by it, that's the fact.... Our meetings, on the last few occasions when we have met, haven't been particularly comfortable. I don't think Peter likes them any better than I do.... One can't force intercourse, Lucy; if it doesn't run easily and smoothly, it had better be left alone. There have been things between us, between Peter's family and my family, that can't be forgotten or put aside by either of us, I suppose; and I don't think Peter wants to be reminded of them by seeing me any more than I do by seeing him. It's—it's so beastly uncomfortable, you know," he added boyishly, ruffling up his hair with his hand; and concluded didactically, "People *must* drift apart if their ways lie in quite different spheres; it's inevitable."

Denis, who had a boyish reticence, had expanded and explained himself more than usual.

Lucy's hand dropped from his knee on to her own.

"I suppose it *is* inevitable," she said, beneath her breath. "I suppose the distance is too great. 'Tis such a long, long way from here to there ... such a long, long way.... Good-night, Denis; I'm going to bed."

She got up slowly, cramped and tired and pale. It was not till she was on her feet that she saw Lord Evelyn sitting in the background, and remembered his presence. She had forgotten him; she had been thinking only of Denis and Peter and herself. She didn't know if he had been listening much; he sat quietly, nursing his knee, saying nothing.

But when Lucy had gone he said to Denis, "You're right, Denis; you're utterly right, not to have anything to do with those swindlers," and, as if in a sudden fresh anger against them, he began again his quick, uneven pacing down the room.

"False through and through," he muttered. "False through and through."

Lucy's face, as she had risen to her feet and said "Good night, Uncle Evelyn," had been so like Peter's as he had last seen it, when Peter had passed him in the doorway at Astleys, that it had taken his breath away.

CHAPTER XVII

QUARRELS IN THE RAIN

In Brook Street the rain fell. It fell straight and disconsolate, unutterably wet, splashing drearily on the paved street between the rows of wet houses. It fell all day, from the dim dawn, through the murky noon, to the dark evening, desolately weeping over a tired city.

Inside number fifty-one, Peggy mended clothes and sang a little song, with Thomas in her lap, and Peter, sitting in the window-seat, knitted Thomas a sweater of Cambridge blue. Peter was getting rather good at knitting. Hilary was there too, but not mending, or knitting, or singing; he was coughing, and complaining of the climate.

"I fancy it is going to be influenza," he observed at intervals, shivering. "I feel extraordinarily weak, and ache all up my back. I fancy I have a high temperature, only Peter has broken the thermometer. You were a hundred and four, I think, Peter, the day you went to bed. I rather expect I am a hundred and five. But I suppose I shall never know, as it is impossible to afford another thermometer. I feel certain it is influenza; and in that case I must give up all hope of getting that job from Pickering, as I cannot possibly go and see him to-morrow. Not but that it would be a detestable job, anyhow; but anything to keep our heads above water.... My headache is now like a hot metal band all round my head, Peggy."

"Poor old boy," said Peggy. "Take some more phenacetine. And do go to bed, Hilary. If you *have* got flu, you'll only make yourself as bad as Peter did by staying up too long. You've neither of you any more sense than Tommy here, nor so much, by a long way, have they, little man? No, Kitty, let him be; you'd only drop him on the floor if I let you, and then he'd break, you know."

Silvio was kneeling up on the window-seat by Peter's side, taking an interest in the doings of the street.

Peggy said, "Well, Larry, what's the news of the great world?"

"It's raining," said Silvio, who had something of the mournful timbre of Hilary's voice in his.

Peggy said, "Oh, darling, be more interesting! I'm horribly afraid you're going to grow up obvious, Larry, and that will never do. What else is it doing?"

"There's a cat in the rain," said Silvio, flattening his nose against the blurred glass, and manifestly inclined to select the sadder aspects of the world's news for retail. That tendency too, perhaps, he inherited from Hilary.

Presently he added, "There's a taxi coming up the street," and Peggy placed Thomas on Peter's knees and came to the window to look. When she had looked she said to Peter, "It must be nearly six o'clock" (the clock gained seventeen minutes a day, so that the time was always a matter for nicer calculation than Peggy could usually afford to give it); "and if Hilary's got flu, I should think Tommy'd be best out of the room.... I haven't easily the time to put him to bed this evening, really."

Peter accepted the suggestion and conveyed his son from the room. As he did so, someone knocked at the front door, and Peggy ran downstairs to open it.

She let in the unhappy noise of the rain and a tall, slim person in a fur coat.

Peggy was surprised, and (most rarely) a little embarrassed. It wasn't the person she had looked for. She even, in her unwonted confusion, let the visitor speak first.

He said, "Is Mr. Peter Margerison in?" frostily, giving her no sign of recognition.

"He is not, Lord Evelyn," said Peggy, hastily. "That is, he is busy with the baby upstairs. Will I take him a message?"

"I shall be glad if you will tell him I have called to see him."

"I will, Lord Evelyn. Will you come up to the drawing-room while I get him?"

Peggy led the way, drawing meanwhile on the resources of a picturesque imagination.

"He may be a little while before he can leave the baby, Lord Evelyn. Poor mite, it's starved with hunger, the way it cries and cries and won't leave off, and Peter has to cheer it."

Lord Evelyn grunted. The steep stairs made him a little short of breath, and not sympathetic.

"And even," went on Peggy, stopping outside the drawing-room door, "even when it does get a feed of milk, it's to-day from one kind of cow, to-morrow from another. Why, you'd think all the cows in England, turn and turn about, supplied that poor child with milk; and you know they get pains from changing. It's not right, poor baby; but what can we and his father do? The same with his scraps of clothes—this weather he'd a right to be having new warm ones—but there he lies crying for the cold in his little thin out-grown things; it brings the tears to one's eyes to see him. And he's not the only one, either. His father's just out of an illness, and keeps a cough on the chest because he can't afford a warm waistcoat or the only cough-mixture that cures him.... But Peter wouldn't like me to be telling you all this. Will you go in there, Lord Evelyn, and wait?"

She paused another moment, her hand on the handle.

"You'll not tell Peter I told you anything. He'd not be pleased. He'll not breathe a word to you of it himself—indeed, he'll probably say it's not so."

Lord Evelyn made no comment; he merely tapped his cane on the floor; he seemed impatient to have the door opened.

"And," added Peggy, "if ever you chanced to be offering him anything—I mean, you might be for giving him a birthday present, or a Xmas present or something sometime—you'd do best to put it as a gift to the baby, or he'll never take it."

Having concluded her diplomacy, she opened the door and ushered him into the room, where Hilary sat with his headache and the children played noisily at horses.

"Lord Evelyn Urquhart come to see Peter," called Peggy into the room. "Come along out of that, children, and keep yourselves quiet somewhere."

She bundled them out and shut the door on Lord Evelyn and Hilary.

Hilary rose dizzily to his feet and bowed. Lord Evelyn returned the courtesy distantly, and stood by the door, as far as possible from his host.

"This is good of you," said Hilary, "to come and see us in our fallen estate. Do sit down."

Lord Evelyn, putting his glass into his eye and turning it upon Hilary as if in astonishment at his impertinence in addressing him, said curtly, "I came to see your half-brother. I had not the least intention, nor the least desire, to see anyone else whatever; nor have I now."

"Quite so," said Hilary, his teeth chattering with fever. (His temperature, though he would never know, as Peter had broken the thermometer, must be anyhow a hundred and three, he was sure.) "Quite so. But that doesn't affect my gratitude to you. Peter's friends are mine. I must thank you for remembering Peter."

Lord Evelyn, presumably not seeing the necessity, was silent.

"We have not met," Hilary went on, passing his hot hand over his fevered brow, where the headache ran all round like a hot metal band, "for a very long time, Lord Evelyn; if we put aside that momentary encounter at Astleys last year." Hilary did put that aside, rather hastily, and went on, "Apart from that, we have not met since we were both in Venice, nearly two years ago. Lord Evelyn, I have often wished to tell you how very deeply I have regretted certain events that came between us there. I think there is a great deal that I might explain to you...."

Lord Evelyn, with averted face, said, "Be good enough to be silent, sir. I have no desire to hear any of your remarks. I have come merely to see your half-brother."

"Of course," said Hilary, who was sensitive, "if you take that line, there is nothing to be said between you and me."

Lord Evelyn acknowledged this admission with a slight inclination of the head.

"Nothing whatever, sir."

So there was silence, till Peter came in, pale and sickly and influenzaish, but with a smile for Lord Evelyn. It was extraordinarily nice of Lord Evelyn, he thought, to have come all the way to Brook Street in the rain to see him.

Lord Evelyn looked at him queerly, intently, out of his short-sighted eyes as they shook hands.

"I wish to talk to you," he remarked, with meaning.

Hilary took the hint, looked proud, said, "I see that my room is preferred to my company," and went away.

When he had gone, Peter said, "Do sit down," but Lord Evelyn took no notice of that. He had come to see Peter in his need, but he had not forgiven him, and he would remain standing in his house. Peter had once hurt him so badly that the mere sight of him quickened his breath and flushed his cheek. He tapped his cane impatiently against his grey spats.

"You're ill," he said, accusingly.

"Oh, I've only had flu," said Peter; "I'm all right now."

"You're ill," Lord Evelyn repeated. "Don't contradict me, sir. You're ill; you're in want; and you're bringing up a baby on insufficient diet. What?"

"Not a bit," said Peter. "I am not in want, nor is Thomas. Thomas' diet is so sufficient that I'm often afraid he'll burst with it."

Lord Evelyn said, "You're probably lying. But if you're not, why d'ye countenance your sister-in-law's begging letters? You're a hypocrite, sir. But that's nothing I didn't know before, you may say. Well, you're right there."

Lord Evelyn's anger was working up. He hadn't known it would be so difficult to talk to Peter and remain calm.

"You want to make a fool of me again," he broke out, "so you join in a lying letter and bring me here on false pretences. At least, I suppose it was really Lucy you thought to bring. You play on Lucy's soft heart, knowing you can squeeze money out of her—and so you can afford to say you've no use for mine. Is that it?"

Peter said, dully looking at his anger as at an ancient play re-staged, "I don't know what you're talking about. I know nothing of any letter. And you don't suppose I should take your money, or Lucy's either. Why should I? I don't want money."

Lord Evelyn was pacing petulantly up and down the shabby carpet, waving his cane as he walked.

"Oh, you know nothing of any letter, don't you. Well, ask your sister-in-law, then; ask that precious brother of yours. Haven't you always chosen to hang on to them and join in their dirty tricks? And now you turn round and say you know nothing of their doings; a pretty story.... Now look here, Mr. Peter Margerison, you've asked for money and you shall take it, d'ye see?"

Peter flung at him, in a queer and quite new hot bitterness and anger (it was perhaps the result of influenza, which has strange after effects). "You've no right to come here and say these things to me. I didn't want you to come; I never asked you to; and now I never want to see you again. Please go, Lord Evelyn."

Lord Evelyn paused in his walk, and stood looking at him for a moment, his lips parted to speak, his hands clasped behind him over the gold head of his cane.

Then, into the ensuing silence, came Lucy, small and pale and wet in her grey furs, and stood like a startled kitten, her wide eyes turning from one angry face to the other.

Peter said to her, in a voice she had never heard from him before, "So you've come too."

Lord Evelyn tittered disagreeably. "Didn't expect her, of course, did you. So unlikely she'd come, after getting a letter like that.... I suppose you're wondering, Lucy, what I'm doing *dans cette galère*."

"No," said Lucy, "I wasn't. I know. You've come to see Peter, like me."

He laughed again. "Yes, that's it. Like you. And now he pretends he won't take the money he asked for, Lucy. Won't be beholden to me at any price. Perhaps he was waiting for you."

Lucy was looking at Peter, who looked so ill and so strange and new. Never before had he looked at her like that, with hard eyes. Peter was angry; the skies had fallen.

She said, and put out her hands to him, "What's the matter, Peter? Don't ... don't look like that.... Oh, you're ill; do sit down; it's so stupid to stand about."

Peter said, his own hands hanging at his sides, "Do you mind going away, both of you. I don't think I want to talk to either of you to-day.... I suppose you've brought money to give me too, Lucy, have you?"

Lucy coloured faintly over her small pale face.

"I won't give you anything you don't like, Peter. But I may give a present to Thomas, mayn't I?"

"No," said Peter, without interest or emotion.

So they stood in silence for a moment, facing each other, Lucy full-handed and impotent before Peter whose empty hands hung closed and unreceiving; Lucy and Peter, who had once been used to go shares and to give and take like two children, and who could give and take no more; and in the silence something oddly vibrated, so that Lord Evelyn, the onlooker, abruptly moved and spoke.

"Come home, Lucy. He's told us he'll have none of us."

Lucy still stood pleading, like a child; then, at Lord Evelyn's touch on her arm, she suddenly began to cry, again like a child, helpless and conquered.

At her tears Peter turned away sharply, and walked to the window.

"Please go," he said. "Please go."

They went, Lucy quietly crying, and Lord Evelyn, suddenly become oddly gentle, comforting her.

At the door he paused for a moment, looked round at Peter, hesitated, took a step back towards him, began to say something.

"Peter...."

Then Peggy came in, followed by Hilary. Lord Evelyn shut his lips lightly, bowed, and followed Lucy downstairs. Peggy went after them to let them out.

Hilary flung himself into a chair.

"Well, Peter? Well?"

Peter turned round from the window, and Hilary started at his face.

"My dear boy, what on earth is the matter?"

Then Peggy came in, her eyes full of dismayed vexation, but laughter twitching at her lips.

"Oh, my dears! What a mood they're in! Lord Evelyn looked at me to destroy me—and Lucy crying as if she'd never stop; I tried to make her take some sal volatile, but he wouldn't let her, but wisked her into her carriage and shut the door in my face. Mercy, what temper!"

The last words may not have had exclusive reference to Lord Evelyn, as Peggy was now looking at Peter in some astonishment and alarm. When Peter looked angry, everyone was so surprised that they wanted to take his temperature and send him to bed. Peggy would have liked to do that now, but really didn't dare.

What had come to the child, she wondered?

"What did they talk about, Peter? A funny thing their coming within half an hour of each other like that, wasn't it. And I never thought to see Lord Evelyn here, I must say. Now I wonder why was Lucy crying and he so cross?"

Peter left her to wonder that, and said merely, "Once for all, I won't have it. You shall *not* beg for money and bring my name into it. It's—it's horrid."

With a weak, childish word his anger seemed to explode and die away. After all, no anger of Peter's could last long. And somehow, illogically, his anger here was more with the Urquharts than with the Margerisons and most with Lucy. One is, of course, most angry, with those who have most power to hurt.

Suddenly feeling rather ill, Peter collapsed into a chair.

Peggy, coming and kneeling by him, half comforting, half reproaching, said, "Oh, Peter darling, you haven't been refusing money, when you know you and Tommy and all of us need it so much?"

Hilary said, "Peter has no regard whatever for what we all need. He simply doesn't care. I suppose now we shall never be able to afford even a new thermometer to replace the one Peter broke. Again, why should it matter to Peter? He took his own temperature all through his illness, and I suppose that is all he cares about. I wonder how much fever I have at this moment. Is my pulse very wild, Peggy?"

"It is not," said Peggy, soothingly, without feeling it. "And I daresay Peter's temperature is as high as yours now, if we knew; he looks like it. Well, Peter, it was stupid of you, my dear, wasn't it, to say no to a present and hurt their feelings that way when they'd been so good as to come in the rain and all. If they offer it again—"

Peter said, "They won't. They won't come here again, ever. They've done with us, I'm glad to say, and we with them. So you needn't write to them again; it will be no use."

Peter was certainly cross, Peggy and Hilary looked at him in surprised disapproval. How silly. Where was the use of having friends if one treated them in this unkind, proud way?

"Peter," said Hilary, "has obviously decided that we are not fit to have anything to do with his grand friends. No doubt he is well-advised—" he looked bitterly round the unkempt room—"and we will certainly take the hint."

Then Peter recovered himself and said, "Oh don't be an ass, Hilary," and laughed dejectedly, and went up to finish putting Thomas to bed.

In the carriage that rolled through the rain from Brook Street to Park Lane, Lord Evelyn Urquhart was saying, "This is the last time; the very last time. Never again do I try to help any Margerison. First I had to listen for full five minutes to the lies of that woman; then to the insufferable remarks of that cad, that swindler, Hilary Margerison, who I firmly believe had an infectious disease which I have no doubt caught," (he was right; he had caught it). "Then in comes Peter and insults me to my face and tells me to clear out of the house. By all means; I have done so, and it will be for good. What, Lucy? There, don't cry, child; they an't worth a tear between the lot of 'em."

But Lucy cried. She, like Peter, was oddly not herself to-day, and cried and cried.

CHAPTER XVIII

THE BREAKING-POINT

The boarding-house suddenly ceased to be. Its long illness ended in natural death. There was a growing feeling among the boarders that no self-respecting person could remain with people whose financial affairs were in the precarious condition of the Margerisons'—people who couldn't pay the butcher, and lived on ill-founded expectations of subsidies. As two years ago the Margerisons had been thrown roughly out of the profession of artistic experts, so now the doors of the boarding-house world were shut upon them. Boarders are like that; intensely respectable.

All the loosed dogs of ill-fortune seemed to be yelping at the Margerisons' heels at once. Hilary, when he recovered from his influenza and went out to look for jobs, couldn't find one. Again and again he was curtly refused employment, by editors and others. Every night he came home a little more bitter than the day before. Peter too, while he lay mending of his breakages, received a letter from the place of business he adorned informing him that it would not trouble him further. He had never been much use to it; he had been taken on at Leslie's request and given a trial; but it could not last for ever, as Peter fair-mindedly admitted.

"Well," he commented, "I suppose one must do something else, eventually. But I shall put off reflecting on that till I can move about more easily."

Hilary said, "We are being hounded out of London as we were hounded out of Venice. It is unbearable. What remains?"

"Nothing, that I can see at the moment," said Peter, laughing weakly.

"Ireland," said Peggy suddenly. "Let's go there. Dublin's worth a dozen of this hideous old black dirty place. You could get work on 'The Nationalist,' Hilary, I do believe, for the sub-editorship's just been given to my cousin Larry Callaghan. Come along to the poor old country, and we'll try our luck again."

"Dublin I believe to be an unspeakable place to live in," said Hilary, but mainly from habit. "Still, I presume one must live somewhere, so ..."

He turned to Peter. "Where shall you and Thomas live?"

Peter flushed slightly. He had supposed that he and Thomas were also to live in the unspeakable Dublin.

"Oh, we haven't quite made up our minds. I must consult Thomas about it."

"But," broke in Peggy, "of course you're coming with us, my dear. What do you mean? You're not surely going to desert us now, Peter?"

Peter glanced at Hilary. Hilary said, pushing his hair, with his restless gesture, from his forehead, "Really, Peggy, we can't drag Peter about after us all our lives; it's hardly fair on him to involve him in all our disasters, when he has more than enough of his own."

"Indeed and he has. Peter's mischancier than you are, Hilary, on the whole, and I will not leave him and Tommy to get lost or broken by themselves. Don't be so silly, Peter; of course you're coming with us."

"I think," said Peter, "that Thomas and I will perhaps stay in London. You see, *I* can't, probably, get work on 'The Nationalist' and it's doubtful what I could do in Dublin. I suppose I can get work of a sort in London; enough to provide Thomas with milk, though possibly not all from one cow."

"I daresay. And who'd look after the mite, I'd like to know, while you're earning his milk?"

"Oh, the landlady, I should think. Everyone likes Thomas; he's remarkably popular."

Afterwards Hilary said to Peggy, "Really, Peggy, I see no reason why Peter should be dragged about with us in the future. The joint *ménage* has not, in the past, been such a success that we need want to perpetuate it. In fact, though, of course, it is pleasant to have Peter in the house...."

"Indeed it is, the darling," put in Peggy.

"One can't deny that disasters have come upon us extraordinarily fast since he came to live with us in Venice two years ago. First he discovered things that annoyed him in my private affairs, which was extremely disagreeable for all of us, and really he was rather unnecessarily officious about that; in fact, I consider that it was owing largely to the line he took that things reached their final very trying *dénouement*. Since then disaster upon disaster has come upon us; Peter's unfortunate marriage, and consequent serious expenses, including the child now left upon his hands (really, you know, that was an exceedingly stupid step that Peter took; I tried to dissuade him at the time, but of course it was no use). And he is so very frequently ill; so am I, you will say"—(Peggy didn't, because Hilary wasn't, as a matter of fact, ill quite so often as he believed)—"but two crocks in a household are twice as inconvenient as one. And now there has been this unpleasant jar with the Urquharts. Peter, by his rudeness to them, has finally severed the connection, and we can hope for nothing from that quarter in future. And I

- 167 -

am not sure that I choose to have living with me a much younger brother who has influential friends of his own in whom he insists that we shall have neither part nor lot. I strongly object to the way Peter spoke to us on that occasion; it was extremely offensive."

"Oh, don't be such a goose, Hilary. The boy only lost his temper for a moment, and I'm sure that happens seldom enough. And as to the rest of it, I don't like the way you speak of him, as if he was the cause of our mischances, and as if his being so mischancey himself wasn't a reason why we should all stick together, and him with that scrap of a child, too; though I will say Peter's a handier creature with a child than anyone would think. I suppose it's the practice he's had handling other costly things that break easy.... Well, have it your own way, Hilary. Only mind, if Peter *wants* to come with us, he surely shall. I'm not going to leave him behind like a left kitten. And I'd love to have him, for he makes sunshine in the house when things are blackest."

"Lately Peter has appeared to me to be rather depressed," said Hilary, and Peggy too had perceived that this was so. It was something so new in Peter that it called for notice.

There was needed no further dispute between Peggy and Hilary, for Peter said that he and Thomas preferred to stay in London.

"I can probably find a job of some sort to keep us. I might with luck get a place as shop-walker. That always looks a glorious life. You merely walk about and say, 'Yes, madam? This way for hose, madam.' Something to live on and nothing to do, as the poet says. But I expect they are difficult places to get, without previous experience. Short of that, I could be one of the men round stations that open people's cab doors and take the luggage out; or even a bus-conductor, who knows? Oh, there are lots of openings. But in Dublin I feel my talents might be lost.... Thomas and I will move into more modest apartments, and go in for plain living and high thinking."

"You poor little dears," said Peggy, and kissed both of them. "Well, it'll be plain living for the lot of us, that's obvious, and lucky too to get that.... I'd love to have you two children with us, but ..."

But Peter, to whom other people's minds were as books that who runs may read, had no intention of coming with them. That faculty of intuition of Peter's had drawbacks as well as advantages. He knew, as well as if Hilary had said so, that Hilary considered their life together a disastrous series of mishaps, largely owing to Peter, and that he did not desire to continue it. He knew precisely what was Denis Urquhart's point of view and state of feelings towards himself and his family, and how unbridgeable that gulf was. He knew why Lucy was stopping away, and would stop away (for if other people's thoughts were to him as pebbles in running water, hers were pebbles seen white and lucid in a still, clear pool. And he knew very well that he relieved Peggy's kind heart when he said he and Thomas would stop in London; for to Peggy anything was better than to worry her poor old Hilary more than need be.

So, before March was out, about St. Cuthbert's day, in fact, Hilary Margerison and his family left England for a more distressful country, to seek their fortunes fresh, and Peter and his family sought modest apartments in a little street behind St. Austin's Church, where the apartments are very modest indeed.

"Are they too modest for you, Thomas?" Peter asked dubiously. "And do you too much hate the Girl?"

The Girl was the landlady's daughter, and undertook for a small consideration to look after Thomas while Peter was out, and feed him at suitable intervals. Thomas and Peter did rather hate her, for she was a slatternly girl, matching her mother and her mother's apartments, and didn't always take her curlers off till the evening, and said "Boo" to Thomas, merely because he was young—a detestable habit, Peter and Thomas considered. Peter had to make a great deal of sensible conversation to Thomas, to make up.

"I'm sorry," Peter apologised, "but, you see, Thomas, it's all we can afford. You don't earn anything at all, and I only earn a pound a week, which is barely enough to keep you in drink. I don't deserve even that, for I don't address envelopes well; but I suppose they know it's such a detestable job that they haven't the face to give me less."

Peter was addressing envelopes because a Robinson relative had given him the job, and he hadn't the nerve to refuse it. He couldn't well refuse it, because of Thomas. Uncompanioned by Thomas he would probably have chosen instead to sweep a crossing or play a barrel-organ, or stand at a street corner with outstretched hat (though this last would only have done for a summer engagement, as Peter didn't like the winds that play round street corners in winter). But Thomas was very much there, and had to be provided for; so Peter copied letters and addressed envelopes and earned twenty shillings weekly, and out of it paid for Thomas's drink and Thomas's Girl and his own food, and beds and a sitting-room and fires and laundry for both, and occasional luxuries in the way of wooden animals for Thomas to play with. So they were not extremely poor; they were respectably well-to-do. For Thomas's sake, Peter supposed it was worth while not to be extremely poor, even though it meant addressing envelopes and living in a great grey prison-house of a city, where one only surmised the first early pushings of the spring beyond the encompassing gloom.

Peter used to tell Thomas about that, in order that he might know something of the joyous world beyond the walls. He told Thomas in March, taking time by the forelock, about the early violets that were going some time to open blue eyes in the ditches by the roads where the spring winds walk; about the blackthorn that would suddenly make a white glory of the woods; about the green, sticky budding of the larches, and the keen sweet smell of them, and the damp fragrance of the roaming wind that would blow over river-flooded fields, smelling of bonfires and wet earth. He took him through the seasons, telling him of the blown golden armies of the daffodils that marched out for Easter, and the fragrant white glory of the may; and the pale pink stars of the hedge-roses, and the yellow joy of buttercup fields wherein cows stand knee-deep and munch, in order to give Thomas sweet white milk.

"Ugh," said Thomas, making a face, and Peter answered, "Yes, I know; sometimes they come upon an onion-flower and eat that, and that's not nice, of course. But mostly it's grass and buttercups and clover." Then he told him of hot July roads, where the soft white dust lies, while the horses and the cows stand up to their middles in cool streams beneath the willows and switch their tails, and the earth dreams through the year's hot noon; and of August, the world's welfare and the earth's warming-pan, and how, in the fayre rivers, swimming is a sweet exercise. "And my birthday comes then. Oh, 'tis the merry time, wherein honest neighbours make good cheer, and God is glorified in his blessings on the earth. Then cometh September, Thomas"—Peter was half talking, half reading out of a book he had got to amuse Thomas—"then cometh September, and then he (that's you, Thomas) doth freshly beginne to garnish his house and make provision of needfull things for to live in winter, which draweth very nere.... There are a few nice things in September; ripe plums and pears and nuts—(no, nuts aren't nice, because our teeth aren't good, are they; at least mine aren't, and you've only got one and a half); but anyhow, plums, and a certain amount of yellow sunshine, and Thomas's birthday. But on the whole it's too near the end of things; and in briefe, I thus conclude of it, I hold it the Winter's forewarning and the Summer's farewell. Adieu.... We won't pursue the year further, my dear; the rest is silence and impenetrable gloom, anyhow in this corner of the world, and doesn't bear thinking about."

Thus did Peter talk to Thomas of an evening, when they sat together after tea over the fire.

Sometimes he told him news of the world of men. One evening he said to him, very gently and pitifully, "Dear old man, your mother's dead. For her sake, one's glad, I suppose. You and I must try to look at it from her point of view. She's escaped from a poor business. Some day I'll read you the letter she wrote to you and me as she lay dying; but not yet, for I never read you sad things, do I? But some day you may be glad to know that she had thoughts for you at the last. She was sorry she left us, Thomas; horribly, dreadfully sorry.... I wish she hadn't been. I wish she could have gone on being happy till the end. It was my fault that she did it, and it didn't even make her happy. And I suppose it killed her at the last; or would she anyhow have escaped that way before long? But I took more care of her than he did.... And now she'll never come back to us. I've thought sometimes, Thomas, that perhaps she would; that perhaps she would get tired of him, so tired that she would leave him and come back to us, and then you'd have had a mother to do for you instead of only me and the Girl. Poor little Thomas; you'll never have a mother now. I'm sorry, sorry, sorry about it. Sorry for you, and sorry for her, and sorry for all of us. It's a pitiful world, Thomas, it seems. I wonder how you're going to get through it."

Never before had he talked to Thomas like that. He had been used to speak to him of new-burnisht joys and a world of treasure. But of late Peter had been conscious of increasing effort in being cheerful before Thomas. It was as if the little too much that breaks had been laid upon him and under it he was breaking. For the first time he was seeing the world not as a glorious treasure-place full of glad things for touch and sight and hearing, full of delightful people and absurd jokes, but as a grey and lonely sea through which one drifted rudderless towards a lee shore. He supposed that there was, somewhere, a lee shore; a place where the winds, having blown their uttermost, ceased to blow, and where wrecked things were cast up at last broken beyond all mending and beyond all struggling, to find the peace of the utterly lost. He had not got there yet; he and his broken boat were struggling in the grey cold waters, which had swept all his cargo from him, bale by bale. From him that hath not shall indeed be taken away even that which he hath.

It was Thomas who caused Peter to think of these things newly; Thomas, who was starting life with so poor a heritage. For Thomas, so like himself, Peter foresaw the same progressive wreckage. Thomas too, having already lost a mother, would lose later all he loved; he would give to some friend all he was and had, and the friend would drop him in the mud and leave him there, and the cold bitterness as of death would go over Thomas's head. He would, perhaps, love a woman too, and the woman would leave him quite alone, not coming near him in his desolation, because he loved her. He would also lose his honour, his profession, and the beautiful things he loved to handle and play with. "And then, when you've lost everything, and perhaps been involved in some of my disgraces, you'll think that at least you and I can stick together and go under together and help each other a little. And I daresay you'll find that I shall say, 'No, I'm going off to Ireland, or Italy, or somewhere; I've had enough of you, and you can jolly well sink or swim by yourself'—so you see you won't have even me to live for in the end, just when you want me most. That's the sort of thing that happens.... Oh, what chance have you?" said Peter very bitterly, huddled, elbows on knees, over the chilly fire, while Thomas slumbered in a shawl on the rug.

Bitterness was so strange in Peter, so odd and new, that Thomas was disturbed by it, and woke and wailed, as if his world was tumbling about his ears.

Peter too felt it strange and new, and laughed a little at it and himself as he comforted Thomas. But his very laughter was new and very dreary. He picked Thomas up in his arms and held him close, a warm little whimpering bundle. Then it was as if the touch of the small live thing that was his own and had no one in the world but him to fend for it woke in him a new instinct. There sprang up in him swiftly, new-born out of the travail of great bitterness, a sharp anger against life, against fate, against the whole universe of nature and man. To lose and lose and lose—how that goes on and on through a lifetime! But at last it seems that the limit is reached, something snaps and breaks, and the loser rises up, philosopher no more, to take and grasp and seize. The lust to possess, to wring something for Thomas and himself out of life that had torn from them so much—it sprang upon him like a wild beast, and fastened deep fangs into his soul and will.

Outside, a small April wind stirred the air of the encompassing city, a faint breath from a better world, seeming to speak of life and hope and new beginnings.

Peter, laying Thomas gently on a chair, went to the open window and leant out, looking into the veil of the unhappy streets that hid an exquisite world. Exquisiteness was surely there, as always. Mightn't he too, he and Thomas, snatch some of it for themselves? The old inborn lust for things concrete, lovely things to handle and hold, caught Peter by the throat. In that hour he could have walked without a scruple into an empty house or shop and carried away what he could of its beauties, and brought them home to Thomas, saying, "Anyhow, here's something for us to go on with." He was in the mood in which some people take to drink, only Peter didn't like any drinks except non-alcoholic ones; or to reckless gambling, only he didn't find gambling amusing; or to some adventure of love, only to Peter love meant one thing only, and that was beyond his reach.

But when he had put Thomas to bed, in his little common cheap night-shirt, he went out into the streets with his weekly earnings in his pockets and spent them. He spent every penny he had. First he went to a florist's and bought daffodils, in great golden sheaves. Then he went to a toyshop and got a splendid family of fluffy beasts, and a musical box, and a Noah's Ark, and a flute. He had spent all his money by then, so he pawned his watch and signet ring and bought Thomas some pretty cambric clothes and a rocking cradle. He had nothing else much to pawn. But he badly wanted some Japanese paintings to put in the place of the pictures that at present adorned the sitting-room. Thomas and he must have something nice and gay to look at, instead of the Royal Family and the Monarch of the Glen and "Grace Sufficient" worked in crewels. So he went into a shop in Holborn and chose some paintings, and ordered them to be sent up, and said, "Please enter them to me," so firmly that they did. Having done that once, he repeated it at several other shops, and sometimes they obeyed him and sometimes said that goods could not be sent up without pre-payment. Pre-payment (or, indeed, as far as Peter could look forward, post-payment) being out of the question, those goods had to be left where they were. But Peter, though handicapped by shabby attire, had an engaging way with him, and most shopmen are trustful and obliging. If they lost by the transaction, thought Peter recklessly, it was their turn to lose, not his. It was his turn to acquire, and he had every intention of doing so. He had a glorious evening, till the shops shut. Then he went home, and found that the daffodils had come, and he filled the room with them, converting its dingy ugliness into a shining glory. Then he took down all the horrible pictures and texts and stacked them behind the sofa, awaiting the arrival of the Japanese paintings. He thought Thomas would like the paintings as much as he did himself. Their room in future should be a bright and pleasant place, fit for human beings to live in. He cleared the chimney-piece of its horrid, tinkling ornaments to leave space for his brown pottery jars full of daffodils. He put the ornaments with the pictures behind the sofa, and when the Girl came in with his supper requested her at her leisure to remove them.

"I have been getting some new pictures, you see," he told her, and was annoyed at the way her round eyes widened. Why shouldn't he get as many new pictures as he chose, without being gaped at?

There was more gaping next day, when his purchases were sent up. He had warned his landlady and the Girl beforehand, that they might not tell the messengers it must be a mistake and send them away, on what would, no doubt be their stupid and impertinent impulse. So they gaped and took them in, and Peter hurried back early from his work and fetched Thomas in to watch him open parcels and admire the contents. He spread bright rugs over the horse-hair sofa and chairs, and flung big soft cushions about them, and said "Hurrah! The first time I've been really comfortable since I left Cambridge." Then he bathed Thomas and put him into a new little soft cambric night-shirt, and put him to bed in the rocking-cradle. Thomas was delighted with it all. He had no doubt inherited Peter's love of all things bright and beautiful, and now for the first time he had them.

"That's more the style, isn't it, old man?" said Peter, stretching himself among cushions in the arm-chair. Thomas agreed that it was, and the two epicureans took their ease among the pleasures of the senses.

"What next?" Peter wondered. "We must have more things still, mustn't we? Nice things of all sorts; not only the ones we can buy. But we must begin with the ones we can buy.... Mrs. Baker will have to wait for her rent for a time; I can't spare any for that.... I've a good mind, Thomas, to take a whole holiday; a long one. Chuck the envelopes and take to living like a lord, on tick. It's wonderful how far tick will carry you, if you try. Muffins for tea, you see, Thomas, only you can't have any. Well, what's the matter? Why shouldn't I have muffins for tea? You've got milk, haven't you, and I'm not getting a share in that. Don't be grudging.... But we want more than muffins and milk, Thomas; and more than cushions and daffodils and nice pictures. We want a good time. We want friends; we want someone to love us; we want a holiday. If Leslie was in England I'd go and say, 'Thomas and I are coming to stay with you for a time, and you've just got to fork out supplies for us and let us spend them.' Leslie would do it, too. But people are always away when one wants them most.... Oh, hang it all, Thomas, I'm not going on with those horrible envelopes; I'm not. I'm going to do things I like. Why shouldn't I? Why *shouldn't* I? Lots of people do; all the best people. I shall give notice to-morrow. No, I shan't; I shall just not turn up, then I shan't be bothered with questions.... And we're not going on with the friends we have here—Mrs. Baker, and the Girl, and the other envelope-gummers. No; we're going to insist on having nice amusing friends to play with; friends who are nicer than we are. The Girl isn't so nice, not by a long way. Rodney is; but he's too busy to be bothered with us much. We want friends of leisure. We will have them; we *will*. Why should we be chucked out and left outside people's doors, just because they're tired of us? The thing that matters is that we're not tired of them.... To-morrow, Thomas, you and I are going down to a place called Astleys, in Berkshire, to visit some friends of ours. If they don't want us, they can just lump us; good for them. Why should they always have only the things they want? Be ready at nine, old man, and we'll catch a train as soon after that as may be."

Thomas laughed, thinking it a splendid plan. He had never seen Astleys in Berkshire, but he knew it to be a good place, from Peter's voice when he mentioned it.

"But I don't want to excite you so late at night," said Peter, "so don't think any more about it, but go to sleep, if you've finished that milk. Does your head ache? Mine does. That's the worst of weak heads; they always ache just when things are getting interesting. But I don't care; we're going to have things—things to like; we're going to get hold of them somehow, if we die in gaol for it; and that's worth a headache or two. Someone says something about having nothing and yet possessing all things; it's one of the things with no meaning that people do say, and that make me so angry. It ought to be having nothing and *then* possessing all things; because that's the way it's going to be with us. Good night, Thomas; you may go to sleep now."

Thomas did so; and Peter lay on the sofa and gazed at the daffodils in the brown jars that filled the room with light.

CHAPTER XIX

THE NEW LIFE

Peter, with Thomas over his shoulder, stepped out of the little station into a radiant April world. Between green, budding hedges, between ditches where blue violets and joyous-eyed primroses peered up out of wet grass, a brown road ran, gleaming with puddles that glinted up at the blue sky and the white clouds that raced before a merry wind.

Peter said, "Do you like it, old man? Do you?" but Thomas's heart was too full for speech. He was seeing the radiant wonderland he had heard of; it crowded upon him, a vivid, many-splendoured thing, and took his breath away. There were golden ducklings by the grassy roadside, and lambs crying to him from the fields, and cows, eating (one hoped) sweet grass, with their little calves beside them. A glorious scene. The gay wind caught Peter by the throat and brought sudden tears to his eyes, so long used to looking on grey streets.

He climbed over a stile in the hedge and took a field path that ran up to a wood—the wood way, as he remembered, to Astleys. Peter had stayed at Astleys more than once in old days, with Denis. He remembered the keen, damp fragrance of the wood in April; the smooth stems of the beeches, standing up out of the mossy ground, and the way the primroses glimmered, moon-like, among the tangled ground-ivy; and the way the birds made every budding bough rock with their clamorous delight. It was a happy wood, full of small creatures and eager happenings and adventurous quests; a fit road to take questers after happiness to their goal. In itself it seemed almost the goal already, so alive was it and full of joy. Was there need to travel further? Very vividly the impression was borne in on Peter (possibly on Thomas too) that there was no need; that here, perhaps round the next twist of the little brown path, was not the way but the achievement.

And, rounding the next bend, they knew it to be so; for above the path, sitting at a beech-tree's foot among creeping ivy, with head thrown back against the smooth grey stem, and gathered primroses in either hand, was Lucy.

Looking round at the sound of feet on the path, she saw them, and smiled a little, not as if surprised, nor as if she had to change the direction of her thought, but taking them into her vision of the spring woods as if they were natural dwellers in it.

Peter stood still on the path and looked up at her and smiled too. He said, "Oh, Lucy, Thomas and I have come."

She bent down towards them, and reached out her hands, dropping the primroses, for Thomas. Peter gave her Thomas, and she laid him on her lap, cradled on her two arms, and smiled, still silently.

Peter sat down on the sloping ground just below her, his back against another tree.

"We've come to see you and Denis. You won't come to see us, so we had to take it into our own hands. We decided, Thomas and I, two days ago, that we weren't going on any longer in this absurd way. We're going to have a good time. So we went out and got things—lots of lovely things. And I've chucked my horrible work. And we've come to see you. Will Denis mind? I can't help it if he does; we've got to do it."

Lucy nodded, understanding. "I know. In thinking about you lately, I've known it was coming to this, rather soon. I didn't quite know when. But I knew you must have a good time."

After a little while she went on, and her clear voice fell strange and tranquil on the soft wood silence:

"What I didn't quite know was whether you would come and take it—the good time—or whether I should have to come and bring it to you. I was going to have come, you know. I had quite settled that. It's taken me a long time to know that I must: but I do know it now."

"You didn't come," said Peter suddenly, and his hands clenched sharply over the ivy trails and tore them out of the earth, and his face whitened to the lips. "All this time ... you didn't come ... you kept away...." The memory of that black emptiness shook him. He hadn't realised till it was nearly over quite how bad it had been, that emptiness.

The two pale faces, so like, were quivering with the same pain, the same keen recognition of it.

"No," Lucy whispered. "I didn't come ... I kept away."

Peter said, steadying his voice, "But now you will. Now I may come to you. Oh, I know why you kept away. You thought it would be less hard for me if I didn't see you. But don't again. It isn't less hard. It's—it's impossible. First Denis, then you. I can't bear it. I only want to see you sometimes; just to feel you're there. I won't be grasping, Lucy."

"Yes," said Lucy calmly, "you will. You're going to be grasping in future. You're going to take and have.... Peter, my dear, haven't you reached the place I've reached yet? Don't you know that between you and me it's got to be all or nothing? I've learnt that now. So I tried nothing. But that won't do. So now it's going to be all.... I'm coming to Thomas and you. We three together will find nice things for one another."

Peter's forehead was on his drawn-up knees. He felt her hand touch his head, and shivered a little.

"Denis," he whispered.

She answered, "Denis has everything. Denis won't miss me among so much. Denis is the luckiest, the most prosperous, the most succeeding person I know. Peter, let me try and tell you about Denis and me."

She paused for a moment, leaning her head back against the beech-tree and looking up wide-eyed at the singing roof overhead.

"You know how it was, I expect," she said, with the confidence they always had in each other's knowledge, that saved so many words. "How Denis came among us, among you and me and father and Felicity and our unprosperous, dingy friends, and how he was all bright and shining and beautiful, and I loved him, partly because he was so bright and beautiful, and a great deal because you did, and you and I have always loved the same things. And so I married him; and at the time, and oh, for ever so long, I didn't understand how it was; how it was all wrong, and how he and I didn't really belong to each other a bit, because he's in one lot of people, and I'm in another. He's in the top lot, that gets things, and I'm in the under lot, with you and father and all the poorer people who don't get things, and have to find life nice in spite of it. I'd deserted really; and father and Felicity knew I had; only I didn't know, or I'd never have done it. I only got to understand gradjully" (Lucy's long words were apt to be a blur, like a child's), "when I saw what a lot of good things Denis and his friends had, and how I had to have them too, 'cause I couldn't get away from them; and oh, Peter, I've felt smothered beneath them! They're so heavy and so rich, and shut people out from the rest of the world that hasn't got them, so that they can't hear or see each other. It's like living in a palace in the middle of dreadful slums, and never caring. Because you *can't* care, however much you try, in the palace, the same as you can if you're down in the middle of the poorness and the emptiness. Wasn't it Christ who said how hardly rich men shall enter into the kingdom of heaven? And it's harder still for them to enter into the other kingdoms, which aren't heaven at all. It's hard for them to step out from where they are and enter anywhere else. Peter, can anyone ever leave their world and go into another. I have failed, you see. Denis would never even begin to try; he wouldn't see any object. I don't believe it can be done. Except perhaps by very great people. And we're not that. People like you and me and Denis belong where we're born and brought up. Even for the ones who try, to change, it's hard. And most of us don't try at all, or care ... Denis hardly cares, really. He's generous with money; he lets me give away as much as I like; but he doesn't care himself. Unhappiness and bad luck and disgrace don't touch him; he doesn't want to have anything to do with them; he doesn't like them. Even his friends, the people he likes, he gets tired of directly they begin to go under. You know that. And it's dreadful, Peter. I hate it, being comfortable up there and not seeing and not hearing and not caring. Seems to me we just live to have a good time. Well, of course, people ought to do that, it's the thing to live for, and I usen't to mind before I was rich, and father and Felicity and you and I had a good time together. But when you're rich and among rich people, and have a good time not because you make it for yourself out of all the common things that everyone shares—the sunshine and the river and the nice things in the streets—but have a special corner of good things marked off for you, then it gets dreadful. 'Tisn't that one thinks one ought to be doing more for other people; I don't think I've that sort of conscience much; only that *I don't belong*. I can't help thinking of all the down-below people, the disreputable, unlucky people, who fail and don't get things, and I know that's where I really belong. It's like being born in one family and going and living in another. You never fit in really; your proper family is calling out to you all the time. Oh, not only because they aren't rich and lucky, but because they really suit you best, in little ways as well as big ways. You understand them, and they understand you. All the butlers and footmen and lady's-maids frighten me so; I don't like telling them to do things; they're so—so solemn and respectable. And I don't like creatures to be killed, and I don't like eating them afterwards. But Denis and his friends and the servants and everyone thinks it's idiotic to be a vegetarian. Denis says vegetarians are nearly all cranks and bounders, and long-haired men or short-haired women. Well, I can't help it; I s'pose that shows where I really and truly belong, though I don't like short-haired women; it's so ugly, and they talk so loud very often. And there it is again; I dislike short hair 'cause of that, but Denis dislikes it 'cause *it isn't done*. That's so often his reason; and he means not done by his partic'lar lot of top-room people.... So you see, Peter, I don't belong there, do I? I don't belong any more than you do."

Peter shook his head. "I never supposed you did, of course."

"Well," she said next, "what you're thinking now is that Denis wants me. He *doesn't*—not much. He's not awf'ly fond of me, Peter; I think he's rather tired of me, 'cause I often want to do tiresome things, that aren't done. I think he knows I don't belong. He's very kind and pleasant always; but he'd be as happy without me, and much happier with another wife who fitted in more. He only took me as a sort of luxury; he didn't really need me. And you do; you and Thomas. You want me much more than he ever did, or ever could. You want me so much that even if Denis did want me a great deal, I should come to you, because you want me more, and because all his life he's had the things he wanted, and now it's your turn. 'Tisn't *fair*. Why shouldn't you have things too—you and Thomas? Thomas and you and I can be happy together with no money and nothing else much; we can make our own good time as we go along, if we have each other. Oh, Peter, let's!"

She bent down to him, reaching out her hands, and Thomas smiled on her lap. So for a moment the three stayed, and the woods were hushed round them, waiting. Then in the green roof above a riot of shrill, sweet triumph broke the hush, and Peter leaped to his feet and laughed.

"Oh, Lucy, let's. Why not? I told Thomas the day before yesterday that we were going to have a good time now. Well, then, let's have it. Who's to prevent it? It's our turn; it's our turn. We'll begin from now and take things and keep them.... Oh, d'you mean it, Lucy? D'you mean you'll come and play with us, for ever and ever?"

"'Course I will," she said, simply, like a child.

He fell on his knees beside her and leant on his hands and peered into Thomas's face.

"Do you hear, Thomas? She's coming; she's coming to us, for always. You wanted her, didn't you? You wanted her nearly as much as I did, only you didn't know it so well.... Oh, Lucy, oh, Lucy, oh, Lucy ... I've wanted you so ..."

"I've wanted you too," she said. "I haven't talked about that part of it, 'cause it's so obvious, and I knew you knew. All the time, even when I thought I cared for Denis, I was only half a person without you. Of course, I always knew that, without thinking much about it, from the time we were babies. Only I didn't know it meant this; I thought it was more like being brother and sister, and that we could both be happy just seeing each other sometimes. It's only rather lately that I've known it had to be everything. There's nothing at all to say about the way we care, Peter, because it's such an old stale thing; it's always been, and I s'pose it always will be. 'Tisn't a new, surprising, sudden thing, like my falling in love with Denis. It's so deep, it's got root right down at the bottom, before we can either of us remember. It's like this ivy that's all over the ground, and out of which all the little flowers and things grow. And when it's like that...."

"Yes," said Peter, "when it's like that, there's only one way to take. What's the good of fighting against life? We're not going to fight any more, Thomas and I. We're going simply to grab everything we can get. The more things the better; I always knew that. Who wants to be a miserable

Franciscan on the desert hills? It's so unutterably profane. Here begins the new life."

They sat in silence together on the creeping, earth-rooted ivy out of which all the little flowers and things grew; and all round them the birds sang how it was spring-time. The fever of the spring was in Peter's blood, flowing through his veins like fire, and he knew only that life was good and lovely and was calling to the three of them to come and live it, to take the April paths together through green woods. The time was not long past, though it seemed endless years ago, when he would have liked them to be four, when he would have liked Denis to come too, because he had so loved Denis that to hurt him and leave him would have been unthinkable. But the time was past. Peter and Lucy had come to the place where they couldn't share and didn't want to, and no love but one matured. They had left civilisation, left friendship, which is part of civilisation, behind, and knew only the primitive, selfish, human love that demands all of body and soul. They needed no words to explain to one another their change of view. For always they had leaped to one another's thoughts and emotions and desires.

Lucy said wistfully, after a time, "Denis will never see us again."

But thoughts of Denis did not, could not, dim the radiant vision of roads running merrily through the country of the spring.

Thomas here said that it was milk-time, and Peter, who had thoughtfully remembered to bring his bottle, produced it from his pocket and applied it, while Lucy looked on and laughed.

"In future," she said, "I shall take over that job."

"I wonder," murmured Peter, "exactly what we contemplate living on. Shall we sell boot-laces on the road, or play a barrel-organ, or what?"

"Oh, anything that's nice. But I've got a little, you know. Father hadn't much, but there was something for Felicity and me. It's seemed nothing, compared with what I've been living on lately; but it will look quite a lot when it's all we've got.... Father'd be glad, Peter, if he knew. He'd say we ought to do it, I know he would. It's partly him I've been hearing all this time, calling and calling to me to come away and live. He did so hate fat and sweetness and all smothering things. They just bored him dreadfully. He wouldn't ever come and stay with us, you know.... Oh, and I've written to Felicity, telling her what I meant to do. I don't quite know what she'll say; nobody ever does know, with Felicity.... Now I'm going back to the house, Peter, and you and Thomas must go back too. But first we'll settle what to do, and when to do it."

It didn't take much settling, between three people who saw no difficulties anywhere, but said simply, "Let us do this," and did it, as children do. But such plans as they thought desirable they made, then parted.

"I shall tell Denis," said Lucy, "I must do that. I'll explain to him all I can, and leave the rest. But not yet. I shall tell him on Sunday night."

"Yes," Peter agreed, simply, while the shadow fell again momentarily on his vision. "You must do that, of course...."

He left it at that; for Denis he had no words.

Lucy got up, and laid Thomas in Peter's arms.

"How much I've talked and talked, Peter. I've never talked so much before, have I? And I s'pose I never will again. But it had to be all said out once. I'm tired of only thinking things, even though I knew you understood. Saying things makes them alive. They're alive now, and always will be. So good-bye."

They stood and looked at one another for a moment in silence, then turned and took their opposite ways.

Peter didn't go back to London till the late afternoon. He had things to show Thomas on this his first day in the country. So he took him a long walk, and Thomas sat in meadows and got a near view of cows and sheep, and saw Peter paddle in a stream and try to catch minnows in an old tin pot that he found.

Another thing that he found, or rather that found them, was a disreputable yellow dog. He was accompanying a tramp and his wife along the road. When the tramp sat down and untied a handkerchief full of apple pie and cold potatoes (tramps have delightful things to eat as a rule) the dog came near and asked for his share, and was violently removed to a distance by the tramp's boot. He cried and ran through the hedge and came upon Peter and Thomas, who were sitting on the other side, in a field. Peter looked over the hedge and said, "Is he yours?" and was told, "Mine! No, 'e ain't. 'E's been follerin' us for miles, and the more I kick 'im the more 'e follers. Wish someone'd pison 'im. I'm sick of 'im." His wife, who had the weary, hopeless, utterly resigned face of some female tramps, said, "'E'll do for 'im soon, my man will," without much interest.

"I'll take him with me," said Peter, and drew the disreputable creature to him and gently rubbed his bruised side, and saw that he had rather a nice face, meant to be cheerful, and friendly and hopeful eyes. Indeed, he must be friendly and hopeful to have followed such companions so far.

"Will you be our dog?" said Peter to him. "Will you come walking with us in future, and have a little bit of whatever we get? And shall we call you San Francesco, because you like disreputable people and love your brother, the sun, and keep company with your little sisters, the fleas? Very good, then. This is Thomas, and you may lick his face very gently, but remember that he is smaller than you and has to be tenderly treated lest he break."

San Francesco stayed with them through the afternoon, and accompanied them back to London, smuggled under a seat, because Peter couldn't afford a ticket for him. He proved a likeable being on further acquaintance, with a merry grin and an amused cock of the eye; obviously one who took the world's vagaries with humorous patience. Peter conveyed him from Paddington to Mary Street with some difficulty, and bought a bone for him from a cat's-meat-what-orfers man, and took him up to the bright and beautiful sitting-room. Then he told his landlady that he was about to leave her.

"It isn't that I'm not satisfied, you know," he added, fearing to hurt her, "but I'm going to give up lodgings altogether. I'm going abroad, to Italy, on Monday."

"*I* see." Mrs. Baker saw everything in a moment. Her young gentleman had obviously been over-spending his income (all these new things must have cost a pretty penny), and had discovered, what many discover, that flight was the only remedy.

"About the rent," she began, "and the bills ..."

Peter said, "Oh, I'll pay you the rent and the bills before I go. I promise I will. But I can't pay much else, you know, Mrs. Baker. So when people come to dun me, tell them I've gone no one knows where. I'm awfully sorry about it, but I've simply no money left."

His smile, as always, softened her, and she nodded.

"I'll deal with 'em, sir ... I knew you was over-spending yourself, as it were; I could have told you, but I didn't like. You'd always lived so cheap and quiet till the day before yesterday; then all these new things so suddenly. Ader and I said as you must 'ave come in for some money, or else as (you'll excuse me, sir) you was touched in the 'ead."

"I wasn't," said Peter. "Not in the least. I wanted the things, so I got them. But now I come to think of it, I shan't want most of them any more, as I'm going away, so I think I'll just return them to the shops they came from. Of course they won't be pleased, but they'll prefer it to losing the money *and* the things, I suppose, won't they. And we haven't spoiled them a bit, except that cushion Francesco has just walked over, and that can be cleaned, I expect. I had to have them, you know, just when I wanted them; I couldn't have borne not to; but I don't really need them any more, because I'm going to have other things now. Oh, I'm talking too much, and you want to be cooking the supper, don't you, and I want to put Thomas to bed."

CHAPTER XX

THE LAST LOSS

Three days later it was Easter Day. In the evening, about half-past nine, when Thomas lay sleeping and Peter was packing the rugs and cushions and pictures he hadn't paid for into brown paper parcels (a tedious job), Rodney came in. Peter hadn't seen him for some time.

"What on earth," said Rodney, lighting his pipe and sitting down, "are you doing with all that upholstery? Has someone been sending you Easter presents? Well, I'm glad you're getting rid of them as speedily as may be."

Peter said ruefully, because he was tired of the business, "The stupid things aren't paid for. So I'm packing them up to be sent back directly the shops open again. I can't afford them, you see. Already most of my belongings are in pawn."

"I see." Rodney wasn't specially struck by this; it was the chronic condition of many of his friends, who were largely of the class who pawn their clothes on Monday and redeem them on Saturday to wear for Sunday, and pawn them again, paying, if they can afford it, a penny extra to have the dresses hung up so that they don't crush.

"A sudden attack of honesty," Rodney commented. "Well, I'm glad, because I don't see what you want to cumber yourself with all those cushions and rugs for. You're quite comfortable enough without them."

Peter said, "Thomas and I wanted nice things to look at. We were tired of horse-hair and 'Grace Sufficient'. Thomas is fastidious."

Rodney put a large finger on Thomas' head.

"Thomas isn't such a fool.... Hullo, there's another of you." Francesco woke and came out of his corner and laid his nose on Rodney's knee with his confiding grin.

"Yes, that's San Francesco. Rather nice, isn't he. He's coming with us too. I called him Francesco instead of Francis that he might feel at home in Italy."

"Oh, in Italy."

Peter hadn't meant to tell Rodney that, because he didn't think that Rodney would approve, and he wanted to avoid an argument. But he had let it out, of course; he could never keep anything in.

"That's where we're going to-morrow, to seek our fortunes. Won't it be rather good in Italy now? We don't know what we shall do when we get there, or where we shall go; but something nice, for sure."

"I'm glad," said Rodney. "It's a good country in the spring. Shall you walk the roads with Thomas slung over your back, or what?"

"I don't know. Partly, I daresay. But we want to find some little place between the hills and the sea, and stay there. Perhaps for always; I don't know. It's going to be extraordinarily nice, anyhow."

Rodney glanced at him, caught by the ring in his voice, a ring he hadn't heard for long. He didn't quite understand Peter. When last he saw him, he had been very far through, alarmingly near the bottom. Was this recovery natural grace, or had something happened? It seemed to Rodney rather admirable, and he looked appreciatively at Peter's cheerful face and happy eyes.

"Good," he said. "Good—splendid!"

And then Peter, meeting his pleased look and understanding it, winced back from it, and coloured, and bent over his brown paper and string. He valued Rodney's appreciation, a thing not easily won. He felt that in this moment he had won it, as he had never won it before. For he knew that Rodney liked pluck, and was thinking him plucky.

Against his will he muttered, half beneath his breath, "Oh, it isn't really what *you* call good. It is good, you know: *I* think it's good; but you won't. You'll call it abominable."

"Oh," said Rodney.

Peter went on, with a new violence, "I know all you'll say about it, so I'm not going to give you the opportunity of saying it till I'm gone. You needn't think I'm going to tell you now and let you tell me I'm wrong. I'm not wrong; and if I am I don't care. Please don't stay any more; I'd rather you weren't here to-night. I don't want to tell you anything; only I had just got to say that, because you were thinking.... Oh, do go now."

Rodney sat quite still and looked at him, into him, through him, beyond him. Then he said, "You needn't tell me anything. I know. Lucy and you are going together."

Peter stood up, rather unsteadily.

"Well? That's not clever. Any fool could have guessed that."

"Yes. And any fool could guess what I'm going to say about it, too. You know it all already, of course...."

Rodney was groping for words, helplessly, blindly.

"Peter, I didn't know you had it in you to be a cad."

Peter was putting books into a portmanteau, and did not answer.

"You mean to do that ... to Denis...."

Peter put in socks and handkerchiefs.

"And to Lucy.... I don't understand you, Peter.... I simply don't understand. Are you mad—or drunk—or didn't I really ever know you in the least?"

Peter stuffed in Thomas' nightgowns, crumpling them hideously.

"Very well," said Rodney, very quietly. "It doesn't particularly matter which it is. In any case you are not going to do it. I shall prevent it."

"You can't," Peter flung at him, crushing a woolly rabbit in among Thomas' clothes.

Rodney sat still and looked at him, resting his chin on his hand; looked into him, through him, beyond him.

"I believe I can," he said simply.

Peter stopped filling the bag, and, still sitting on the floor by it, delivered himself at last.

"We care for each other. Isn't that to count, then? We always have cared for each other. Are we to do without each other for always? We want each other, we need each other. Denis doesn't need Lucy. He never did; not as I do. Are Lucy and I to do without each other, living only half a life, because of him? I tell you, I'm sick to death of doing without things. The time has come when it won't do any more, and I'm going to take what I can. I think I would rob anyone quite cheerfully if he had what I wanted. A few days ago I did rob; I bought things I knew I couldn't pay for. I'm sending them back now simply because I don't want them any more, not because I'm sorry I took them. It was fair I should take them; it was my turn to have things, mine and Thomas's. And now I'm going to take this, and keep it, till it's taken away from me. I daresay it will be taken away soon; my things always are. Everything has broken and gone, one thing after another, all my life—all the things I've cared for. I'm tired of it. I was sick of it by the time I was ten years old, sick of always getting ill or smashed up; and that's gone on ever since, and people have always thought, I know, 'Oh, it's only him, he never minds anything, he doesn't count, he's just a crock, and his only use is to play the fool for us.' But I did mind; I did. And I only played the fool because it would have been drearier still not to, and because there was always something amusing left to laugh at, not because I didn't mind. And then I cared for Denis as ... Oh, but you know how I cared for Denis. He was the most bright and splendid thing I knew in all the splendid world ... and he chucked me, because everything went wrong that could go wrong between us without my fault ... and our friendship was spoilt.... And I cared for Hilary and Peggy; and they would go and do things to spoil all our lives, and the more I tried, like an ass, to help, the more I seemed to mess things up, till the crash came, and we all went to bits together. And we had to give up the only work we liked—and I did love mine so—and slave at things we hated. And still we kept sinking and sinking, and crashing on worse and worse rocks, till we hadn't a sound piece left to float us. And then, when I thought at least we could go down together, they went away and left me behind. So I'd failed there too, hopelessly. I always have failed in everything I've tried. I tried to make Rhoda happy, but that failed too. She left me; and now she's dead, and Thomas hasn't any mother at all.... And Lucy ... whom I'd cared for since before I could remember ... and I'd always thought, without thinking about it, that some day of course we should be together... Lucy left me, and our caring became wrong, so that at last we didn't care to see one another at all. And then it was as if hell had opened and let us in. The other things hadn't counted like that; health, money, beautiful things, interesting work, honour, friends, marriage, even Denis—they'd all collapsed and I did mind, horribly. But not like that. As long as I could see Lucy sometimes, I could go on—and I had Thomas too, though I don't know why he hasn't collapsed yet. But at last, quite suddenly, when the emptiness and the losing had been getting to seem worse and worse for a long time, they became so bad that they were impossible. I got angry; it was for Thomas more than for myself, I think; and I said it should end. I said I would take things; steal them, if I couldn't get them by fair means. And I went down to Astleys, to see them, to tell them it must end. And in the woods I met Lucy. And she'd been getting to know too that it must end, for her sake as well as for mine.... And so we're going to end it, and begin again. We're going to be happy, because life is too jolly to miss."

Peter ended defiantly, and flung his razor in among the socks.

Rodney had listened quietly, his eyes on Peter's profile. When he stayed silent, Peter supposed that he had at last convinced him of the unbreakable strength of his purpose for iniquity, and that he would give him up and go away. After a minute he turned and looked up at Rodney, and said, "Now do you see that it's no good?"

Rodney took out his pipe and knocked it out and put it away before he answered:

"I'm glad you've said all that, Peter. Not that I didn't know it all before; of course I did. When I said at first that I didn't understand you, I was lying. I did understand, perfectly well. But I'm glad you've said it, because it's well to know that you realise it so clearly yourself. It saves my explaining it to you. It gives us a common knowledge to start on. And now may *I* talk for a little, please? No, not for a little; for some time."

"Go on," said Peter. "But it's no use, you know.... What do you mean by our common knowledge? The knowledge that I'm a failure?"

Rodney nodded. "Precisely that. You've stated the case so clearly yourself— in outline, for you've left out a great deal, of course—that really it doesn't leave much for me to say. Let's leave you alone for the moment. I want to talk about other people. There are other people in the world besides ourselves, of course, improbable as the fact occasionally seems. The fact, I mean, that it's a world not of individual units but of closely connected masses of people, not one of whom stands alone. One can't detach oneself; one's got to be in with one camp or another. The world's full of different and opposing camps—worse luck. There are the beauty-lovers and the beauty-scorners, and all the fluctuating masses in between, like most of us, who love some aspects of it and scorn others. There are the well-meaning and the ill-meaning—and again the incoherent cross-benchers, who mean a little good and a little harm and for the most part mean nothing at all either way. Again, there are what people call the well-bred, the ill-bred, and of course the half-bred. An idiotic division that, because what do we know, any of us, of breeding, that we should call it good or bad? But there it is; a most well-marked division in everyone's eyes. And (and now I'm getting to the point) there are the rich and the poor—or call them, rather, the Haves and the Have-nots. I don't mean with regard to money particularly, though that comes in. But it's an all-round, thing. It's an undoubted fact, and one there's no getting round, that some people are born with the acquiring faculty, and others with the losing. Most of us, of course, are in the half-way house, and win and lose in fairly average proportions. But some of us seem marked out either for the one or for the other. I know personally a good many in both camps. Many more of the Have-nots, though, because I prefer to cultivate their acquaintance. There's a great deal to be done for the Haves too; they need, I fancy, all the assistance they can get if they're not to become prosperity-rotten. The Have-Nots haven't that danger; but they've plenty of dangers of their own; and, well, I suppose it's a question of taste, and that I prefer them. Anyhow, I do know a great many. People, you understand, with nothing at all that seems to make life tolerable. Destitutes, incapables, outcasts, slaves to their own lusts or to a grinding economic system or to some other cruelty of fate or men. Whatever the immediate cause of their ill-fortune may be, its underlying, fundamental cause is their own inherent faculty for failure and loss, their incompetence to take and hold the good things of life. You know the stale old hackneyed cry of the anti-socialists, how it would be no use equalising conditions because each man would soon return again to his original state. It's true in a deeper sense than they mean. You might equalise economic conditions as much as you please, but you'd never equalise fundamental conditions; you'd never turn the poor into the rich, the Have-Nots into the Haves. You know I'm not a Socialist. I don't want to see a futile attempt to throw down barriers and merge all camps in one indeterminate army who don't know what they mean or where they're going. I'm not a Socialist, because I don't believe in a universal outward prosperity. I mean, I don't want it; I should have no use for it. I'm holding no brief for the rich; I've nothing to say about them just now; and anyhow you and I have no concern with them." Rodney pulled himself back from the edge of a topic on which he was apt to become readily vehement. "But Socialism isn't the way out for them any more than it's the way out for the poor; it's got, I believe, to be by individual renunciation that their salvation will come; by their giving up, and stripping bare, and going down one by one and empty-handed into the common highways, to take their share of hardness like men. It will be extraordinarily difficult. Changing one's camp is. It's so difficult as to be all but impossible. Perhaps you've read the Bible story of the young man with great possessions, and how it was said, 'With men it is impossible...' Well, the tradition, true or false, goes that in the end he did it; gave up his possessions and became financially poor. But we don't know, even if that's true, what else he kept of his wealth; a good deal, I daresay, that wasn't money or material goods. One can't tell. What we do know is that to cross that dividing line, to change one's camp, is a nearly impossible thing. Someone says, 'That division, the division of those who have and those who have not, runs so deep as almost to run to the bottom.' The great division, he calls it, between those who seize and those who lose. Well, the Haves aren't always seizers, I think; often—more often, perhaps—they have only to move tranquilly through life and let gifts drop into their hands. It's pleasant to see, if we are not in a mood to be jarred. It's often attractive. It was mainly that that attracted you long ago in Denis Urquhart. The need and the want in you, who got little and lost much, was somehow vicariously satisfied by the gifts he received from fortune; by his beauty and strength and good luck and power of winning and keeping. He was pleasant in your eyes, because of these gifts of his; and, indeed, they made of him a pleasant person, since he had nothing to be unpleasant about. So your emptiness found pleasure in his fullness, your poverty in his riches, your weakness in his strength, and you loved him. And I think if anything could (yet) have redeemed him, have saved him from his prosperity, it would have been your love. But instead of letting it drag him down into the scrum and the pity and the battle of life, he turned away from it and kept it at a distance, and shut himself more closely between his protecting walls of luxury and well-being. Then, again, Lucy gave him his chance; but he hasn't (so far) followed her love either. She'd have led him, if she could, out of the protecting, confining walls, into the open, where people are struggling and perishing for lack of a little pity; but he wouldn't. So far the time hasn't been ripe for his saving; his day is still to come. It's up to all of us who care for him—and can any of us help it?—to save him from himself. And chiefly it's your job and Lucy's. You can do your part now only by clearing out of the way, and leaving Lucy to do hers. She will do it, I firmly believe, in the end, if you give her time. Lucy, I know, for I have seen it when I have been with her, has been troubled about her own removal from the arena, about her own being confined between walls so that she can't hear the people outside calling; but that is mere egotism. She can hear and see all right; she has all her senses, and she will never stop using them. It's her business to be concerned for Denis, who is blind and deaf. It's her business to use her own caring to make him care. She's got to drag him out, not to let herself be shut inside with him. It can be done, and Lucy, if anyone in the world, can do it—if she doesn't give up and shirk. Lucy, if anyone in the world, has the right touch, the right loosing power, to set Denis free. I think that you too have the touch and the power—but you mustn't use yours; the time for that is gone by. Yours is the much harder business of clearing out of the way. If you ever loved Denis, you will do that."

He paused and looked at Peter, who was still sitting on the floor, motionless, with bent head.

"May I go on?" said Rodney, and Peter answered nothing.

Rodney looked away again out of the window into a grey night sky that hid the Easter moon, and went on, gently. He was tired of talking; his discourse had been already nearly as long as an average woman; but he went on deliberately talking and talking, to give Peter time.

"So, you see, that is an excellent reason—to you it is, I believe, the incontrovertible reason—why you should once more give up and lose, and not take. But, deeper than that, to me more insurmountable than that, is the true reason, which is simply that that very thing—to lose, to do without—is your business in life, as you've said yourself. It's your profession. You are in the camp of the Have-Nots; you belong there. You can't desert. You can't step out and go over to the enemy. If you did, if you could (only you can't) it would be a betrayal. And, whatever you gained, you'd lose by it what you have at present—your fellowship with the other unfortunates. Isn't that a thing worth having? Isn't it something to be down on the ground with the poor and empty-handed, not above them, where you can't hear them crying and laughing? Would you, if you could, be one of the prosperous, who don't care? Would you, if you could, be one of those who have their joy in life ready-made and put into their hands, instead of one of the poor craftsmen who have to make their own? What's the gaiety of the saints? Not the pleasant cheerfulness of the Denis Urquharts and their kind, who have things, but the gaiety, in the teeth of circumstances, of St. Francis and his paupers, who have nothing and yet possess all things. That's your gaiety; the gaiety that plays the fool, as you put it, looking into the very eyes of agony and death; that loses and laughs and makes others laugh in the last ditch; the gaiety of those who drop all cargoes, fortune and good name and love, overboard lightly, and still spread sail to the winds and voyage, and when they're driven by the winds at last onto a lee shore, derelicts clinging to a broken wreck, find on the shore coloured shells to play with and still are gay. That's your gaiety, as I've always known it and loved it. Are you going to chuck that gaiety away, and rise up full of the lust to possess, and take and grasp and plunder? Are you going to desert the empty-handed legion, whose van you've marched in all your life, and join the prosperous?" Rodney broke off for a moment, as if he waited for an answer. He rose from his chair and began to walk about the room, speaking again, with a more alright vehemence. "Oh, you may think this is mere romance, fancy, sentiment, what you will. But it isn't. It's deadly, solid truth. You can't grasp. You can't try to change your camp. You—and Lucy too, for she's in the same camp—wouldn't be happy, to put it at its simplest. You'd know all the time that you'd shirked, deserted, been false to your business. You'd be fishes out of water, with the knowledge that you'd taken for your own pleasure something that someone else ought to have had. It isn't in either of you to do it. You must leave such work to the Haves. Why, what happens the first time you try it on? You have to send back the goods you've tried to appropriate to where they came from. It would be the same always. You don't know *how* to possess. Then in heaven's name leave possessing alone, and stick to the job you are good at—doing without. For you are good at that. You always have been, except just for just one short interlude, which will pass like an illness and leave you well again. Believe me, it will. I don't know when, or how soon; but I do know that sometime you will be happy again, with the things, the coloured shells, so to speak, that you find still when all the winds and storms have done their worst and all your cargoes are broken wrecks at your feet. It will be then, in that last emptiness, that you'll come to terms with disaster, and play the fool again to amuse yourself and the other derelicts, because, when there's nothing else left, there's always laughter."

Rodney had walked to the window, and now stood looking out at the dim, luminous night, wherein, shrouded, the Easter moon dwelt in the heart of shadows. From many churches, many clocks chimed the hour. Rodney spoke once more, slowly, leaning out into the shadowy night.

"Through this week," he said, "they have been watching in those churches a supreme renouncement, the ultimate agony of giving up, the last triumph of utter loss. I'm not going to talk about that; it's not my business or my right ... But it surely counts, that giving up whatever we may or may not believe about it. It shines, a terrible counsel of perfection for those who have, burning and hurting. But for those who have not, it doesn't burn and hurt; it shines to cheer and comfort; it is the banner of the leader of the losing legion, lifted up that the rest may follow after. Does that help at all?... Perhaps at this moment nothing helps at all.... Have I said enough? Need I go on?"

Peter's voice, flat and dead, spoke out of the shadow of the dim room.

"You have said enough. You need not go on."

Then Rodney turned and saw him, sitting still on the floor by the half-packed bag, with the yellow dog sleeping against him. In the dim light his face looked pale and pinched like a dead man's.

"You've done your work," the flat voice said. "You've taken it away—the new life we so wanted. You've shown that it can't be. You're quite right. And you're right too that nothing helps at all.... Because of Denis, I can't do this. But I find no good in emptiness; why should I? I want to have things and enjoy them, at this moment, more desperately than you, who praise emptiness and doing without, ever wanted anything."

"I am aware of that," said Rodney.

"You've got in the way," said Peter, looking up at the tall gaunt figure by the window; and anger shook him. "You've stepped in and spoilt it all. Yes, you needn't be afraid; you've spoilt it quite irrevocably. You knew that to mention Denis was enough to do that. I was trying to forget him; I could have, till it was too late. You can go home now and feel quite easy; you've done your job. There's to be no new life for me, or Thomas, or Lucy, or Francesco—only the same old emptiness. The same old ... oh, damn!"

Peter, who never swore, that ugly violence being repugnant to his nature, swore now, and woke Francesco, who put up his head to lick his friend's face. But Peter pushed him away, surprising him violently, and caught at his half-filled bag and snatched at the contents and flung them on the top of one another on the floor. They lay in a jumbled chaos—Thomas's clothes and Peter's socks and razor and Thomas's rabbit and Peter's books; and Francesco snuffled among them and tossed them about, thinking it a new game.

"Go away now." Peter flung out the words like another oath. "Go away to your poverty which you like, and leave us to ours which we hate. There's no more left for you to take away from us; it's all gone. Unless you'd like me to throw Thomas out of the window, since you think breakages are so good."

Rodney merely said, "I'm not going away just yet. Could you let me stay here for the night and sleep on the sofa? It's late to go back to-night."

"Sleep where you like," said Peter. "There's the bed. I don't want it."

But Rodney stretched himself instead on the horse-hair sofa. He said no more, knowing that the time for words was past. He lay tired and quiet, with closed eyes, knowing how Peter and the other disreputable forsaken outcast sat together huddled on the floor through the dim night, till the dawn looked palely in and showed them both fallen asleep, Peter's head resting on Francesco's yellow back.

It was Rodney who got up stiffly from his hard resting-place in the dark unlovely morning, and made tea over Peter's spirit-lamp for both of them. Peter woke later, and drank it mechanically. Then he looked at Rodney and said, "I'm horribly stiff. Why did neither of us go to bed?" He was pale and heavy-eyed, and violent no more, but very quiet and tired, as if, accepting, he was sinking deep in grey and cold seas, that numbed resistance and drowned words.

The milk came in, and Peter gave Thomas to drink; and on the heels of the milk came the post, and a letter for Peter.

"I suppose," said Peter dully, as he opened it, "she too has found out that it can't be done."

The letter said: "Peter, we can't do it. I am horribly, horribly sorry, but I know it now for certain. Perhaps you know it too, by now. Because the reason is in you, not in me. It is that you love Denis too much. So you couldn't be happy. I want you to be happy, more than I want anything in the world, but it can't be this way. Please, dear Peter, be happy sometime; please, please be happy. I love you always—if that helps at all.—Lucy."

Peter let the note fall on the floor, and stood with bent head by the side of Thomas's crib, while Thomas guggled his milk.

"Two minds with but a single thought," he remarked, in that new, dreary voice of his. "As always.... Well, it saves trouble. And we're utterly safe now, you see; doubly safe. You can go home in peace."

Then Rodney, knowing that he could be no more use, left the three derelicts together.

CHAPTER XXI

ON THE SHORE

There is a shore along which the world flowers, one long sweet garden strip, between the olive-grey hills and the very blue sea. Like nosegays in the garden the towns are set, blooming in their many colours, linked by the white road running above blue water. For vagabonds in April the poppies riot scarlet by the white road's edge, and the last of the hawthorn lingers like melting snow, and over the garden walls the purple veils of the wistaria drift like twilight mist. Over the garden walls, too, the sweetness of the orange and lemon blossom floats into the road, and the frangipani sends delicate wafts down, and the red and white roses toss and hang as if they had brimmed over from sheer exuberance. If a door in one of the walls chance to stand ajar, vagabonds on the road may look in and see an Eden, unimaginably sweet, aflame with oleanders and pomegranate blossom, and white like snow with tall lilies.

The road itself is good, bordered on one side by the garden sweetness and the blossoms that foam like wave-crests over the walls, on the other breaking down to a steep hill-slope where all the wild flowers of spring star the grassy terraces, singing at the twisted feet of the olives that give them grey shadow. So the hillside runs steeply down to where at its rocky base the blue waves murmur. All down the coast the road turns and twists and climbs and dips, above little lovely bays and through little gay towns, caught between mountains and blue water. For those who want a bed, the hush of the moonlit olives that shadow the terraced slopes gives sweeter sleep than the inns of the towns, and the crooning of the quiet sea is a gentler lullaby than the noises of streets, and the sweetness of the myrtle blossom is better to breathe than the warm air of rooms. To wander in spring beneath the sun by day and the moon by night along the sea's edge is a good life, a beautiful life, a cheerful and certainly an amusing life. Social adventures crowd the road. There are pleasant people along this shore of little blue bays. Besides the ordinary natives of the towns and the country-side, and besides the residents in the hotels (whose uses to vagabonds are purely financial) there is on this shore a drifting and incalculable population, heterogeneous, yet with a note of character common to all. A population cosmopolitan and shifting, living from hand to mouth, vagrants of the road or of the street corner, finding life a warm and easy thing in this long garden shut between hills and sea. So warm and lovely and easy a garden is it that it has for that reason become a lee shore; a shore where the sick and the sad and the frail and the unfortunate are driven by the winds of adversity to find a sheltered peace. On the shore all things may be given up; there is no need to hold with effort any possession, even life itself, for all things become gifts, easily bestowed and tranquilly received. You may live on extremely little there, and win that little lightly. You may sell things along the road for some dealer, or for yourself—plaster casts, mosaic brooches, picture postcards, needlework of divers colours. If you have a small cart drawn by a small donkey, you are a lucky man, and can carry your wares about in it and sell them at the hotels, or in the towns at fair-time. If you possess an infant son, you can carry him also about in the cart, and he will enjoy it. Also, if your conversation is like the sun's, with a friendly aspect to good and bad, you will find many friends to beguile the way. You may pick them up at fairs, on *festa* days, like blackberries.

On Santa Caterina's day, the 30th of April, there is a great *festa* in the coast towns. They hold the saint in especial honour on this shore, for she did much kindness there in plague-time. Vagabonds with wares to sell have a good day. There was, on one Santa Caterina's day, a young man, with a small donkey-cart and a small child and a disreputable yellow dog, who was selling embroidery. He had worked it himself; he was working at it even now, in the piazza at Varenzano, when not otherwise engaged. But a fair is too pleasantly distracting a thing to allow of much needlework being done in the middle of it. There are so many interesting things. There are the roulette tables, round which interested but cautious groups stand, while the owners indefatigably and invitingly twirl. The gambling instinct is not excessively developed in Varenzano. There was, of course, the usual resolute and solitary player, who stood through the hours silently laying one halfpenny after another on clubs, untempted to any deviation or any alteration of stake, except that on the infrequent occasions when it really turned out clubs he stolidly laid and lost his gained halfpennies by the other. By nine o'clock in the morning he had become a character; spectators nudged new-comers and pointed him out, with "*Sempre fiori, quello.*" The young man with the embroidery was sorry about him; he had an expression as if he were losing more halfpence than he could well afford. The young man himself lost all the stakes he made; but he didn't gamble much, knowing himself not lucky. Instead, he watched the fluctuating fortunes of a vivacious and beautiful youth near him, who flung on his stakes with a lavish gesture of dare-devil extravagance, that implied that he was putting his fortune to the touch to win or lose it all. It was a relief to notice that his stakes were seldom more than threepence. When he lost, he swore softly to himself: "*Dio mio, mio Dio, Dio mio,*" and then turned courteously to the embroidery-seller, who was English, with a free interpretation—"In Engliss, bai George." This seemed to the embroidery-seller to be true politeness in misfortune. The beautiful youth seemed to be a person of many languages; his most frequent interjection was, "*Dio mio—* Holy Moses—oh hang!*" After which he would add an apology, addressed to the embroidery-seller, who had a certain air of refined innocence, "*Bestemmiar, no. Brutto bestemmiare. Non gli piace, no,*" and resume his game.

Peter, who was selling embroidery, liked him so much that he followed him when he went to try his luck at the cigar game. Here Peter, who never smoked, won two black and snake-like cigars, which he presented to the beautiful young man, who received them with immense cordiality. A little later the young man, whose name was Livio, involved himself in a violent quarrel with the cigar banker, watched by an amused, placid and impartial crowd of spectators. Peter knew Livio to have the right on his side, because the banker had an unpleasant face and Livio accused him of being not only a Venetian but a Freemason. The banker in response remarked that he was not going to stay to be insulted by a Ligurian thief, and with violent gestures unscrewed his tin lady and her bunch of real lemons and put away his board. Livio burst into a studied and insulting shout of laughter, stopped abruptly without remembering to bring it to a proper finish, and began to be pleasant to the embroidery-seller, speaking broken American English with a strong nasal twang.

"My name is Livio Ceresole. Bin in America; the States. All over the place. Chicago, 'Frisco, Pullman cars, dollars—*you* know. Learnt Engliss there. Very fine country; I *should* smile." He did so, and looked so amiable and so engaging that the embroidery-seller smiled back, thinking what a beautiful person he was. He had the petulant, half sensuous, spoilt-boy beauty of a young Antinuous, with a rakish touch added by the angle of his hat and his snappy American idioms.

So it came about that those two threw in their lots for a time. There was something about the embroidery-seller that drew these casual friendships readily to him; he was engaging, with a great innocence of aspect and gentleness of demeanour, and a friendly smile that sweetened the world, and a lovable gift of amusement.

He had been wandering on this shore for now six months, and had friends in most of the towns. One cannot help making them; the people there are, for the most part, so pleasant. A third-class railway carriage, vilely lighted and full of desperately uncomfortable wooden seats, and so full of warm air and bad tobacco smoke that Peter often felt sick before the train moved (he always did so, in any train, soon after) was yet full of agreeable people, merry and sociable and engagingly witty, and, whether achieving wit or not, with a warm welcome for anything that had that intention. There is a special brand of charm, of humour, of infectious and friendly mirth, and of exceeding personal beauty, that is only fully known by those who travel third in Italy.

From Varenzano on this *festa* day in the golden afternoon the embroidery-seller and his donkey-cart and his small son and his yellow dog and Livio Ceresole walked to Castoleto. Livio, who had a sweet voice, sang snatches of melody in many languages; doggerel songs, vulgarities from musical comedies, melodies of the street corner; and the singer's voice redeemed and made music of them all. He was practising his songs for use at the hotels, where he sang and played the banjo in the evenings, to add to his income. He told Peter that he was, at the moment, ruined.

"In Engliss," he translated, "stony-broke." A shop he had kept in Genoa had failed, so he was thrown upon the roads.

"You too are travelling, without a home, for gain?" he inferred. "You are one of us other unfortunates, you and the little child. Poor little one!"

"Oh, he likes it," said Peter. "So do I. We don't want a home. This is better."

"Not so bad," Livio admitted, "when one can live. But we should like to make our fortunes, isn't it so?"

Peter said he didn't know. There seemed so little prospect of it that the question was purely academical.

They were coming to Castoleto. Livio stopped, and proceeded to pay attention to his personal appearance, moistening a fragment of yesterday's "Corriere della Sera" in his mouth, and applying it with vigour to his dusty boots. When they shone to his satisfaction, he produced from his pocket a comb and a minute hand-mirror, and arranged his crisp waves of dark hair to a gentlemanly neatness. Then he replaced his pseudo-panama hat, with the slight inclination to the left side that seemed to him suitable, re-tied his pale blue tie, and passed the mirror to Peter, who went through similar operations.

"Castoleto will be gay for the *festa*," Livio said. "Things doing," he interpreted; adding, "Christopher Columbus born there; found America. Very big man; yes, *sir.*"

Peter said he supposed so.

Livio added, resuming his own tongue, "Santa Caterina da Siena visited Castoleto. Are you a Christian?"

"Oh, well," said Peter, who found the subject difficult, and was not good at thinking out difficult things. Livio nodded. "One doesn't want much church, of course; that's best for the women. But so many English aren't Christians at all, but heretics."

They came into Castoleto, which is a small place where the sea washes a shingly shore just below the town, and the narrow streets smell of fish and other things. Livio waved his hand towards a large new hotel that stood imposingly on the hill just behind the town.

"There we will go this evening, I with my music, you with your embroideries." That seemed a good plan. Till then they separated, Livio going to try his fortune at the fair, and Peter and Thomas and Francesco and Suor Clara (the donkey) establishing themselves on the shore by the edge of the waveless sea. There Peter got out of the cart a tea-caddy and a spirit lamp and made tea (he was always rather unhappy if he missed his tea) and ate biscuits, and gave Thomas—now an interested and cheerful person of a year and a half old—milk and sopped biscuit, and produced a bone for Francesco and carrots for Clara, and so they all had tea.

It was the hour when the sun dips below the western arm of hills that shuts the little bay, leaving behind it two lakes of pure gold, above and below. The sea burned like a great golden sheet of liquid glass spreading, smooth and limpid, from east to west, and swaying with a gentle hushing sound to and fro which was all the motion it had for waves. From moment to moment it changed; the living gold melted into green and blue opal tints, tender like twilight.

"After tea we'll go paddling," Peter told Thomas. "And then perhaps we'll get a fisherman to take us out while he drops his net. Santa Caterina should give good fishing."

In the town they were having a procession. Peter heard the chanting as they passed, saw, through the archways into the streets, glimpses of it. He heard their plaintive hymn that entreated pity:

"Difendi, O Caterina
Da peste, fame e guerra,
Il popol di Cartoleto
In mare e in terra..."

Above the hymn rose the howls of little St. John the Baptist, who had been, no doubt, suddenly mastered by his too high-spirited lamb and upset on to his face, so that his mother had to rush from out the crowd to comfort him and brush the dust from his curls that had been a-curling in papers these three weeks past.

It was no doubt a beautiful procession, and Peter and Thomas loved processions, but they had seen one that morning at Varenzano, so they were content to see and hear this from a distance.

Why, Peter speculated, do we not elsewhere thus beautify and sanctify our villages and cities and country places? Why do they not, in fishing hamlets of a colder clime, thus bring luck to their fishing, thus summon the dear saints to keep and guard their shores? Why, Peter for the hundredth time questioned, do we miss so much gaiety, so much loveliness, so much grace, that other and wiser people have?

Peter shook his head over it.

"A sad business, Thomas. But here we are, you and I, and let us be thankful. Thankful for this lovely country set with pleasant towns and religious manners and nice people, and for the colour and smoothness of the sea we're going paddling in, and for our nice tea. *Are* you thankful, Thomas? Yes, I'm sure you are."

Someone, passing behind them, said with surprise, "Is that *you*, Margerison?"

Peter, looking round, his tin mug in one hand and a biscuit in the other, recognised an old schoolfellow. He was standing on the beach staring at the tea-party—the four disreputable vagabonds and their cart.

Peter laughed. It rather amused him to come into sudden contact with the respectable; they were always so much surprised. He had rather liked this man. Some people had good-temperedly despised him for a molly-coddle; he had been a delicate boy, and had cherished himself rather. Peter, delicate himself, incapable of despising anyone, and with a heart that went out to all unfortunates, had been, in a mild and casual way, his friend. Looking into his face now, Peter was struck to sorrow and compassion, because it was the face of a man who had accepted death, and to whom life gave no more gifts, not even the peace of the lee shore. It was a restless face, with hollow cheeks unnaturally flushed, and bitter, querulous lips. His surprise at seeing Peter and his vagabond equipment made him cough.

When he had done coughing, he said, "What *are* you doing, Margerison?"

Peter said he was having tea. "Have you had yours? I've got another mug somewhere—a china one."

As he declined with thanks, Peter thought, "He's dying. Oh, poor chap, how ghastly for him," and his immense pity made him even gentler than usual. He couldn't say, "How are you?" because he knew; he couldn't say, "Isn't this a nice place?" because Ashe must leave it so soon; he couldn't say, "I am having a good time," because Ashe would have no more good times, and, Peter suspected, had had few.

What he did say was, "This is Thomas. And this is San Francesco, and this is Suor Clara. They're all mine. Do you like their faces?"

Ashe looked at Francesco, and said, "Rather a mongrel, isn't he?" and Peter took the comment as condemning the four of them, and divined in Ashe the respectability of the sheltered life, and was compassionate again. Ashe cared, during the brief space of time allotted to him, to be respectably dressed; he cared to lead what he would call a decent life. Peter, in his disreputability, felt like a man in the open air who looks into the prison of a sick-room.

Ashe said he was staying at Varenzano with his mother, and they were passing through Castoleto on the way back from their afternoon's drive.

"It's lungs, you know. They don't give me much chance—the doctors, I mean. It's warm and sheltered on this coast, so I have to be here. I'd rather be here, I suppose, than doing a beef-and-snow cure in one of those ghastly places. But it's a bore hanging round and doing nothing. I'd as soon it ended straight off."

Ashamed of having been so communicative (but Peter was used to people being unreserved with him, and never thought it odd), he changed the subject.

"Are you on the tramp, or what? Is it comfortable?"

"Very," said Peter, "and interesting."

"*Is* it interesting? How long are you going on with it? When are you going home?"

"Oh, this is as much home as anywhere else, you know. I don't see any reason for leaving it yet. We all like it. I've no money, you see, and life is cheap here, and warm and nice."

"Cheap and warm and nice...." Ashe repeated it, vaguely surprised. He hadn't realised that Peter was one of the permanently destitute, and tramping not from pleasure but from necessity.

"What do you *do*?" he asked curiously, seeing that Peter was not at all embarrassed.

"Oh, nothing very much. A little needlework, which I sell as I go along. And various sorts of peddling, sometimes. I'm going up to the hotel this evening, to try and make the people there buy things from me. And we just play about, you know, and enjoy the roads and the towns and the fairs and the seashore. It's all fun."

Ashe laughed and made himself cough.

"You awfully queer person! You really like it, living like that?... But even I don't like it, you know, living shut away from life in this corner, though I've money enough to be comfortable with. Should I like it, your life, I wonder? You're not bored, it seems. I always am. What is it you like so much?"

Peter said, lots of things. No, he wasn't bored; things were too amusing for that.

They couldn't get any further, because Ashe's mother called him from the carriage in the road. She too looked tired, and had sad eyes.

Peter looked after them with compassion. They were wasting their little time together terribly, being sad when they should have found, in these last few months or years of life, quiet fun on the warm shore where they had come to make loss less bitter.

Tea being over, he went paddling, with Thomas laughing on his shoulder, till it was Thomas's bedtime. Then he put Thomas away in his warm corner of the cart, and Livio joined him, and they had supper together at a *trattoria*, and then climbed the road between vineyards and lemon gardens up to the new white hotel.

Livio, as they walked, practised his repertory of songs, singing melodious snatches in the lemon-scented dusk. They came to the hotel, and found that the inhabitants were sitting round little tables in the dim garden, having their coffee by the light of hanging lanterns.

From out of the dusk Livio struck his mandolin and sweetly sang. Peter meanwhile wandered round from group to group displaying his wares by the pink light of the lanterns. He met with some success; he really embroidered rather nicely, and people were good-natured and kind to the pale-faced, delicate-looking young man who smiled with his very blue, friendly eyes. There was always an element in Peter that inspired pity; one divined in him a merry unfortunate.

The people in the hotel were of many races—French, Italian, German, and one English family. Castoleto is not an Anglo-Saxon resort; it is small and of no reputation, and not as yet Anglicised. Probably the one English family in the hotel was motoring down the coast, and only staying for one night.

Peter, in his course round the garden, came suddenly within earshot of cultured English voices, and heard some one laugh. Then a voice, soft in quality, with casual, pleasant, unemphasised cadence, said, "Considering these vile roads, she's running extraordinarily well. Really, something ought to be done about the roads, though; it's absolutely disgraceful. Blake says ..." one of the things that chauffeurs do say, and that Peter did not listen to.

Peter had stopped suddenly where he was when the speaker had laughed. Of the many personal attributes of man, some may become slurred out of all character, disguised and levelled down among the herd, blurred with time, robbed of individuality. Faces may be so lost and blurred, almost beyond the recognition of those who have loved them. But who ever forgot a friend's laugh, or lost the character of his own? If Ulysses had laughed when he came back to Ithaca, his dog would have missed his eternal distinction.

Soft, rather low, a thing not detached from the sentence it broke into, but rather breaking out of it, and merging then into words again—Peter had carried it in his ears for ten years. Was there ever any man but one who laughed quite so?

Looking down the garden, he saw them, sitting under a pergola, half-veiled by the purple drifts of the wistaria that hung in trails between them and him. Through its twilight screen he saw Denis in a dinner-jacket, leaning back in a cane chair, his elbow on its arm, a cigarette in his raised hand, speaking. The light from a big yellow lantern swinging above them lit his clear profile, gleamed on his fair hair. Opposite him was Lucy, in a white frock, her elbows on a little table, her chin in her two hands, her eyes wide and grey and full of the wonder of the twilight. And beyond her sat Lord Evelyn, leaning back with closed eyes, a cigar in his delicate white hand.

Peter stood and looked, and a little faint, doubtful smile twitched at his lips, as at a dear, familiar sight long unseen. Should he approach? Should he speak? For a moment he hung in doubt.

Then he turned away. He had no part with them, nor they with him. His part—Rodney had said it once—was to clear out.

Livio, close to him, was twanging his mandolin and singing some absurd melody:

"Ah, Signor!"
"Scusi, Signora?"
"È forae il mio marito,
Da molti anni smarrito?..."

Peter broke in softly, "Livio, I go. I have had enough."

Livio's eyebrows rose; he shrugged his shoulders, but continued his singing. He, anyhow, had not yet had enough of such a good-natured audience.

Peter slipped out of the garden into the white road than ran down between the grey mystery of the olive groves to the little dirty fishing-town and the dark, quiet sea. In the eastern sky there was a faint shimmer, a disturbance of the deep, star-lit blue, a pallor that heralded the rising of the moon. But as yet the world lay in its mysterious dusk.

Peter, his feet stirring on the white dust of the road, drew in the breath of the lemon-grown, pine-grown, myrtle-sweet hills, and the keen saltness of the sea, and the fishiness of the little, lit, clamorous town on its edge. In the town there was singing, raucous and merry. Behind in the garden there was singing, melodious and absurd. It echoes fleeted down the road.

"Ah, Signor!""Scusi,
Signora?"
"È forse il mio marrito..."

Peter sat on the low white wall to watch the moon rise. And for a moment the bitter smell of the soft dust on the road was in his nostrils, and he was taken back into a past bitterness, when the world had been dust to his feet, dust to his touch, dust in his throat, so that he had lain dust-buried, and choked for breath, and found none. This time a year ago he had lain so, and for many months after that. Those months had graved lines on his face— lines perhaps on his soul—that all the quiet, gay years could not smooth out. For the peace of the lee shore is not a thing easily won; to let go and drift before the storms wheresoever they drive needs a hard schooling; to lose comes first, and to laugh long after.

The dust Peter's feet had stirred settled down; and now, instead of its faint bitterness, the sweetness of the evening hills stole about. And over the still sea the white moon rose, glorious, triumphant, and straight from her to Peter, cleaving the dark waters, her bright road ran.

Peter went down into the little, merry town.

He and Thomas slept at an inn that night. Livio joined them there next morning at breakfast. He said, "You were foolish to leave the hotel so soon. I got a good sum of money. There was an English family, that gave me a good reward. My music pleased them. The English are always generous and extravagant. Oh, Dio, I forgot; one of them sent you this note by me. He explained nothing; he said, 'Is he that was with you your friend? Then give him this note.' Did he perhaps know you of old, or did he merely perceive that you were of his country? I know nothing. One does not read the letters entrusted to one for one's friends. Here it is."

He handed Peter a folded-up piece of notepaper. Opening it, Peter read, scrawled unsteadily in pencil, "Come and see me to-morrow morning. I shall be alone." E.P.U.

"He followed me to the garden door as I went away," continued Livio, "and gave it me secretly. I fancy he did not mean his companions to know. You will go?"

Peter smiled, and Livio looked momentarily embarrassed.

"Oh, you know, it came open in my hand; and understanding the language so well, it leaped to my eyes. I knew you would not mind. You will go and see this milord? He *is* a milord, for I heard the waiter address him."

"Yes," said Peter. "I will go and see him."

An hour later he was climbing the white road again in the morning sunshine.

Asking at the hotel for Lord Evelyn Urquhart, he was taken through the garden to a wistaria-hung summer-house. The porter indicated it to him and departed, and Peter, through the purple veils, saw Lord Evelyn reclining in a long cane chair, smoking the eternal cigarette and reading a French novel.

He looked up as Peter's shadow fell between him and the sun, and dropped the yellow book with a slight start. For a moment neither of them spoke; they looked at each other in silence, the pale, shabby, dusty youth with his vivid eyes; the frail, foppish, middle-aged, worn-out man, with his pale face twitching a little and his near-sighted eyes screwed up, as if he was startled, or dazzled, or trying hard to see something.

The next moment Lord Evelyn put out a slim, fine hand.

"How are you, Peter Margerison? Sit down and talk to me."

Peter sat down in the chair beside him.

Lord Evelyn said, "I'm quite alone this morning. Denis and Lucy have motored to Genoa. I join them there this afternoon.... You didn't know last night that I saw you."

"No," said Peter. "I believed that none of you had seen me. I didn't want you to; so I came away."

Lord Evelyn nodded. "Quite so; quite so. I understood that. And I didn't mention you to the others. Indeed, I didn't mean to take any notice of you at all; but at the end I changed my mind, and sent for you to come. I believe I'm right in thinking that your wish is to keep out of the way of our family."

"Yes," said Peter.

"You're right. You've been very right indeed. There's nothing else you could have done, all this time." Peter glanced at him quickly, to see what he knew, and saw.

Lord Evelyn saw the questioning glance.

"Oh, yes, yes, boy. Of course, I knew about you and Lucy. I'm not such a blind fool as I've sometimes been thought in the past—eh, Peter Margerison? I always knew you cared for Lucy; and I knew she cared for you. And I knew when she and you all but went off together. I asked Lucy; I can read the child's eyes better than books, you see. I read it, and I asked her, and she admitted it."

"It was you who stopped her," said Peter quietly.

Lord Evelyn tapped his fingers on his chair arm.

"I'm not a moralist; anything but a moralist, y'know. But as a man of the world, with some experience, I knew that couldn't be. So I told her the truth."

"The truth?" Peter wondered.

"Yes, boy, the truth. The only truth that mattered to Lucy. That you couldn't be happy that way. That you loved Denis too much to be happy that way. When I said it, she knew it. 'Deed, I believe she'd known it before, in her heart. So she wrote to you, and ended that foolish idea. You know now that she was right, I think?"

"I knew it then. I was just going to telegraph to her not to come when I got her letter. No, I didn't know she was right; but I knew we couldn't do it. I didn't know it for myself, either; I had to be told. When I was told, I knew it."

"Ah." Lord Evelyn looked at the pale face, that had suddenly taken a look of age, as of one who looks back into a past bitterness.

"Ah." He looked in silence for a moment, then said, "You've been through a bad time, Peter."

Peter's face twitched suddenly, and he answered nothing.

"All those months," said Lord Evelyn, and his high, unsteady voice shook with a curious tremor, "all that summer, you were in hell."

Peter gave no denial.

"I knew it," said Lord Evelyn. "And you never answered the letter I wrote you."

"No," said Peter slowly. "I answered no letters at all, I think. I don't remember exactly what I did, through that summer. I suppose I lived— because here I am. And I suppose I kept Thomas alive—because he's here too. But for the rest—I don't know. I hated everyone and everything. I believe Rodney used to come and see me sometimes; but I didn't care.... Oh, what's the good of talking about it? It's over now."

Lord Evelyn was shading his face with a shaking hand.

"Poor boy," he muttered to himself. "Poor boy. Poor boy."

Peter, recovering his normal self, said, "You've been awfully good to me, Lord Evelyn. I've behaved very badly to you, I believe. Thanks most awfully for everything. But don't pity me now, because I've all I want."

"Happy, are you?" Lord Evelyn looked up at him again, searchingly.

"Quite happy." Peter's smile was reassuring.

"The dooce you are!" Lord Evelyn murmured. "Well, I believe you.... Look here, young Peter, I've a proposal to make. In the first place, is it over, that silly business of yours and Lucy's? Can you meet without upsetting each other?"

Peter considered for a moment.

"Yes; I think we can. I suppose I shall always care—I always have—but now that we've made up our minds that it won't do ... accepted it, you know.... Oh, yes, I think we could meet, as far as that goes."

Lord Evelyn nodded approval.

"Very good, very good. Now listen to me. You're on the roads, aren't you, without a penny, you and your boy?"

"Yes. I make a little as I go along, you know. One doesn't need much here. We're quite comfortable."

"Are you, indeed?... Well now, I see no reason why you shouldn't be more comfortable still. I want you to come and live with me."

Peter startled, looked up, and coloured. Then he smiled.

"It's most frightfully good of you...."

"Rubbish, rubbish." Lord Evelyn testily waved his words aside. "'Tisn't for your sake. It's for mine. I want your company.... My good boy, haven't you ever guessed, all these years, that I rather like your company? That was why I was so angry when you and your precious brother made a fool of me long ago. It hurt, because I liked you, Peter Margerison. That was why I couldn't forgive you. Demme! I don't think I've forgiven you yet, nor ever shall.

That is why I came and insulted you so badly one day as you remember. That's why I've such a soft place for Lucy, who's got your laugh and your voice and your tricks of talk, and looks at me with your white face. That's why I wasn't going to let her and you make young fools of yourselves together. That, I suppose, is why I know all the time what you're feeling; why I knew you were in hell all last summer; why I saw you, though I'm such a blinde bat now, last night, when neither Denis nor Lucy did. And that's why I want you and your boy to come and keep me company now, till the end."

Peter put out his hand and took Lord Evelyn's.

"I don't know what I can say to thank you. I do appreciate it, you know, more than anything that's ever happened to me before. I can't think how you can be so awfully nice to me...."

"Enough, enough," said Lord Evelyn. "Will you or won't you? Yes or no?"

Peter at that gave his answer quickly.

"No. I can't, you know."

Lord Evelyn turned on him sharply.

"You *won't?* The devil take it!"

"It's like this," said Peter, disturbed and apologetic, "we don't want to lead what's called respectable lives, Thomas and I. We don't want to be well-off—to live with well-off people. We—we can't, d'you see. It's not the way we're made. We don't belong. We're meant just to drift about the bottom, like this, and pick up a living anyhow."

"The boy's a fool," remarked Lord Evelyn, throwing back his head and staring at the roof.

Peter, who hated to wound, went on, "If we could share the life of any rich person, it would be you."

"Good Lord, I'm not rich. Wish I were. Rich!"

"Oh, but you are, you know. You're what *we* mean by rich.... And it's not only that. There's Denis and Lucy too. We've parted ways, and I do think it's best we shouldn't meet much. What's the good of beginning again to want things one can't have? I might, you know; and it would hurt. I don't now. I've given it all up. I don't want money; I don't want Denis's affection ... or Lucy ... or any of the things I have wanted, and that I've lost. I'm happy without them; without anything but what one finds to play with here as one goes along. One finds good things, you know—friends, and sunshine, and beauty, and enough minestra to go on with, and sheltered places on the shore to boil one's kettle in. I'm happy. Wouldn't it be madness to leave it and go out and begin having and wanting things again?"

Lord Evelyn had been listening with a curious expression of comprehension struggling with impatience.

"And the boy?" he said. "D'you suppose there'll never come a time when you want for the boy more than you can give him here, in these dirty little towns you like so much?"

"Oh," said Peter, "how can one look ahead? Depend on it, if Thomas is one of the people who are born to have things, he will have them. And if he's not, he won't, whatever I try to get for him. He's only one and a half now; so at least there's time before we need think of that. He's happy at present with what he's got."

"And is it your purpose, then, to spend all your life—anyhow, many years—in these parts, selling needlework?"

"I've no purpose," said Peter. "I must see what turns up. No, I daresay I shall try England again some time. But, wherever I am, I think I know now what is the happy way to live, for people like me. We're no use, you see, people like me; we make a poor job at the game, and we keep failing and coming bad croppers and getting hurt and in general making a mess of things. But at least we can be happy. We can't make our lives sublime, and departing leave behind us footprints on the sands of time—oh, I don't think I want to, in the least—but we can make a fairly good time for ourselves and a few other people out of the things we have. That's what we're doing, Thomas and I. And it's good enough."

Lord Evelyn looked at him long in silence, with his narrowed, searching eyes, that seemed always to be looking for something in his face and finding it there.

Then he sighed a little, and Peter, struck through by remorse, saw how old he looked in that moment.

"How it takes one back—takes one back," muttered Lord Evelyn.

Then he turned abruptly on Peter.

"Lest you get conceited, young Peter, with me begging for your company and being kindly refused, I'll tell you something. I loved your mother; my brother's wife. Did you ever guess that?—guess why I liked you a good deal?"

"Yes," said Peter, and Lord Evelyn started.

"You did? Demme! that's her again. She always guessed everything, and so did you. She guessed I cared.... You're her own child—only she was lovely, you know, and you're not, don't think it.... Well, she had her follies, like you—a romantic child, she always was.... You must go your own way, young Peter. I'll not hinder or help you till you want me.... And now I'm tired; I've talked too much. I'm not going to ask you to lunch with me, for I don't want you. Leave me now."

Peter paused for a moment still. He wanted to ask questions, and could not.

"Well, what now? Oh, I see; you want the latest news of your Denis and Lucy. Well, they're doing as well as can be expected. Denis—I need hardly say, need I?—flourishes like the green bay tree in all his works. He's happy, like you. No, not like you a bit; he's got things to be happy about; his happiness isn't a reasonless lunacy; it's got a sound bottom to it. The boy is a fine boy, probably going to be nearly as beautiful as Denis, but with Lucy's eyes. And Lucy's happy enough, I hope. Knows Denis inside and out, you know, and has accepted him, for better or worse. I don't believe she's pining for you, if that's what you want to know. You may be somewhere deep down at the bottom of her always—shouldn't wonder if you are—but she gives the top of her to Denis all right—and more than that to the boy—and all of her to life and living, as she always did and always must. You two children seem to be tied to life with stronger ropes than most people, an't you. Sylvia was, before you. Not to any one thing in life, or to many things, but just to life itself. So go and live it in your own way, and don't bother me any more. You've tired me out."

Peter said good-bye, and went. He loved Lord Evelyn, and his eyes were sad because he had thrown back his offer on his hands. He didn't think Lord Evelyn had many more years before him, though he was only fifty-five; and for a moment he wondered whether he couldn't, after all, accept that offer till the end came. He even, at the garden wall, hung for a moment in doubt, with the echo of that high, wistful voice in his ears.

But before him the white road ran down from the olive-grey hills to the little gay town by the blue sea's edge, and the sweetness of the scented hills in the May sunshine caught him by the throat, and, questioning no more, he took the road.

He loved Lord Evelyn; but the life he offered was not for Peter, not for Thomas as yet; though Thomas, in the years to come, should choose his own path. At present there was for both of them the merry, shifting life of the roads, the passing friendships, lightly made, lightly loosed, the olive hills, silver like ghostly armies in the pale moonlight, the sweetness of the starry flowers at their twisted stems, the sudden blue bays that laughed below bends of the road, the cities, like many-coloured nosegays on a pale chain, the intimate sweetness of lemon gardens by day and night, the happy morning on the hills and sea.

For these—Peter analysed the distinction—are, or may be, for all alike. There is no grabbing here; a man may share the overflowing sun not with one but with all. The down-at-heels, limping, broken, army of the Have-Nots are not denied such beauty and such peace as this, if they will but take it and be glad. The lust to possess here finds no fulfilment; having nothing, yet possessing all things, the empty-handed legion laughs along its way. The last, the gayest, the most hilarious laughter begins when, destitute utterly, the wrecked pick up coloured shells upon the lee shore. For there are shells enough and to spare for all; there is no grasping here.

Peter, with a mind at ease and Francesco grinning at his heels, sauntered down the warm, dusty road to find Thomas and have lunch.

CPSIA information can be obtained
at www.ICGtesting.com
Printed in the USA
LVHW040551081222
734780LV00030B/932

9 789356 716629